The Garments of Caean was described in 'F...
Review' as a surrealistic space ...
as hyper-Vancean.

'Fluent, singular, and ...
William Gibson

'Bayley has produced an ... ...tion,
a literary party trick. I fou... ...he book with an
appreciative chuckle.'
Frederick Patten

'The popularity of the science adventure story occasionally
causes one to forget that science fiction is also a literature of
ideas. Bayley has not forgotten, however, and he also knows
that the two are not incompatible.'
Roger Zelazny

'Bayley has a delightfully fertile imagination, formulating his
preposterous concepts with seeming ease, then slotting them
into his vigorous narratives and developing them with such
thoroughness that any reader with a sense of wonder cannot
fail to be carried along by the sheer intellectual stimulus of
the ideas.'
Chris Evans

The Pillars of Eternity
and
The Garments of Caean

Barrington J. Bayley was born in Birmingham in 1937 and began writing science fiction in his early teens. After national service in the RAF and various jobs, he began as a general freelance writer on features, stories, serials and picture strips, mostly in the juvenile field. Finally returning to straight SF, his stories appear in magazines such as *New Worlds*. His first major novel to be published in Britain was *The Soul of the Robot* (1976), which was followed by *Star Virus*, *Empire of Two Worlds* and *Collision with Chronos*. He currently lives in Telford, Shropshire.

Also available in Pan Books by Barrington J. Bayley

The Fall of Chronopolis *and* Collision with Chronos

Barrington J. Bayley

The Pillars of Eternity
and
The Garments of Caean

Pan Books
London, Sydney and Auckland

The Garments of Caean first published in Great Britain 1978 by Fontana
The Pillars of Eternity first published in USA 1982 by Daw Books Inc.
This omnibus edition published 1989 by Pan Books Ltd,
Cavaye Place, London SW10 9PG

9 8 7 6 5 4 3 2 1

©Barrington J. Bayley 1978, 1982

ISBN 0 330 30835 1

Typeset by Selectmove Ltd, London.
Printed and bound in Great Britain by
Courier International, Tiptree, Essex.

This book is sold subject to the condition that it
shall not, by way of trade or otherwise, be lent, re-sold,
hired out, or otherwise circulated without the publisher's prior
consent in any form of binding or cover other than that in which
it is published and without a similar condition including this
condition being imposed on the subsequent purchaser

Contents

The Pillars
of Eternity

1

He came slowly down the arcaded avenue that led from the landing ground. He was a blunt, stocky man encased in a modsuit, the ribbed, scruffy appearance of which might have caused some to think of him as an old trader who had grown careless about his equipment. They would have been wrong: though the modsuit was standard wear for shipkeepers, adaptable to a variety of gravities, he would have been happy to shuck it off like a torn jacket. His muscles were lithe and flexible, though now beginning to stiffen a little, for in his youth he had often scorned the use of a modsuit altogether, and he had trodden many worlds. His face was clearly unaccustomed to expressing emotion: impassive, square, pockmarked, jutting forward from the collar of the suit and surmounted by shorn grey hair. A perceptive person might have seen it as a face that masked suffering. This man, such a person might have said, has known pain, and has not overcome it. But there were unlikely to be such persons here in Hondora. A trader's town, on a planet whose culture was all borrowed from other sources, had little room for sensitivity. Here people would notice only how much he could be induced to bend in price, would ask only where he had been, where he was able to go. They would take more interest in his ship than in himself.

His ship. They would do well, he might have said to himself, to look at his ship.

Joachim Boaz was how he named himself. Captain was how he styled himself, preferring the archaism over the more modern 'shipkeeper'. There was a reason for this eccentricity. He did not see himself as his ship's keeper. Quite the reverse.

The air had a balmy, lemony quality, like aerial sherbet. It was distinctive of class-C planets, and resulted from the overlarge yellow suns that abounded in the region, or more properly speaking from the mixture of secondary gases in the atmosphere, gases which such suns exuded when they expelled the material that was to form planetary systems. Captain Boaz drew the tangy breeze deep into his lungs. He cast a lingering glance at the luminous, sulphur-colored sky. He liked it here, to the extent he ever liked anything.

The arcade was fringed with fragrant tree blossoms. He pressed on, ignoring any who passed him on the avenue, and shortly came to the edge of the town. Youths and girls gazed languidly through the shaded entrances of service rooms. Stray wisps of conversation drifted to him, scarcely noticed by him but nevertheless recorded in his brain and simultaneously transmitted to his ship which stood parked a mile away. '*Choc me one more style . . .*' '*. . . wild one . . .*' '*. . . the rad gap's closed up in Ariadne now . . . can't get through . . .*' '*. . . have you ever killed a girl like me before? . . .*'

In the meantime his ship was transmitting subliminal signals to him, guiding him with unheard suggestions. He was prompted to enter a drum-shaped room where men in dhotis and togas sat on benches against the walls. Some drank, some sniffed yellow powder, some talked to breastless girls draped in loose shifts. Walls and ceiling were bare of ornament. They were the colour of chalk, except at the rear where an ochrous red tunnel gaped, serving robots shifting from foot to foot in its mouth.

In the center of the room was a circular table occupied by five men, four of them shipkeepers, by the signs on their chests. The other was a merchant with cargoes to be moved.

Pausing, Captain Boaz waited to be noticed. Eyes swivelled, saw his modsuit, his cargo carrier's sign.

'Will you join us, shipkeeper?' called the merchant jovially. 'The game is better the more the players.'

Idly Boaz thought: for you it is. He took a vacant seat, and spoke in a dour tone. 'I can take a load Harkio way. Nowhere else.'

'Harkio?' the merchant squeaked in surprise. Boaz was breaking an unspoken rule of contract bargaining by stating his intentions at the outset like this. The other players gave him glances of disapproval.

'Yes, I might have something in that quarter,' the merchant said smoothly. 'Will you sit this round out, then? We'll come to it.'

Boaz nodded. He took a small deck of picture cards from his pocket and began to shuffle them in a habitual, self-calming ritual. Those present would recognize the cards and know him for a colonnader.

He relaxed, inspecting a card occasionally. Games were played with such cards once. That was long ago, when a card deck could be depended on to stay inert and not play tricks at the behest of its owner.

A slot in the center of the table disgorged the card pack's equivalent: shiny cubes an inch on a side, guaranteed fully randomized by the house. The merchant was banker. He took a cube; the others each took one. They all examined the facets for the symbols that in a few moments appeared there.

Boaz ignored the proceedings and concentrated on his cards. No one seemed to know how game bargaining had begun; but shipkeepers were generally born gamblers and, after all, it was only a logical extension of haggling. The shipkeepers made bids that represented what they would be prepared to carry a cargo for. The merchant tried to drive them down by calling their bluff. In the last resort it was the cards that decided.

It could mean that a shipkeeper would have to carry a cargo for below cost. Or he could collect an exorbitant fee. Usually, however, matters worked out reasonably enough.

The merchant gave a grunt of satisfaction as he held up his cube, the signs flashing from it in pastel colors. 'Excellent, Rodrige. You will be able to afford a holiday after this trip! Now, then. The Ariadne gap is closed up, I hear. For the time being I shall hold my Ariadne-vectored goods in store; perhaps the gap will open up again. Now let us see

. . . Harkio!' He looked up at Boaz. 'Your name, shipkeeper?'

'I am Captain Joachim Boaz,' Boaz said.

'Ah! How quaint! What is the load capacity of your ship?'

'Two and one-fifth milliards.'

'That should suffice. Let us play.'

Rodrige, who in fact had achieved a worse deal than he had hoped for, left the table with a sour face. Captain Boaz spoke again.

'I do not wish to play; I am not in the mood for it. I will take your cargo for the cost of the fuel plus a point eight per cent for depreciation.'

The merchant's face showed pleasure when he received this offer. The shipkeepers gave Boaz looks of malice. He was joyriding, taking a cargo simply to finance himself as a passenger on his own ship. 'That might be agreeable . . . any other offers, gentlemen?'

'What could there be?' muttered one bitterly. They left, allowing Boaz to feel their dislike.

When they had gone a look of anxiety crossed the merchant's features. 'Your ship . . . is it sound? I do not know you. Are you qualified?'

The barest hint of a smile almost came to Boaz. He pulled an identibloc from his pocket. The merchant's face smoothed out and became bland as he read it. 'Ah yes . . . that should do . . .'

'My ship is open to your inspection.'

'I will rely on your experience, good shipkeeper – or should I call you "Captain", eh? Ha ha! Well, then, Harkio. I have a consignment of Boems for Schloss III.'

'Boems?' said Boaz.

'Something wrong, Captain?' the merchant enquired.

A moral struggle ensued within Captain Boaz. He had always refused to take Boems before. Some philosophers classed them as sentient beings. In which case to traffic in them would involve him in slavery.

'I am not sure I can do it.'

'What? Ah, I see your problem. You are a colonnader, are you not? You follow an ethical code. Luckily I am a sceptic in gnostical matters. Well, you need not worry. These Boems have no conscious process. It has been scrambled out of them, if any ever existed. They would classify as corpses.'

'Then what use are they?'

'Oh, they can perform many functions of the simpler sort,' explained the merchant in good humour. 'They are used mainly in children's toys. Does that clear it up for you?'

Boaz decided. He was keen to get to Harkio.

'It's agreed.'

'Good. Now let me see . . . hmm, hmm.' The merchant was computing the figures with his adp implant. 'The Boems amass one point seven eight milliards. What's the mass of your ship?'

Boaz told him. The merchant worked out how many fuel sticks the trip would need, added a little leeway, reckoned the cost plus Boaz's depreciation.

'Two hundred and twenty-eight point one eight nine psalters,' he mutterd. Captain Boaz nodded, having simultaneously done the same calculation on his own adplant. The merchant wrote out a contract on a vissheet, finishing with a flourish. Each touched it to his forehead, recording his body odour as a signature of compliance with the terms. The merchant counted out some domino-like coins from a bag on his lap, giving them to Boaz wrapped in a cloth.

'Here you are, then. My goods will be delivered tomorrow morning.'

He left, looking satisfied. For a while Captain Boaz sat alone at the table, the folded cloth of money in his hand, watching the fizzy sunshine filter through the open doorway.

A nymphgirl who had been drinking on a side bench stood up suddenly, discarded her shift and began to dance naked. Her body was hairless, narrow-waisted and without breasts. She was just like a girl child enlarged to the size of a full-grown woman. It was the current fashion in Hondora, again a fashion imported from nearby worlds.

The girl stopped dancing when a robot stepped quietly from the red tunnel to place a hand on her shoulder. 'You must not do that here, madam. This is a place of business. For that, you must go to other establishments.'

Wordlessly she picked up her shift. Glancing scornfully around her, she stalked out.

Captain Boaz rose to address the robot. 'Where can I get ship fuel?'

'The nearest stockist is close by, sir,' the robot said, turning its smooth face toward him. 'Proceed down the avenue and take the second turning on the right. Proceed further a hundred yards. The stockist's name is Samsam.'

Boaz quit the room and again walked the arcade, going deeper into Hondora. Further down, the avenue became more lively, assailing him with motley smells and noises. Metal clashing, food frying, the aromas of a hundred mingled drugs and perfumes. He heard laughter, screams of mirth, the tinkling sounds of soft music. Men and nymphgirls spilled out of doorless openings and chased one another, kicking up the orange dust of the unpaved concourse.

Under shimmering awnings merchandise was displayed on glittering trays: foods, sweetmeats, drugs, trinkets, garments, a thousand intricate artifacts. Captain Boaz's step faltered. He had come to a stall offering Boems for sale. The pale micelike slabs were piled carelessly in the trays, their crystalline ridges jammed into one another.

Were they decerebrated or not? Captain Boaz looked away and strode on.

The side street was quieter. Samsam's was an unprepossessing shop without windows or display stall. Inside it was dim and cool.

The shopkeeper shuffled out from the back, blinking. 'Yes?'

'Good day.' Captain Boaz presented his credentials and placed the money on the counter. 'I need fuel sticks. I'm told you charge standard price, otherwise I'll go elsewhere.'

'Oh, yes indeed.'

The old man leaned across the counter, and his voice fell. 'I can get you some for less, if you like.'

'Thank you, no. I want no stolen merchandise, and no inferior fuel. Give me good rods.'

The shopkeeper turned to the shelves behind the counter that were stacked with sticks. 'What size?'

'X20. Give me five full-length, and one you'll have to cut.'

'What d'you want it cut to, then?' The man selected sticks and laid them on the counter.

'Give me thirty-seven over a hundred,' Boaz said, stating a fraction.

'Oh, I don't cut to anything less than an inch,' the shopkeeper grumbled. 'I can't get rid of scraps like that.'

'Very well, give me four over ten,' Boaz said impatiently. The man picked up a stick and took it to a cutting machine at the end of the counter. He put it in the grip, calibrated it, and set the blade to whining at high speed through the yellow rod.

While this happened Boaz picked up another of the rods and ran his eye along it as if testing the straightness of an arrow. It was about two feet long and two inches in diameter. It sparkled like sugar frosting and was rough to the touch.

The special kind of energy that resided in the rods was put there by a very expensive process. Each one would carry two milliards of shipweight a distance of ten light-years. Boaz unfolded the cloth that contained his money and counted out rectangular coins while the shopkeeper placed the sticks in a carrying bag. He received the change, thanked the vendor and stepped back out into the lemon sunshine.

Halfway down the side street, his ship told him he was being stalked. He tucked the fuel sticks under his arm. It was those they were after. About a minute later, his ship reported the attack was imminent.

Then a spring lasso snaked out from the nearby wall, jerking him off balance. Like a paper box, a section of wall folded in and revealed a narrow alley, and in it two men, one wielding the lasso and hauling Boaz inward, the other shifting from foot to foot with hands reaching out, like a wrestler looking for a hold.

For a moment Boaz could not deploy his strength. Still clutching the fuel sticks, he was dragged into the alley. Only then was he able to grab the lasso with his free hand, seizing it by the haft and pulling the man down on top of him.

For a stocky, modsuited man, his subsequent speed was a surprise to his attackers. He rolled, and was on his feet, in almost the same movement delivering a kick to the lasso man's coccyx, snapping his spine.

The man gave a bubbling moan, face down and moving his arms like a crippled insect. He would not live long. Boaz turned to face the second robber over the semi-paralysed form of his comrade. The man had a gun. Boaz saw a snarl of fear, felt heat as the beam struck his chest.

But this sensation was measured in microseconds. Two miles away on the landing ground Boaz's ship was responding to the events impinging on his body. Billions upon billions of digital pulses passed down the tight directional beam it maintained, and set about arranging his body's defences. The lethal shot from the thief's gun was diverted, dissipated in a thin blaze of light.

Taking one step forward with the fuel sticks still under his arm, Captain Boaz tore the gun from the mugger's grasp, smashing its handle against the wall so that the charge pack broke open and tossing it aside. The thief backed away with a glance to his rear. The alley was a dead end, probably constructed specifically for the purpose of robbers.

'We weren't going to hurt you, shipkeeper,' he pleaded quickly. 'We only wanted your fuel sticks.'

'Liar. That was a kill shot.'

'Look what you did to my friend —'

He could not evade Boaz, who grabbed him by the front of his toga and forced him to his knees, still using only one hand. Then he took him by the throat.

Just as Boaz began to throttle him, a transformation came over the thief's face. His terror dissolved into a dreamy leer, and he looked up at Boaz.

'You goin' to kill me?' he asked breathlessly.

Boaz glanced at the still moaning form behind him. Abruptly he saw his posture in a new light, and he did not like it. He withdrew his hand. The robber sagged, looked relieved, disappointed, edgy.

No expression at all showed on Boaz's face. He backed out of the alley, turned, and set off for the main avenue.

He came again to the ship ground. A few dozen ships dotted the flat, three-mile-square expanse. They loomed and seemed to drift on the hazy air. A few were half-heartedly streamlined for a swift getaway, but most ship designers did not consider the small saving in fuel worth the trouble and ungainly shapes abounded.

Evening was coming on. The sun was low and on the sky's opposite horizon a few stars showed. Overhead was an unusual sight; this system was irregular in its planetary formation, and the planet was actually the binary satellite of a gas giant. It could be seen glowing palely in the effervescent sky, its rings clearly visible.

The ship ground was a raised plateau. From its vantage the landscape and the town were laid out like a map. Captain Boaz paused to look at it. Why was it, he wondered, that on nearly all man-inhabited worlds he had visited he received this same feeling of universe old and in decline? A universe experiencing a soft autumn, wearing out, losing vitality. Could the universe really be approaching its end, when it would dissolve in mind-fire? Or was it only human society that exuded such decay?

He reminded himself that the impression could not be other than subjective: it emanated from its own feelings. Such a belief had arisen before, when in fact mankind had been very young, as he knew from reading the works of philosophers and historians such as Plutarch, Lucretius and Marcus Aurelius, who had lived before there was even a machine civilization. They too had concluded, for reasons that seemed trivial now, that the world was in its dotage, and they, it was evident, had stood on some hill as Boaz did now, and saw the fey melancholy that seemed to invest everything and even to drift down from the stars.

It said something for Captain Boaz's character that he could muse in so pensive a manner just after having killed one man, barely refraining from killing another. It was not that he was a cruel or heartless man; on the contrary his adherence to colonnade philosophy gave him a strictly ethical outlook. But, in comparison with what he had known, it simply did not seem important. They had come against him, and that was that.

A flowing tread-rail carried him up the ship's side to the manport. Inside, he went to the engine cabin, where he busied himself with checking out the fuel sticks, measuring their straightness (vital for smooth performance) and sampling their peculiar energy, which alone could send a ship faster than light. Finally he slammed them into the empty induction tubes (on landing there had been less than an inch of stick left).

He went to the main cabin and prepared himself a simple meal of the special foods he ate. He felt at home. The metal, the processors, the adp, the transmitters, enwrapped him. He was inside his ship like a babe inside the womb. No longer did it need to protect him from afar; there was no fear of distance, no narrow control-beam. Its emanations regulated his nervous system, his perceptions, carefully preserved him from harm, and did it all by means of a suffused ambiance of constant signalling that filled the air around him.

His ship; it was his tragedy, and his salvation, and his hope. It reached out its gentle hands and maintained him for as long as he remained within range. It gave him abnormal strength and immunity from many weapons. At ten miles its efficacy began to fade and he would fall ill. At fifteen miles he would die, in a horrible agony that was a repetition of the agony he could remember.

And the ship, just as it could reach out to regulate his ravaged body, could also reach out with its subtle beams to tell him what was happening elsewhere. Boaz settled himself in a low armchair, and without really meaning to, found himself indulging in the random spying he would sometimes resort to as a means of diverting his mind from the broodings that threatened to overwhelm him. His mind seemed to drift, as if in a waking dream, through the streets and buildings of Hondora. The sun was down; the day's business was over. The town was giving itself over to the pursuits that mainly interested its habitants: the pursuits of aimless pleasure.

The ship's beams lunged softly, undetectably, through metal, through walls of lithoplaster, paint and HCferric. Boaz perceived the interior of a crowded bar. Nymphgirls danced in the centre of the room, rarely with men, who held back and drank solidly.

His perspective shifted, zoomed in on a booth at the far end. A tough-looking man sat at a narrow table, a tankard in front of him. His face was broad and flat, with a spade jaw, squashed nose and widely separated eyes, as if it had been hit with a mallet. Sharing the table with him was a girl with long red hair, red lips, long cheeks. Her movements were mobile; she gestured and shifted as she talked, quite unlike her stolid partner.

There had been tease-play between them. Boaz saw that they had only met that night, but she was seeking a relationship. He was less enthusiastic, offhanded but not dismissive. Consequently they needled one another.

He looked at her in annoyance. 'I keep thinking I've met you before. I have, haven't I?'

'Have you?'

'Ah, I don't know.' He drawled his words, scarcely moved his jaw when he spoke. 'Maybe it was your sister. You got a sister?'

'Maybe.'

'Yah – I guess it was somebody else. There are a million girls like you. I've had a hundred, at least.'

She leaned close, looked up at him from under long lashes. Her mouth hung open lasciviously. 'You ever kill a girl like me?'

'I've killed lots of girls.'

Boaz became sleepy. He dozed. The man and the girl danced, drank, drifted in and out of his awareness. There was a certain savage intensity developing between them. When he came fully awake again they were in a private room, facing one another across the mattressed floor like animals ready to pounce on one another. Both were naked.

Suddenly her eyes hardened. 'You *have* killed somebody like me before. I'm Jodie. Remember?'

He looked uncertain, flexing his muscled body in impatience. 'Jodie? But your face. It's not the same. Not quite, anyway.'

She looked triumphant. 'I'm altered. A hormonal imbalance in the tank. Too much thyroid. But I'm Jodie all right – and I remember.' Her voice became fervid. '*God, how I remember!*'

With a darting movement she bent to her discarded clothing and came up with a coiled tendril of an object. It was a parawhip. Her hair swung about her shoulders as she straightened. Her words came in gasps. 'I've got kinky thinking about it. But this time it's going to be different. This time, *I'm going to kill you!*'

The whip sang out to reach for the man's nerves and incapacitate him for her pleasure. But he was too quick for her. He sidestepped. Then he sprang, caught her wrist and twisted her arm, catching the handle of the whip with his other hand as it fell from her grasp.

'Sorry, honey, I don't go for that clone stuff.' His voice was gruff and hot. 'There's only one way I want to stay alive. For *you*, though –'

His big hand around her throat, he forced her to the floor. Boaz signalled the ship to withdraw from the scene. His *voyeurism* drew the line at sex murder; he found it distasteful.

The girl had a clone body stashed away somewhere. A transmitter was in her brain, something like the one in Boaz's ship, but much, much simpler. Moment by moment it fed her experiences into the sleeping clone. When she died the clone would wake up. It would have all her memories, including the memory of dying. Jodie resurrected.

Sex killing had become a fashionable cult among the sated pleasure-seekers of this region, who found through it the acme of a connection long known to psychologists: the connection between sex and death. They said there was no ecstasy to match it, because there was nothing fake about it. The original *did* die, genuinely, forever. The sense of continuity belonged only to the new, awakened clone.

At least that was most people thought. Boaz wasn't so sure. He believed that there was such a thing as the soul, and that it was not spatially limited. Perhaps it followed along with the identical memory. Just the same, he did not like the death cult. The clone's memory of sex death caused it to seek the same experience over again. It was a vicious circle of perversion.

Boaz himself had no clone body. He would have welcomed death if it could have helped him. But it could not help him. It would still leave the past, where his agony lay.

He slept, still slumped in the armchair. After ten hours he awoke to find the merchant's trucks arriving. Even before he roused himself his ship robots had put out a derrick and were clambering down the side of the hull. He followed, and watched them hoist the crates into the hold.

He opened the last crate. Inside were Boems, from a unique planet where crystalline growths proliferated to a fantastic degree. Boems were simply the most advanced form of this growth. Whether they were simply natural crystals with a better than adp complexity or evolved living forms, sentient but non-motile, had never been established. One could converse with them, using the right kind of modem, but the responses could equally be a processing of the inquirer's own information as genuine.

Whatever the truth, they made useful control systems. Put a Boem in a cybernetic device and it became almost a person – hence the attraction for the toy industry, even for those cerebrally scrambled. Manufactured adp, on the other hand, lacked spontaneity.

Boaz had no way of knowing whether those were in fact scrambled, as the merchant had promised, but it was far too late for him to be able to reconsider the contract. He would have to deliver the cargo before attending to any quest of his own. Such was the law.

He put his odour to the delivery note. The trucks rolled away, the robots climbed back inside, the derrick withdrew. Captain Boaz mounted the tread-rail and took himself to the flight cabin. The first of the fuel sticks was sparked and began to deliver its energy. Slowly, the cargo carrier rose through the lemon-colored sky.

2

Once Boaz was among the blazing lights that were stars and the curtains of splendour that were stretches of dust and gas, there was nothing to distract him. As his ship sped through the galactic realm he had little to do but sit, and as he sat he brooded, and when he brooded the past could not help but well up. Onplanet he could always direct his attention elsewhere. But here there was only the ship and the void.

The faint drone of the ship engine was a constant background. His attention, even when resisting at first, found itself flicking from one to another of the images that bubbled up to claim it.

Memory took over.

Captain Joachim Boaz had not always borne that name. His original name had been a single word, a curse, a nickname, a word he would not bother to articulate now; it did not seem like him any more. Born in the warrens of Corsair, he had never known a father and saw little of his mother. From the age of ten he had been alone, trying to join one of the conduit gangs, as the packs of juveniles who terrorized the warrens were called.

But Boaz was ill-fated from birth. He was born deformed, his spine twisted, his limbs warped, unable to walk but only to hump himself along with a stout stick he held in both hands, and which was also his defence against the kicks and blows he received from young and old alike. He never was accepted by any gang, though he ran with any that would tolerate him, able to get up a fair speed as he lolloped along with his stick.

Unable to share in the thievery and robbery by which the conduit gangs survived, he spent much of his time begging at the spaceport. By the time he was fifteen he had conceived an ambition: he wanted to be a shipkeeper. Those straight-backed, steady-eyed men, owners of their own ships, able to go anywhere, were heroes to him as they strode about the spaceground. They were less liable to kick him aside with a well-shod boot than were space passengers, mechanics or even company crewmen;

more inclined to give him a coin instead. Dimly Boaz guessed that there was more to the universe than Corsair's brutish, pitiless society. When he saw a ship soar up into the blue (Corsair had a blue sky) he thought of escape.

When he was sixteen, it happened. Boaz came humping out of the conduit onto a shadowed corner of the spaceground. Half a dozen Slashers, the conduit gang he avoided most, were chasing him, shouting his name at him, the name he hated, the name that described what he was.

He might even have got away from them had not a pylon been in his way. With his mode of locomotion he could not change direction easily at speed. It gave one of them a chance to head him off. His stick was kicked from under him and went skittering away. He scrabbled after it, but they had him now. They put a prong on him to hear him scream.

He only felt one jolt. Then a change came over the scene. The Slashers paused, their yells cut short. The prong was suspended in midair. Boaz raised his eyes as he lay on the floor of the spaceground. He saw a pair of bare feet, above them bare ankles and legs bare up to the mid-thigh. Then the hem of a chiton, a toga-like garment that draped loosely from the shoulders.

It was a garment worn by professional people who did not have to work much. The young Boaz peered up over his humped, twisted shoulder. Above the white fabric of the chiton he saw blue eyes gazing from a clean-shaven face with hair cut neatly across the forehead.

The stranger must have stepped from behind the pylon. The Slashers could have dealt with him easily, but they seemed too surprised to act for the moment. The conduit gangs had a tacit agreement with the port managers: they did not molest off-world visitors on the spaceground itself. Yet that did not seem to be all that was restraining them. There was something in the unflinching look of the newcomer that was overpowering.

He made a sweeping gesture with his arm. 'Be off with you.'

They did not move at once but after a few moments, with surly glances, they made their way back to the conduit. The stranger retrieved Boaz's stick and handed it to him. Boaz planted its end on the floor and hauled himself up it until he was as nearly upright as he could be. He came not far above the stranger's waist.

'Thank you, sir. If you could spare a small coin, sir . . .'

The man in the chiton ignored his automatically replayed spiel. He was looking Boaz over with a professional eye.

'Were you born in that condition, young man?'

Nervously Boaz took one hand off his stick to clutch his ragged tunic protectively to him, bunching it up at his throat. 'Yes, sir,' he whispered.

'Have you ever seen a doctor?'

'A doctor, sir?'

Boaz scarcely knew what a doctor was. Sickness on Corsair was as rare as congenital disorder; natural selection had bred it out.

'A doctor is someone who mends a body that has gone wrong.' The man spoke patiently, at once understanding the extent of Boaz's ignorance.

'No, sir.' Boaz held out his hand but then, perceiving that he was to be given nothing, made as if to shuffle off.

'Wait,' the man said. 'I wish to talk to you. Follow me.'

Wonderingly Boaz obeyed. He felt peculiar and out of place as the man escorted him into one of the hotels lining the spaceground. Soon he found himself in a well-lit, well-furnished room. It was all strange to him; he was not used to furnished interiors.

The man spoke, but not to Boaz. A minute later a servitor appeared and delivered a covered tray. Inside it was an oval plate of spiced food. The man invited Boaz to eat.

The food was delicious, but scant in quantity. Boaz did not guess that this was because his host, seeing his half-starved features, did not wish to overburden his stomach. With it was a fizzy drink, the sort Boaz liked and bought often. He gulped it greedily.

The man in the chiton let him finish before beginning to talk to him again. 'Your body can be mended,' he told him. 'Your bones can be remade and straightened. Your tissues can be stimulated and adjusted, so that you will attain your proper growth. Did you not know this?'

Boaz shook his head. He had never even thought about it.

'The process is, of course, very costly.'

The stranger was making some sort of pitch, that much Boaz knew very well. But what it was he could want from him was a total mystery. He listened while the man continued in his mild, factual voice. He could see to it that Boaz got the required treatment, he said. He was prepared to take Boaz off Corsair and to a planet where friends of his, skilled doctors, would straighten out his body. But he was not making this offer only to help Boaz. There was something he wanted out of it, too – something that could be greatly to Boaz's advantage if all went well. If not – well, the risk was a small one, it was unlikely that anything would go wrong that could not be put right. At the worst the experiment would fail, but they would still ensure that Boaz ended up with good bones. He promised Boaz that.

The price Boaz had to pay for these benefits was that he was to be used as an experimental subject. In fact, the orthopedic surgeons – bonemakers, the man called them – would replace Boaz's entire skeleton. In place of his poor twisted bones, they would insert bones they had made themselves. These would be as good as natural bones in strength and durability, and they would contain marrow for making blood. But they would have a lot of silicon in them. Every gram of this silicon would comprise adp.

'Do you know what adp is?' the man asked him.

Boaz shook his head. The man shrugged. 'Automatic data processing. It is what all machines work by. The servitor that brought you your meal. Every type of control system.' He tapped his brow. 'The implant in my skull that allows me to calculate beyond limit. In effect, your whole skeleton will consist of microprocessing. It will be like a second person within you, with new perceptions, new feelings, new abilities. Except that there will be no second person there. These benefits will be all yours, whenever you wish to make use of them.

'This is the natural direction for human evolution to take. The brain is not large enough, even with adplants added. Silicon bones provide the room for extra processes, while still doubling as a skeleton. So far the technique has been developed using animals . . . the vital stage of adaptation to human beings has been delayed while we waited for one of us to volunteer as a subject . . . You, however, could solve our little problem. You are unusual; there are not many congenitally deformed people in the galaxy.'

'Why'd you come to Corsair looking for someone like me? 'Cause there are no doctors here?'

'I did not come to Corsair looking for anything. This spaceport is a stop-over point; I shall be here for a few hours waiting for my connection to Aurelius. It is by simple good fortune that I found you – good fortune for us both, I hope.'

Later, Boaz was to compare these silicon bones with the Boems, the crystalline adp that grew naturally. It had made him think that perhaps Boems weren't sentient after all, any more than the bones were.

The sixteen-year-old beggar boy had not understood everything the bonemaker said to him. Later he was to find that fullness of explanation was an ethical consideration on the other's part. To estimate another's level of comprehension was arrogance, since it was nearly always to underestimate his mental capacity. Civilized standards required that all the facts be made available for the listener to understand or not, as the case may be.

In fact, the bonemaker's talk of new perceptions went right over Boaz's head. But he understood clearly that the stranger was offering to take him off Corsair, and besides that was offering him hope of a kind he had never dared to contemplate.

But why should he trust this chiton-wearing offworlder, a man whose class was despised in the warrens because of the ease and comfort of its life-style? Boaz had a reason, which he could not articulate but which told on him as he sat across from his host. All the man's words and actions were careful and deliberate, yet they displayed no desire to impress. He had not once smiled at Boaz. He had not tried to apply persuasion. He had put facts, and had left it to Boaz to decide. It was the first time in his life that Boaz had been treated as an equal.

He decided.

'I'll come with you,' he said.

The bonemaker's name was Hyton. When asked his, the boy simply went even paler than usual and looked away. Hyton did not inquire again; and Boaz found that he could manage without a name. In a week they were on Aurelius, and here his horizons expanded swiftly.

His first change of perspective came almost immediately. He was confused by the unfailing courtesy shown him by the men into whose charge he had delivered himself. When the time came for physical examination, he flinched as they approached him, and could barely refrain from cowering.

The specialist (it was another, not Hyton) team leader smiled. 'There was once a civilization, you know,' he said to Boaz, 'in which a malformed person was not at all an object of contempt. Rather, he was pitied, and given special deference.'

Boaz gaped.

'Matters are different now, of course. I have no doubt you have been abused a great deal.'

He nodded, as though the silent youth had given him some answer. 'Nature has taken over. Compassion is to some extent artificial, a product of urban life. It is more normal for a malformed specimen to be attacked and driven out by the community. That is how it is with animals, and so it is with the village mentality into which most of civilization has declined.'

'And what of you?' Boaz challenged.

Again the bonemaker smiled. 'We are what are known as "colonnaders",' he replied.

Boaz had never heard of colonnade philosophy, and this news meant nothing to him. But it was important, he was told, that he should be instructed in it. Silicon bones were intended for people of philosophic attainment, and it was necessary to test out their effects as completely as possible.

Aurelius was in fact the planet from which colonnade philosophy had emanated. After examining him, the bonemakers proclaimed that lengthy preparation would be needed before the final operation. Suitable bones would have to be manufactured to his dimensions, and besides there was much in his musculature to be rectified. Meantime they carried out some temporary corrective work. Boaz could now walk with a limp, again with the help of a stick, though his leg muscles were assisted by calipers and fired by adplants.

Hyton took him to Theta, the city in the equatorial sunbelt which was the home of colonnade thought. Colonnaders did not, in fact, call themselves colonnaders at all. The word was a popularism, coined from Theta's distinctive architectural feature – its immensely long and spacious colonnades and peristyles which made the flower-decked city so delightful. To themselves, the colonnaders were merely philosophers – 'lovers of wisdom'.

Along these airy pathways Boaz learned the refined pleasure of cool discourse. Aurelius was yet another class-C planet: another with a lemon sherbet sky, investing the colonnades with a crocus-colored radiance, as though the stone itself were soaked in saffron. Gazing down the endless perspectives was like staring into a benign infinity, while unfamiliar and marvellous ideas suffused Boaz's brain.

Hyton introduced him to a man called Madrigo, whom he was eventually to look upon as his mentor. Madrigo paid no attention to his lack of experience in the world; he informed him from the start that this was of no moment. At first Boaz was inclined, more or less by a reflex learned on Corsair, to seek small advantages for himself, even to try to manipulate those around him. But this quickly faded when it met with no response.

Instead he began to emulate the behaviour of the people around him: the dispassionate considerateness, the assumption of good will on the part of others – for all conscious beings, Madrigo assured him, were in reality common citizens of a single city, the city of the universe.

But most important of all was the attitude Madrigo taught him to adopt toward himself. The mental condition striven for by colonnader training was known as ataraxy; undisturbed consciousness, or stoical indifference to events.

'Everything is transitory, everything is arbitrary, yet at the same time everything is inevitable,' Madrigo told him. 'Whatever happens to you must be borne, without resentment if bad, without glee if good. Your own unconditioned consciousness is the secret of life.'

'You can't help your feelings,' Boaz mumbled.

'That is why you are here. You will learn to recognize your feelings, and not to be ruled by them. It will come.'

And he *did* learn. Guided by Madrigo, he made what was to him an amazing discovery: that his own feelings were *not* the most important things in the world, not even to himself. He learned to detach himself from troublesome emotions, to treat them as objects external to himself. When he did this, he found that his senses grew a little sharper, his attention span a little longer. Gradually, too, he found that behind the cruder kind of emotions, based on desire or the thwarting of it, were feelings of a broader sort – warmth toward others, pleasure that was softer, more voluptuous. These, too, Madrigo warned him, he must not become attached to. He must always remember that the world was, in a sense, illusory.

Boaz balked at this. 'It seems pretty real to me,' he sniffed.

'So it is; it is real, but it is not self-sustaining. Everything that happens passes, and fades, and so it is as if it had never been – until it happens again.'

Boaz did not understand what Madrigo meant by these last words until, some time later, he came to know something of colonnader cosmology. The world consisted in reality of *mind-fire*, their term for a kind of undifferentiated consciousness. Something happened in this mind-fire; it began to attenuate here and thicken there, becoming uneven. From this movement there began to differentiate out the physical elements. The sidereal universe evolved, and the elements combined in countless ways. Yet mind-fire was always there, even if reduced in quantity and quality, and it coarsened itself sufficiently to become *individual* consciousness, manifest in organic creatures.

This was how the universe came into being, congealed, as it were, out of mind-fire. But only for a period. After an unknown number of billions of years it entered a phase of collapse until eventually it was consumed by fire – mind-fire, the purest form of fire imaginable. The elements dissolved into it, sinking back to the latent state. Thus the world came to an end. But not forever. After a similarly protracted period of time the process began again, *exactly as before*. The manifest universe re-emerged just as it had already been. Every atom, every individual, every event recurred, identical in every detail. Nothing ever changed, from eternity to eternity.

The cosmic oscillation was fundamental: two pillars of universal stability. Indeed they were but the first instance of the basic law of polarity on which all manifest existence depended.

Fond of symbolism, the colonnaders represented this law in terms of two upright pillars, one positive, one negative. And there were names for them dating back to ancient lore: *Joachim* and *Boaz*.

The crippled lad found these conceptions awesome. On a more personal level they solved a problem for him. Since coming to Theta he had given thought to the choosing of a new name for himself. The trouble was that all names he heard sounded like someone else, not himself. But now, ignoring any possible accusation of false grandeur, he decided to give himself names representative of his rebirth as a person, and besides that indicative of the new mental horizons opening before him.

He named himself *Joachim Boaz*.

His old life was finished, and he put all thought of Corsair behind. Three months later, the bonemakers announced that they were ready to perform the operation.

His heart beating (he was not yet so trained in ataraxy that he did not feel prey to fear), he submitted himself to pre-med. His body was purged of poisons and waste matter. He was meticulously cleaned and shaved. It was explained to him that he would be unconscious for ten weeks. After the skeleton replacement, he would lie in a tank where his muscles would be coaxed into adjusting themselves to his new, straightened frame. There would be a subsequent operation in which the new bones would be connected up to his nervous system. Finally, completely healed, he would be taken from the tank and allowed a further short term of recuperation. Only then would his higher brain functions be switched back on. He would awaken between crisp sheets in a fresh room with the scent of flowers wafting through an open window, and he would be new.

And so it was.

Boaz stirred in his chair. He thought he had fallen asleep and had been dreaming, but no, he was only remembering. There was a remedy for memory. It could be selectively excised by surgery or by electrical manipulation of the brain's storage areas. New memories could be introduced, even. One could have a new past, become a new, different person with different experiences. There were cults that practiced this rewriting of past life. But Boaz, a man of rigid personal integrity, had never even considered it. Life was real, and only memories that were based on real episodes counted. To accept other memories was to live in a dream, and from a dream, even if it took half of eternity, one must eventually awaken . . .

The thought evoked a painful emotion in him, and in response the ship stirred. It was always busy, always worrying both over itself and over Boaz – they both were its province. He heard a faint hum, a click, the quietest whisper of some change of state taking place in the ever-watchful mechanisms. Then he sank into the vivid hallucinatory quality of his memories again. . . .

There was no mirror in the recuperation center. He asked for one, but they told him to be patient. First he had to learn to balance, to walk, to get used to himself. What of the bone functions? he asked. They were not switched on. He would be shown how later.

Just by looking down at himself he could see he was differently shaped. Looking around him, he could see he stood in a different relationship to his environment. No longer was his form a cowering one. He was tall: nearly as tall as most people. His spine was erect. His limbs moved freely.

His musculature was marvellously flexible and strong. It was a new, delightful experience to be able to poise his body on one foot, to stride across a room, to bend and reach out without danger of falling over. But it was remarkable how quickly he adjusted to his new condition. To his surprise, it was no longer new after a day or two; it was normal.

Only then did they bring in mirrors.

After a week they took him back to the operating theatre and put him to sleep to check out his bones on the mass of testing equipment they had there. It was like switching on a new kind of engine; if it didn't run right, there could be damage.

He woke up back in the recuperation center. Hyton was there to greet him. Everything was in order. The switching on could begin.

It was something he had to do himself, but he had to be shown how, and it was necessary to be cautious. In all, the bones had eight functions; but for the present he was to be shown only the preservation function and the felicity function, and the latter he would only be shown how to raise to Grade Three on a scale of ten.

The preservation function was simple off/on. It was, however, the only function intended to be left permanently on, and it was, moreover, the greatest triumph of the bonemaker's art so far. By supplementing the natural repair systems, it endowed the physical organism with an unprecedented ability to withstand shock and injury, even rendering organs capable of regenerating themselves to some extent, after the manner of the liver (previously the only organ able to do so). It prolonged life, slowing the biological clock.

The felicity function was of a psychological type. It engendered a state that would also be obtained – but temporarily – through the use of drugs, and which was faintly foreshadowed in the side effects of the mental exercises Boaz had received from Madrigo. Like them, the function worked on the feelings. Hyton also referred to it as 'the joy function.'

Its action was to open a direct conduit between sensory perception and emotional life. The sight of any scene or object, the hearing of any sound, was greeted with feelings of joy, wonderment, pleasure, happiness. Nothing was bland or mundane. The universe came to life: it glowed with radiance and meaning, from every drop of water to every spacious landscape.

The felicity function was, as Hyton had promised, like possessing another mode of perception. Boaz chuckled with delight as he gazed around him at setting two. The even, light tangerine color of the wall – how hopeful, how genial it was! The flashing mirror, with its surround of sheened bluemetal – why, it struck him at once with its sense of self-confidence, its ability to return and project images of any hue! It warmed his heart to see it!

And when he looked out of the window at the garden beyond and at the daffodil sun low in the sky – the ravishing scene made his heart burst with happiness. Just to know that all this *existed!*

'May I raise to setting three?' he asked.

'Very well, but be careful.'

Switching was accomplished by means of mentally intoned syllables. So far, Boaz had been told six – two on/off pairs and the two additional settings for felicity. In his mind he spoke the syllable for the third setting – and immediately gasped at the shock-flood of emotion that the glowing, blazing scene before his eyes evoked in him. Hastily he reverted to setting two.

'You must raise any function only to the level that your consciousness is able to handle,' Hyton warned him. 'The danger with silicon bones is of being swamped, even eradicated, by the strength of some of the functions. Generally speaking we shall install bones only in people who have had philosophical training.'

Boaz switched off felicity and came down to ground level. 'What are the other functions?'

Hyton smiled. 'There is adjusted chronaxy, which alters the minimum duration of nervous excitability and therefore controls the time sense by lengthening or shortening the specious present. There is also adjusted rheobase, which alters the galvanic threshold of nervous excitability; this heightens or lowers the intensity of sensory impressions. By the same token adjusted rheobase should affect the range of mental associations, provoking new chains of thought – as to that, we shall see.' He paused before continuing. 'There is also a sexually oriented function which I will not go into now. Then there is the kinesthetic function which makes one more alert to movement and the shapes of edges much as certain predatory animals are; dances should prove particularly entertaining when viewed with this function. . . .'

Hyton chattered on, but Boaz understood scarcely a word of what he was saying. 'Why isn't there an ataraxy function?' he asked.

'Ataraxy is not a function,' Hyton told him. 'It is a primary condition. You have eight-function bones; they are experimental to a degree. Later models may have more functions, but ataraxy will not be one of them. Nor can it be.'

Hyton paused again. 'That is why you must be introduced gradually to the effects of these functions. They are designed to be used in a condition of high ataraxy, or your mind could be blown. For that reason fail-safe fuses are installed, but just the same . . . we estimate that your functions should be switched on gradually over a period of years.'

'Years?' the young Boaz said. He sounded alarmed. 'How many *years* am I supposed to stay here?'

There was nothing they could do to hold him, short of unethical imprisonment. All his early years his true character, cowed and beaten, had been given no chance to express itself. Now he was freed of the harshness of

Corsair; his true nature was beginning to show, and it turned out that his character was an impetuous one. He yearned to roam, and his restlessness became a knot of frustration that could not tolerate any restraint.

He stuck it out for two months, during which time he learned to handle the felicity function up to setting four. Then he announced that he was going.

Hyton tried to persuade him against it; Madrigo made no attempt to do so. Boaz was adamant. He was eager to experience life; the remaining control syllables could wait until he was ready. He promised only that while he was away he would strive at all times for ataraxy, and that he would return so that the experiment could continue.

He went. And he did the bonemakers a great service.

He found out their basic mistake.

To own his own ship was still his goal, but for that he would need extensive financial credit. Meantime he entered the cargo trade as a hired hand, serving first on a cheap tatty scow with her tubes half rotted, then working his way up to the larger lines. He *did* gain experience of life, on a score of worlds, and the galaxy was as colorful as anything he could have imagined. . . . Sometimes he would feel sorry for his tormentors back on Corsair. They, like him, would be grown men and women now, but it was unlikely that many of them would have got offplanet. To imagine their no doubt dreary lives gave him a feeling of vengeful satisfaction that only his philosophical training prevented him from revelling in. . . .

He kept his promise. As the years passed, he did go back to Aurelius, several times, and spent months at a time there. Mostly, though, it was Madrigo who gave him his attention. The bonemakers, disappointed at not finding him permanently at their disposal, had located new, more co-operative subjects. Hyton himself, in fact, had been installed with silicon bones, and the number of bonemen and bonewomen was increasing. Still, Boaz could boast of being the first. They checked him out, debriefed him, gave him a few more syllables, the first settings of other functions. Meantime, Boaz saved as hard as he could. . . .

No longer so young, he grew mature. . . .

. . . day 29, month 3, year 716 standard time. . . .

H819 was an anomalous planet. It was lifeless, but it had a breathable atmosphere, if you didn't mind breathing in sulphides along with it or else wore an air filter. The oxygen was belched out by numerous volcanoes whose intense heat apparently split some underground oxide such as water. Boaz arrived there as a crewman on a ship bringing equipment to an alchemical research station. The company he worked for had decided to switch him to another ship, so he was left onplanet to wait for his new berth to pick him up.

He remembered craggy cliffs and burning cones, nothing moving except the constant movement of rocks dislodged by frequent ground tremors. . . .

Alchemy was not a popular sect. Colonnader cosmology was the one most universally respected in man-inhabited space; the most scientific, the most proven. And while it had its variants and deviations, alchemy was not one of them. Alchemists were famous for spreading noxious and dangerous gases, dusts and radiations through their ill-considered experiments, and were forbidden to practice their art on more worlds than not; hence this station on a dead world where they could harm no one but themselves. In place of the stoical calm of the colonnaders, they had a reputation for mental aberration and reckless improvisation, for being unable to restrain their burning zeal for chemical discovery.

By now sufficiently schooled in philosophy to be able to call himself a colonnader, Boaz felt curious about doctrines that were rivals of his own. Alchemical work was exotic enough for him to feel attracted to the alchemists despite their dour and over-intense manner. He became friendly with Dorsuse, the chief artifex at the station, and this individual indulged him to the extent of using him as an untrained assistant in the main laboratory.

The alchemists were indeed contemptuous of danger. Their skin was discoloured and bore the marks and scars of many strange burns and lacerations. Boaz alone took the precaution of wearing a face mask in the mercury-laden, vapour-drenched air of the laboratory, and many were those present whose breath came in gasps or whose limbs shook from the intake of similar unholy mixtures over the years.

Boaz counted himself lucky. Since coming to the planet the team of adepts had been preparing a singularly arcane experiment, and it was about to come to culmination. Dorsuse had promised to take him to the firepit to witness the climax.

The object of the operation was to isolate a particularly potent and rarefied form of fire as the alchemists understood the element. They called it *ethereal fire*. According to them, its existence was so far hypothetical only. The firepit, dug by the alchemists themselves, was lined with mica and diamond laminate. For nearly a standard year they had been slowly dripping into it a mixture made up of more than forty substances, including plutonium, electronium (a form of matter whose nuclear protons had been replaced by positrons; the substance was electrically neutral but incredibly light, and capable of numerous fanciful molecular configurations impossible for normal matter), mercury which had been treated by a secret process known only to alchemists, and other substances which they also claimed were not known by orthodox science.

The real secret, Dorsuse assured him, lay in the measured proportions by which the ingredients were slowly introduced to one another. A century of experimentation, he told Boaz, had gone into the formula that was now being tried. It was calculated that on the 29th of month three, the meld would be complete, all the ingredients being exactly tempered and suffused. The result should be ethereal fire.

Boaz was excited. With Dorsuse and two other alchemists, he stood on the overhanging observation platform on the lip of the pit. Down below was a faint orange-green radiance from a cloudlike mass.

He was wearing dark goggles Dorsuse had given him. The alchemists had goggles, too, but careless as ever, they left them dangling around their necks. On an impulse Boaz tore off his goggles too, and gloried in the stinging sensation in his eyes as the glow fell on them.

He wanted to make the most of this. He switched on rheobase setting three, felicity setting two (he didn't want to lose control by setting too high). Preservation, of course, was already on. He never switched it off.

Glow, glow, orange and green. The now-familiar intensification of vision due to lowered rheobase hit him (lowering the rheobase threshold intensified sensation; raising rheobase dimmed it). The depth of the pit, with its dark, round, brooding walls, the nascent life of the cloudy mass, made him heady with anticipation.

'I think the light is increasing,' Dorsuse said.

Another of the alchemists nodded. 'Do you think we shall be on schedule this time?'

'Schedule' was an obsessive word with Boaz's hosts. Their theory of chemical operations contained a time factor. Ordinary chemical reactions, which took place immediately or in seconds or minutes, were in their parlance 'vulgar' or 'common.' The arcane chemical processes took place over time spans of days, months, years, even decades (there was a legend of an alchemical reaction that took more than six hundred standard years to take place). The sought-for transformation of substance, however, usually happened suddenly at the end of this time, and was supposed to be predictable to within seconds. This was what was implied by 'schedule.' In fact, an alchemical operation was likely to involve a whole sequence of colour changes, transitions between solid, liquid, gas and plasma, or other signs Boaz was not familiar with, all consequent on the continued application of the enlivening energy source, and if any single one of them failed to occur on time the whole procedure was deemed abortive.

For all that, there was a great deal of self-glorification in the alchemists' own descriptions of their art. Though they would speak airily of predicting the outcome of years-long operations to 'within seconds,' in practice they could rarely calibrate their schedules to less than a calendar day.

'Yes, it is increasing,' Dorsuse said. He leaned out over the parapet, craning his neck to get a better view.

'Is there any danger?' Boaz asked tentatively. 'How will the ether-fire manifest itself?'

'Well, we can always get out of the way if anything alarming looks about to happen. . . .'

As he spoke the incandescent mass exploded. It reared up the well of the pit in a gaseous flash. The platform supports were burned through in an instant. Down fell the platform and its occupants. The ethereal fire (for that was what it truly was) boiled over the rim in a foaming, expanding mushroom head of light.

Paradoxically, it was indescribably beautiful: a golden, radiant, softly roaring incandescence. Boaz knew this because he did not disappear into the depths of the pit as did the others. They must have been killed in a split second. He, by contrast, grabbed the lip of the pit as he fell, and with a strength he should not have possessed he hung on.

The gentle, beautiful light was not all he knew as he hung there. Ethereal fire only *looked* beautiful, with a beauty that masked its inner horror, its antipathy to all organic life. It was fire upon fire, fire within fire, fire impounded, compounded, almost playful in its ability to torture without limit, penetrating his body to the core, to the bones in fact, infusing every cell to some degree.

Boaz should have died within two or three seconds. So would he have, had he been engulfed in ordinary fire, for the heat was intense. His flesh would have turned to shreds of carbon and even his bones, those shining silicon bones, would have melted.

But ethereal fire was subtle, rarefied, as tenuous as perfume. It burned in a way that ordinary heat did not. The chemical changes attendant upon combustion took place but leisurely in its presence (the observation platform had been charred to disintegration; it should have been vaporized). Boaz, likewise, burned *slowly* with a burning that soaked deep into his body, into his mind, into his feelings.

Yet if that were all he had to suffer, he might have died in not too large a fraction of a minute. But it was not all. He also had silicon bones.

Nature bestows one merciful beneficence on the living creatures she generates and touches with waking consciousness. She so arranges their nervous systems that there is a limit to the degree of suffering they can endure. When agony or terror reach a certain traumatic point, the organism immunizes itself against further horror by means of daze, unconsciousness or death. Shock is the ultimate guarantee. The heart stops, blood leaves the brain, catatonia develops.

That was the mistake of the bonemakers, who proved themselves less wise than nature.

For the whole ten minutes that Boaz was engulfed in ethereal fire, his preservation function kept his ravaged body working after a fashion. It kept the blood pumping, the nerve cells firing. It insisted, with an implacable preprogrammed will, that the ascending reticular system which brings alertness to the brain should not close down.

Boaz was conscious the whole time.

Not only that, he was on rheobase setting three. Put simply, lowered rheobase meant hyperaesthesia. Every sensation was felt with an unnatural keenness – every datum of pain had that extra edge. Not only that, he was on felicity setting two. Everything he received with his senses was being shunted to his emotions.

Boaz grabbled in his mind. Instant insanity might have been a refuge of sorts, but the preservation function was charged with maintaining not only his physical but also his psychological health. Mental coherence was another matter, however. He called on his bones to help him, trying to mouth trigger syllables as though screaming prayers to the gods.

He was too overwhelmed with pain to have any real control over what his mind pronounced. The heat had probably affected the bone functions, too. Because he did not even have the syllable for what followed.

Felicity retuned itself to setting eight – three settings higher than the bonemakers had allowed him to experience.

His burden of physical agony, already inconceivable in terms of what human awareness can be expected to survive, crashed through the remaining gates of his mind to take possession of the entire gamut of his emotions. Pain that had already stripped his consciousness bare, that burned and whipped him, that transcended all thought or explanation, that became a living entity, a personality that spoke to him, played with him, raped him, punished him with its enfolding caresses, now had access to the 'joy function' – a reservoir of positive emotional energy. It instantly turned that energy negative.

Misery would have been too bland a word to describe the rivers of ultimate horror that flooded and ran through Boaz. It is not often that emotional pain can equal physical pain of even a normal kind. Yet he knew grief that arose from and was the equal of his physical torment. There were no hidden parts to Joachim now. Not a thought, not a feeling, not a memory was not dredged up and drenched permanently in that grief. He howled his suffering until that howl echoed in an emptiness which was his own self, and that self contracted around

and became only one thing. PAIN, AGONY, SUFFER-
ING, GRIEF, *repeated and repeated and repeated, forever
and ever. Amen.*

The alchemists in the distance heard his screams.
They listened to them with curiosity and fascination.
How could screams be so seemingly endless in content?
How could they seem so much like a new language, for
a new world? When the ethereal fire at length dissipated
(rising through the atmosphere and into space, they said,
seeking its proper abode among the stars) they ventured
cautiously closer. They found the blackened form of
Boaz still clinging as if in rigor mortis to the laminated
diamond-and-mica lip of the pit. He wasn't screaming
now; the preservation function had robbed him of the
physical strength to do so as it commandeered every erg
of energy in its desperate fight to keep him alive. They
presumed he was dead, of course. They scooped up his
charred body and placed it on a wooden board. Then,
amazed to find he was still breathing, they carried him
into their small surgery, but appeared to think the case
hopeless and did nothing for him.

As chance would have it the company ship put down
to pick him up only an hour later. The ship's robot doctor, observing that he did not immediately die, consulted
Boaz's medical record. Then it did its duty and informed
the captain of *his* duty. Boaz was delivered, still suffering,
to the bonemakers twenty light-years away.

The bonemakers, in turn, did their duty as they saw
it. They set about to repair Boaz. The task was more
massive than any they had yet envisioned; it made the
mere making of silicon bones seem easy.

And indeed, bones were of no use in a case like
this. Every cell, every nerve, every gland, every single metabolic process would have to be closely and
permanently regulated by artificial means; truly speaking, Boaz's entire somatic integrity was gone, and would
never in future be able to stave off total collapse. On the
other hand, all the adp that would be needed could never

be packed inside Boaz's frame, not even using bones – and even if some means of incorporating could be found, the bonemakers would have decided firmly against it. So fine were the attunements that were required that bringing the processors into physical contiguity with the ruined *soma* would in short order have led to functional coalescence. Boaz would no longer have been human.

So regulators and *soma* had to be separate, and to house everything necessary to keep his destroyed body miraculously walking, digesting, feeling and thinking would take a building the size of a small dwelling.

But that would effectively have imprisoned him within a radius of a few miles. The bonemakers chose another course. They felt they owed it to Boaz to do more than merely heal him. They owed him something in recompense.

Knowing of his ambitions, they bought him a ship. A newly built cargo ship, crew-robotized (independent ship-keepers disliked hiring employees), with range enough to allow him to roam almost anywhere, provided he could find cargoes to pay his way. And into that ship they put all the processing. Into it they put the transceivers that linked him to this secret brain, larger than any natural brain since it undertook to keep biological functions running that should have been able to run themselves. The ship was, in fact, a preservation function, but one far more capacious and more penetrating than that put earlier into his silicon bones. Correspondingly, it gave him a survivability that was unparalleled.

The bonemakers' unheated apologies still rang in Boaz's ears. They admitted to having made a serious mistake. It might comfort him to know that other bonemen would benefit from his experience. Future models would have an automatic cutoff on the preservation function to render the owner unconscious beyond a set level of pain, or even to permit him to die. And they were calling in all bones installed so far for modification.

While Boaz and the bonemakers could never be quits, they had done all they could for him. In their opinion he was still far better off than when they had first picked him up off that Corsair spaceground.

His bones, they informed him, were still operable. It made no difference to Boaz. He had never used them since.

Captain Boaz groaned out loud.
AGONY – AGONY – AGONY –
Normal physical pain, however bad, is mentally un-recoverable once it is over. That it happened can be recollected, the nervous system can be permanently depressed by it, but the memory carries no storage facility whereby the experience of it can be relived.

Emotional pain, however, the mind *can* remember, and relive. Boaz's pain had not been normal. It had been physical and emotional all at once, supernal physical pain married to emotional pain of like intensity. And the memory of it bubbled up unbidden, again and again.

And yet such memory was not the worst of it; burden-some though it was, it was but a pale copy of the origi-nal. Worse was *knowledge*. The knowledge that it had happened.

In the doctrine of an extinct religion the wicked were consigned after death to a lake of supernatural fire. This fire burned a thousand times more intensely than ordi-nary fire, and was a thousand times more agonizing. Yet it burned without consuming, and those cast into it burned forever.

Boaz understood the description. He had been dipped into the lake of hellfire.

As if in dim after-image to the brilliant pain-flash, he remembered when, after a long time spent in the medibath, his tissues were mended and he emerged as a lumpy, scarred version of his former self – but only physically. Psychologically he was broken.

Then began the visits of Madrigo, his mentor. Methodically, with sure touches, he began the job of reconstituting Boaz's shattered mentality. Boaz could hear now the mentor's quiet, sympathetic voice. Ataraxy was all. A contented life was impossible without it. Everything that happened, no matter how good or how bad, must simply be accepted, with equanimity.

Madrigo agreed that some experiences were dread enough to overcome even the most highly controlled human consciousness, and Boaz had been through something that could destroy any normal psyche utterly. Without philosophy there would be no hope for him. But there *was* philosophy, and the mind, in the last analysis, was stronger than all, simply because it was eternal while experiences were only temporary.

Ataraxy must be striven for. Pleasure and pain, however intense the degree, must never be acknowledged as a master.

'After all, are not your chosen names *Joachim* and *Boaz*, the two pillars of universal stability?'

'Yes,' said Boaz, 'but I am beginning to curse those names. . . .'

'Take the large view,' the mentor told him. 'When the world ends, when all is absorbed in mind-fire, your accident will take on a different aspect. It will not seem fearsome, then.'

'No!' Boaz protested with a passion that broke through the resolve that Madrigo had patiently been building in him. 'I do not believe mind-fire sees experience as illusory or unreal – that would be to render the creation meaningless! The world is real, mentor, you have taught me that. My sufferings were real! They cannot be mitigated by a change of view!'

To that, Madrigo remained silent.

Boaz slumped in his chair, head and shoulders slouched forward as though he were about to fall out of it. The memories faded, then disintegrated and flew apart like a flock of birds startled by a gunshot.

A set of luminous dials on the wall of the cabin quivered. From the drive down below a fuzzy whine, his constant companion, permeated the cabin.

A chime gonged. It was time to change the fuel rods.

With an effort he lurched reluctantly up from his chair. He flexed his stiffened limbs, and turned up the cabin's dim lighting.

He scanned the dials. He would soon be in Harkio.

Then he would know whether the lead he had was worth anything or not.

3

BY THIS EDICT:

Experimentation aimed at the establishment of travel through time is forbidden UNDER PAIN OF DEATH.

Experimentation aimed at control over the time flow is forbidden UNDER PAIN OF DEATH.

Experimentation aimed at retrieving objects from past or future states is forbidden UNDER PAIN OF DEATH.

Experimentation aimed at gaining direct consciousness of or retrieving information from past or future states is forbidden UNDER PAIN OF DEATH.

Possession of any artifact or natural object exhibiting one or more of the above properties is forbidden UNDER PAIN OF DEATH. Possession of any document containing explicit data relating thereto is forbidden UNDER PAIN OF DEATH.

Acts of experimentation, research or inquiry into the nature of time are forbidden UNDER PAIN OF LIFE IMPRISONMENT OR DEATH unless with the express permission of the Office of Scientific Regulation. Publication of confirmed or theoretical data relating thereto is forbidden UNDER PAIN OF LIFE IMPRISONMENT

OR DEATH unless with the express permission of the Office of Scientific Regulation.

(Bearing the seal of the
Department of Law Propagation)

Gare Romrey left Karti's in a hurry, leaving his friends there feeling decidedly less friendly. Outplanet in a rented *Stardiver*, he paused within call range just before going into hype, and dialled through. Being what he was, he was quite unable to resist this last look back.

Karti's Dive Infee Club came up on the cage plate, sour light from the ceiling strips falling on stained walls and tattered furniture. The bar was sticky with spilled drinks to which adhered ash from waft sticks. Only about half a dozen people were visible – the others had decamped in an effort to stop Romrey from reaching the ship ground. They crowded the screen when they realized who was bleeping them.

Up front was the thin-faced redheaded kosher pimp with the archaic cognomen of Jericho Junkie. Romrey flashed him a quick smile.

'I thought I'd just explain, boys—'

'He's offplanet,' someone behind Jericho muttered. The purveyor ponce (he supplied a specialized sexual taste involving a rare genetic type of woman, a certain drug and a specially treated aphrodisiac food) glared at Romrey with hot eyes. '*One* chance, Romrey. You've got *one chance* to get back here with the cube. Otherwise—'

'This, you mean?' Romrey held up the half-inch-sized memory cube which Jericho had been selling by lottery and which he had filched just before the numbers were about to be called. 'You've got to trust me, boys. I thought of a better plan, that's all. I asked myself what would happen if one of you won the cube. What would you do with it? Go out there and try to land on Meirjain?' He shook his head. 'It would be a fiasco. *Me*, now—I can handle a job like that. When I get back I'll split the incomings with you.'

Snorts of indignation expressed a general disbelief in his last pronouncement. 'Whoever won the cube could have sold it,' Jericho said.

Romrey shook his head again. 'Negative thinking. This way I – we – strike big.'

A bull-shouldered alec shoved Jericho aside and thrust his jaw out at Romrey, who recognized him as Ossuco, a carcass dealer. 'We know where you're going, you rat, and we'll catch up with you. I got a feeling *I* would have drawn that ticket. I'd like to know what makes *you* think you could get away with it.'

Romrey picked up the pack of cards lying on the control board and fanned them open, holding them up before the cage screen. '*These* told me to do it.'

He let them gawp for a moment at the numbered picture cards, before he cut them off.

Then he swivelled his seat to face the engine controls. He gripped the manual handles and pushed them forward. Energy spurted from the fuel rods as the *Stardiver* put on speed. With a shudder he hit c; then he was riding smoothly, heading for the centre of the Harkio region where it nearly touched the Brilliancy Cluster.

He was grinning with pleasure when he switched to auto. He always enjoyed going through c on manual.

The journey to Sarsuce would take a few days. He picked up the memory cube again and plugged it into the *'diver's* starmap. The Brilliancy Cluster came up on the navigation screen. The view was from Sarsuce, or rather from Sarsuce's sun, the Econosphere planet nearest to the cluster. A red arrow blinked on and off, pointing out the spot where Meirjain was due to make its appearance. At the bottom of the screen ran boxed lines of figures, including a date.

Absentmindedly Romrey reached into the larder chute and took out a pinana. He peeled off the orange-hued skin while he studied the screen. It was his favorite fruit: a banana into which the flavor of pineapple had been delicately, genetically blended.

The cluster was, to be sure, a beautiful if familiar sight. Romrey's attention focused on the red arrow, surrounded as it was by piles of vari-colored stars. He read the data box, making a rough estimate of times and distances.

How many other people had this data? It was supposed to be rare, but –

Jericho Junkie claimed to have got it during a trip to Sarsuce, from the Meirjain tracker himself. Romrey turned from the screen. One hand picked up the deck of cards again, and expertly laid out a row while he bit into the pinana. He frowned as he tried to interpret the sequence. The Inverted Man reversed, followed by the ten of laser rods, followed by the eight of ciboria. . . . He stopped, puzzled. Deceit, leading to fulfilment.

Reading the future was not his forte. Reading a course of action, though, was easier – and in that regard what he had told Jericho was true. The cards *had* instructed him to rob the lottery, although the idea, of course, had been in his mind already.

Romrey, in recent years, had hit upon a practice which relieved life of much of its anxiety. Whenever he came to a point of uncertainty, he consulted the cards, and he did whatever he believed they were telling him to do. If the issue could be reduced to a simple *yes* or *no*, of course, then so much the better.

There was a heady, almost delirious pleasure in not being responsible for his own decisions anymore.

He thought of the poor cruds in Karti's. Planet-huggers for the most part, scarcely been off Kleggisae. A ponce, a carcass dealer, assorted alecs who had found ways of living off the Econosphere Welfare Bureau. Not a prospector among them.

Strictly speaking Romrey wasn't a prospector either. He called himself 'a trader with wide interests.' But the thought of landing on Meirjain the Wanderer didn't frighten him, and neither did the competition. Neither did he necessarily think of himself as a liar. Would he be generous to his erstwhile friends and colleagues in the

Karti Dive Infee, as he had promised, if he made out on Meirjain? Maybe he would, maybe he wouldn't.

He would let the cards decide.

And if they decided against, Ossuco could look for him in every sextile of the Econosphere for all he cared.

Thoughtfully, self-indulgently, he munched the pinana.

In half a standard day Captain Joachim Boaz's business in Harkio was completed. He delivered his cargo, collected the small tail fee, and took off again for Sarsuce, the natural jumping-off point for the Brilliancy Cluster.

Through a hazy atmosphere and what seemed an untypical drove of traffic, he descended onto the ship ground at Wildhart, Sarsuce's largest city – though not the capital, since Sarsuce had none. It was the kind of town he seemed to have spent half his life in, with an atmosphere that did not give him the feeling of being in an authentic place at all, but more like a transit district, a place at the junction of other places, a boom town that had somehow outlived its usefulness so that even to claim a name for itself smacked of fraud. The deception was never more transparent than now. The ship ground was uncommonly full, and Boaz was hard put to squeeze a place for his ship in it. The port proctor's clerk took his fee with an unfriendly brusqueness, as though Boaz were forcing him to connive in something immoral. And when he walked into Wildhart itself the excitement was palpable.

Boaz scowled. All these strangers. He did not like to be one of a crowd, and it was certain they were mostly after the same thing he was – though for different reasons.

The sun slanted from the west. But overhead there hung what appeared to be a giant bauble in the sky, like a lantern hung from a festival tree; a hundred times larger than the sun itself, and glowing palely with a multihued mass of point sources, even in broad daylight. That was the Brilliancy Cluster, with its estimated eight thousand closepacked stars, the place where *pure* prospectors went.

It had no settled planets, no properly mapped interior – in fact not a lot of planets at all, since nearly all its stars had quirkishly opted to form planetless double, triple and quadruple sun systems.

But it did have one very famous planet, a planet of fable that until now had been seen only once: Meirjain the Wanderer, a planet which had no sun of its own but which instead swung from star to star like an interstellar comet, weaving an apparently random path within the cluster.

On average the stars of Brilliancy were only light-hours apart, allowing Meirjain to steer a miraculous, sinuous course which gave it an equable climate for nearly all the time. This remarkable feat was taken as evidence that the Wanderer's motion was the result of artifice, though not everyone thought so – the astronomer Ashojin had calculated that Meirjain followed a thermal isocline due to the competing geodesics of surrounding stars. In fact very little could be stated of the Wanderer with certainty. It had been discovered three centuries ago. Men had landed on it, had sampled its treasures. Then, through the carelessness or ignorance of its discoverers, it had been allowed to disappear again, melting untrackably into the Brilliancy Cluster like a molecule of sugar in coloured water.

And now, three centuries later, word had it that the Wanderer had been sighted again; its course tracked to the point where it would emerge on the edge of the Cluster in the gravisphere of a particular star. Which star, and when, was what all these people were here to find out.

Boaz pushed his way through a jostling crowd of naked nymphgirls, purveyors, vendors, steer narks and mod-suited shipkeepers – some of them cargo carriers like himself, perhaps, but more likely prospectors. He ignored the overhead adholo flashes which tried to beam enticing images into the retinas of his eyes. He moved down the avenue – it seemed that every town he stopped in had an avenue just like this one, as though there were only one town in the whole galaxy, capable of manifesting itself everywhere – until he came to the arcaded entrance of a rest room.

He turned into it. The room was large and dome-shaped. It was as if he were back in Hondora, except that this place was busier. He found an empty table and sat down, signing a robot to bring him a drink while he surveyed the people around him.

Information was being offered here, his ship told him. Sipping the milky cocoin the robot delivered, he became aware of someone at his elbow. A small man, his body swathed in buff and orange bands, slipped into the chair opposite. Boaz disliked him immediately. His smile was too ingratiating.

'Good day, shipkeeper!' the stranger said jovially. 'Looking to land on Meirjain?'

'What is it to you?' Boaz became aware that the man had followed him from the ship ground.

'Most people who come in are looking for it. You know what the hottest property around here is, I suppose?'

'No.'

'The hottest property is numbers. Co-ordinate numbers. That tell you where and when Meirjain will appear.'

The swathed man turned to indicate a table in the centre of the room where a dumpy, togaed individual sat talking desultorily with two others and toying with a set of gambling cubes. His eyes were downcast. Boaz recognized him as a person who spent most of his time *waiting*. Waiting for the right customer to come along.

'See that alec over there? He has the numbers. He's one of about ten people on Sarsuce who have them. But it's information that costs a *lot*.'

'Why should it? Meirjain will become visible soon.'

'Not soon enough. Haven't you heard?' The other raised his eyebrows. 'The Wanderer's been put off-limits. An econosphere cruiser is on its way. Nobody is going to get down on Meirjain that isn't able to jump the gun and get to the co-ordinate point ahead of that cruiser. So you see, it's the co-ordinates or nothing.'

'This is a wild story. I don't believe you.'

The man sighed. 'How blunt. It's almost quaint, really. You needn't believe *me*.' He reached into a swathe and placed a news card on the table, tracing his finger round the dial. 'See for yourself.'

Boaz picked up the thin wafer. The holoflash hit his retinas. In urgent, colored script, he read: ALL CITIZENS ARE ADVISED AND WARNED THAT THE PLANET KNOWN AS 'MEIRJAIN THE WANDERER' AND ASSOCIATED WITHIN THE LIMIT OF THE BRILLIANCY CLUSTER IS BY ORDER OF THE DEPARTMENT OF LOCATIONAL AFFAIRS PLACED UNDER ABSOLUTE PROHIBITION. NO LANDING IS TO BE MADE ON SAID PLANET NOR ANY SCAN CARRIED OUT EXCEPT BY OFFICIAL ORDER. PENALTIES WILL BE POSTED IN THE AMOUNT OF TWENTY YEARS LABOUR OR FIVE HUNDRED THOUSAND PSALTERS. . . .

Thoughtfully he laid down the card. The penalties were largely bluff. The econosphere, as the great rambling empire of man-inhabited space called itself, was in a state of semi-disintegration; spasmodically tyrannous, but just as often unable to impose any effective government whatsoever over innumerable worlds. The government would depend on the arriving cruiser to enforce the edict. . . .

'If you still don't believe me,' his informant said softly, 'there's a public announcement on every two-hour.'

'In these circumstances,' Boaz pointed out, '*no* one is going to land on Meirjain.'

'Some people reckon they can. Econosphere law doesn't count for a lot in this neck of the woods; that cruiser has a long way to come. Word has it that those who know in advance where the Wanderer is due will beat the law to the drop.'

Boaz's mind turned to what might be behind the ban, which bore all the hallmarks of official panic. There was uncounted wealth on Meirjain; its dead civilization was a treasure house. But most valuable of all, of course, were what Boaz was after – time-jewels, gems able to refract light through time as well as space. It was the only known example of time modification by physical – and probably artificial – means.

Something about these gems frightened the econosphere government, Boaz reasoned. He had tried to track down some of the jewels that had been taken from the Wanderer on the first landing three centuries ago. To all intents and purposes they had vanished from existence, hidden away, secreted – perhaps even destroyed, he suspected – by government agencies.

His conclusion gave him hope. If the authorities feared the gems, then they had a use. . . .

'The alec's name is Hansard,' Boaz's informant was saying. 'Do you want me to talk to him?'

'I don't have money in the amount he would probably ask.'

'You have a ship. A fine ship.'

Boaz grunted. 'Without a ship, what good are co-ordinates?'

'Leave it to me.'

While Boaz watched, the swathed man walked to Hansard and leaned over to talk to him. Hansard glanced at Boaz, a perfunctory, predatory glance. He nodded, as his eyes returned to the table.

The swathed man beckoned. The others left the table as Boaz stepped over and took the seat that was offered. Hansard's gaze flicked up to him and back to his cubes again. He was smiling to himself.

'A fine ship you have, I'm told. What's its name?'

'It's my ship; it doesn't need a name.'

'Well, never mind. . . .'

Hansard scattered the play blocks and reached in his pocket. He pulled out a memory cube and held it up. 'I had four of these. I've got two left. I paid good money for them and I'd like to make a profit, but I'm not adamant about it. I place it in the lap of the gods.'

'That's normal commercial practice.'

'Correct. I'm a gambler. Double or quits. One throw. If you win, you have the numbers and you still have your ship so you can use them. If I win, I take your ship. You won't have any use for the numbers then, anyway.'

'I guess not,' Boaz said. The idea that he would gamble with his ship as a stake caused him a wry amusement. He had known this was all wrong from the outset, and now the beam that stretched out to him from the ship ground confirmed it.

He cheats; the blocks are loaded, his ship whispered to him. And then: *Also, his merchandise is worthless*.

As a thief, Hansard was stupid. He piled cons on top of one another, multiplying the risk to himself.

'You're overdoing it,' Boaz said aloud. 'A good swindle doesn't need redundancy.'

He rose and strode away. Back in the avenue the public announcement was beginning. CITIZENS ARE ADVISED AND WARNED. . . . Passersby paused, glanced up to let the flashing letters strike their eyes the better, then walked on unconcerned.

Boaz had the picture now. Wildhart would be crawling with dealers offering fake coordinates. And the real coordinates? How many people had those? Half a dozen? Two or three? Or only one?

He felt little doubt that the story of the race with the government cruiser was true. Otherwise there would be little demand for co-ordinates at all.

It was beginning to look like a problem.

Romrey had forgotten how kinky the fringe planets were. In former empires depravity had festered first in the central urban areas. In the econosphere, it seemed instead to arise in the nearly lawless peripheral provinces, working its way inward to eat steadily away at the fabric of morality.

The girl had picked him up at an eatery on the night of his arrival. The eatery served spicecrab, a dish banned on many conservative worlds whose flesh contained compounds related to L-dopamine and alpha androstinol. Romrey had damned the expense. In his euphoria at arriving on Sarsuce he had wanted to try something new.

But what the girl, whose name was Mace, hungered for was *too* new as far as he was concerned. The alpha androstinol had done its stuff (that was why she had gone there: to find a man whose pheromones excited her). But later, when they rented a play room not even the L-dopa could carry him through the scene she wanted. She wanted him to kill her.

Romrey had never done that before. The idea repelled him. And he told her so. Perversely (maybe it was the spicecrab again) his refusal excited her even more.

Since then, she had been pursuing him. In eateries, in drinking houses, in the street, hanging around outside the door of his lodging, she would sidle up to him. '*Kill me,*' she would whisper in his ear. It was a determined kind of seduction he found horrifying. As if he were the one who was to be defiled.

In one way, he supposed, he could see some sense in it. On the night of their first meeting Mace had told him she was a bonewoman. Bone people were usually colonnaders, and colonnaders believed that consciousness – mind-fire, as they called it – was not limited by space or time. She probably had no real conception of personal extinction; she thought her same consciousness would awaken in the clone body she had somewhere.

A colonnader had once explained it to him in terms of the death and rebirth of the universe. 'We never die, really,' he had said. 'When we are resurrected in the next turn of the wheel, it's our own same consciousness that lives again.'

Romrey was sceptical. He wondered, though, whether Mace's clone also had silicon bones. That would mean she had a lot of money. . . .

He had resolved to ignore her until she eventually wearied of the game, but he had not reckoned on a deadly trick she had up her sleeve. He awoke one night and became aware that someone was in his room, moving clumsily.

He waved his hand at the service panel, flooding the room with light. Mace was there, naked, her voluptuous breasts flopping (she did not follow the breastless nymph-girl fashion). As the light came on, her hand went to her hair and pulled out what appeared to be a strand. The strand stiffened and went silvery. It was a paraknife.

In almost the same instant she flung herself toward the bed. Romrey rolled aside. The knife stabbed down where he had been and sliced his shoulder. He hardly felt it at first. Then the stinging pain and the sight of his dripping blood brought his senses to a furious awakening.

'*You bitch!*'

They stood facing one another over the bed. She still pointed the paraknife at him, her shoulders hunched. Her face was slack. Her lips drooped, in a way that made him imagine something lascivious was dripping from them.

Then she began to giggle. 'I'm going to have you,' she told him. 'You'll have to kill me, because if you don't *I'm going to kill you!* It's you or me – get it?'

Gasping with passion and fright, she lunged at him again. He retreated, but she clambered over the bed to get at him. 'You'd better do it,' she breathed. 'You'd better do it now. Or I'll get you sooner or later. Creep up on you – stick it in – bet you got no other body to wake up in. Right?'

'Right,' he said harshly. He caught her wrists in his hand, holding the knife away from him, while she kicked desperately at his crotch with vermilion-painted toes. A rage was boiling up in him to think how close to death he might have been, accompanied by a feeling of heat and a pounding in his ears – an unfamiliar reaction he would not have guessed he could make.

'All right.' His words came thickly. 'If that's how you want it—'

He twisted her hand, forcing her to drop the knife. He punched her in the stomach. She folded up on the bed. He fell on her. A mist was before his eyes as he felt his hands go round her throat.

Passing on the avenue a few yards distant, Captain Joachim Boaz paused.

The ship's beams were sweeping the district, searching for information. What they brought him in this instance was far from what he sought, but it caught his attention just the same.

The scene was the distasteful kind he had glanced at on many occasions and then turned away from. He would have done so now except for one extra piece of information. The beam told him: *She has no replacement body.* Then: *He believes she has.*

Boaz hesitated, of a mind to keep to his own business and passs on, but his colonnader training told on him. He turned into an alley that ran through a small maze of rented rooming shacks. His ship told him when he had come to the right place; told him what was happening behind the lithoplast wall. The entrance was on the other side of the building, and he judged there was no time to go looking for it.

He called on the ship to flood his tissues with toughness and strength. He attacked the thin wall with the edge of his hand, chopping right through it in three sharp blows. Then dust and frayed fragments were raining down about him as, like some kind of demolition engine, he burst through the partition and confronted the startled pair.

Romrey rose slowly from the bed. To him, Boaz must have been a frightening sight, and he began to edge toward the cupboard where he kept his gun.

Boaz raised a monitory hand.

'You should be warned that you are laying yourself open to a charge of murder,' he rumbled.

Romrey huffed, momentarily overcoming his surprise. 'What are you talking about? It's legal here.'

'Only when the terminated party has a working linked-up clone.'

'What?' Romrey murmured. His eyes sought Mace's. 'But don't you have . . .?'

Mace was rubbing her neck. She winced. Then she shrugged.

'So I'm tired of life. So what?'

'And what about *me?*' Romrey's anger returned. He bent over her, his fist raised in her face. 'I would have gone to the chamber for you!'

'Be gallant. Say I'm worth it.'

Mace slipped from under him and stepped to where she had dropped some clothes near the door. Deftly she slipped into a shiftlike robe, smoothing it down. She pulled up her hair and tied it in a snood.

Boaz stared at her. Through her ostentatious uncon-cern, certain facts were visible. First, very fine white lines in the skin, unnoticeable by most but discernible to Boaz, told him she had silicon bones. But that did not mean she was a colonnader – though still rare, bones were being acquired by more and more people these days, not all of them colonnaders.

Boaz did not think she was a colonnader. The stoical quality of ataraxy was not in her face. In his judgement she was pure epicurean, and lived for the senses.

And, yes, she was tired of life. She had chosen an exotic style of suicide without a thought for the consequences for her victim – something a colannader would never do.

While she dressed momentary looks of concentration came to her face, suggesting to Boaz that she was switch-ing off her bone functions one by one, detumescing from a plateau that had never been reached. Was she relieved – or just disappointed? He tore his gaze away as the man spoke.

'Are you law enforcement?'

Boaz smiled faintly. 'Not the law you are talking about. No, I am nothing official.'

The man was peering through the hole Boaz had made in the wall, as if expecting to see something there. 'What other kind of law is there?'

'He's talking about cosmic ethical law,' the woman said acidly. 'He's just a goddamned busybody. A fully boned, paid-up, stuck-up ethical pain in the neck.' Boaz realized she took his supernormal strength for evidence that he, too, wore silicon bones in his body, and she had put two and two together.

'I'm surprised you ever got replaced, with your attitude,' he told her. 'Replaced' was how bone people referred to their transformation.

'The surgeon wasn't a colonnader either. See, busybody? The ethic is disintegrating.'

'Perhaps that is why you wish to end your life? Those who devised silicon bones intended them for people with philosophical training.'

'Maybe.' The tiredness in the girl's eyes struck Boaz. The man, meanwhile, looked from her to Boaz in bewilderment.

'Look here,' he said to Boaz, 'thanks for saving my neck, but why don't you two lunatics just clear off and let me get some sleep?'

'As you wish,' Boaz said. He made for the door, but then the ever-present ship beam, emanating from a processing load that all this time had been sifting and guessing with the data it was collecting from the scene, made a suggestion.

Both of them could be useful to you.

He turned. 'Could it be you are here on Sarsuce waiting for the Wanderer?'

Romrey made a wry face. 'Sure. And I've got co-ordinates, too.'

'False ones?'

'Probably. But how would I know? I brought them back in Iridan.'

'They are fake. It is almost certain.' Boaz turned to Mace. 'And you?'

She tossed her head. 'Why would someone with a yen for extinction be searching for anything – except death?'

Boaz waited. She relented. 'All right. Not me, I don't give a damn for anything. I belong to a man called Radalce Obsoc. One more collector's item. He wants to get down to Meirjain. He wants it bad.'

Boaz picked out only what was relevant from her cryptic comments. 'You belong to him. Is that why you want to die?'

'Maybe. I've been with him a long time. I just felt tired.'

'Your will to live has been drained away through indulgence in the senses.'

'Maybe. But then I'm into pleasure, not power like you.'

It was understandable that she should misjudge him. Boaz surveyed them both. They were an unlikely pair.

'There might be some benefit in our working together.'

Romrey had worked his way through bewilderment and incredulity. Now he was merely puzzled. 'How?'

'You are aware that it is going to be very difficult to land on Meirjain without knowing the position of its appearance beforehand. We can take it that all those co-ordinates offered here in Wildhart and elsewhere are false, and indeed in such circumstances it would be impossible to identify the real ones among the fake. Special talents are needed to track down who has the real ones. A detective could do it, perhaps. . . .'

'Obsoc already hired a detective,' Mace said. 'He got nowhere.'

'So what are these special talents, and why do we have them?' Romrey asked acidly.

Boaz stood motionless. He had no answer.

'You can read the future, maybe?' Romrey persisted.

Seriously, Boaz shook his head. 'By no means.'

'*I* can read the future,' Romrey said.

*

Boaz watched carefully as he reached into a drawer in the bedside table. 'I read the future with these,' he said. 'And I'm going to read it now.'

He had taken out a deck of cards and proceeded to lay out ten of them on the table, after a quick shuffle. 'The issue is a simple one. Do I throw in with you, or do I not?' Romrey's lean face was intent as he laid down the cards. 'A positive answer is a score that's above average. Negative, below average.'

Briefly he reckoned up. 'Well, that's fairly positive. A hundred and one. It looks like we're partners, whoever you are. And who the hell are you, anyway?'

'I am Captain Joachim Boaz.'

'Shipkeeper?'

'Yes.' Boaz was gazing at the cards with interest. As Romrey swept them up and laid them down, he stepped over to examine them, glancing at Romrey for permission.

'They're colonnader cards,' Romrey told him.

Boaz thumbed through them. 'Not colonnader,' he stated. 'This is a perverted set, muddied with occultism.'

There were in fact many variants on the original colannade pack (itself reconstructed from a pre-scientific pack of great antiquity), most of them produced by deviant philosophical or arcane sects. This one was typical. Artistically it was very accomplished, but the images were altered and adorned with additional symbolism which was often incorrect and also tended to obliterate much of the carefully inculcated subtlety of the original. The Priestess, for instance, a simple but enormously potent figure in the true colannade version, was here cluttered with a number of extraneous signs – in her hair, in her right hand, under her left foot. These symbols were drawn from the aberrant occultism of the sect that had construed them, and in that sense had meaning. But to a colonnader they were simply irrelevant.

'So you base your decisions on simple chance?' he said to Romrey. 'Play cubes would be sufficient for that.'

'Not on chance, no.' Romrey shook his head. 'That's no ordinary deck of cards. Look closely at the material. The cards have adp in them.'

'All such cards do – these, for instance.' With a slow movement Boaz brought out his own deck. 'To make the pictures move.'

'No, no, these have much more. They are *all* adp.'

The cards had a micalike finish. They were, as Romrey had said, made of adp substance, much like silicon bones.

'These are magical cards,' Romrey said. 'Mystic cards. They respond to events going on around them. They are never wrong. In fact, they can *create* events too.'

'Yes, if you are improvident enough to let them guide all your actions,' Boaz remarked.

He had to admit that the cards had a charm all of their own. Even the aberrant symbolism added up to a certain bizarre profundity. And he reminded himself that some of the deviant sects, as they passed down the hidden lanes and by-ways of thought, often made surprising discoveries.

Just the same, his background made him sceptical of Romrey's claims, so much so that his lip curled.

However, his ship had presumably, during its surveillance of the city over the past few days, seen this man using the cards for divination – something which true colonnaders looked upon as pure superstition. If his ship took it seriously, then so did Boaz.

Romrey began pulling on some garments. Boaz turned to the woman. 'And what can your man Obsoc contribute?'

'Him?' She rolled her eyes to the ceiling. 'Money. He's rich. He's got his own big yacht orbiting up there, and it's armed, pretty heavily. Probably it could even take on that government cruiser that's coming.'

'Can you arrange a meeting with him?'

'If he thinks you can do him any good.'

Boaz nodded. Events had changed rapidly for all three of them in the past few minutes, he thought. But people were used to fast transitions, in this modern world.

Radalce Obsoc was a tall, stooped man with bulging eyes. His nose was small and hooked, exactly like an owl's beak, and his thin-lipped mouth was equally small.

His appearance was in curious contrast with the red-haired sensuous-looking Mace Meare, as Boaz had come to know her. Their relationship, however, was not hard to fathom. She was a paid pleasure girl, on permanent contract.

The pleasure, it was undertood, was to be hers. Obsoc himself was not a sensuous man: he was a collector, his passions cerebral, who required to have among his possessions a beautiful woman who could plumb the depths of erotic delight. Silicon bones gave Mace that, and Obsoc's enjoyment was the voyeur's one of watching her attain the transports of that delight – with whom, or what, or by herself (Obsoc had a complete collection of sexual appurtenances) did not matter. Boaz doubted if he ever actually touched her himself.

Obsoc collected many things, but his real passion was for jewels. He practically raged at Boaz when he spoke of them. He possessed, he said, specimens of all *but one* of the nine thousand and thirty-four known gem classifications, including the largest natural diamond ever found, weighing over half a ton (this was a mere curiosity, since single-crystal diamonds of up to twenty tons had been synthesized). His cold store contained the complete range of low-temperature gems, including rare varieties of ice of surpassing beauty, produced only under the freak conditions of isolated sunless planets (and far exceeding his half-ton diamond in value). He had an impact technetium sapphire – one of the only two specimens ever found. No price could be put upon his collection; it was unique. He had stipulated that it was to remain intact after his death, and he doubted if any individual would be wealthy enough to buy it. It would, perhaps, become a trust to the glory of the econosphere.

'There is but one gem, sir, that I do not possess,' he said in almost ferocious tones to Boaz, 'and that is a time-gem from Meirjain the Wanderer. The lack of it makes an intolerable gap in my collection, and I am determined to repair it. Furthermore, the fewer are in circulation the better pleased I shall be. Present circumstances, therefore, meet with my approval to some extent – if all goes well.'

'You'd like it better if you could be the only one to land on Meirjain, I suppose?' Romrey interjected.

'You grasp my meaning quite correctly. But you need fear no treachery on my part. I have an unbending sense of probity, and will deal loyally with all members of our little party.'

They were in the main cabin of Boaz's ship. He strongly disliked entertaining strangers, or indeed anyone, within this, his private domain (it was like inviting someone into his own body), but the proposed exercise called for it.

He sat next to Romrey at the small circular table. To his left was Mace, and opposite him was Obsoc. Romrey was expertly shuffling his cards. 'Are you ready, Captain?'

Curtly Boaz nodded.

'Then we must all concentrate. You especially, Captain. Concentrate on what it is we're looking for.'

For Boaz that was easy, despite his feeling slightly ridiculous about the proceedings. He had been obliged to swallow his scepticism in order to make the experiment, which consisted of marrying the cards' reputed function with his ship's special data-gathering ability. Also, he had been obliged to divulge something of that ability. The other three now had some idea – though not a complete one – that it was the ship that kept Boaz alive.

Romrey made a brief salutation, raising his hand perpendicular to his face in a cryptic sign. 'To the force that orders events.'

Slowly Romrey began to lay down cards, speaking as he did. 'This deck was issued by the Carborundum Order, which I don't think exists any more. Anyway I was never a member of it – I'm a straight sort of alec, really. I don't even know what carborundum means.'

'It is a carbon compound once used for polishing,' Boaz supplied quietly. 'The Carborundum Order taught a technique they termed "polishing the mirror". The mirror being the mirror of mind.'

'Is that so? Well, to get down to it, in the Carborundum deck the four suits stand, among other things, for the four points of the compass on planets that have a magnetic field. So we ought to be able to locate which part of the city to look in.'

'If our man is in Wildhart at all,' Mace pointed out.

Romrey had dealt five cards. 'He is,' he said, pointing to the first, which was the Vehicle, showing a gorgeous chariot-like ship surging through space, sometimes dipping into planetary atmospheres, past shining cities or even under oceans.

'This is the perfect card of assent and victory,' he said. 'It tells us we are right in our assumption. Now, we have two picture cards and three suit cards – two wings, and one cubes. Wings predominate, and stand for north. Therefore he is in the north of the city. But cubes are also present, and they stand for west. So he's in the northwest, or more probably the north-northwest.'

He peered thoughtfully at the other picture card, as though hoping for some extra clue in its motions. It was the Inverted Man. 'Note that his head enters a deep shaft. It could mean that our target is underground.' He darted a look at Boaz. 'Can your beams reach down there?'

'It depends how deep,' Boaz said. 'Shall I begin?'

Romrey hesitated, fingered the next card in the deck, then pushed it back. 'OK.'

Boaz slumped, his fist falling to the table with a thump.

He called on his ship, and down below them the innards of one of the big casings geared up, sending beams lunging softly forth. Out, out, up into towers, down into basements, sorting through a collage of Wildhart's innumerable private scenes.

As on previous occasions, Boaz noted to himself how repetitious were those scenes. Human life centred around only a few activities. People ate, drank, slept, quarrelled, fought, made love, gambled, studied, worked. It was like a number matrix in which nearly all the numbers were the same. But of course this was Wildhart, a border town. In a hundred places around the city men and women were submitting to sex death. There was much robbery, as well as murder – a crime cheapened today by its erotic associations. As well as debauchery in all its most inventive forms.

After getting his bearings, Boaz followed Romrey's suggestion and concentrated on the substreet levels, muttering a monologue to which Romrey listened intently while laying down more cards, trying to interpret them into suggestions as to which direction Boaz should veer in.

Such a rapid, bewildering overseeing of the life of the city was tiring. And frustrating. After an hour Boaz stopped, exhausted. They had got nowhere.

'This is no use,' he said. 'We are making fools of ourselves with those cards.'

'I don't reckon so.'

'It is ridiculous. I grant they have a lot of adp. So what? *How can that affect their order when shuffled?*'

Romrey frowned. 'I heard something about that once, but I didn't understand it. These cards are locked into the structure of the world somehow. They are never wrong, provided you trust them. But sometimes you have to do a rerun.'

Boaz snorted, glancing scornfully first at Obsoc and then at Mace. Romrey was shuffling again. 'We'll start from the beginning,' he decided stubbornly.

Once more he laid down five cards. The first was the Vehicle. 'Again the Vehicle!' he announced triumphantly. 'Again the Inverted Man! But look here.'

The hand was uncannily similar to the first one, so much so that Boaz suspected sleight of hand. There were two picture cards and three suit cards. And two of the suit cards were wings, as before. But the other was laser rods, not cubes.

'The first reading misled us,' Romrey muttered. 'Of course – the cubes had a low value, and was not reliable. Here we have the nine of rods, which is more definitive. The co-ordinates are to be found in the north-northeast, not north-northwest.'

Wearily Boaz took up the hunt again. And suddenly he seemed to go in rapport with Romrey. He was telling him where he was and what he saw, and Romrey was slapping down card after card, telling him which way to move and whether he was getting closer or farther.

Romrey himself seemed to go into a daze. He held each hand of five fanned before his face as if playing one of the old games like poker or gin-rummy. And he talked, spinning a story out of the cards, sometimes seeming to be ahead of Boaz. Like an invisible spirit, the shipkeeper moved into a semi-derelict area, drifting past broken walls of HCferric that inadequately hid the derelict human beings who sheltered behind them, gliding over dusty unused roadways littered with urban detritus.

Again and again the Inverted Man was turning up, like a flashing locator signal. It told them that Boaz was warm. Then he went through the wall of what appeared to be a deserted warehouse. The ship had found something there, he knew. Mouldy abandoned bales of some sort of fibre were stacked to one side. Without pause, the floor rose up to him. He went through it, down into a series of cellars.

One of them had been converted into makeshift living quarters. On a low couch lay a sleeping figure. Beside it, on the floor, was a dish containing a white powder.

Boaz scanned the rest of the room. There was little furniture. The one door bore steel bonds and at the four corners of the room were antennaed boxes. These were guard devices which, to the credit of his ship, the search beams did not appear to have triggered.

This is the man, the ship told him, *who went into the Brilliancy Cluster and detected Meirjain. He has the data.*

'I've found him,' Boaz said out loud.

The other three leaned close. 'Have you fixed the location?' Obsoc asked.

'I can find it again.'

'Who is he?' asked Mace curiously.

'A prospector. He's drugged right now. I think he's an addict. It looks like plutosnow.'

'Oh, by the Fire,' Mace said, unconscious of using the colonnader oath, 'no wonder he didn't make it to Meirjain first time.' The effects of plutosnow were erratic. It produced bursts of unusual energy and ability, interspersed with an almost total lack of will. Anything achieved by its use usually had to be finished by somebody else.

'Perhaps the whole story is a fantasy he started,' Obsoc suggested worriedly. 'Perhaps Meirjain is not due to appear.'

'I doubt it,' Boaz said. 'One side effect of plustosnow is an aversion to untruth. This character may have opened his mouth too much and then holed up for his own protection. Or else he gave the numbers to a few people and then holed up.'

'If the econosphere takes it seriously, so can we,' Romrey said.

Boaz nodded agreement. He looked at Obsoc. It was now up to the trillionaire to play his part and organize the seizure of the needed information. In the circumstances it scarcely seemed necessary. Boaz felt he could take the cellar on his own.

Obsoc's grasp on realities, however, betokened more than a nodding acquaintances with such operations. 'We must move carefully,' he said with a grave air. 'There are men in Wildhart whose interest in this matter matches our own, and they are totally ruthless. Did you know that the Hat Brothers are here? Also Father Larry and his girls. Perhaps you do not know of these people. I assure you they are very resourceful and they will be watching to see if anyone is about to make a move. Yes. . . . Then of course the econosphere undoubtedly has agents here, though whether they command any resources worth speaking of is a different matter.' He pondered. 'I take it he has defences?'

'There is a guard system. I didn't see anything else.'

'I will hire some people who know how to deal with these things. Meanwhile you'd better give me the exact location.'

The collector attended closely while Boaz drew a rough map and described the warehouse. 'Good. Well, our work here would seem to be finished. Are you coming, Mace, my dear?'

The girl looked almost appealingly at Boaz. 'I'll follow you a little later, Radalce. I'd like to rest here a while longer – if you don't mind, Captain Boaz.'

Though he would have preferred her to go, Boaz shrugged his consent. Obsoc looked his craggy body up and down, an obvious thought dawning on him. 'Well, enjoy yourself, my dear. I'll send the runabout back for you.'

He and Romrey left. When Boaz came back from seeing them down the flowrail she was still sitting at the table. As he came close her hand glided up and gently stroked his leg.

He drew back. 'You must not do that, Mace. You cannot expect to entice me into dalliance.'

'You're not *that* much of a colonnader!'

'So to speak.'

'But you have bones. How can you refuse such pleasure?'

'I never use my bones, Mace. They have been switched off for many years.'

'A stoic indeed!'

'Pleasure is a poor thing to me. My life is set in one direction.'

'Oh, you're a mystic, bent on self-transcendence,' she

said, misunderstanding him. 'But that puzzles me. Here you are going all out after time-gems. It could only be for the money. Greed for money doesn't square with sensual abstention – does it?'

'It is not for money.'

'Then what?' She frowned.

'Never mind.' Boaz waved his hand in annoyance. 'You wished to end your life.'

'And you interfered. That was very sanctimonious of you.'

'It was not because of you. You tried to implicate someone else, in a way that would have had harmful consequences for them. That was unfair.'

She looked unabashed.

'Do you still intend to end your life?'

She smiled self-consciously, as though wanting to avoid the subject. 'There's no such things,' she said flippantly. 'You're a colonnader, you know that. The world returns, and we return with it. There is no death.'

'You are not a colonnader.'

'I don't have to be. Everybody knows it's true. Science has proved it.'

'Yes, that is so.' He paused, deliberating, before he spoke again. 'But as a consideration, it is too abstract an idea for most people. Even if they take it seriously, the prospect of dreamless sleep for the next nine hundred trillion years is sufficient inducement for the intended suicide. So I ask you again: is it still your intention?'

'I don't know.' She dropped her eyes to the table. 'When you came bursting in like that, it sort of broke my rhythm.'

'Is death really the only thrill left?'

'Well it's one thrill anyway.' She glanced up at him again. Her eyes were mischievous. 'Want me to tell you what it's like?'

'Not now,' Boaz said. 'Not now. And leave Romrey alone, as far as that is concerned.'

*

Approaching the warehouse unseen was a problem. Obsoc's hirelings had picked out a route which minimized the open ground to be crossed, and they carried gadgets which were supposed to keep the guard devices silent, but it was still debatable whether the party would enter undetected.

It was night and Sarsuce was moonless, but the placing of the Brilliancy Cluster was such as to send a glow through the whole atmosphere, so that every solid object was surrounded by a haze of shadow. Boaz stirred, crouching behind a low wall, and watched the three raiders as they edged into the light of Brilliancy.

Romrey was crouched stock-still beside him, peering over the wall with the intentness of a stoat. Obsoc was not present; he awaited their report back in his apartment.

The raiders raced suddenly across the stone-strewn ground to fetch up like shadows against the warehouse wall. As they went, something caused Boaz to look to the right of the building. He saw a human figure in a close-fitting catsuit flit away, loping with head down. 'Look,' he whispered to Romrey. But then it was gone.

A billow of fine dust expanded from the base of the warehouse as the team disintegrated a hole in it. 'They're going in,' Romrey whispered hoarsely. Boaz could feel his excitement. They watched as two men went inside. The third man paused, waited, then beckoned to Boaz and Romrey. They scrambled over the wall and ran lightly to join the team.

The interior of the warehouse was as Boaz had already seen it. Obsoc's men, wearing light energy armour, moved across the floor, holding out ring antennae parallel to it. They were looking for the trapdoor entrance. One of them, a bland-faced, plump man, abruptly stopped and held up a hand.

'Here it is,' he murmured, 'but it's too well protected.'

'We'll dust in through the floor,' one of his companions said, referring to the disintegration process. He pulled out a grenade.

'Wait.' The other was listening to his readings through an earphone. A look of surprise crossed his face. 'It's already been opened. We can go through.'

'He forgot to lock it?'

Already Boaz could guess how events were turning out. But he said nothing while the three cautiously opened the thick hinged plate, alert for traps, and lowered themselves into the cellar below. He followed, and then Romrey. It was as he expected.

The plump man was inspecting a prone body on the matted floor. 'He's dead,' he announced. 'Sonic gun.' It was the prospector Boaz had seen asleep on the couch.

'I saw someone run off just as we got here,' he informed.

'Damn. Somebody beat us to it.'

'Maybe they missed it,' Romrey said anxiously. 'Look around. Look for a memory cube.'

'We'll look. But we won't find it. This was an official killing.' Another of the hirelings picked up a card from the floor. It bore a silver eagle – the emblem of the econosphere. 'A government agent was here.'

'Most likely there never was any external record,' the third raider said. 'He probably carried the data in his adplant.'

'Can you be sure that card's genuine?' Boaz asked querulously.

'It's genuine.' The hired raider sounded resigned as he examined the document, tilting it in the light to read ingrained patterns. 'These are pretty difficult to forge. And eco agents always leave them after an enforcement job.'

'It's a way of displaying the long arm of the ecosphere,' the other raider said in all seriousness. He flipped open a communicator. 'Shall I report to our employer, or will you?'

'I'll do it.' He took the communicator and began to press out Obsoc's code.

Romrey was standing over the body of the murdered

man, shaking his head. 'The government certainly does want to keep Meirjain off limits, to just wipe this poor alec out like this. I wonder what they're afraid of?'

The leader of the hirelings shrugged. 'It beats me. The people who got down last time didn't find anything so dangerous, from what I've heard. They all came back in one piece.'

Boaz got through to Obsoc. On the matt-like surface of the screen he could see the lounge of his apartment, though Obsoc did not show himself. His dry, petulant voice came through. 'Yes? How is it?'

'This is Captain Boaz, Citizen Obsoc,' Boaz said politely. 'I'm afraid it isn't any use. A government agent got here before us. Almost certainly the data has been wiped out. It probably doesn't exist anywhere now.'

'It doesn't matter,' Obsoc's voice said. 'Not in the least. Something has happened in the last few minutes.'

He paused. 'There's a blanket broadcast coming out of Brilliancy. It must be from Meirjain. It gives the emergence co-ordinates. They're common property now.'

'But that doesn't make sense!' exclaimed Romrey, striding over. 'What does it mean?'

'It means,' said Obsoc, 'that something on Meirjain wants people to go there.'

4

Madrigo, on Boaz's last visit to Theta, had been pleased by the extent of his seeming recovery. It had almost been a trial to disabuse him.

In his memory, emblazoned there like poignant signs of an existence that might have been, Boaz saw the immense colonnades stretching to the horizon, the benign sherbet-like atmosphere fading into the crocus-coloured sky. He smelled the delightful yet calming fragrances of the place. By his side walked Madrigo, that rock of assurance.

'I can see from your manner that you have proved the supremacy of mind, Boaz,' he said. 'You have conquered your ill fate.'

'I have not conquered it,' said Boaz.

And it was true. Boaz's rock-steady personality, like the modsuit he now always wore – like, on the somatic level, his strong and craggy body – was armour. Character armour, permitting him to function in the real world, but protecting a core of absolute horror.

It was Madrigo himself who had helped create this armour. Without colonnader knowledge of the mind the task would have been impossible. By the same token, it was Madrigo who was now fooled by it.

'I chose ill when I selected my names,' Boaz said. 'They augur a destiny I would avoid. . .'

He spoke on, outlining his great fear. Madrigo nodded, and looked serious.

And then Boaz put his question. It would, for a fact, have been hard to find a more audacious question. It was the first time he had ever seen his mentor appear startled.

He waited.

'What you plan is quite impossible,' said Madrigo when he was sure he had understood Boaz's intention. 'Nothing can ever be changed. If it were otherwise, your names would be lies.'

Then Boaz knew that no human being, not even his wise and kindly mentor, would or could help him, and the utter loneliness of his mission overwhelmed him.

Boaz pushed the memory away, inasmuch as it could be pushed, into the burning coffers of his mind. He had checked the fuel rods to see that they were delivering their energy evenly. Now he carried out a similar but less practical ritual – inspecting those parts of the ship with which he was in somatic integration.

Apart from the space taken up by the engines, the hold, living quarters and astrogation, there were four decks devoted to keeping Boaz alive. The ship was constructed on the principle of 'holistic integration,' which meant that no system in it was left entirely unaffected by what happened in any other system. Boaz, in other words, was entirely a part of the ship. When the engines exerted themselves, he could feel it in his guts. When the ship changed state or direction, he experienced a momentary feeling of vertigo.

The somatic system, as the bonemakers called it, was all-enveloping. It extended through the walls of his living quarters and into the working parts of the ship. Its main bulk, however, lay in the four decks crammed with dull-coloured casings. When he moved among them, Boaz had the feeling of moving within his own body – for this, in a sense more real than flesh and blood, *was* his body. Even his consci ousness was maintained here.

Normal adp was silent; but this was not. Boaz did not fully comprehend the reason why, but it whirred and clicked in a constant mutter of mechanical conversation – although he knew it had no moving parts.

On each casing was a check screen. Moving from casing to casing, Boaz stared in fascination at the symbols that flickered ceaselessly on the glowing green plates. The bonemakers had taught him the meanings of some of those symbols, though in actuality there was no need for him to look at them at all. The somatic system was entirely selfsupervising.

The reason for the existence of the screens, as for his daily inspection of them, was that they constituted a reminder of where his health lay. Otherwise there was a danger (the bonemakers believed) that he might forget, and wander out of the ship's range despite the warning bleeps that would be transmitted to him were he to do so.

Last of all he went to the transmitters on the fourth level. It was an extraordinary sensation to stand there. The beams were at maximum penetration (though very nearly parallel and coherent, their strength weakened with distance due to loss of intelligibility on passing through a material medium. Each inch of emanating beam was like a computer system in its own right). Boaz had the feeling that a strong, invigorating light shone through his body, filling him with health and power.

The temptation was to spend long periods of time there, but it was a temptation he resisted every day. Quickly and efficiently he carried out his checks (to which there was a more practical point than with the processors, the transmitters being more liable to deterioration) and withdrew.

He went back to his cabin.

'Nearly there now,' the ship whispered to him.

'Show me.'

Boaz settled in his armchair. Dispensing with artificial displays, the ship fed his mind with an image of the Brilliancy Cluster through which he was now moving. A crimson circle pinpointed the star which it was expected would be host to the wandering planet.

Flecks of bright purple were a swarm of other ships migrating purposefully toward the same location. Some were far ahead of others – as soon as it was realized the broadcast from Brilliancy had to be genuine, they had started taking off from Sarsuce like fleas leaving a drowning dog. In the rush nobody had paused to dwell on who had sent the broadcast, or why.

'After the gold,' Boaz muttered to himself. 'All after the gold.' It was an old saying from a time when gold had been a valuable metal and men had stampeded for any chance of laying their hands on it.

He was going to be among the stragglers getting there. There were operators in the vicinity with very fast ships, and he had delayed some hours before taking off.

But Meirjain was a big planet, and he had the advantage that he did not want as much as they did. Boaz, in his gloomy way, was feeling fairly optimistic.

★

The ship woke him from his troubled sleep. A minor note of urgency pervaded the summons, and Boaz came instantly to a sitting position in the armchair that served him in place of a bed.

'Look,' said the ship.

Again a picture in his mind – or rather, a montage of pictures. A planet, its surface mottled purple, blue and mauve, fretted with a filigree of other colours – gold, silver, scarlet. It was warmed by a yellow sun with a hint of blue; a sun, he recognized, that offered the full spectrum of colors accessible to the human eye.

In diagrammatized form he saw what the naked eye would not see: scores of ships in orbit. Their outlines flickered in his vision. Many of them he could remember seeing on Wildhart ship ground.

'Why haven't they gone down?' he asked.

'They can't,' his ship told him.

'Why not?'

'I have called *The Sedulous Seeker* for you.'

The Sedulous Seeker, Radalce Obsoc's yacht, was as fast as anything flying and would have been among the first vessels to arrive. Obsoc's image rose before Boaz's mind's eye, a sumptuous lounge providing a background. Mace lolled on a couch, her eyes closed.

The collector's bulging eyes glistened. 'Good day, shipkeeper. You got here at last.'

'What happened?' Boaz asked. 'Is no one down?'

'No one has been able to get down.' Obsoc's mouth twitched. 'Plenty have tried. The atmosphere is impossible to penetrate.'

Boaz was silent; he left it to his puzzled expression to ask the question.

'My engineer tells me the planet is surrounded by a "reverse inertial field",' Obsoc supplied. 'Though in my view he is simply covering up ignorance with clever words.'

'It doesn't make sense,' Boaz said slowly.

'For Meirjain to be inaccessible? Presumably it makes sense to whatever intelligence is manipulating us in this fashion. There is something down there, shipkeeper, and it is playing games with us.'

'We can't hang around here forever,' Boaz said. 'The cruiser will be on us in a few standard days.'

'The cruiser may not *necessarily* have things all its own way. We have a regular orbital town here, Shipkeeper Boaz, and some firepower.' Obsoc frowned. 'The real problem is whether anything is going to come of this exercise. You may care to add your voice to an attempt to find a way out of the impasse. We are holding a meeting to see if there might be some way forward.'

'Who will be at this meeting?'

'Some of those who have tried to penetrate the barrier. Also some scientific minds who are among us.' Obsoc paused. 'Also it has not been possible to exclude some of the more forceful personalities present. I should warn you that they are people of the most dangerous sort. Tempers are frayed; there has already been fighting.'

'And who is holding it?'

'It will take place aboard my yacht. The quarters here are particularly commodious. Heave to in three standard hours if you are interested.'

'All right,' Boaz decided. 'I'll be there.'

The image disappeared from his projective imagination. 'Instructions?' the ship queried.

'Continue orbit.'

Boaz looked again at the planet below. For some reason the events taking place did not arouse his curiosity. He merely found the mystery annoying.

With an aggrieved sigh, he went back to sleep.

The ships were beginning to gather when Boaz approached *The Sedulous Seeker*. A crowd of them, of all shapes and sizes, stretched about the sleek, elegant form of the yacht. He recognized Romrey's natty *Stardiver* nestling close under the belly of the bigger spaceship, its access tube dangling. Romrey, it appeared, had already joined the party.

A voice sounded in his head, not Obsoc's but a crewman's or else a machine's. 'Citizen Obsoc welcomes you aboard, Shipkeeper Boaz.'

His ship conveyed his thanks for him. He clambered down to the port, from where an access tube was already reaching out to join up with a similar tube from the star yacht. As soon as they were sealed the lid flicked up to allow him to enter.

The distance to the yacht was about fifty yards. The inertial gravity field did not operate outside the skin of the ship and once in the tube he was in free fall, pulling himself along by means of handholds. Then, as he passed the midpoint, he came down to the floor with a bump. He might have guessed, he thought ruefully, that a man as wealthy as Obsoc would have gravity even in an access tube.

The farther lid flicked up as he reached it. A solicitous robot helped him through the port. 'Citizen Obsoc is in the main lounge, sir,' it said, in the same voice Boaz had heard earlier. 'If you will follow me.'

The corridor was panelled with honeywood, an organic fibrous substance with an intriguing texture which had highlights of silver in it. A thick-piled carpet made walking a silent, mossy experience. It was quite unlike the hard though sometimes springy floors he was used to.

The robot ushered him into the lounge. Radalce Obsoc stepped politely forward to greet him.

Boaz gazed about him. Walls and ceiling were patterned in fretted gold. There was little furniture. He got the idea most of it had been removed, perhaps to make more room, perhaps to avoid risk of damage to Obsoc's valuable antiques. There were about a dozen people present, including Romrey who sat talking with a young man while a fat, bland woman watched them both. He had been invited, presumably, on the strength of the partnership the three of them had recently enjoyed. Obsoc, perhaps uniquely among those who had flocked to Wildhart, had a sense of propriety.

'You won't accommodate everybody here,' he remarked.

'You refer to the ships outside? They gather like insects around honey. Word has gone around. But I have invited only twenty-six persons in all.' He lowered his tone. 'Over there is Larry with two of his girls. You must, of course, take care not to annoy them.'

Surreptitiously he gestured to a huge man, big-boned, with the hard, aggressive face of a mobster, who stood by a table. He was flanked by two junoesque women as large as himself, younger but with a striking family resemblance – the same large-boned jaw, the flashing, challenging eyes. They would be taken for Larry's sisters or daughters. They were, Boaz knew, his clones, genetically male like himself but somatically female, having been given hormone treatment in the foetus stage. Larry's entire gang consisted of such girls, of whom he had an unknown number. Now, like most of the other guests, he stood awkwardly, impatiently sipping from a glass.

Boaz's attention was caught by the opening of another door farther along the lounge. This time it was the Hat Brothers who entered. Obsoc rushed immediately to receive them.

The Hat Brothers might also have been taken for clones, but were in fact naturally identical twins. Their appearance together was striking not so much for their lookalike features as for the black, wide-brimmed hats they both wore. The story of those metal hats was well known. Boaz was aware that the psychopathology of the professional criminal involved a passion for strong family relationships – as witness the Larry gang. The brothers' hats were welded to their skulls. Bestowed on them by their father, they were transceivers for relaying mental activity, tuned and coded only to one another. Each brother experienced all the thoughts and feelings of the other, and this had been the case since their early years. They were, in effect, one mind with two bodies.

It was an unsettling sensation to be in the presence of the brothers. Boaz watched as, walking in step, they traversed the lounge to reach the drinks table. People moved furtively out of their path. As they passed near Larry and his girls, ignoring them, there was a definite air of tension.

Deftly, like two android robots operated by a single controller, they took a drink apiece from the table top and turned to face the room.

'All right!' barked one in an acid voice. 'Let's get started!'

'We're not all here yet,' growled Larry, his voice testy.

'It's not our liking to be kept waiting,' the Hat Brother said. Then his twin, as if continuing the same speech (which was likely pointed to the young man who had been talking with Romrey). '*You* tried to get down, and got farther than most. You're an engineer too, we hear.'

'And *you*,' continued his brother, pointing to another man, bearded, in a crimson tunic, 'you're a physicist.' The twins looked around the now silent gathering. 'We've enough here to be starting with. If there are any ideas, let's have them.'

One of Larry's girls suddenly strode across the room. She raised her fist at the last brother to speak. 'If you think you can push us around—'

'Ladies! Gentlemen! Please!' Obsoc pressed himself forward supplicatingly. 'We must not quarrel. We are here to co-operate.'

There was a smile of amusement hovering around Larry's thin, hard lips. He beckoned to his girl. She rejoined him.

At that moment the robot servant opened the door again. Several more people entered, including, Boaz noted to his faint surprise, a nymphgirl wearing a gauzy shift.

Obsoc turned, then reached out his arm to disengage her from the group. 'May I introduce Neavy Hirester? Though you may not think it to look at her, she is an expert on inertial field.'

Looking at her, the Hat Brothers smiled ironically. 'Really? Now that's something we didn't know. And where did you train, girl?'

'I didn't train,' Neavy answered in a cool voice. 'I had it adplanted.'

'An adplant doesn't make you an *expert*,' the Hat Brother said. 'An *expert* is somebody who understands what he's talking about. Like my brother and I are *experts* at seeing to it that people do—'

'*Shut up, Hat*,' grated Larry. He turned to Neavy, 'You've worked with fields?'

She nodded. 'I was servicing generators before—'

'—you started servicing *people!*' another voice finished for her, and laughed.

Boaz wondered what urge it was that had brought the girl to Meirjain. That she was unusual among nymphgirls – who as a rule lived only for uncomplicated sensual pleasure – was attested by her having specialist technical knowledge, albeit adplanted.

What of the others, for that matter? For her it was probably a simple desire for quick wealth, as it was with Romrey. But for some of the others – like the Hat Brothers, and the Larry Family – there had to be more to it. They were already wealthy. What kind of greedy craving was it that made them want even more wealth, at whatever risk?

Neavy was speaking. 'The Meirjain barrier is quite clearly an inertial field, like the artificial gravity in a spaceship except that it resists the approach of matter instead of attracting it. And except that it's much more powerful, of course. Now it's not commonly appreciated by laymen that artificial fields of this type have a breaking point. It will be pretty high in a planet-sized field this strong, but I think we might give it a try.'

'How?' Larry asked. Once she had started talking they all seemed intrigued by the idea of taking technical advice from her.

'The field is designed to keep ships out. Ergo, it will be designed to withstand any normal ship propulsion unit. So we lash up a number of units on one ship and try to go through.' She paused. 'I calculate that where an inertial field is used as a repulsor instead of an attractor, puncturing it will have a bubble effect. It will disintegrate – until the generator can build it up again.'

'That's not an advantage,' Obsoc pointed out. 'It's not in our interest to clear the way for all that mob out there.' He waved his hand to take in the raggle-taggle fleet gathered around his yacht.

'We won't be able to do anything about it,' the girl pointed out.

Boaz spoke up. 'There's another aspect to all this. The sequence of events puzzles me. A broadcast from the Wanderer practically invites us here, but then an inertial field stops us from getting down. Someone is playing games with us.'

Larry pulled a face. 'Nobody is there. There first expeditions reported no intelligent life. Only dead civilization.'

His girls nodded approvingly, inadvertently advertising that he had already talked over this point with them.

'Then to what do you attribute both the broadcast and the field?' one of the Hat Brothers asked archly.

'Some left-over machine is doing it. At random, for no reason.'

'I'd say that's a good explanation,' the young man Romrey had been talking to offered anxiously. His face was serious. 'There used to be a saying in the Academy – when events contradict one another, put it down to nature or machine, not consciousness.'

What academy he referred to wasn't clear, but his contribution was ignored as though he had never spoken. Boaz sensed something happening between Larry and the Hat Brothers. He tensed, but the outcome, when it fell out, took him by surprise.

Larry looked straight at the nearest brother and raised his eyebrows. In return, both brothers nodded.

'Things need simplifying,' the brother farthest from him said, though he was looking the other way and couldn't have seen Larry's signal. For a moment the three men stood motionless, eyes glazed.

'How do we do that?' the nymphgirl asked. No one seemed to have noticed the exchange between the men. The Hat Brother's remark was received, with only slight bewilderment, as continuing the previous conversation.

It was, Boaz supposed, to be expected – treachery, combinations between enemies, anything that could bestow an unfair advantage even though, on the face of it, probably no one would gain anything anyway. Was Obsoc party to this, or had he innocently invited a viper to his bosom?

But what was it Larry and the Hat Brothers planned? Simply to shoot down everyone present. Boaz reached out in his mind to draw extra defensive strength over the beam from his ship – but at that moment the ship itself spoke to him:

Extreme danger. Return immediately.

He was puzzled by the message. He could not imagine what threat to him there was here that the ship could not help him handle. Larry was doing nothing, merely smiling to himself, while the brothers gazed in bored fashion at the floor.

He was about to ask the ship for an explanation when a shout from the far end of the lounge directed him to the answer. A big wall screen had come on, probably activated by a robot on the yacht's bridge.

The gathered swarm of small ships was on the screen. Moving through them, firing in all directions with what looked like proton broadbeams, came two slightly larger vessels, almost certainly those belonging to the Hat Brothers and to Larry and his girls.

It now became urgently clear to Boaz what the danger was. It was not directly to him. *It was to his ship.* His ship, without which he was dead. This had been prearranged; while seeming to do nothing, Larry and the Hat Brothers had been sending go signals to their vessels.

The scene was little short of carnage. Very few of the starcraft had weapons, and those that were manned got under way and fled in panic. Others – mostly those whose occupants were aboard *The Sedulous Seeker* – floated passively and were junked by the withering effect of high-velocity proton pulses.

While seeing this, Boaz was on his way to the exit. There the robot which had admitted him barred his path.

'Sir, I strongly urge you not to leave the ship. It is not safe out there.'

'Get out of my way!' Boaz bawled.

'Sir, for your own safety I cannot allow you to pass. Citizen Obsoc would be most distressed if you came to harm on his account.'

Boaz paused, turning to see what happened in the lounge behind him. Everyone now realized what was afoot. Some recognized the identity of the attacking ships. But just as they might have been thinking of doing something about it, they were pre-empted by Larry's girls. Parawhips in hand, they stepped toward the gathering their motions animal and predatory, sending the thin whips singing out warningly over the heads of those present.

The Hat Brothers entered into the act, too. Producing numbnerve guns, they separated to dance down opposite sides of the lounge. Watching them move was fascinating. It was not a walk, not a lope, but more like a beautifully co-ordinated balletic performance. Boaz realized that they enjoyed moving together. *Phut, phut* went the hazy blue spheres of static they sent rebounding through the lounge from the muzzles of their guns, again taking care not to aim at anyone.

'Don't anybody move,' said a brother in a confident, low-timbred voice. 'When we've cleared the riffraff away we'll carry out the nymphgirl's plan.'

'My ship!' screamed someone. Boaz waited to see no more. He pushed aside the robot, who did not have the strength to restrain a human being anyway, and ran down the corridor.

Others had got the idea of trying to save their craft by the time he reached the skin of the ship, but he had no difficulty in sending the signal that automatically reconnected the access tubes. Wondering what he would do if a proton beam accidentally sliced through the tunnel, he hauled himself swiftly along it and in minutes had regained his own ship.

As with most vessels, there was no external armament and it was imperative to get out of danger as quickly as possible. Ordering the ship to bring him an image of surrounding space, he went to his cabin.

The long shaft of Obsoc's yacht floated fifty yards away. In the other direction was a scene of chaos. With scarcely a thought from Boaz, the ship disconnected and was about to withdraw the access tube, when he noticed a figure floating near the dangling end of another access tube farther along *The Sedulous Seeker*.

The figure, wearing an emergency space cape and twisting slowly, looked familiar. 'Give me a closer look at that,' Boaz ordered.

The picture zoomed in his mind. As he had thought, it was Romrey. Panning the image, Boaz found the wreck of his *Stardiver*. Romrey must have been trying to reach it, and had somehow fallen out of the end of the tube. Very careless of him.

Boaz knew he should be steering his ship away from here without delay. But there was never a time when ethics could be entirely overridden. He nudged the ship closer and ordered the tube extended toward the stranded man.

Suddenly the ship spoke to him again, with a note of even greater urgency: *Attention. A government cruiser approaches.*

'What?' Boaz spoke out loud in his startlement. 'But it isn't due for another two standard days.'

Whoever made that assessment was mistaken, or mischievous. It is here.

'Let me see.'

From a purely rational point of view the ensuing images were confusing, but Boaz was used to the semi-diagrammatic way of representation his ship sometimes adopted. He saw Romrey reaching for the access tube, ridiculously waving his arms and legs as though swimming toward it (like most people, he had practically no experience of free fall). He saw the scattering, damaged cloud of space craft, as though from a different viewpoint imposed on the first. And imposed on *that*, he saw the fully armed econosphere cruiser, more than twice as large as Obsoc's yacht, its form functional and ungainly – ugly, in fact – swiftly moving in to enforce the government edict which everyone here had defied.

The montage fused into one coherent picture as the cruiser darted sharklike among the still-disorganized crowd of ships, the official blazon – a starburst with eight glowing rays – clearly visible on its flanks. The servants of the econosphere were notoriously unfastidious about how they achieved their aims. The cruiser opened fire from the start, ruthlessly selecting targets with a view to chasing away anyone trying to land on the planet that loomed to one side of the scene. Its heavy-duty beams immediately vaporized three ships. Its staff was probably surprised, however, to see the eerie blue glow of a magnetic defense screen abruptly surround *The Sedulous Seeker*. The yacht returned fire and began to accelerate, sliding around the gorgeous curve of Meirjain.

The two ships that earlier had been firing on the assembly followed suit – presumably because Larry and the Hat Brothers were still aboard Obsoc's yacht. They, too, opened up on the now pursuing cruiser. In seconds all four vessels had disappeared over the horizon.

But they would soon be back. 'Seal the tube and haul it in quickly,' Boaz ordered. 'This is all a dead loss. We shall have to withdraw.'

It is being done, the ship said. Then: *A message is coming through. Listen.*

Once again a set of interpreted images impinged on Boaz's consciousness. When the crowd of ships scattered in panic, one of them had gone plunging down toward the planet. Now, from within the atmosphere, an excited voice was broadcasting from that ship:

'*The screen is down. I'm getting through! The screen's vanished, everybody! I'm going right on down!*'

Wryly Boaz reflected that the broadcaster was doing himself little good by making this announcement. Probably he had been betrayed by a sudden excess of enthusiasm and a misplaced sense of camaraderie with his fellow prospectors. But whoever he was, Boaz felt grateful for his mistake. A note of triumph entered his feelings.

Your guest is aboard, the ship informed him.

'Take us down,' Boaz said. 'We're landing on Meirjain.'

5

The descent had been hasty, the need to escape the enforcer cruiser's ravening beams overriding any interest Boaz felt in the enlarging landscape. The cruiser, shooting ships out of the sky as it came back round the curve of the planet, *The Sedulous Seeker* fleeing before it, had followed the mob as far as the troposphere – before returning again to orbit. *The Sedulous Seeker* and its two sudden allies, the armed ships belonging to Larry and the

Hat Brothers, had soon abandoned their abortive attempt to put the cruiser out of action and, outgunned, had also dived into the atmosphere.

Vast patches of gold and silver, interspersing a less brilliant background of lavender and violet, had slid below. The prospectors, including Boaz, had all made an instinctive dash for darkness, zipping in a drove over the terminator before scattering. In fact the cruiser would be able to scan the night as well as the day, and for that matter probably had orders not to fire on the surface of Meirjain. But people felt safer in the dark. Boaz, like the others, sought cover, landing in what looked like the leeward side of a cliff.

No one would move until daylight came. Boaz calculated that the hours of waiting would be useful, putting the commander of the government cruiser in a more passive mode. He would probably take no further action until the prospector tried to leave the planet – then their problems would begin in earnest.

Boaz reminisced, skulking within his ship.

'*What you plan is quite impossible. Nothing can ever be changed.*'

These words of Madrigo, uttered at Boaz's last meeting with him, were often replayed in the shipkeeper's mind. They dropped into his consciousness now, provoking as usual a response that he knew was perverse. They should have affected him like drops of slow poison, steadily depressing him into senselessness. Instead, they infected him with a kind of manic exhilaration. Insane stubbornness, irrational determination, gave his will a hard edge. When last had man pitted himself against the gods?

Romrey sat watching Boaz curiously from the other side of the small cabin. The shipkeeper had rebuffed all his attempts to engage in conversation. He sat slouched over a table, moodily fondling his deck of colonnader cards while waiting for Meirjain's new sun to come up. The totality of his self-absorption reminded Romrey of someone on a run-up to suicide—*real* suicide, not clone-backed self-immolation.

What *was* it, he wondered, that Boaz was after? He gestured to the cards. 'You have a deck, too. Are they anything like mine?'

Boaz shook his head. 'Nothing like,' he muttered. Actually Romrey would have found little difference, but for Boaz there was no comparison. In his cards the symbolism was pure and elegant, with none of the carborundum deck's florid arcanery. They were philosophical, not occult. Neither did he expect any mysterious help from them, as Romrey did from his.

He stopped at the card called the Universe. One way which the colonnader cards differed from the degraded decks was that however familiar the images became they seemed fresh and new each time one looked at them. Boaz could still intuit original nuances, even after years of study.

The Universe showed a city set on an island, amid a wavy blue-green sea. Gaily-garbed people thronged the balconies, traversed the walkways, ascended and descended the upthrusting towers, appeared briefly at countless windows. The meaning of the card was relatively simple (though a wealth of more technical ideas was encoded in the shapes and numbers of its towers and shafts). It expressed the basic colonnader idea that the universe was an organized whole, and that all sentient beings in it were, so to speak, citizens of a common *polis*.

Boaz thumbed out two more cards: the Priestess, which was the Universe's complementary card at the other end of the twenty-one card sequence, and Strength, which as the middle pivotal card of the whole sequence linked them together. The three cards comprised a potent triad. The Priestess was a card of ceaseless allure and enchantment. She sat on a throne, smiling in benign, pleased fashion at the beholder. The pillars *Joachim* and *Boaz* flanked her rear, the space between them screened by a veil merging with the wimple she wore as a headdress. On her lap lay an open book, whose pages she turned one by one, unendingly. Each leaf of this book, the reverse of which was left blank, bore exactly the same image: a miniature of the card called the Universe. It was complete in every detail, every tower, every traverse, every citizen, every tiny motion. Again and again the city reappeared, absolutely unvarying from page to page, vanishing for the moment that the leaf was turned.

Thus was the doctrine of the world's eternal recurrence explicated.

Strength, the card through which the other two interacted was also a female card. A willowy woman, wearing a flowing gown, stood on a bare landscape. Her face was serene and gentle. In her two hands she held the jaws of a lion, which somehow seemed to merge with or emerge from her pelvis.

Some called the card Nature, or the Strength of Nature. Others Force, or Conservation. Few without colonnader training knew what it really signified: the obdurate rock-steadiness of natural forces, which were absolutely self-regulating in the cosmic context, and which could not be made to swerve or alter by a single iota.

Madrigo had explained: 'Imagine a force which whenever it acts calls into play a countervailing force which instantly dampens it down. Such a force would display no positive characteristic, and would be undetectable. It would be indistinguishable from empty void. And yet it might be nature's ultimate force that maintains all others.

'Such a force exists. It is indeed the ultimate conserving force, the absolute bedrock of nature. It cannot be detected. Neither can it be interfered with, even in the least degree. . . '

Boaz laid out the three cards in a triangle. Here was the Priestess, the birth of the universe when the twin pillars of existence separated from one another and matter unfolded from potentiality, just like a book opening. Here was the Universe: the world-city itself, no more than a detail in the Priestess. And here, at the other corner of the triangle, was Strength, the linking card. This explained, to the superior understanding, why it was that the world could only exist in the mode of eternal repetition, for otherwise there would be no unity to nature, no strength. . . .

The cards distressed him and he rose from the occasional table where he had been seated, to go pacing about the narrow space.

Eternal recurrence . . . it was his burden. Should it not be everyone's? What was more depressing than that one's life must be repeated endlessly, to the last unalterable syllable? . . . But to the common man this knowledge had no meaning, he realized. It was an equation in a book. Only to a philosopher, to Boaz who had had the sure proof of the equation shown to him, for whom it had become a part of everyday thought, was it as real as yesterday, tomorrow, or today.

His stricken look amazed Romrey. He stared up at the shipkeeper. 'What's wrong?' he asked. 'Did you see something in the cards?'

'If you like,' Boaz answered brusquely.

'You know,' Romrey said, after a thoughtful pause, 'it's probably not good manners after you saved my life, but I'm curious about you. You look like one lonely man to me.'

Words came from Boaz before he had to time to check them. 'Loneliness: an abyss without a bottom, into which to fall, without limit. So it must be.'

The intensity of Boaz's pronouncement took Romrey aback slightly. 'Nobody need be that alone,' he said. 'I wonder if you'd mind telling me what you're hoping to find here on the Wanderer. It's probably not money, like the rest of us.'

When Boaz ignored him, he slipped his carborundum cards out of his pocket. 'Well, maybe *these* can tell me,' he said, and began to shuffle preparatory to dealing them out for a reading.

He had half feared that Boaz would react to his temerity by turning him out onto the surface to fend for himself, regardless of colonnader ethics. Boaz, indeed, seemed angry. He knocked the cards from Romrey's hand.

'This trash will tell you nothing.' He spoke thickly. 'Your pack has not the depth. Very well, you importuning thief, I will tell you. Who knows, perhaps you have the intelligence to understand it. But first you must be able to understand that there could be a man who has suffered in a way unknown by any other being in the history of creation. Could you believe in inconceivable suffering? Does it sound like a melodramatic exaggeration? No, it is literally true, and I am that man. I will not explain how, except to say that science, in seeking greater good, has wrought the greatest ever evil, and that the school of mental calm is responsible for such agony as to make calm impossible. All my actions are directed toward escaping from this agony. And that is why I am on Meirjain.'

'You suffer it *now?*' Romrey inquired.

'It is in the past.' Boaz turned away to hide his haunted eyes.

'Then you already have escaped it,' Romrey said, puzzled. He shrugged. 'If the memory is unbearable, you could always have it erased.'

'No!' Boaz turned to Romrey again. His expression was savage. 'Don't you see? The universe repeats. Everything that has gone before must come again, and again, forever and ever. It lies before me.'

'Yes, of course,' muttered Romrey, though he showed by his quizzical expression that the idea was barely comprehensible to him.

Suddenly he laughed softly. 'It *is* time-gems you're after, then! You want time travel, right? To travel back and change what happened . . . whatever it was. . . .'

'The past? Why change the past?' Boaz shook his head. 'You disappoint me, Gare. Do you know nothing of cosmology? *The future is the past.* Because the future has already occurred, countless times in the past. What has been must be, again and again. Do you see, Gare? *What has been must be, again and again.* I must change the *future*, abolish predestination, put time on a new track.'

'Past, present or future, everybody knows time is immutable – predestined, as you put it. The world goes from phase to phase of the same eternal cycle. It's a law.'

'Time has been immutable till *now*.' Boaz slammed his fist on the table, causing the cards he had laid there to jump. 'You are wrong. It is not a law. It is a circumstance. Nature is strong, but not omnipotent. Indeed, her strength can be used against her.'

It was on this point that all his hopes were pinned. He had studied all the data obtained by scientists, and all the arguments of the philosophers, and he had concluded that nothing made predestination an absolute law. It was a consequence of the strength of nature, that was all. The sheer weight of the universe, so to speak, caused events to run an identical course with each manifestation. If someone could be strong enough, or clever enough. . . .

'If one small detail in present time can be altered,' he went on, 'then eventually all will be altered. The tiniest deviation can only accumulate, until there are untold results.' His voice shook. 'If only somewhere in the whole vast universe, some little flower can be caused to have seven petals instead of eight! If one lone electron orbit acquires one quantum of energy more or less! Then the next manifestation of the world will not be identical to this one, and the next one will be different again. The nature of cause and effect must make it so. Then,' he added dreamily, 'my prison will be shattered. I shall have a chance to be spared that torment.'

'It might mean you don't exist at all, next time,' Romrey ruminated.

'Gladly, gladly!'

'Mankind might not exist either.'

'What does it matter? Conceivably the whole universe will never exist again. There might be just nothing, for ever and ever. Or it might take a wholly new form, in which matter itself will be different. I do not care one jot about it. All I care is that—'

Boaz halted, his fist clenched. A knowing look had come over Romrey's face. He spread his legs so that the colonnader cards that Boaz had knocked on the floor became visible.

The cards had fallen in a mass, faces down. Only one card had separated and lay face up. Romrey bent and retrieved it. It pictured a stone tower in the instant of being shattered by a massive lightning bolt or gush of energy. From its buckling height a lone figure tumbled head first.

Romrey said sourly, 'So we have a reading after all. This card is something of a mystery. There's no general agreement on its meaning. Some people call it "the Universe Buster". If that's right, you've interpreted it nicely.'

Staring at the card, Boaz said, 'It symbolizes simultaneous creation and destruction, in the colonnader deck.'

They fell silent. How Sisyphean, Boaz wondered for the thousandth time, was his task? The time-gems gave some prospect of hope – yet how often had he spent his life in this quest, only for the rock of his labours to roll back down to its resting place at his death?

In a sense, he was forced to admit that the hopelessness of his quest was the very essence of it. Its audacity, its irrational grandiosity, gave point to his existence. He pursued only because life offered no other possibility. . . .

Romrey, meanwhile, was having thoughts of his own. He knew now, after what he had just heard, that Joachim Boaz was quite insane.

Together, without speaking, they waited for the dawn.

It came first as a glow that suffused the darkness, then as a sudden blaze. Surveying the scene through the ship's sensors, Boaz saw at once that he had misjudged his surroundings when landing in the darkness, but he decided that the ship might as well stay put for the present. The atmosphere checked as breathable, just as previous explorers had reported – though as a different sun had then warmed the planet, the datum was not necessarily reliable.

Boaz got busy, getting together a tool kit and float sledge. 'If you like, we'll go together.'

Romrey nodded.

'We'll make a short reconnoitre to start with,' Boaz continued. 'As you may have guessed, there is a limit to how far I can wander from my ship. You may be useful to me in that regard.'

No mist rose from the ground to greet the burgeoning yellow sun as they descended the tread-rail. The air was perfectly clear, the landscape shining. The sky was like none either man had ever seen: it seemed to be of no single colour, but glimmered patchily, mauve, blue, pink, shot through with channels and outlines of brighter colours, like a reflection of the planet's surface as it had appeared from space—which it probably was, thought Boaz, wondering what combination of upper atmosphere gases might bring about such a refractive trick.

But it was the ground below that held the greatest surprise. It was not ground but a floor, stretching indistinctly toward the horizon. It shone, it gleamed, it was brilliant but with a soft brilliance. It was pure yellow. As soon as they set foot on it Boaz took a cutting tool from his kit. In moments he had cut out a cavity in which yellow shadows gleamed. Wonderingly he massaged in his hands the lump he had cut. It was so malleable he could bend it where it was not too thick, needing to summon only a little strength over his integration beam.

He tested the metal with a chemical assay. Gold. Purest gold. The plain was made of it. Now that he looked close he could see that it was marked with a checkerboard of fine, barely visible etched lines.

Romrey eyed the sample without interest. Though neither of them had ever seen gold used so lavishly, it was, like every other natural element except radium and technetium, too low in value to be worth taking.

What everyone now scattered around Meirjain was after was the incredibly rare, the new, the unexpected, small in bulk and huge in desirability – like time-gems. . . .

Boaz threw aside the lump and directed Romrey's attention to what, on landing, he had taken to be an uneven cliff wall behind them.

It was not a cliff wall. It was definitely artificial. It was a bulging, rounded hull, reddish gold in hue but studded and decorated with baroque traceries the colour of ruby, cobalt, copper and amber. The two men were too close to the gigantic structure to gain any clear idea of its nature, and Boaz gestured to Romrey to mount the float sled. Together they glided over the gold floor for a distance of about a mile.

Looking back, it was just possible to see what the 'cliff' was. It was, Boaz was sure, a ship, though conceivably it might have been a fixed building of fantastic shape. But what a ship! No econosphere spacedock, nor the yards of any past or present civilization in Boaz's ken had ever constructed or planned a vessel remotely like it in size and magnificence. Its height was about a mile, but it rested lengthways on immense ornate runners, and its length was about three miles. Its form was everywhere gently rounded, though its sides, as near as Boaz could judge, were nearly parallel near the center. As the sun rose, at an angle to the horizon, the light slid along the shining bulk disclosing a richness of age, and of sheer wealth.

And that was not all. On either side of it were similar ships, forming a rank from horizon to horizon. This was a parking ground.

'By the gods,' Romrey muttered. 'Just look at that. I wonder if the other people who came to the Wanderer found anything like this?'

'There's no saying. Most information about what was found here was suppressed. Not that there seems to have been all that much of it in the first place. They only stayed a few hours.'

'Yeah, I know. A slingshot orbit. When they came back, Meirjain was gone and they never tracked it again – until now. Phew.' A greedy look came over Romrey's face. 'We've got to get inside one of those things.'

'Later, perhaps,' frowned Boaz. He was looking in the opposite direction. Near the horizon, which was about three miles away, was a different type of structure. It looked rather like a miniature city built of purple blocks, towers and various other shapes that were indistinct at this distance. Although it could have been an industrial plant or some such artifact, it did have more of the appearance of a permanent dwelling than the monstrous vessel – although, paradoxically, it also seemed smaller.

'That might be a better place to look, at first,' he observed.

He was about to put the sledge in motion again when Romrey gave an alarmed grunt and pointed to the sky. Limned against the confusing multicoloured backdrop was a slender shape, which as they watched enlarged itself into the elegant outline of Radalce Obsoc's yacht. Boaz stayed his hand on the controls of the float sledge. *The Sedulous Seeker* hovered, moved to and fro slightly, then put down not half a mile away.

'What do you think?' Romrey asked. 'This isn't coincidence.'

'Not with a whole planet to fly to.'

'I'm not going to like it if all those people are aboard. Especially you-know-who.'

Boaz was prepared to deal mortally with the persons Romrey referred to, if he had to. He decided it was an issue best faced up to now rather than left until later. He put the sledge on a steady glide and swept toward the portal of the yacht. It opened even before they reached it.

Obsoc appeared in the entrance as they stepped off the sledge. He was blinking rapidly and his face showed obvious strain. 'Oh, come in, come in, both of you,' he entreated in a high-pitched voice. 'You don't know how glad I am to see you. It's been simply dreadful.'

'Are the others with you?' Boaz asked him.

'Ach!' Obsoc put his hand to his forehead. 'Only Neavy. And I think she's dying.'

He led them into the main lounge. Neavy Hirester lay on a couch, attended by one of the yacht robots which had been given a medical programme. Mace was kneeling beside her, a hand on her brow.

No one else was present in the lounge. Boaz noticed, however, the dark bloodstains on the carpet.

He and Romrey stepped near the couch. Neavy's eyes were closed, and she appeared unconscious. She was very pale. Her clothing was open and the robot was binding an ugly cut with a surgical instrument.

'It isn't really any use,' Mace said, glancing up. 'She's lost too much blood, and we haven't got any.'

'What did it?'

'Parawhips. Those damned girls. She's got some really deep lacerations. Haemorrhaged like mad.'

Boaz turned to Obsoc. 'How did you find us?'

'My robots tracked you down. I hope you don't mind our turning up like this. I feel shaken, citizens, I don't mind telling you – what a business!'

'What happened?' asked Romrey.

'As soon as they realized the barrier was down Larry and the Hat Brothers started fighting. They just didn't care – they were killing anyone. They would have killed us too, if our robots hadn't helped us to hide. One of Larry's girls was killed, too. Luckily their own ships came down for them, and they left.'

'You mean everyone else is dead, except Neavy?'

Obsoc nodded. 'Everyone. Oh, what a business! The carnage!'

'Where are the bodies?'

'I got the robots to throw them out.' Obsoc rubbed his eyes, as if very tired, then leaned against a table. 'This is dreadful. What am I doing here? I have risked my life – for what? For the satisfaction of ownership! And yet I would do it again. My friends, you probably do not understand these things. You cannot comprehend the compulsion that comes over the impassioned collector.'

'It is the same as any other vice,' Boaz said absently. 'The object of it is largely irrelevant.' He reflected. 'You haven't seen anything more of the econosphere ship?'

'No. It won't bother us while we're down here.'

'I think she's going,' Mace said sadly.

The robot paused, then felt a pulse, probed for a heart-beat, and finally applied a little flat meter box to the girl's temple. It straightened.

'She has died, sir,' it said to Obsoc.

Obsoc sighed, a trifle ostentatiously. 'All right, put her outside.'

Romrey stirred. 'I don't think I like the idea of a corpse lying around the place.'

'Oh, all right.' Obsoc gestured to the robot. 'Put her in the freezer. You can dispose of her later.' The robot bent and, with obvious difficulty (robots generally were quite frail), lifted the dead girl in its arms and carried her out.

'I wonder if she has a clone,' Mace said dreamily. 'The trouble is, it's probably light-years away. It won't receive her death signal.'

The men ignored her. Obsoc's manner suddenly changed and became brisk as he spoke to the other two. 'Well, gentlemen, from the look of it you were about to do some exploring. You've noticed those gigantic ships, I suppose? From the air you can see hundreds of them! And that's not all. This planet is a fairyland. It's quite unbelievable. How the race that did all this could have died out I just don't know.'

'We were heading for the citylike structure,' Boaz said. 'I suppose you have a suggestion to make?'

Obsoc shrugged. He looked uncertain, and Boaz realized that he was frightened. He wanted the other two to find the goods for him.

'Perhaps we can be most useful to one another when it comes to leaving,' Boaz offered. 'There is still the cruiser to be got past.'

'And the time-gems?' Obsoc queried anxiously.

'If we find any, we'll share them.'

'Good! And if there should be other finds, other jewels, hitherto unknown, perhaps—'

'We'll have to talk about it,' Romrey said sourly. 'Maybe you'll have to do some exploring yourself.' He turned to the exit. 'Well, how about it, shipkeeper? We're wasting time.'

They left. Outside, Boaz put the sledge in motion again, and they set off for their goal. As they came closer, some first impressions of the 'city' were dispelled. On the one hand it began to seem more machine-like, the blocks and pipes taking on the appearance of components of a mechanism. On the other, the purple colour resolved itself into a pointillism of colours which glittered like tinsel, all merging at a distance into the one luminous purple. There was an eerie beauty to it that threatened to befuddle the senses – or at least Boaz thought so. From the restlessness of his companion he guessed that Romrey was simply filling himself with excited thoughts of riches.

A low wall, about three feet in height, surrounded the city. He floated the sledge over it, then set down and stepped out, looking around him. He touched the wall; it had a roughened surface, every wrinkle of which was a different colour. He was not surprised at the apparently perfect state of preservation of what they had seen so far. Only primitive civilizations built with materials that decayed. It was another question whether the long-dead inhabitants had left behind them any energy sources that were also non-degradable. If so, it was remotely possible that even the ships looming behind them were still work-able.

Neither was it the first time that Boaz had stood amid the works of an alien culture. His search for a means to change time had led him to many strange places. He lifted his gaze and surveyed what turned out to be a tangle of pylons, snaking pipelike shapes, oddly formed blocks, figures from some twisted geometry.

'There's something queer about this place,' Romrey said.

'I know what you mean.' Boaz picked on a spot and tried to follow a pipe, oval in cross-section, as it veered among the towers of the 'city'. He soon lost it.

There was a topological oddness to it all. While it obviously existed in the normal three dimensions of space, it reminded him more than anything of sketches and models that were meant to represent forms in four-dimensional space. The thought gave him a feeling of excitement that subjectively, he guessed, was much like Romrey's delirium of greed for wealth.

He looked back. His ship was a small grey shape against the golden balloon of the Meirjain giant. It was already some miles away, and there was no saying whether there might not be materials in the 'city' that would prove impervious to its beams, or at least that might attenuate them. He issued a silent command: *Follow*. Obediently the ship lifted itself, soared past *The Sedulous Seeker* (which unlike Boaz's ship had a horizontal landing attitude) and put down half a mile away.

Romrey observed the move in silence. 'Let's move,' Boaz said. 'If we find any doors, we might be able to tell what kind of place this is.'

Romrey stepped down from the sledge, which dutifully trailed after them as they moved deeper into the 'city'. Soon it engulfed them. The sky seemed to disappear, its colours merging with those of the structures that rose and danced all around them. His surroundings began to seem forbidding to Boaz. He was telling himself that they were wasting their time here, and that they would do better to search elsewhere, when a cry of 'Hey!' came from Romrey.

He had found an entrance to one of the blocklike buildings, shaped like a man-sized door. The aperture was too small to admit the sledge. Leaving it parked outside, Boaz followed his companion through.

Inside, the darkness was almost complete. Boaz switched on a torch and held it aloft. By its fierce radiance he saw that they were in an empty chamber, cube-shape but with rounded corners. In the opposite wall was another entrance, this time oval but also of a size to admit a man.

Romrey peered through it. 'It's a tunnel.'

Boaz joined him, twisting the ring on the torch to produce a beam. There was nothing to be seen in the tunnel, which after a few yards curved out of sight.

Pausing, Boaz told himself that poking into any chance corner was perhaps not the best way of persuading this fabled world to reveal its treasures. A more reliable method might be to trust his ship's spy beams. While Romrey urged him to go down the tunnel, he summoned up the ship, asking which way he should go.

The ship spoke, but mingled with the message was a note that was unfamiliar: *Go forward.*

He stepped through the opening, beckoning Romrey to follow.

They moved cautiously, for what seemed a long time. There was no apparent sense to the oval corridor's convolutions: it turned this way and that, it dipped, it rose, it slanted at random oblique angles, it turned – so Boaz suspected – back on itself. Then, as he was about to suggest they retrace their steps, it delivered them to a low-ceilinged, boat-shaped chamber, about the size of the lounge in Radalce Obsoc's yacht.

Returning the torch to an all-round lamp, he took quick stock of the room. The walls were of a matt lavender louvred with close-set ribs which followed the curve of the chamber like the ribs of a sail-driven water boat. Placed along the center of the chamber were about half a dozen closed chests, or coffers. A storage place, perhaps?

Romrey dashed to the chests and threw open the unresisting lid of the first one he came to. He drew his breath in sharply, dipped in a hand and pulled out something that glittered.

It looked at first like a silver spider's web. But its threads seemed to flow and reorganize themselves constantly as Romrey held it up to the light, turned it over and examined it through an eyeglass.

'I don't know what this stuff is. Never seen anything like it before.'

Boaz was not listening to him. He was receiving a message, which at first he thought came from his ship – but no, it was that other, unfamiliar note which minutes before had mingled with the ship's voice.

Here, little Mudworm, is the treasure you seek.

Mudworm! That hated name – the name he had not heard all these years, the original name he had been given by his enemies – where had it come from now? What was speaking to him?

With the words, there was an instruction. He was directed to the third chest in the row. Moving to it, he saw that it had a transparent lid. Not only that, but a square in the ceiling over it was also transparent, and light – daylight, as far as he could tell – shone down onto the cask below.

Through the crystalline lid, he saw a layer of what appeared to be large diamonds.

The use of his earlier name had provoked turbulent and unpleasant feelings in Boaz. Nevertheless he forced himself to be calm, and lifted the lid.

The gems, about a hundred of them, were laid on something resembling velvet. Each was faceted, and about an inch and a half in diameter. Boaz picked one up, turned it over, let it catch the light.

Romrey was suddenly at his elbow, the silver spider web dangling from his hand. 'What's that? Is it . . .?'

For answer, Boaz brought the gem close to his face to peer into it. One could see reflections in the facets, tiny little pictures. He brought it closer to his eye, looking as though through a lens.

And he saw himself and Romrey, coasting over the yellow plain on the float sledge, reaching the 'city', dismounting. . .

A scene from the recent past.

Now he understood why this chest had a transparent lid, why the light shone on it from outside. Time-gems refracted light through time. From the past, from the future. The overhead panel brought it light from the city's environs.

But a scene from the past could be explained by other means than time transference. He turned to another facet. And saw himself again.

He saw Romrey, too, but something was wrong. Romrey was standing like a statue, staring ahead of him as if frozen. In the scene Boaz himself seemed disturbed. He staggered, peered close at Romrey, reached out his arm to touch him. . .

The picture faded.

A warning?

'What did you see?' asked Romrey. He reached past Boaz and picked up another gem, focusing his gaze into it as Boaz had done. For a while both men were absorbed in the tiny picture shows.

It was strange that images so minuscule, and presumably bounced around the interiors of the gems at random, should be so clear. The gems themselves were as limpid as water, except where glints and sparkles flashed through them – and as these glints enlarged themselves, as the facets were turned, the scenes came suddenly into focus, never lasting more than a few seconds before vanishing.

If the glimpses were all from past and future time, then the range was immense; somehow Boaz had expected it to encompass a few hours or minutes only – perhaps no more than seconds or a part of a second. Briefly he saw a perfect little landscape with a yellow sun and wavy, frondlike trees swishing over dusty ground. Flowerlike creatures walked in groups beneath those trees. . . . Now he saw one of the golden ships flying. It swept over Meirjain's fantastic landscape, then soared upward, disappearing in a sky that was blue rather than mottled.

Boaz snatched up another gem and examined it for scenes also. He was greedy for evidence of time transference. But fascinating though the little cameos were, nothing seemed to distinguish one jewel from another.

'Let's get 'em,' Romrey exclaimed feverishly. They scooped the gems up, pouring them into their belt pouches. Then Romrey turned his attention to the other chests.

Boaz stood where he was. He had retained the last gem in his hand and was staring into it. He turned the stone ever so slightly, until a tiny scene came into focus.

For the first time the scene was within the chamber itself. The six chests were being carried into it and laid down in a row, just as he and Romrey had found them. The work was being done by humanoid, olive-skinned creatures who were completely naked except for silver circlets around their waists. The humanish impression was completely destroyed, however, by their faces, which more than anything resembled the head of an Egyptian ibis. . .

It was wholly coincidence, a startled Boaz decided, that the ibis also figured in a colonnader card entitled the Stellar Realm. . .

He tried to hold the scene, but his fingers trembled and he lost it.

He dropped the gem in his pouch.

He felt frightened. He did not know who or what had spoken to him a short while ago. He presumed it was a thought from his own mind (perhaps even some sinister stray datum from his ship?); he wanted to stay and explore further, at the same time fighting an urge to leave, now, with what he had found.

What happened next was terrifying, yet so unexpected and bewildering that, paradoxically, it was robbed of its terror. He was seized. He felt something pick him up and *move* him, like a chess piece. He hurtled up the winding tunnel, *which was still lit by the beam of his torch*. An astonishing flurry of sights, thoughts, words and sensations dizzied past him.

He stood in the lounge of Obsoc's yacht. 'Perhaps we can be most useful to one another when it comes to leaving,' he said to the anxious collector. 'There is still the cruiser to be got past.'

'And the time-gems?'

'If we find any, we'll share them round.'

'Good!' Obsoc's eyes gleamed. 'And if there should be other finds – '

Once again the chess piece was moved from square to square. Boaz was picked up, whisked across the board. Flashing squares of yellow gold. A kaleidoscope of impressions, like a vid recording played a hundred times too fast. The jewel chamber. Purple blocks. Words, feelings. Flashing squares of yellow gold.

He stood in the lounge of Obsoc's yacht. He spoke to one of the yacht robots. 'Take off and enter circumpolar orbit, achieving stable velocity over the magnetic north pole. Meanwhile broadcast a surrender message to the government cruiser. With luck they will intercept you rather than shoot you down, and you can gain medical assistance for your master and his friends.'

The robot inclined its head in understanding. Boaz turned to go, and in turning was moved off again, even faster than before. He was in the storage chamber. Romrey had stuffed his pouches full and shook loose a carry-bag, which he also proceeded to fill.

'This is where they kept their valuables, all right. I don't recognize a single gem-stone, not a single metal – if they are metals. Come on, get your share.'

'Let's go.'

'Go?'

Boaz was mad with elation. 'I knew it was true,' he murmured. Already he understood that he had travelled through time, to the past, then to the future, and now back to the present. 'The answer is here.'

But he felt a terrible fear that whatever power it was that had seized him would carry him out of the range of his ship's healing beams. That would be the end of him – in the agony he was doing all this to avoid.

'I'm going back to the ship,' he said. 'Do what you like.'

'Well, all right. But let's get a couple of these chests to the sledge.'

'I'm going straight back.' Boaz turned and started back up the tunnel. Twisting and turning, he eventually gained the outside, to find that Romrey was not far behind him.

'What's the matter with you?' Romrey said. 'We were doing fine.'

Boaz ignored him and made his way through the complex's eye-straining shapes, signing the sledge to follow. There was a fact that up to now he had been too numbed to admit, but that now was bursting upon him.

It was as if the unreality of a dream had imposed itself on real experience, and as in a dream logic had been short-circuited. But now logic was back, bringing with it a single, luminous inference. *Meirjain was not uninhabited.* He had been projected into his past, then into his future, he presumed (in the hastiness of his thought he found no time to wonder what was implied by his future instructions to the yacht robot). Ergo, beings existed here who had mastered time travel, probably the same ibis-headed beings he had seen in the time-gem.

Unless a machine had accomplished it, acting at random? Possible, he thought, but unlikely.

Romrey joined him as he stepped over the wall and turned his back on the complex. They saw that a third prospector ship had landed on the plain, a little way in front of his own. Like *The Sedulous Seeker* it was horizontal in line, but much smaller and sleeker.

'I don't like this,' Romrey breathed. 'That's the Hat Brothers' ship.'

And even as he spoke the figures of the two brothers were already emerging, distinctive in their dark garments and wide-brimmed hats. Romrey came abreast of Boaz, who stood still. 'They must have followed Obsoc here,' he said. 'They probably imagine he knows something they don't about time-gems.'

'Fools,' Boaz muttered. 'The time-gems are all over the planet. How else could we have found them so easily?'

Giving a nervous smile, Romrey took his deck of cards out of a pocket. 'You are too sceptical, shipkeeper. It was these cards that led us to the gems. They create events, remember? I told you they were effective.'

'Don't you know the econosphere regulates against magic charms?' Boaz replied acidly. 'Never mind. I will deal with the Hat Brothers. Come along.'

He had meant to move off toward *The Sedulous Seeker*. But before he could take the first step a sensation like a sudden and crushing blow made him gasp and stagger. It was as if a huge shadow stood over him, as if a great weight, a gigantic foot, were stamping down to crush him like an insect. And yet the blow was not physical at all. It was mental, a blow at his consciousness.

He gave a choking cry. Instantly the ship was coming to his aid. He felt the integrative machinery gearing up, reaching out, casting about for the source of the attack. Briefly he had the peculiar sensation of being frozen in a block of ice. Then a titanic struggle, an unbearable tension, permeated his body. It was total war, interspersed, to his amazement, with fragmentary, whispered comments:

'*Special measures necessary. . . . Total opposition. . . . The impact has radius vectors in the negative dimension. . . .*'

He was hearing the ship talking to itself as it sought to save him! Never before had he experienced *that!* On and on the voices went, debating, conferring, deciding – and all, he realized later, in a split second of time. Then a moment of horror as the ship, as if demoralized, consulted him:

'*You may submit, if you wish.*'

'*No!*' Boaz shouted. He knew in his heart that it would be the end of him if he surrendered to the assault. He felt the ship rally and try again. He staggered once more, forgot where he was for an instant, and then was suddenly still.

It was over, except for a feeling of inner pressure which betokened an extra vigilance from the ship.

Apart from that, what had changed?

Romrey had changed. The prospector stood stock-still, like a statue. His eyes stared. Boaz passed a hand before them. Nothing.

He touched Romrey's cheek. The flesh was hard and smooth, like stone.

Experimentally he nudged the rocklike body, then pushed it gently. Romrey toppled over, clanked dully to the floor of gold. Not a finger had shifted position.

Whatever had attacked Boaz, and been fought off by his ship, had attacked Romrey too. Boaz allowed his gaze to wander to three newly landed ships parked on the golden, shining landscape. The Hat Brothers stood staring at one another, or seeming to. They were utterly motionless.

He framed a question, staring at *The Sedulous Seeker*. '*The same,*' his ship answered, with an alacrity that showed it had already checked the yacht on its own initiative. Briefly it brought Boaz a cameo of Obsoc and Mace sitting together, also motionless.

Boaz came to a quick decision. He would take the stiffened bodies of Romrey, Obsoc and Mace aboard his ship and take off immediately, taking his chance on getting past the econosphere cruiser. In his haste he forgot, for the moment, his advance knowledge of his future words to the yacht robot. When he remembered them it was already too late to do anything, for the chess game began again. Once more Boaz was a manipulated piece. Once more he went through a dizzying sequence of impressions, too fast for him to be able to take in, in which colours, images and sounds flashed past.

But in what sense was he now being moved? He sensed that it was not just in time – perhaps not in time at all. After scant seconds all went black. He seemed to be hurtling down a dark tunnel. Then he was still, but in darkness, into which a yellow glow spread slowly.

The darkness fled, revealing that he stood in a dome-shaped chamber. Around him stood five or six of the ibis-headed creatures he had seen in the time-gem. They regarded him calmly, with beady eyes, their beaklike faces gleaming. They were, on average, a little shorter than a man, and their thin, smoothly muscled, olive-colored bodies appeared youthful, like the bodies of young girls – for, he noticed, they all lacked anything resembling male sex organs. The silver circlets around their waists, which comprised their only adornment, seemed, now that Boaz saw them more closely, to be in ceaseless motion, as if made of flowing quicksilver.

Despite the ordeal he had just been through, he did not feel particularly afraid of them. It was, however, a habituated response. He had encountered intelligent aliens several times before, and had come to learn that in general they were apt to offer him less threat than were strangers of his own species.

He did, on the other hand, feel awe. These were the beings who could manipulate time, to whom time was no more than an additional spatial dimension. They were, in other words, *four-dimensional beings*.

In comparison with ordinary creatures like Boaz, who crawled like worms from one moment to the next, that made them like gods. Were they, in fact, gods? And was not the ibis head, he recalled with an inward shudder, a symbol of the ancient god Thoth, said to have shown and explained the colonnader card pack to mankind long ago, before the technical age?

Once Boaz had asked Madrigo if there were gods. Madrigo had answered: 'There may be; it has not been settled. But if there are then they are transient and limited beings, as we are. More intelligent, more potent, with a consciousness whose relation to matter is perhaps somewhat different from ours, but that is all. One should not,' he had added, 'be afraid of any entity.'

'They will not be immortal?' Boaz had asked.

'All beings are immortal,' Madrigo had reminded him. 'But like us, the gods must live and die.'

The creature facing Boaz made a cryptic gesture, touching a finger to its flattened forehead. With the same flowing motion it turned, with an open hand indicating the curved wall behind it. Then the entire group turned, and filed out of the chamber to Boaz's left.

Boaz could not see the door they exited by. But in front of him, where there had been only blank wall a moment before, there was now an arched opening. A purple cloth screened the opening, waving slightly as if in a breeze. He stepped forward, touched the cloth – which wasn't there. There was just the feeling of something silky, like warm oil, touching his skin, and his hand went right through.

Boldly he walked through the screen, and stopped. He had entered a circular chamber like the first, but smaller. The walls and curved roof were of the same texture he had seen in the 'city' – indeed, Boaz guessed that he was in fact back in the mysterious complex. This chamber, however, contained more by way of furniture, though he could only guess at the functions of the three or four cabinet-like objects standing on the floor.

On a raised, cushioned dais in the center of the room there sat, cross-legged, another of the ibis-headed aliens. At first sight it seemed indistinguishable from the others. But for some reason, as he looked at it, Boaz gained an impression of immense age and experience. Furthermore, as the beady, expressionless eyes stared back, he felt like a puddle into which some lofty entity was poking a finger, so that the ripples radiated out into every crevice of his being and were reflected back. There was absolutely no doubt of it: the creature was inspecting his mind.

'Come in, little Mudworm.'

Again the hated nickname which, among so many other factors, had helped make his life a misery in the Corsair warrens.

The voice was mature, full, human, – and male. Hearing it was a trifle odd. One imagined it was spoken by the creature facing him, but the curved, tubelike beak was clearly unsuited to human speech, and the creature's head had not moved. The voice had emanated from empty air.

In spite of the irrational displeasure he felt at the reference to his early years, excitement mounted in Boaz. He had been given an interview with the inhabitants of Meirjain – with the time-gods, as he already thought of them! He could ask questions! He was close to learning what he needed to know!

'So you know our language,' he began.

'Or you have been made to understand ours. What difference does it make? Come closer, Mudworm. Do not hover by the door.'

'My name is Joachim Boaz,' Boaz said sternly. But he obeyed, moving closer. The voice chuckled.

'Aggressive self-assertiveness, as ever with your species. Very well, Joachim Boaz, as you will.'

'What shall I call you?' Boaz asked.

'I am myself. I need no name. Does that answer sound familiar to you?'

'No.'

'It should. It is similar to an answer you once gave when asked the name of your ship.'

'But we are not ships.'

'Are *you* not? What are you without one?'

The creature clearly knew all about him. It was disconcerting to be so mentally naked. 'I have questions,' Boaz said. 'But you already know what they are.'

'You have questions. But discourse cannot be tacit. The mind must express itself.'

Boaz almost smiled. It was a remark Madrigo himself might have made. The thought provoked Boaz into dipping his hand in a pocket and coming out with the colonnader pack. Expertly he flipped through the cards until coming to the Stellar Realm, which showed a naked woman pouring out water onto a landscape from two jugs. Behind her, an ibis was taking flight from an evergreen tree.

He held out the card before the Meirjain creature, pointing to the ibis. 'First,' he said excitedly, 'did your species have contact with mine long ago? This picture is centuries old. Note the head of the bird. It symbolizes the god of all the sciences. Perhaps *you* taught *us* the beginnings. . . .'

His voice trailed off. The ibis-headed man leaned forward and inspected the card. 'Yes, there is certainly a resemblance,' the voice said. 'But it means nothing. It is simply a matter of convergent evolution, arising from the manner of feeding. The general shape of my head is a commonly occurring one, as is the shape of yours. As for whether any of my colleagues visited your planets long ago, I have no idea. You have seen the big ships outside? They were mainly used for visiting foreign galaxies. But they have been laid up for a long time now.'

Slowly Boaz put away the cards. He had forgotten all about Romrey and the others. The big, big question hung in his mind, and he was afraid to speak it.

He stood silent, dumb. The ibis-headed man's artificial voice spoke again, softly.

'Yes, I can help you, Joachim Boaz. But I wonder if you really want it, little Mudworm.'

'You know I want it!' Boaz burst out. 'It is all I want. You have conquered time! You can tell me how –'

He stopped, realizing the ridiculousness of his position, seeing how he had been reduced to helplessness. Why should these creatures help him? What interest had they in his mad scheme? And yet there was no way he could disguise his intention.

'Yes?' the voice said. 'I can tell you how to alter time, you were about to say? There I can only disappoint you,

Joachim Boaz. We cannot alter time, whether past, present or future. Time is inexorable.'

'But I have *experienced* it!'

'Have you? Think. All I did was move your consciousness along your time-line. I can take you into your past, and a little way – only a little way – into your future. In the same way we can refract light through time, by means of the time-gems. Yes, the past and the future can be known. But as for altering anything – no. Does this sound like a paradox? It isn't really. I shall explain. As you have guessed, we are four-dimensional beings. But only in a sense. We have learned to do what I did for you – to move back and forth over our time-lines, though only to a limited degree into the future. No time transfer was involved in bringing you into this dwelling, incidentally. We merely put you through a displacement vortex, which is our normal way of travelling about the planet.

'You might think that the foreknowledge this gives us, by governing our actions, enables us to control and alter future time – but no. Everything that happens in my future is already a result of this foreknowledge. It cannot be changed. Our time-travelling ability is, itself, part of the predestined cosmic pattern.'

Boaz stared at the ibis-headed man, a familiar burdensome feeling coming over him. 'What is the good of such a faculty?' he asked.

'It adds an extra dimension to life, as you can appreciate. To return to the past is more efficient than memory, which is apt to be unreliable. Experience of the future is also more useful than mere prediction.'

'You have some machinery for accomplishing this mental projection through time?'

'It is a mental discipline. There is no machinery for it.'

'Would you teach it to me?'

'You could never learn it. Your brain is too different.'

The right adplants, or else the right silicon bones, might rectify that, Boaz thought. But if what he had just been told was true, there would probably be little point in it. The time-gems in his pocket still seemed to offer him most hope. Whatever the ibis-headed man said, they were proof that there *was* a physical means of manipulating time.

'Then I thank you for your information. I would like to leave now.'

'No, you cannot leave yet, Joachim Boaz. I have something more to tell you.'

The ibis-headed man shifted slightly. His head turned, as if to glance at something on the wall, and for a moment Boaz saw the strange face in profile, looking exactly like the Egyptian bird in the colonnader card.

'Let me tell you what brought you here, what brought all the others here who landed in the last few hours. You see, I am very old. My species conquered the aging process long ago. My body will die only when accidental and unrepairable damage on the cellular level reaches a lethal accumulation – which will happen eventually, of course. Now, beings that live a long time are liable to develop special hobbies, so as to while away the period of their existence. My hobby is alien psychology. As our steerable planet wanders through the galaxy I made it my business to study the mental features of the various species we come across from time to time. This, let me add, is my own hobby. My friends and colleagues, some of whom you have just met, follow other interests. . .

'But to come back to the point, Joachim Boaz. We have been in this star cluster for a while now, long enough for me to notice that your species possesses a certain psychological peculiarity. This quirk could be summed up as *obsessiveness*. Never have I met a race with such a capacity for letting the mind become possessed with a desire or idea. It intrigues me considerably.

'So I decided to collect a few suitable specimens for study. Ordinary specimens were no good, I wanted those in whom this obsessive quirk is developed to a high degree. So I set up a *fly trap*. You know what a fly trap is? On your worlds you have troublesome insects, so you set a trap for them with something sweet and sticky. The sweetness attracts them, and the stickiness stops them from getting away. The flies cannot resist the sweetness, so they are bound to get caught. Do you see how I caught you all, little fly? You are all obsessed in one way or another – with greed, with desire for possession, with other, more interesting needs. . . . and Meirjain the Wanderer became the irresistible lure for you all! The ploy might be a convenient way of ridding your society of its undesirable elements – criminality, you see, is unusual among intelligent species. My own motive is not altruistic, however. I now have an adequate number of suitable specimens for future study.'

'Then those people – are still alive?'

'Alive and fully conscious. But conscious in an unaccustomed way. What else do you do with flies? You swat them. That is what I have done with the people who came here seeking their own ends. I stopped their consciousness at one moment of time. They live timelessly now, experiencing only that one moment, thinking their last thought, feeling their last feeling, seeing whatever happened in that instant. This mode of consciousness will be most strange for one of your kind. For me, of course, it is only a matter of convenience, a means of storage.'

'Why are their bodies so stiff?'

'Their bodies persist, even though consciousness is locked in the past. They are rigid because the electrical forces between molecules have been rendered incapable of change.'

'But it didn't work with me, did it?'

'No. Your ship saved you. It is a remarkable phenomenon. And you yourself are by far the most interesting of the specimens, Joachim Boaz. That is why I have brought you here. The others all have minds that, when we come down to it, are petty in their concerns. But you! You have set yourself to change time itself, to negate the whole universe if need be. Could any obsession be so grandiose?

You have set yourself to fight Hercules, to pull the legs from under Atlas, to wrestle with Mother Kali, to joust with Jesus, to battle with Ialdabaoth. . . .'

Though he vaguely recognized the other names, only Atlas and Hercules were familiar to Boaz. They were ancient, cruder versions of the colonnader image of strength, or nature. 'And you, I suppose, will tell me it is impossible,' he said in a surly tone.

'Could it be possible? After all, a bacterium can slay a man. But to do that it must multiply itself indefinitely, and there is only one Joachim Boaz. Besides, a bacterium and a man are of almost the same size, when compared with the ratio between you and nature. And there is something else you must understand, Joachim Boaz. Even those gods I mentioned are powerless to change anything. They are powerless because they do not exist. All that exists is natural force, and in the last resort, the unconditioned consciousness that comes into its own between successive world manifestations. But even this super-personal consciousness can neither change anything nor even decide to change anything. It is only the real world made latent, and the real world is changeless. So you see, in your madness you are striving for the absolutely impossible.

'And yet I tell you, Joachim Boaz, that there is a way you can do it.'

The narrow curved beak, so nearly motionless while they had been talking, dipped as if in thought. Boaz found that he could not speak, so great was the tension within him, and after a while the ibis-headed man continued: 'Let me paint you a picture. You are walking down a street in one of your towns. The street forks both left and right. Both routes bring you to the ship ground where your ship is parked. Both routes take about the same time. Always at this moment, throughout all eternity, you have taken the left turn. *Can you now take the right turn instead?*'

'It is all that is needed,' Boaz admitted. 'I know this.'

'But have you never tried to force yourself, in some such small action, to do *something new?*'

'Of course!' Boaz was familiar with this frustrating and futile exercise. A distressed frown crossed his face. 'It is impossible to know! One can never remember what one's future action is supposed to be!'

'That is right. You cannot remember that you have lived before. You do not know what is supposed to happen. What you cannot remember, you cannot alter. Perhaps it would be easy to act differently if you could remember – who knows? But you cannot, so instead you look to science, to a mechanical device that can alter time for you. But you can never succeed that way, Joachim Boaz. No inanimate device can do it for you. *You must do it yourself.* You as you are cannot do it. The super-personal consciousness that keeps guard in the night of the world cannot do it. If it can be done at all, it can be done only by a new kind of consciousness – one that is personal, residing in a living creature, and yet *remembers*. Such a consciousness would be more intense than the abstract consciousness from which the world was originally made. It could act differently.'

'This is all very well,' Boaz rumbled, pondering as he listened, 'but I don't have this new consciousness. And although I have received mental training, I have never heard of it before.'

'Of course not. If it existed, the world would not repeat from phase to phase with such absolute precision. But you *can* have it, Joachim Boaz – if you are brave enough.'

'I am brave enough,' Boaz said immediately. 'Tell me how.'

'Are you? We shall see. Only a god could change the course of the universe, and in effect you are asking how to become a god, the first ever to exist, since there have been no gods up to now. Very well, I will tell you. To become a god you must bear the unbearable. What brought you to this extraordinary idea, in the first place? Transcendental pain! It opened the door to a new idea, a new vision.

For a fact, it was an event never intended by nature. All these ages it has lain as a minute but imperceptible chink in nature's armour, a tiny flaw that conceivably could lead to her being overthrown. But the experience broke you, Joachim Boaz. You were unable to bear it; human consciousness is not strong enough.

'Nevertheless you must bear it. Only if an experience of that order can be faced, contained, endured without losing control, can the human mind transcend itself. And if it transcends itself, it transcends nature. I tell you, Joachim Boaz, this event would be unique, unprecedented in the history of the cosmos. You could be catapulted into a new order of being. *You would remember,* Joachim Boaz. *You would remember,* and remembering, you could alter what you remember. The world around you would become a machine under your control.'

Boaz nodded, wondering what Madrigo would make of this.

But the news was not good enough for him. 'You are telling me to wait, to be patient until the next manifestation of the world – and then to meet my misfortune in a different frame of mind. Your proposal is ludicrous.'

'That is not what I propose, Joachim Boaz. There is no need to wait. With my help, you can do it now. I can return you to that horrendous event. *I can backtrack your consciousness through time, so that you live through it again.* But this time you must be prepared to conquer it.

'Well?' the ibis beak lifted challengingly. The small black eyes glittered.

When the shocking meaning of what the alien was offering came home to him, Boaz felt as though someone had punched him unexpectedly in the stomach. He flinched, he trembled, he was aghast.

'No. You can't expect – you couldn't expect me to agree to that—'

'You are afraid. It is natural. And yet you know that eventually it must come again, an unknown number of times, as the wheel turns. This is your chance to face it knowingly. Success is only a conceivable possibility, of course, not a guarantee. Perhaps you will triumph, perhaps you will sink into the final insanity. But to become a god, you must have the daring of a god.'

An irrational hatred of the ibis-headed man arose in Boaz, and with it an ungovernable panic. He was terrified that the alien might carry out the plan without permission. When he spoke, it was in a choking voice.

'Plainly there is a limit to your knowledge. You imagine that I – or anyone – could face *that*. It is not the way. There must be another way.'

'There is no other way. You will accomplish nothing unless you conquer your fear. Fear rules you, little Mudworm. Fear drives you to everything. But it does not matter what I say to you. You will continue to convince yourself that a miracle can be worked by purely material means. I knew already that this would be the outcome. Think how often you have been given this one opportunity which you lack the courage to seize.'

'How dare you say that to me.' Boaz was sobbing. 'You have not suffered as I have.'

'The worm would become a god. But the worm had not the heart of a god. Go then, little Mudworm, and live out your useless life. I have finished studying you.'

Boaz was enraged. He did not know, in that moment, whether he would attack the ibis-headed man or flee through the screen at his back. In any event, a black funnel formed suddenly in the air before him. He felt himself moving, traversing countless dizzying scenes as before.

Stillness again. He was standing on the plain of gold, which shone in the light of the yellow sun. The Hat Brothers stood near their ship, which was made tiny by the huge and gorgeous alien ships far off. A little farther away was Boaz's alien ship, with *The Sedulous Seeker* behind it.

How much freedom would the ibis-headed man permit him? He shook off rage, shook off the sick feeling of having failed a crucial test. He shook off the resentment and contempt he felt for anyone, man or alien, who told him to endure what he was certain no being could endure.

He had the time-gems. He had an assurance, from his conversation with the ibis-headed man, that his quest was not *totally* hopeless, however qualified that statement might be. He could go forward.

He had to think how to leave Meirjain unmolested by the government cruiser. After only a moment's deliberation he lifted Romrey's statuelike body onto the sledge and set off for *The Sedulous Seeker*.

He could not resist slowing down as he passed the Hat Brothers. They were staring sightlessly at one another. As the time-swat jointly hit them, it must have been the last thing they did. That mutual look was now made timeless.

At the yacht Obsoc's robots greeted him worriedly with concerned news of Obsoc and Mace, neither of whom, it seemed, could be roused. Boaz directed the sledge into the lounge, where he briefly inspected the two.

He spoke to one of the yacht robots. 'Take off and enter circumpolar orbit, achieving stable velocity over the magnetic north pole. Meanwhile broadcast a surrender message to the government cruiser. With luck they will intercept you rather than shoot you down, and you can gain medical assistance for your master and his friends.'

The robot inclined its head in understanding. Boaz turned to go, then paused. Already he had saved Mace from self-destruction. By his ethic, he had an obligation to her.

He did not think the time-stop would prove permanent or incurable once they were away from Meirjain. But her future with Obsoc would probably land her in the same psychological state as before.

'Move the girl onto my sledge,' he ordered the robots. He left the yacht with her, and minutes later was aboard his own ship. He watched *The Sedulous Seeker* lift off. When he gauged that the econosphere cruiser would be moving to intercept it, he ordered his own ship up.

In the opposite direction, he hurtled in a low, flat trajectory. Over the south magnetic pole he piled on power and shot away from the planet, using it to screen his ship. Soon he was through the *c* barrier and safe.

Only then did he realize he had forgotten something. He should have taken Romrey's time-gems from his belt pouch. Romrey, if he did come out of time-stop, was going to be in deep trouble over those gems.

6

The matter of the meeting was so secret that all but three of those present would be subjected to memory elision before leaving the building. The privileged three had ordered the meeting. Two were econospheric councillors. The third, a man with steady blue eyes and an impassive gaze, was the heavily adplanted Director of the Department of Scientific Affairs. All three were members of the Cabal, the inner and semi-secret society by means of which the econospheric government buffered and protected its business.

Seated triumvirate fashion on the traditional raised dais, they loomed like judges over the dozen or more advisers squatting on cushions arranged in a horseshoe on the floor. These, too, were nearly all government employees – scientists, philosophers, policemen. The exception was a quiet individual who had been brought all the way from the famed colonnader planet of Aurelius. To him the trio paid a more discernible, if grudging, respect.

Not until they had settled themselves were the advisers informed that they were to discuss infringements of Article 70898/1/5: *Regulations Concerning the Measurement of Time*. It was in these regulations, so as not to draw undue attention to it, that the prohibition on time research was buried. The first stage of the meeting, officially called 'Presentation of the Problem,' was nearly over. The gathering was watching a recording of a police interrogation, and on the holocast a lean-faced man, still younger rather than middle-aged, swayed drunkenly in the straps of the chair that held him. His mind was being played back with no less trouble than a voice tape.

Gare Romrey was that man, recovered from time-stop, charged with possession of prohibited artifacts, all legal rights waived in the interests of state security. 'The man's crazy,' he was mumbling. 'The craziest alec I ever came across. By the cards, I was glad to get away from him. . . .'

The picture faded as Romrey slumped. The whole story had been drained from him.

Into the silence that followed, Cere Chai Hebron, the Scientific Director, spoke. 'From the information obtained from this man, from the other criminal Radalce Obsoc whose confession you have also seen, and from the robots who accompanied the latter, a probability analysis has been made of the period the fugitive Joachim Boaz spent upon the wandering planet. It is estimated with a weighted probability of around sixty-eight percent that the fugitive gained some information concerning time control that could not be perceived by his companion Romrey – remember Romrey's puzzlement that Boaz decided to leave the alien complex so abruptly, at a point where it might seem the search was most in prospect of greater success. Added to this, possession of the time-refractive gems itself opens up the likelihood of illegal experimentation, with a weighted probability of nearly ninety-seven percent that prohibited data will be obtained – data, incidentally, not available to the authorities themselves, since previously all circulating time-gems had been confiscated and placed under interdict.

'It might be asked why an expedition of foray is not sent to Meirjain to ascertain the validity of these conclusions. The fact is that although less than a standard year has passed since the events in question took place, the planet has already disappeared back into the Brilliancy Cluster and has proved unlocatable.

'I now ask Citizen Orskov, Dean of Moss Corporated Laboratories, to speak.'

The designated academic, grey-haired, with a mild manner and a slight nervous affliction that caused him to jerk his head a little as he spoke, did not rise. 'A few months ago we were asked by the Department to make a fresh examination of the Mirror Theorem,' he began. 'For the benefit of those who may not be acquainted with it, the Mirror Theorem describes the motions of point masses through eternity. Put briefly, it states that if an intersection is made at any arbitrary moment in time, the world-lines produced by the future configurations of the totality of point masses in the universe will be an identical reflection of the past configurations. In less technical language, the theorem proves, given a sufficiently long span of time, the periodic recurrence of the universe.

'Philosophically speaking there has always been a missing piece in this theorem. It deals with a closed system. Its prediction that the future will exactly repeat the past arises from the mechanical determinism inherent in the movements of masses. For a loose illustration of this principle, we can refer to its earliest historical exposition by the prescientific philosopher Lucretius. Working purely with inductive, observational methods, Lucretius produced an account of nature that in many respects was remarkably correct. He pictured the universe as consisting of particles or atoms falling through an endless void. As they fell the particles collided, tangled with and parted from one another, and the impermanent configurations that resulted comprised the worlds and their contents. Since the particles must eternally continue to fall, and since the number of possible configurations is limited, it follows that the same configurations, that is, the same worlds, beings and events, must recur again and again.

'For Lucretius's perpetual falling we can substitute its modern equivalent, the law of conservation of mass and energy which, in general terms, represents the endless momentum inherent in matter. What the Mirror Theorem lacks, however, is any term showing that the theorem is rigorous. The theorem is valid not of necessity, but simply because what it describes *is* a closed system. It has yet to be shown what would happen were an extraneous factor, by some unimaginable means, to be inserted into this system. What could be extraneous to the universe, you may ask? That is why this feature of the Mirror Theorem has never been taken seriously, and why to all intents and purposes the theorem has been regarded as rigorous.

'Nevertheless, it is thought that the configurations exhibited by our universe in its lifetime do *not* exhaust all *possible* configurations, and therefore alternative universes are at least conceivable.'

With that, the academic sat silent, nodding to himself and smiling.

'Well, and what did your examination yield?' Director Hebron prodded impatiently.

'Hm? Oh yes. So sorry. No change. We could not prove the rigorousness of the Mirror Theorem. The mutability of time remains theoretically possible.'

One of the econospheric councillors nodded gravely, and took up the theme. 'Extraordinary though it may seem, this is the possibility we must seriously consider. Ever since the non-rigorousness of the Mirror Theorem was discovered, we have had to take account of the fact that there *might*, however low the order of probability, be a means whereby the unfolding progression of events could be turned aside. We know what this means, do we not? It means that the magnificent stability which the econosphere enjoys, and which is guaranteed eternal by cosmic recurrence, could be nullified. The next manifestation of the world could be one in which the econosphere does not exist, in which none of us exists.

The time regulations are there to guard against this remote possibility.'

What grotesque grandiosity, thought Madrigo as he listened to the discussion. It was a case of political ideology arrogating cosmic proportions to itself – a peculiarly gross overestimate of the importance of mankind.

The econosphere, slowly but steadily falling into decay, already owing its grandeur to the past rather than to present vigor, still retained its traditional creed of permanence and stability. From colonnader philosophy it had borrowed the idea of the eternal city and applied it, not to the sidereal realm of the galaxies, which was its proper meaning, but to its own existence. Faced with the knowledge that it must eventually collapse and disappear, it found its salvation in the greater and absolute permanence of cosmic recurrence. The econosphere would never perish, because ultimately nothing ever did.

Now its leaders had conceived a paranoiac suspicion that the course of nature, even on this the vastest of scales, could be interfered with. It reminded Madrigo of psychopathological religions of the past, which had gone so far as to put individuals on trial for 'sabotage against God'.

A question was being raised by the scientists on the floor. Nothing, they pointed out, lay outside nature. How, therefore, could the human mind find the fresh impulse that could lead it to alter time, even if it were technically feasible? Did that not contradict the principle of predetermination, which was supposed to govern human actions as well as everything else?

'The determinacy of nature has never been absolutely established, either,' the Dean of Moss Corporated Laboratories responded diffidently. 'If temporal mutability is possible, then it shows that nature, to some degree, perhaps hidden until now, is potentially indeterminate.'

'Nevertheless, we would be faced with the incredible fact that this individual, this shipkeeper Joachim Boaz, must already have come in possession of some mental quality that is uniquely new, if he is to have any prospect of success. The indeterminacy of nature must already have shown itself.'

This remark came, in a more forthright manner, from a man wearing the collar of the Research Tabulation Branch of the Department of Scientific Affairs. He apparently had the ear of Director Hebron, for the latter nodded approvingly. 'As you say, there is something interesting here. We know, of course, how the fugitive came to conceive his ambition. It arose from his very unusual experience, an accidental combination of silicon bone functions and the pain-feeling function of the sensorium. It must be assumed that it is this that has introduced an indeterminate note into nature, if indeed any exists. . . .' Abruptly he turned to a burly, big-bellied figure in grey uniform who previously had not spoken. 'How much pain can one experience? Is it known?'

The person he addressed was Chief of the Rectification Branch of the Department of Police, the arm of the police force charged more than any other with the impossible task of enforcing the econosphere's political laws. For a moment the police chief looked embarrassed; then he recovered himself and his lip curled in a half-smile of ill-veiled relish.

'This question has received some investigation, of course,' he said in an impressively heavy baritone. 'The problem has always been to maintain the subject's consciousness while continuing to increment pain levels. Consequently the absolute limit of pain has never been reached by us, surprising though that might seem. The silicon bone gimmick sounds like a good one. I'll see that it's followed up.'

'Please do not do so,' Hebron said politely but firmly. 'At least not for the present, until we can clear this whole matter up. We do not want any more Joachim Boazes wandering around.'

Throughout the conference Hebron had been glancing at Madrigo, as if expecting him to take part in the exchanges. Madrigo rose to his feet now, in defiance of established protocol which required those on the floor to remain seated.

'Allow me to introduce myself,' he said, gathering in the folds of his cyclas. 'I know more than any of you about this man you are discussing. I was his mentor in Aurelius.'

He paused, while his gaze traveled coolly over the gathering. 'Firstly, let me say that any properly trained colonnader like myself will regard your talk regarding alterations to nature as simple foolishness. It is what one can expect from pure scientists. They become hypnotized by their ability to calculate, they allow themselves to become lost in the byways of a logical maze, and so they lose their sense of proportion. They forget, too, that all their science is founded on deeper philosophical ideas. And from the standpoint of genuine philosophy, I can tell you categorically that there can be no alteration to the predestination of time. Whatever happens, the next universe will be an exact reproduction of this one.

'As for Joachim Boaz, I am sorry to say that his truly harrowing experience has broken his mind, so that he is now even beyond my help. I am certain that he is quite insane, with no vestige of ataraxy. To conjoin in his delusions is undignified in a department of government.'

An initial silence followed Madrigo's words. Then a babble of argument began. One of the econospheric ministers raised his hand, at which the noise stopped.

He conferred briefly with his two colleagues, in tones which the others could not decipher. Then he turned back to face the gathering.

'The sense of the meeting is that a situation exists where a derangement of the structure of time could be possible,' he said coldly, 'and that this constitutes a threat to the econosphere. We order that the individual Joachim Boaz be found and destroyed. The colonnader' – he cast an unfriendly glance at Madrigo – 'is to be held until that is done, for any further assistance he can render.'

Hearing of his pending detention, Madrigo understood that its main purpose was to prevent him from getting a warning to Boaz – even though, on the face of it, memory elision would render it unnecessary. Econosphere officials had a sometimes exaggerated respect for the mental abilities of colonnaders.

He noted, as the meeting broke up, that the police chief's eyes gleamed with the prospect of the hunt. Even though he, too, after the next few minutes, would not know why the man he hunted was a danger to society.

7

'This is a nice one,' said Mace.

Boaz had left his colonnader cards on the table. Mace had been sorting idly through them, and now was inspecting Major Arcanum number twenty. It was the card called Unveiling. Specifically, the veil that in the card called the Priestess had hung between the pillars *Joachim* and *Boaz* had now been drawn aside and was draped along one edge of the card. The scene it revealed was unworldly. A mythical semi-human figure, with richly pinioned wings half unfolded to extend rakishly along its back, hovered in a horizontal posture over an indistinct landscape. The 'angel', as the figure was called, held to its lips a long, slender trumpet that itself seemed to float endlessly over this same landscape, so elongated was it. The trumpet evidently gave voice to a powerful blast, of a force so great that the group of people who threw up their hands in its path was being dispersed.

Dissolution was the meaning of the card: it depicted, in parabolical language, the time when the universe would collapse into fire and come to an end. The pillars of existence would fall into one another, and the latent, unmanifest eons would begin.

The slight movement of the ship stopped. It had completed its short journey across the ship ground and had entered an underground parking shed. Boaz had taken this precaution to try to reduce the possibility of early discovery by the authorities.

From his armchair, he looked across the table at Mace. They had been together for nearly a year now, hiding in space or on fringe worlds to evade the police hunt which he was sure would be taking place. She had come out of time-stop when they were exactly ten light-hours from Meirjain, and she had told him, when she was able to speak, what it was like to be trapped in one moment in time: an experience which, perhaps, could only be comprehended, and that only partially, by a boneman or woman who had experienced the elongated time sense of altered chronaxy. It had clearly had an effect on her, giving her eyes a drugged, haunted look which faded only after some days.

He should have parted company with her, but he had not. He sensed that she had not yet shaken off the wish to commit suicide, and his colonnader obligations still told on him. He had embarked on a course of mental therapy, of the kind that had so deftly been practiced on him when he was a boy in Theta, and of whose methods his subsequent training had given him some knowledge.

It was odd, he admitted, that a man bent on total self-obliteration should, in passing, bother to mend the self-feeling of someone else. Mace, of course, had no idea that any form of process was being practiced on her. Colonnader techniques were not that formal. All she knew was that she had close discussions with Boaz, and that somehow her attitude toward herself gradually changed.

They had come to know one another well in the past year. Boaz, his tongue loosened perhaps by his earlier disclosure to Gare Romrey, as well as by the confidentiality of the therapist-patient relationship, had even confessed the nature of his mission to Mace.

She had listened with fascination, and none of the criticism or uncomprehending blame he could have expected from most. 'But what does your mentor say to this?' she asked eventually.

'Madrigo?' Boaz made a wry face. 'He thinks I have fallen victim to cachexia. He does not admit the possibility of what I am trying to do.'

'Cachexia?'

'Mental disturbance. An ill-conditioned state of mind. When colonnaders use the term, it betokens a particularly serious kind of mental illness.'

'Do *you* think you could have it?'

'Of course I have it. The mistake is in thinking it is based on delusion. True, all other cases of cachexia *are* based on delusion. But in me it is based on reality. A reality deeper than any that underpins sanity. Not even Madrigo understands that.'

He sighed, the conversation coming briefly to his memory, and rose. 'It is time for me to find my friends, Mace. You may go into the city if you wish. Or remain here. You have your own key.'

She nodded, and carried on sorting through the cards. Boaz hesitated; he would have liked to ask her for them, preferring to have them with him always, but decided it would be impolite. He left the ship, passed up the flow-elevator to the surface, and ventured cautiously onto the street.

He had wondered if he could have handled events better on Meirjain, but could see no ethical way in which he could have prevented his identity from becoming known to the authorities. Since then he was almost certainly a fugitive (although he had heard no official posting of his name) and the necessity of maintaining close proximity to his ship was proving a decided disadvantage. It was, in fact, the main reason why he had delayed events by nearly a year while he skulked on the edge of the econosphere, only now reckoning it relatively safe to come to Kathundra, a member of the Central Clique of worlds, a seat of government, though only one of several, a centre of science and learning, and home of vices more sophisticated and depraved than raw boundary planets had yet imagined.

Mace, he imagined, would have a good time here. At other ports of call he had sometimes had occasion in passing to glance at her erotic adventures during his voyeuristic surveys.

She had once, with some eagerness, offered herself to him, but he had been obliged to decline. When he shut down his bone functions long ago, he had relinquished all sexual feeling with them.

He took a deep breath. At last he was on the planet Kathundra, in the city of Kathundra (on all Clique worlds the capital bore the same name as the planet). Here, within the ten miles of freedom his ship allowed him, was the man who all these years had been waiting for him.

He strolled for a while through the glittering walkways, interrogating his ship with orders to ascertain whether he was under observation. Because his shabby modsuit identified him as an outworld visitor, he was constantly beset by commercial adflashes and come-ons, as well as accosted by various individuals offering services likely to be sought by the tourist, and all of which he rudely refused. Finally satisfied that he had done all he could, he entered a travel agency. Kathundra boasted a modern transport system working on the instantaneous acceleration principle – an adaptation of star drive – and all he had to do was wait his turn at a line of stage chambers, dial a number and step inside. The door slid shut behind him, sealing the ceramic-lined cubicle with a hiss. He was seized in a complex field of uni-directional electrostatic forces which separated ever so slightly the positive and negative charges of every atom in his body. Other, more powerful uni-directional fields were added, acting on those charges and accelerating Boaz down a ceramic-lined tunnel. He passed through perhaps thirty switching points in the process of being routed to his destination, his velocity retarded or accelerated in each case so as to slot him in with millions of others passing through those same points. Boaz was not aware of what was happening, of course. The entire process, involving a roundabout journey of perhaps ten miles, took place in the standard interval of one-twentieth of a second. All he was conscious of was that a light came on and the cubicle number on the wall suddenly changed. He stepped out into the house of Aban Ebarak.

For a moment Boaz felt slightly dizzy, a consequence of the generally excellent transport system unique to him. While he was in the acceleration fields his ship's beams, though they were able to track him, were vitiated in their integrative functions. If he were trapped in the system for, say, a matter of minutes, he would probably die.

He stood in a small vestibule. To one side a broad window (which Boaz knew to be genuine, not a display) revealed that the scientist Ebarak's house was half a mile up a tower block and gave a breathtaking view of the jungle of shafts which was Kathundra. Ebarak himself was not in evidence, though Boaz had received the acceptance signal before stepping into the stage chamber. The scientist had in fact, been expecting him for days.

Pausing to recover from the journey, he moved to a door and opened it, disclosing a neat study. Ebarak was within, poring over a reading screen. He looked up at the intrusion, a smallish, tidy man, with a pale face, chiselled nose, and mild blue eyes, which, when they were directed at anything or anyone, seemed to turn flint-hard.

'Ah, hello, Joachim. Sorry I wasn't on hand to greet you. I was just reading up on some material here. The memory gets a bit rusty, you know.' Ebarak was one of many scientists who did not trust adplants too far, believing them to make the intellect lazy. He did not have a single memory adplant and only a standard type of adplanted calculator. The book he was reading on the screen, Boaz saw, was one on the econosphere's index of prohibited texts: Whitlaw's *Cases of Relativistic Event Reversal*. It dealt with the way in which time order could seemingly be reversed in small, insignificant ways as a result of the relativity laws.

The scientist killed the screen as he stood up. His mouth firmed. 'Have you got them with you?'

'I have.' Boaz took a pouch from a pocket of his modsuit. He handed it to Ebarak, who loosened the cord at the neck and poured out a number of gems onto the palm of his hand.

'They look so ordinary, don't they?' he murmured.

Laying the pouch on his desk, he picked up a gem between thumb and finger and brought it close to his eye, peering intently. After a moment in which he rolled the gem to tilt facet after facet, Ebarak saw a tiny scene. He saw himself, in his laboratory, fitting something gem-sized into an instrument with a long, shiny barrel.

He smiled. He was, he realized, looking a few minutes into his own future.

It was not the first time he had seen such gems. Briefly he had begun to investigate two specimens brought back from the first landings on Meirjain, before the Scientific Ministry for which he then worked had closed down all such work in panic and impounded the jewels. He believed they had been destroyed.

'Thank you,' he said with feeling. 'Thank you.'

'When shall I see you again?'

'Call me in a few days. Better leave now. I want to get down to work.'

'Yes, of course.' Shyly, hesitantly, Boaz turned to go. He would have liked to stay, to watch or assist his co-conspirator, but he knew that Ebarak did not want him there, and besides, the longer he stayed the more he increased the danger to the scientist.

He dialled the same travel agency he had come by and emerged, only slightly unsteady, back onto the walkway. For some time he drifted with the throng as before. Then he entered an eating house, sat and watched the passersby through the transparent frontage. As he knew from his previous visit, when he had sought and eventually made the acquaintance of Aban Ebarak, Kathundra was a place of affected mannerisms. People who met on the street greeted one another with exaggerated gestures and flourishes. Which, he supposed, made the offhanded casualness of Ebarak a distinctive mark of individuality.

After a while he returned to his ship. Mace was not there. He sat in his armchair, relaxed, and fell into a semi-doze. Without any prompting on his part, the ship began to send out its spy-beams, bringing him the habitual montage of scenes from the surrounding city.

He paid them only a fraction of his attention; he was like a man who kept the video switched on all the time. He showed a little more interest when the beam brought him a picture of Mace. It was hardly a coincidence, especially in a city of such size. Boaz had realized that the ship showed him Mace much more often than chance would account for. It was, he reasoned, obeying his subconscious wish to keep watch over her.

Usually he did not linger over her escapades, but this time some unformed impulse made him hold the image steady. Mace was in a private room with two others, a man and a woman. The woman was voluptuous like Mace, with heavy breasts and hips: the nymphgirl fashion was long out of date here on Kathundra. All three were naked, except that the man and woman wore gas masks. And they were spraying some kind of pearly mist over Mace from nozzles they held in their hands. The mist billowed over her skin and seemed to be absorbed by it. It drifted in her mouth and nostrils. As all this happened, her face took on a look of extraordinary, ever-increasing ecstasy.

Boaz knew that the mist was a sex-enhancing drug. He knew, too, from the look on Mace's face, that she had switched on several of her bone functions.

The man and woman put aside the nozzles, ripped off their gas masks, and fell together on Mace. In moments all three were squirming and rocking together. Boaz, seeing the incredible intensity of the pleasure Mace was experiencing, was struck by a totally new thought which brought him instantly to wakefulness.

Could there be, to the horrendous *negative* experience that had ruined his life, a *positive* one of equal intensity? Was it possible to know pleasure, or happiness, in the same degree in which he had known pain and misery?

Could *that* be his salvation? Could there be a cancelling of effects?

Gradually he faded out Mace's continuing transports of delight. He ordered the spy-beam withdrawn from the city and then sat alone in the darkness. It seemed a wonder to him that he had never considered this before. After all, equilibrium was one of the basic principles of the colonnader card pack. . . .

But no. The idea was fanciful, absurd. It seemed that his long cohabitation with the girl was causing his mind to wander.

He began thinking about the time-gems, and to wonder instead if Aban Ebarak would make any progress.

8

Two local days later Abab Ebarak received another visit, this time entirely unannounced.

But it was not without forewarning. He had rigged up a simple apparatus to project the images flashing so unpredictably from the time-gems onto a screen (though he had not, yet, worked out a way to capture a gem's output on all facets simultaneously). On the screen, the door of the laboratory opened and a tall slender figure, wearing a hooded street cloak clasped at the throat, entered. Ebarak was able to study the face for several seconds before the image faded.

By resuming the investigation so rudely interrupted years before, he had been able to calibrate the angle through which light was refracted on entering a gem. The scene he was witnessing registered a time bracket of five minutes either way of the present. Since it had not happened yet, it would happen shortly.

Patiently he waited, until a small sound came from the other side of the door.

'Come in, Cere,' he called without turning his head.

The door opened and in walked Cere Chai Hebron, Director of the Department of Scientific Affairs, and econospheric Cabal member.

'How did you recognize me?' Hebron said in genuine surprise. He undid his cloak's throat-clasp, threw back the hood and pulled a flat, flesh-coloured device from the side of his neck. Immediately his face began to change its appearance, no longer pulled into a false shape by the device's neurological control over his facial muscles. The real face that now showed was pale and finely chiselled, like Ebarak's, but unlike his it had a sultriness about the mouth, a hint of passion about the eyes, when Hebron listened or spoke intently.

'The eyes, Cere,' Ebarak said. 'You forgot to disguise the eyes. That gadget couldn't fool me.' He was amused. A survey had once revealed that thirty-eight percent of scientific workers – a far higher percentage than chance could account for – had eyes of the same cool blue hue. There was still argument over what the finding meant.

Hebron sighed. It was a habit of people of his class to disguise themselves when moving alone in public. In this case he had an additional reason for doing so. He was putting himself at risk by being here at all.

'There's something else,' Ebarak said. 'You probably imagine I saw you come into the vestibule through a monitor. I didn't. I watched you enter this laboratory – in advance.'

He spun a wheel, backtracking the recorder and running the scene again for Hebron's benefit.

'Time-gem?' Hebron asked, staring at the few seconds of action in fascination.

'Yes. You already know I have them, of course. That's what brings you here.' He paused. 'It would make a good warning system, if it could be made reliable.'

'But productive of paradoxes?' Hebron suggested as the scene faded.

'Oh, I don't think so. Paradoxes don't exist in the real world.' Ebarak turned away from the screen, switched off the apparatus and swivelled to face Hebron. 'I would have got word to you that I have the gems. You know that, don't you?'

'Do I?' said Hebron acidly. Feeling the heat of the laboratory, he removed his cloak. Draping it over one arm, he stared down at Ebarak in schoolmasterly fashion. 'You should have let me know *immediately*. This matter has been given top priority. It is only a matter of time before Orm's bloodhounds track you down, and this Joachim Boaz, too. I shall protect you for as long as I can, but it would be easier if you had confided in me.'

'Orm?'

'He's now chief of the Rectification Branch. And he's a brute, I promise you.'

'How did you find out I have the gems?'

'My own people have been watching you. You met Boaz once, years ago. It seemed possible he would seek your help.'

Ebarak raised his eyebrows. 'You knew of my acquaintance with Boaz?'

'You told me, at the time.'

'Did I?' said Ebarak vaguely. His eyes glazed in a vain effort at recollection. This time it was Hebron's turn to smile, partly with exasperation. Scorning memory adplants, Ebarak was prone to these blank spots in his knowledge of past details.

'How many gems did Boaz give you?' Hebron asked.

'Twelve. But I believe he may have more.'

'Let me see one.'

A trifle reluctantly, Ebarak went to a safe, bent to its audio plate where he quietly hummed a series of tones, and opened the thick metal door. He took out the pouch Boaz had given him, carefully extracted a gem, and handed it to Hebron.

The Director lifted the gem to the light, peering into its depths. He rolled it, chuckling.

'It's genuine! And so clear! This is like old times, Aban! This time let's try to ensure that they stay in our possession.'

He handed back the gem. 'But we must get properly organized. I hope you didn't have thoughts of working on your own? You'll get nowhere that way. What's needed is teamwork.' He stroked his jaw thoughtfully. 'Also your facilities here are too limited – quite apart from what will happen if *Orm* learns of your past relationship with Boaz.'

Ebarak swivelled his chair so that he was in profile to the Director and gazed into the distance, as though not wanting to hear what Hebron had said. Hebron leaned back against a workbench, supporting himself with his hands, and scrutinized his old friend. 'I see you are displeased.'

'It's just that I'm not convinced people with philosophical commitments can produce good scientific work,' Ebarak said in a neutral tone.

Hebron was not offended. 'The pure scientist, as ever! Excellent. It is why we value you.'

'Also I do not share this aim of yours.'

'Do you not? Yet you seem willing to work toward its accomplishment . . . Yes, I know, it is disinterested research where you are concerned. The pure search for knowledge. And yet the great transformation might be achieved. Temporal mutation might become possible. Think what you will have unleashed on the world! Recklessness of that order, simply in the quest for knowledge, borders on a philosophical commitment all of its own.'

'Except that these gems may not lead to what you want. I have no reason to think they do.'

'And have you communicated that belief to Boaz? After all, *his* aim is the same as mine.'

'He is a man obsessed, in a way that even you are not. He forms his own opinions.'

'And you exploit that obsession to get what *you* want. You see, we all use each other. In this case you have no choice but to work with my team. You need me to ward off Orm – if I can. Otherwise I do not think you will live long enough to contemplate, in your intellectual purity, the new knowledge of time you may glean from these gems.'

Ebarak turned his head sharply toward the Director. 'Do *you* never contemplate the risks you are taking? You are a member of the Cabal, yet you are committing what amounts to state treason. I do not think *you* will suffer a simple death, when you are found out. They will make a terrible example of you.'

'I *will* enjoy a simple death,' Hebron said quietly. 'It is already arranged. I assure you I am not oblivious to the risk. As for why I take it, your friend Joachim Boaz understands it even if you do not. *He* believes it is possible to lift the dead hand of predestination. Do you never feel it pressing down on your every deed, Aban? Does the impossibility of original action never depress you?'

'No, because what you are saying is philosophy, in other words, it is imagination.'

'It is fact. What a stubborn refusal to appreciate reality!'

'Your lack of caution amazes me, nevertheless,' Ebarak persisted mildly. 'Being such a prominent figure, you are skimming very close to the event horizon.' He was using a contemporary figure of speech that, in an earlier age, might have emerged as 'skating on thin ice'.

'Oh, but I am a powerful man, Aban. You must rely on obscurity for your protection, but I can employ econosphere resources to avoid discovery. Besides, it is now a matter of urgency. There is something I might as well tell you. You said to me once that even if a way to alter predestination could be found, the changes that could be made would be trivial. I have put some of the best brains in the econosphere to work on just that point, and what they say is this: a small change in *this* universe will effect a total change in the next one. Changes wrought in the current manifestation may well be trivial, as you predict – perhaps even imperceptible. But it is during the latent period, not the material one, that the consequences of those changes work themselves through. Here is an analogy: immerse alum crystals in water, heat it and the crystals will dissolve and disappear. Cool the solution again, and the crystals will reappear *in the same formation as before*. But what if the solution is stirred while hot? Then the case is not the same. The crystals will arrange themselves differently on their next materialization.'

Ebarak listened closely while Hebron went on: 'So you see, Aban, there is a race on. Whoever succeeds in this thing will have the key to unimaginable power, if it can be controlled. I sense that it *will* succeed; the process is under way. But by whom will it be accomplished? If your work does not produce results then Joachim Boaz, for instance, will go elsewhere, and perhaps, eventually, he will succeed. So if we die, still not masters of our fates, we cannot be sure what will become of us in our next resurrection, and perhaps as individuals we will cease to exist at all, forever.

'Tell me,' he said after a long pause, 'did Boaz have a woman with him?'

'He had no one with him.'

'There is evidence that he had a woman with him when he fled Meirjain. Is he residing in the City?'

'I believe so.'

'He has a deficiency, a physical dependence on his spaceship. He is unable to stray far from it . . . his ship may even be hidden somewhere near the ship ground. I will investigate . . .'

He dropped his eyes and fell silent. Ebarak said nothing. Hebron, he knew, was thinking that the woman he had mentioned would be a good source of information about

Boaz. But he did not want to feel curious about what such a line of inquiry entailed.

Idly he switched on the projector again. A picture formed on the screen, snatched from out of near-time. With relief he saw a cloaked and hooded Hebron, a few minutes in the future, depart from his laboratory.

Exuding an odour of sweat laden with pheromonic musk, Eystrach Orm moved down the line of young men bent over their monitor desks. As he passed, each junior policeman felt a tremor of terror mingled with lust.

Everyone who worked in that department had to come to terms with Orm's tastes. He liked young men, but he liked them to be heterosexual, and to overpower their natural repugnance for his advances. Dismay, horror and unwilling but irresistible attraction were for him an indispensable sexual recipe. To this end he used not only his rank, not only his impressive physical presence, but also crudely chemical means. The scent he wore contained concentrated organic compounds that overcame almost any male's resistance.

'Sir.'

'Yes?' Orm strode to a monitor who had raised his arm. He bent to the screen, placing his hands on the youth's shoulders and squeezing slightly as he brought his head close to his.

'Look, sir.' The policeman was twisting slide-dials, trying to sort the signal he had traced from the rest of the city's traffic and bring it up on the screen.

Orm frowned at the flickering, fading pattern in pastel colors that was brought to the screen. 'It looks like noise. Probably just reflection.'

This section prided itself on being able to intercept any beamed signal in the city. 'That's what I thought it was, sir – a double reflection, it's so faint. The general traffic completely hides it normally. But—'

'Yes?' Orm's hand was fondling his subordinate's neck.

'It has a constant level, sir. It must be a deliberate output.'

'But it's too low. It isn't a useful signal.'

'No sir. But I can't understand its multiplexing either.'

'Keep on it. Let me know if you need a filter-booster.'

'Yes sir.'

Orm's hand dropped from the policeman's neck. He prowled away, left the monitor room and came to where the outworld reports were being sifted. 'Well?'

Seated at a datagrator was an officer wearing silver braid. His eyes looked dazed as he rapidly absorbed the results that were being fed to his adplant through a silver nerve in his thumb. At the same time a broad-angle holdisplay was before him, though Orm couldn't see it from where he stood.

The officer came out of his near-trance. 'It's shaping up, sir. Two positive placings, a significant curve of probables over the year. It looks as if he's moving in this direction.'

'Eh? The cheeky bastard.' Orm studied a dataplate the officer handed him. The difficulty in these cases sprang from the total lack of migration or trade controls on nearly every planet of the econosphere. A man could land and take off without anybody bothering him, and could even pay his shipground dues without leaving a record of his identity. Despite that, detective work was straighforward. One simply collected, through a far-flung plethora of spies, informers and data machines, a billion or more small facts which were analysed statistically. It always brought results, given enough time. Amazingly trivial objects could be tracked, such as items of cargo.

'Do you think he could actually be *here*?' Orm asked wonderingly. 'In Kathundra?' It seemed irresponsibly reckless – unless the desperate shipkeeper had a reason good enough to risk it.

He thought of the mysterious minimum-power signals the monitor had picked up. There could be a connection with the physical reliance the ex-colonnader was supposed to have on his converted cargo ship. The prisoner Romrey had spoken of its unusual communication system.

If Boaz was already in Kathundra, then Orm's quarry was trapped.

'We might snuff out this one sooner than we thought,' he said with a purr of pleasure. He smiled, feeling a touch of excitement, the excitement of a chase nearing its end. Excitement caused him to sweat more, and as his evaporating perspiration cast extra pheromonic volatiles into the air, his sexual presence became all the stronger.

Moving with the burly grace of a puma, he padded back to the monitor room.

9

'Look.'

Captain Joachim Boaz awoke.

He was alone in the ship. Mace had not been there for over three days, but that was no surprise. Her absences were becoming longer.

He did not answer. But he felt, impinging on his brain, one end of a very long stick. That stick was a spy-beam that extended seven miles or more.

The other end of the beam showed him Mace. At first he wondered why the ship had roused him just to show him one more of her erotic episodes. It was a good part of a minute before he realized that this time something else was happening.

Mace was bound to a chair by clasps. Nearby two men sat, wearing the loose flowing garments associated with the high-ranking and leisured classes. It was the apparel that had confused Boaz at first. The men did not look like policemen.

One leaned toward Mace, listening intently. And Mace was talking. It was evident she was drugged. Drugs that could get a person eagerly to tell all, on any subject, without inhibition or hint of falsehood, were legion.

'What's the range?' he asked. The answer was what he expected: just over seven miles. 'Show me where.'

The ship fed a route map to his brain, storing it in his adplant. Boaz wasted no time in getting ready. He pulled on his modsuit, and went to the storeroom. He selected a hand gun and a cutting beamer, both of which he tucked into two of the many recesses of the suit.

He went to a cupboard, opened a flask, and drank a long draught of glucose-rich nutrient syrup.

'Get up onto the ground,' he ordered the ship, 'and be ready to take off when I return.'

The ship robots were busying themselves when he left. He made his way to the travel agency just outside the ship ground, and dialled a small ten-booth agency whose number he had to get from the directory after consulting the map in his mind.

He emerged on a nearly deserted walkway. At his back, the blank wall of a building seemed to extend forever. Before him, on the other side of the walkway, a tangled vista of rectilinear shafts gave the usual view of the three-dimensional urban jungle that was Kathundra, interspersed with lamp-suns that relieved the gloom of the lower city and created a glowing haze.

He paused with eyes closed, waiting for the wave of sickness that ran through his body to fade. Then he turned left and walked along the wall until coming to the entrance he knew would be there.

The huge blank-walled building was multifunctional. In it were several thousand dwellings, businesses, work-shops, private clubs, dens and enterprises of all sorts, slotted into a mazelike inner structure. What they all had in common was a measure of secrecy. The building had no internal addresses, and all its force-transport numbers were unlisted. The only way to find any of the apartments was to be given a travel number or already to know the way there. For such privacy, the rentees paid highly.

But it was no protection against Joachim Boaz. He moved into the lobby, which was a long tunnel, square in cross-section, the wells roughened and grey and punctuated with elevator gates and the openings of flow-corridors. A tomblike quiet prevailed. The air was dead and oppressive.

Along the flowing floors of silent corridors, down in silently running elevators, Boaz came to a grey, numberless door. He took out the cutting beamer and began to trace out a rough square around the lock.

The tool's nearly invisible radiation blade, carrying very little heat but maximum penetrating power, sliced into the metal. The main difficulty with a cutting beam was that the shear line was so thin that metals tended to bond themselves back together after the beam had passed. To prevent this Boaz placed a sucker pad against the section and jiggled it slightly until, the cutting complete, it came away altogether.

He knew that an alarm would go off as the door opened. Beyond it was an empty room. He crossed it at a run, and almost without losing momentum smashed into a second door with a booted foot and a fist.

The plastic panel shattered under the impact of his ship-enhanced strength. Kicking his way through the fragments, he emerged into the second room, putting away the cutting beam and taking out his hand gun.

During his long years of dependence on his ship Boaz had become used to foreknowledge. He already knew what he would find in the room. The interrogation was over. Mace, still held by clasps, lolled in the chair. The two robed men, who moments before had been sitting pensively, had risen at the sound of the alarm and now stared at Boaz with a lack of reaction that was curious until one realized that, after all, there was little they could do about what was happening. Boaz blocked the only exit. Neither man was armed. Usually, people in the addressless building saw little need for protection other than simply being there.

The taller of the two was a man with blue eyes that were clear and direct. With raised eyebrows, he coolly appraised the intruder.

'Captain Joachim Boaz, I presume?' he said after a moment's hesitation.

'How do you know me?' Boaz asked gruffly.

'You look the part, Captain. I admit, I had not anticipated that you would turn up here. You are even more resourceful than I had thought.'

Boaz used his gun to wave both men to the rear of the room. The use of the archaism 'Captain' in place of 'shipkeeper' disconcerted him slightly. He stepped to Mace, taking hold of her face in a thick hand and directing her eyes to him. She stared up without recognition.

He released the clasps on her wrists and waist. 'Stand up,' he ordered. When she did not respond he hauled her to her feet. Unsteadily she stayed on her feet, leaning on his shoulder. He backed away, guiding her toward the door, keeping the gun trained on her interrogators.

'Stop,' the taller man said.

Boaz's plan was to leave by the transport cubicle he had seen in the other room. Regretfully he was thinking to himself that he would have to kill these two first. But he halted.

Something in the situation was odd.

Apart from the lack of formal dress, apart from the furtive location, there was the behaviour between the two men. The smaller individual with sandy hair and a snub nose had said nothing and seemed unready to take any initiative, looking to the other as a disciple toward a master.

Boaz recognized that look. It was a feature of many philosophic or occult groups, whose members were apt to fall into what Madrigo had termed thelemic transfer – the surrender of the individual's personal will to the superiors in the order.

'I take it you are government?' he queried.

'Yes and no. Let me introduce myself. I am Cere Chai Hebron, Director of the Department of Scientific Affairs. My friend here' – he indicated the other – 'also works for the government. But today neither of us is acting in an official capacity. We are, to put it bluntly, committing a crime, as you are.'

He smiled, without mirth but in an apparent attempt to win Boaz's confidence. 'I think you should listen to me. Without my help you stand little chance of leaving Kathundra alive. You see, it is not simply a matter of illegal possession of alien artifacts. I am sure you have little idea of the alarm with which the government regards your very existence, or of the effort that is being put into tracking you down.'

A bundle of questions arose in Boaz's mind. In particular he wondered how these people had found Mace. But then it occurred to him that this man Hebron, if that was his real name, could be doing nothing more than feeding him information gained from Mace herself. Perhaps she was the victim of a random kidnapping, snatched to satisfy the festering lusts or warped hobbies of pleasure-sated Kathundrans. The man was evidently trying to delay him, and every extra moment spent here increased his danger.

He started back again. 'At least let me call Aban Ebarak here to talk to you,' Hebron said hurriedly.

Again Boaz stopped. That name could not have come from Mace.

'You know Ebarak?'

'Indeed. You and I are collaborators, in a way.'

'What is his number?'

Hebron recited a string of digits, which Boaz matched against the number he held in his adplant. He nodded, but was still suspicious. 'Come here,' he said.

Beckoning them into the other room, he dialled. After a short wait Ebarak appeared on the vision plate by the side of the booth which was inset into the wall. Boaz pushed Hebron before it.

'Do you know this man?'

Guardedly Ebarak nodded. 'Yes. He's a Cabal Director.'

'What can I expect from him?'

Ebarak, reluctant to say anything incriminating over a public service, looked ill-at-ease. 'You could say he's on our side,' he murmured eventually.

'Then we're coming through. Stand by.'

'I was suggesting Aban come *here*,' Hebron said diffidently.

'Get in the booth, both of you.'

Still at gunpoint, they obeyed. After dispatching them Boaz dialled again, pulled Mace in after him, and stepped out with her in Ebarak's vestibule.

Only the scientist was present. 'They've gone into the lounge,' he said. 'You will join us?'

'They gave Mace a truth drug. Bring her round for me.'

'Bring her in here.'

He led Boaz into the laboratory and helped him lower Mace into a chair. Disappearing into a storeroom, he returned a few moments later with a hypodermic into which he measured a tiny amount of colourless fluid.

With a faint hiss the drug went into Mace's bloodstream. 'She'll be all right. Don't suppose he gave her anything to hurt her, anyway.'

'Do you mind telling me what this is all about?'

Ebarak smiled wryly. 'Philosophy again. A human preoccupation that seems capable of producing an endless variety of fanatics.'

'I had guessed it,' Boaz muttered.

Mace seemed to have fallen asleep. Ebarak arranged her limbs more comfortably in the deep armchair. 'You see, the government, including the Cabal itself, has unwittingly become host to a secret occult society, and its beliefs are treasonable. Cere Hebron, the tall fellow in the next room, is Director of this society. He is also Director of the Department of Scientific Affairs.' He shrugged. 'I haven't been able to tell you this before, but we have both, to some extent, been under his protection. I have also been obliged to collaborate with his society in the matter of research into the time-gems.'

'These treasonable beliefs concern time?' Boaz asked.

'Yes. The society's aims are broadly speaking the same as your own. But the philosophical background is quite different.'

Unseen by Ebarak, Cere Chai Hebron had slipped into the laboratory while he spoke. 'That is right, Captain Boaz,' he said quietly. 'And yet you, I gather, should be able to appreciate that background.'

'What "philosophy" is it that makes it necessary to kidnap an innocent woman?' Boaz demanded brusquely.

'I make no apology,' Hebron replied, unperturbed. 'The Great Work is of such magnitude that any act committed in pursuit of it is praiseworthy. As it is, I took your friend so as to gain an insight into your good self, Captain. And I am glad that I did.'

He moved closer, without a glance at Mace. His gaze on Boaz was open and disconcerting. 'Listen closely, and I will explain our doctrine. We reject that colonnader teaching on the absoluteness of mind-fire. We believe it is not a state of ultimate consciousness, but only a kind of limpid sleep, a clear, calm quiescence. The whole universe is in this state of quiescence, whether in its latent or its manifest phase. Essentially, it consists of the fact that nothing ever changes. The Mirror Theorem proves this. It is what we call predestination. But what does predestination signify? To those of us in the society it merely signifies that existence has not yet evolved true consciousness and will. What consciousness does exist, either as pure mind-fire or as the smaller consciousness that is present in every one of us, is passive and not in command of itself.

'In this condition, the universe resembles a flower, or some other plant, that blossoms by day and closes up by night, and does nothing more. This opening and closing, of course, symbolizes the manifest and latent stages of the world. So it has been for no one knows how long.

'But it will not remain so forever. The universe is capable of further development. There is a higher destiny – to evolve a new, more intense consciousness that is not quiescent, but which instead is capable of change and innovation. Only creatures possessing individual consciousness can take this step, and doubtless this is the reason why such creatures – organic creatures – exist. We believe it is man's specific duty to generate the new consciousness. We are the acme of creation. But we are still conditioned by the material universe. We can, if we choose, become its masters.'

Boaz turned his face away. It was no wonder Hebron was interested in him, he thought. He remembered Gare Romrey. It was more than likely he had disclosed Boaz's quest under interrogation.

'You see how closely our ambitions match, Captain,' Hebron went on. 'The difference is that you seek only escape. You have not grasped that the goal is rather a glorious new adventure. To create wholly new events! To control time, space and materiality!' His eyes shone. 'To become, in a word, *gods*. That is our future – a future outside the dead time we are used to.

'And yet if anyone has earned a place in our society, it is you, Captain,' Hebron added calmly. 'You see, I have learned all about you from your girl. On Meirjain you met the ibis-headed man, who told you the secret of attaining super-consciousness.' He gestured. 'All this technical research is unnecessary. The secret is in the *will*. If you can descend into hell, and emerge unbroken, you will become a god.'

'Except that no one could do it,' Boaz said bitterly.

'Not even if it is the *only* way? Think, Boaz. We are a madcap species. Some man, somewhere, must brave that which cannot be faced. Perhaps it will be our society that implements the ibis-headed man's instructions.'

'You will not implement it. If you try, you will fail. You could not endure that agony. I could not. No one can, and if either your aim or mine depends on it the cause is lost.'

'In any case,' he said after a pause, 'are you not guilty of a failure of perspective? The universe has spawned millions of species, any of whom might be candidates for this transformation you speak of. More likely than ourselves, for instance, might be the ibis-headed people.'

Hebron laughed. 'Have you not committed the same hubris, Captain? Why should *you* be the only mite who can move a mountain? Yet that has not deterred you. We believe that man *is* unique. Time and again it has been shown that other races, while they may be advanced intellectually, lack man's daring. The ibis-headed man tried to denigrate this forceful quality of ours by calling it obsessiveness. Yet because of it, our guess is that it is man's destiny to be the inheritor of the new universe. Look!'

Suddenly he held up his open hand, palm outward. He seemed to concentrate for a moment or two, and on the pale palm words appeared, standing out blood-red:

WHO
DARES
WINS

'Our identifying motto. A willed stigma, made visible by mental effort. You may bear this stigma, if you choose.'

'I take it *you* do not adhere to this doctrine?' Boaz said to Ebarak.

Ebarak's wry smile returned. 'I'm a scientist,' he said. He rapped his knuckles on the workbench, producing a hollow drumming sound. 'Matter and force are what are real, not ideas. As for belief without proof, I've no time for that.'

Hebron waved his hand, allowing the motto to fade. 'Aban's is a shallow attitude. Science rests on philosophical thought; it is nothing without it. Your own mentor pointed that out to me, Captain. But I detect, somehow, that you are not with us.'

'That's right,' Boaz said. He did not like the look of Hebron, or the sound of his philosophical society, which he sensed was ruthlessness personified. 'Your teaching is interesting, but my aims are purely negative. I don't care about the future of existence, on whatever plane.'

Hebron gave no sign of disappointment. 'We are bound to work together, nevertheless.' He turned to Ebarak. 'I was going to contact you today anyway. Orm is on the point of tracking down Captain Boaz. He may well discover his connection with you, too. I can't delay matters long – you had both better get out. Best, in fact, if we move the whole operation to a fringe planet I have selected.' He turned back to Boaz. 'Gems, equipment and most of the staff will leave by separate ships in separate directions. You leave first. You can join up with us later.'

'And why should I allow *you* to dictate my actions?' Boaz responded in an unfriendly tone.

The Director smiled. 'Can you be so ignorant? Are you unaware of *why* time research is banned? It is because whatever Aban may say about it, government scientists *do* think that time mutation is possible. The Cabal is a traditionalist institution, just like any government anywhere. In its eyes time research threatens destruction. So if I tell you that the Rectification Branch has orders to hunt you down with unusual vigour, you will realize that you took an enormous risk in coming here. Perhaps I will return to my office today and be informed that your ship has already been traced to Kathundra. For a few hours I can delay its seizure, but no more. So do as I say, take your girl and go where I tell you – before it is too late.'

The news startled Boaz. It made him feel vulnerable, reminding him that the surrounding city was, in effect, hostile territory – and that he was miles from his ship, linked to it only by its subtle beams. Could these alone be enough to break his cover? Until now he had not thought so. He had presumed that the government of the decaying econosphere would not have the latest technical refinements in its armoury, and that the integrator beams would remain invisible. But then he had taken only routine methods of surveillance into account . . .

He found it bewildering that the totally private nature of his mission to change time should have been breached. That other minds considered it valid, that it was a secret political issue, made the concept seem paradoxically unreal. He doubted, too, that he had any real friends here. Hebron's co-operative attitude was probably connected with the fact that Boaz still had a hoard of time-gems in his possession.

Mace stirred, opened her eyes abruptly and stared about her in alarm.

Boaz placed a reassuring hand on her shoulder. 'All right,' he said, speaking to Hebron, 'we'll do as you say.'

10

Again, lemon-sherbet skies. Again, sitting on a hill to contemplate a fading universe.

Except that it was a different hill, and a different town sprawling below it. Except that this time Mace was beside him, and that his thoughts and feelings were, comparatively, confused.

'You took a long time getting here,' she said.

'I made a mistake,' he told her. 'I stopped over at Al-Kadron to buy fuel rods. I was spotted by Rectification Branch agents. I had to kill three of them.'

It was soon after leaving Kathundra that he had parted company with Mace, feeling that the risk of capture was too great and should not involve her. But she had insisted on a rendezvous. When he arrived on Chaunce, the planet chosen by Hebron, it was to find her waiting.

His delayed, wandering course – he had taken eight standard months in getting here – was not entirely due to caution. In a deeper sense, Boaz had lost his way. Now, when he should at last have been feeling some hope of success in his mission, it was as if the quest itself had deserted him, and the iron-hard certainty in his soul seemed, despite himself, to waver, and all his efforts to seem trivial and useless.

'I think Hebron is here,' Mace told him.

He looked at her in surprise. 'What makes you think that?'

'Ebarak was acting shifty the last time I saw him, and there were some official people about. I got the idea Hebron had arrived to see how the research was going. Ebarak wouldn't tell me that, of course.'

Boaz grunted. He had already seen Ebarak himself, and the scientist had said nothing of this.

Hebron was probably disappointed in Ebarak's results so far. Scientifically, they were exciting – but they came nowhere near satisfying the exalted ambitions of the Director and his group.

'They've created a new future-myth,' Boaz murmured. 'The myth of an operator-controlled universe, with man as the operator.' He shook his head. 'Men as the new gods of a new universe. What an absurd notion. Anthropomorphism carried to the ultimate degree. It's the best piece of squirrelling I've heard.'

'Squirrelling?'

'Sorry.' Mace would not know the word; it was a technical term of obscure derivation. 'Losing sane perspective. Going nuts.' His words sounded despairing. 'What I mean is, in my view Hebron's crew are barely sane, and probably actually deranged. It's a ludicrous spectacle.'

Mace began to laugh, unpleasantly, mockingly. It startled him, and he turned to her, disconcerted.

'You're some alec, Joachim. You see derangement clearly in their case, but you're incapable of seeing the same thing in yourself. It's comic!'

'What are you saying?'

'Well, isn't your objective the same as theirs, basically, and just as egocentric? I agree, they are mad. But by the same token so must you be.'

'It was never conceivable that you could understand me,' Boaz said, averting his face again, and feeling disappointed at her lack of sympathy.

'Why not? Because I'm uneducated? Just the same, I'm a *bonewoman*, remember.' She stood up and moved in front of him, brashly confronting him. Her big breasts fell bulkily in her shift as she leaned toward him. Her face was annoyed and admonishing. 'Why don't you just *drop* it? Why don't you stop pitying yourself? There's still time left to *live!*'

'Live? It is living that's the trouble.' Boaz's voice sounded burdened. He didn't know why he was again taking the trouble to explain himself to her. It was the first time since his childhood that anyone's derision had affected him. 'As you said, you have no proper education in philosophy. For that reason you don't quite comprehend that an unbearable past is to be feared – because it is also the future.'

'Here we go again.' Mace waved her hand. 'Philosophy's all junk, do you hear me? *Junk*. How do you *know* the past repeats itself? It's only a theory. It's only what people *think*. Perhaps the world *doesn't* repeat itself the way you say it does. Perhaps it just goes on and on forever, changing all the time.'

'It's been scientifically proved.'

To Boaz's vast surprise Mace uttered a sound of disgust and kicked him as hard as she could in the shin. 'If you could list everything that's been "scientifically proved" and still turned out wrong, it would make the world's longest book. All the scientists do is play around with ideas they get from philosophers. Some deep-thinking alec says, "the world is made of lemons and bananas". So the scientists get busy and start calculating, until they come up with some "equation" that tells you how many lemons and how many bananas there are. Fifteen million lemons and nineteen million bananas, or something. And there's your proof. What fools you people are.'

Boaz did not look up. One part of him dismissed what Mace was saying as shallow ignorance. But another part of him, the part that had felt shaken and uneasy over recent months, saw in it an unfamiliar viewpoint that jolted his perception of things.

How did he know? How could he be *certain* that cosmic recurrence was true? How could anyone?

Could a bacterium, however hard it tried, ever chart the cycles of cosmic evolution?

Surveying the town below, he recalled that other occasion when he had noted how the econosphere's fading glory seemed, in the human imagination, to invest the universe itself with an aura of nostalgia – a subjective impression that could only be delusory, given the span of cosmic life. By the same token, was not the whole scope of human thought also inapplicable to the universal immensity? Against that immensity, was not any idea, however trivial and shallow, like the seedy charm of the town below? It was a novel thought, a shocking thought, but suddenly he could not understand why it had never occurred to him that behind all the teachings of Madrigo, so steeped in ataraxy, so rational, so wise – a rock of sanity, a paragon of the intellect – there might lurk a single ineradicable fact of human knowledge: that no one knew anything.

If the colonnaders were wrong, his burden was lifted. A surge of joy jolted through him at the prospect. Free of fear! Free of return to pain! Free to live, and then to live no more!

How was it that Mace's harsh, uneducated words could, in the space of moments, rip open his garment of decades of stubborn brooding? No, it could not be . . . an ignorant, suicidal girl could not know better than Madrigo . . .

He became aware that, unknown to himself, he had taken his colonnader cards from his pocket and was sifting them idly through his hands. He glanced down, faced with the appalling new impression that these superb, numinous symbols were after all pure invention . . . Then Mace snatched them from him and flung them away. He saw them go fluttering over the cyan grass of the hilltop.

Next, she swiftly unfastened her shift and let it fall from her body, revealing her nakedness. He saw from the exalted, ecstatic look in her eye that she was switching on her bone functions one by one. She leaned close to him, her hands resting on his shoulders, the aroma of her rising from her body, her plump, firm breasts, nipples erect, filling his vision.

'Forget it all, Joachim,' she hissed. 'Remember you are a boneman. Come on! Switch on your bones! Feel them glowing within you!'

He sat motionless, not responding. She placed her cheek against his. 'Philosophy isn't real. But what bones give you, *that's* real. Ever since it happened, you haven't allowed yourself anything good, Joachim. That's the trouble. You must learn to *enjoy*. That's the only way to wipe out the past.'

Boaz, his picture of himself and the world, were all adrift. At present he had no sexual feeling. But to Mace's cajoling he answered at last by dredging from his memory the all-but-forgotten controlling syllables.

It was like remembering flavours lost in the past. *Felicity* came on: for the first time in many years he knew the joy of emotion and sensation linked together, of delight at the sight of his surroundings, at sounds and smells, at the sigh of air on his skin. *Adjusted rheobase* came on, and everything he perceived became sharper and more vivid than an unboned man would have thought possible. *Adjusted chronaxy* slowed his time sense. Mace, as she edged closer to him, was performing a vast balletic dance in which every slight movement, every pore of her skin, took part.

At her urging whisper, the sex function came on.

She was helping him out of the modsuit, out of the sheathlike undergarment. 'Higher,' she moaned. 'Take it all the way. You can stand it.'

Her hands ran over his ravaged skin. He obeyed her, pushing all the settings higher and higher, to maximum, until his mind dizzied with the assault of impressions and sensations, and the aid of the ship was necessary to maintain his sanity.

Oh, it was madness! It was a seething cauldron of desire, a world of endless eroticism, a delirium of delight that snatched away his identity and put in place of it – pleasure! Infinite excitement! She grappled with him until they scarcely knew which was which, and in a dazzling flashing fog of arousal he felt his ship, visible on the level ground to one side of the town, gearing itself up, getting ready to raise his phallus – which he would not have been able to do without its help, although it had never been called upon to accomplish this for him before.

A hard, bulky object filled his being, a tower of strength. Then – penetration. Now it filled her being too, dominant, lunging.

Into fire. Into a burning, seething, hopeful world.

The light gravity of Chaunce made Cere Chai Hebron feel slightly unsteady. To increase his weight marginally he wore a slimmed modsuit, scarcely more bulky than a chemise and hose, but this too lacked comfort. He liked his raiment to be loose and flowing.

But for the news of Boaz's arrival he would have returned to Kathundra by now. 'That is his ship, you say?' he said. He pointed through the recessed upper-story window, over the roofs of the town to the space vessel that distinguished itself by its tall, rounded form among the more ungainly shapes of the ship ground.

'Yes, Grand Master. That is his ship.'

A dozen members of *Thelema*, seated in formal convention, faced Grand Master Hebron. Nine of them had been hastily summoned from Kathundra and had arrived only that morning. Hebron turned from the window and resumed his seat, twirling the toga he wore over his modsuit around him.

'Those of us who came earlier,' he said, 'have evaluated the work carried out by Citizen Ebarak and our own scientists on the time artifacts.' He hesitated. 'Our scientists have not been called to this meeting, for tactical reasons. It is best that what I have to tell you should not reach the ears of Ebarak.

'The results are disappointing. It is unlikely that the time-gems will be of any help in achieving our aims. But then, I had reached this conclusion even before the work was moved to Chaunce. As you know, we have gained new information. Through suffering, the mind of man may become the mind of a god.'

Not a hint of reaction came from his followers (all men – women were not permitted into the higher ranks of Thelema) as he reminded them of the nature of their quest. Their discipline, which included restraint in the expression of feeling, was good. 'The secret lies, then, not in some technical resource, but in the strength of our own will. But can suffering of the requisite intensity be mastered? It must of necessity be transcendent and therefore unendurable. One individual *has* known this degree of suffering, but failed to be transformed: the shipkeeper Joachim Boaz, a strange man who was marked ineradicably by his experience.'

He paused for almost ten seconds, then in the growing silence said: 'It is true to say that Boaz is not really a man at all. His body is incapable of sustaining its own life. It is dependent on adp machinery within his ship, which integrates his every somatic function over a communication beam. The ship, rather than the walking man, is the bodily Boaz.'

He again indicated the window, in which Boaz's ship, not far away on the ship ground, was neatly framed. Hebron did not know that at that moment it was assisting

Boaz in an ecstasy of a wholly positive nature. 'We have a unique opportunity for researching the true means to attaining transcendental consciousness. Control that ship, and we control Boaz. That gives us the means to use him as an experimental subject. It is said that the alien being on Meirjain offered to reintroduce Boaz to his agony, so he could attempt to overcome it. Though he did not have the courage to accept, we can force the issue on him, again and again if need be. Since he failed the test once he will do so again; but in so doing he will provide us with valuable data. This is indispensable if we are to prepare ourselves for the same trial.'

Hebron stopped, looking the meeting over in the manner that tacitly allowed questions. 'Why should this particular individual be valuable to us?' someone asked.

'For two reasons: he is uniquely controllable, and he has already been close to the transcendental state. He is a natural subject for research into it.'

'And what if our manipulations should, after all, cause him to cross the barrier?' someone else asked. 'Our position might be unenviable.'

Hebron smiled. 'We are playing with fire,' he agreed. 'Mind-fire, to be exact. Anyone who is afraid has no place in *Thelema*.'

He nodded to the one nearest him, who then read out a list of names from among those newly arrived from Kathundra: the attack team.

'Our task is simple,' Hebron told them. 'You will break into the Boaz ship and gain control over the equipment there, using the apparatus you brought with you. You must analyse it before he can return to confront you – he is a fierce adversary if opposed. Once you succeed, he can do nothing by himself.'

The small man who had helped Hebron with the interrogation of Mace spoke. 'Is there not a moral issue here?'

'Why should there be?' Hebron said, his tone supercilious. 'Who will judge a god?'

In another part of the town (which was much like Hondora, the town Boaz had been thinking of a few minutes earlier) a smaller meeting took place. The Rectification Branch colonel had not arrived on Chaunce in uniform but he donned it now, feeling more secure, stronger, in the shiny black and green, in the broad utensil belt and slant hat.

The room was small and low-ceilinged, shielded against every known spy-ray. Every police station in the econosphere had such a room. 'It is confirmed, then,' he said to the three non-uniformed agents with him. 'The quarry is here.'

'He is here, sir.' The agents, though large of build, had an anonymous blankness about them. They were selected for it: it was supposed to make their activities more invisible. The colonel wasn't sure if the ploy wasn't sometimes counterproductive: put several of them together, and their ordinariness became almost glaring.

'This is a matter of importance,' he said. 'I can tell you that I have come straight from the Chief. Orm's orders are that Boaz is to be liquidated outright. No attempt at arrest.'

'There are problems in either case, sir.'

'Yes . . . he is a difficult man to stop. If we were in Kathundra, now, it would be different.' He chuckled. The police in Kathundra had a secret right of control over the force-transport network. Any citizen under observation could, at any time he entered a travel booth, be switched straight to a police cell or killing chamber, or even circulated endlessly through the system for as long as need be . . . 'But there is an easier way,' he went on. 'This creature Boaz has a grave deficiency. He is a man on remote: his ship keeps him alive. To destroy him, one should destroy his ship, preferably choosing a time when the two are separated . . .'

They spoke further, laying plans and appointing a time. In actual fact the plotting of Boaz's course had been firming up for more than a standard month: that Chaunce would be his final destination had been extrapolated in advance. Police Chief Orm had gleefully told the colonel an even more interesting fact: Chaunce had a secret visitor, a government minister no less, though Orm was not at liberty to name him. Nevertheless when he made his report it would be to the full Cabal, and someone very important had better have a damned good explanation . . . Treason in high places was a crime for which Police Chief Orm had particular relish.

11

No longer was Boaz fighting a figment. For the first time, perhaps, since he had wakened in the city of Theta with a new, straight skeleton, with silicon bones that promised a new future, he knew a measure of happiness.

He was in a fun room with Mace, just off the main arcade of the sprawling, blossom-smelling town. The room itself was a work of art: walls a delicate shade of yellow, embossed with a frieze which could give the occupants enough suggestions to last a week; carpeted and furnished with a softness that made it seem a playland. An everchanging spectrum of perfumes made the air continually fresh and pleasant. Subliminal sounds – inaudible to those whose senses were not heightened by silicon bones – fed one's sense of well being with constant, encouraging music.

They had rested, and now were ready to begin again. Mace smiled, and touched his naked shoulder. 'Your body has qualities,' she said, 'that are yours alone.'

He looked down at his craggy self. She did not mention that perpetual virility was one of them: that was not unique – it was available by a simple piece of surgery. More important to him, in any case, was the new virility that had come to his mind.

That dreadful past, of course, was still there. But he

could now bring himself to have the memory erased if he wished, flushed from his psyche. In fact, he had decided not to. Mace had shown him another way, another goal.

He would seek pleasure the equal of that pain! Even now he could not help but put it in philosophical terms. In the colonnader cards the principle of justice, or equilibrium, was all important. If such a principle truly existed in the universe, then his agony *must* be balanced by an equal *positive* experience able to cancel its evil effects!

He had not mentioned this piece of reasoning to Mace. She would only have laughed. It was a wonder to him, a marvel, that all she had done was to open his eyes to what any untutored workman, nymphgirl or shopkeeper could have told him – that because a body of ideas was impressive, and had the backing of civilization and classical discourse, did not make it true.

She opened her palm. In it rested four little filter plugs, two pink, two pale blue. 'The blue ones are for men,' she said. 'Put them in.'

He took them and, following her example, inserted them in his nostrils. 'Now we spray each other,' she said. 'Remember to breathe through your nose.'

She handed him a blue spray-gun that she took from a cushion, taking a pink one herself. Her selective nose filters protected her from the highly charged male-directed pheromonic molecules she puffed at him; his kept out the female-directed chemicals he puffed at her.

Standing only a couple of feet apart, they drenched each other. She threw back her head as she silently set her bone functions. She tossed aside the spray-gun, discarded the nose filters. She threw open her arms.

'Bones!' she screeched quietly. 'Your bones, Boaz!'

Excitedly, he began to rise, and rise yet higher.

The low, single sun was casting long probing fingers across the ship ground when three large men, wearing the garb of technicians, approached an unusually upright cargo ship. They paused at the bottom of the tread-rail.

Then one stepped on, his hand inside his tunic, holding the stock of the heat-and-shock pistol with which to force the hatch. As the rail started to flow the others stepped on after him, ready with hand weapons to deal with any defensive robots, the last man carrying the case of thermal grenades.

At the top, he received a surprise.

The hatch lock was already blown.

He signed the others to be cautious, then eased the hatch open and stepped through, placing his feet with cat-like quietness. He was on a between-decks gallery. A ship robot lay on the floor, limbs awry. It had a blast hole through its chest.

The others followed him in. 'Someone's been here before us,' he murmured. 'They could still be on board.'

'Probably common robbers.'

'Then they can go with the rest of it. Come on.'

Their main job was to make sure they blew both the transmitter and the processors. But this was a custom-built ship; it had not been possible to obtain a design print. He went through a door at the end of the gallery and found himself on a deck that was, he guessed, over the hold.

His eyes quickly adjusted to the dim light. The deck had a crammed appearance. It seemed to be made up of corridors whose walls were dull-coloured casings that whirred and clicked. On each casing was a dully glowing green check screen, so that the whole deck was filled with the eerie luminescence – the only light there was, apparently.

At the end of the first corridor two men, clad in black cat-suits, knelt by a flat box shape. Part of a casing had been cut away, and the innards connected to the box by adp-fibres. The nearby green screen was oscillating wildly.

'Police,' the Rectification Branch man announced in a cold voice. 'On your feet, keep your hands in sight.'

The two jumped up, eyes flicking from the pale,

indistinguishable faces of the Branch men to the guns they held. 'We are on official business,' said one.

'Whose?'

There was no answer. Though incurious as to the truth of the claim, the Branch man was slightly mollified. 'Get out fast,' he said. 'This ship is to be destroyed.'

The other's eyes widened in alarm. 'No! It's ours! It has to be preserved—'

There came a noise from behind the casing. Another cat-suited figure came around the bend of the corridor. This one was armed with a force gun.

The Branch men did not wait. Two of them opened fire. The unarmed victims before them cried out in panic and cringed, flinging out their arms in a useless, self-defensive reflex. WHO DARES WINS glared briefly on the palms of their hands, before they fell.

The third Branch man did not see the stigmata. He was crouched down between two casings and was opening his box of thermal grenades.

Mace was anointing his body with oil when Boaz first began to feel prodromic flashes of discomfort.

His bone settings were high, so high it was as if he were transported to another world. Yet it was a world in which Mace was present with him, into which they had entered together. In that world she had said to him: this is the future for mankind. We are like a new species, we bone people. Others cannot understand it. Hebron, Ebarak, they do not have bones. You can tell it. Everything about them is dull.

And, yes, it was true. It was true that new powers glowed within one, that the world was transfigured. That those without bones were to be pitied.

He moved a foot or two away from her, trying to identify the new source of physical unease.

Then unseen fire suddenly enveloped him, moving in a flash from the soles of his feet to the crown of this head. His ship screamed to him, one last cataclysmic message.

COLLAPSE

He knew in an instant that nothing could save him. He had failed to evade the Rectification Branch. His ship was being destroyed. All the work of the bonemakers, whose skill and resource had made of him again a functioning human entity, was being undone piece by piece as the regulating departments of the ship went out one by one. He took a step forward, and seemed, howling, to move as through a crystal lattice of pain. Too late, he realized he had unthinkingly keyed in *all* his bone functions, including – just as on that far-off day on the edge of the alchemists' firepit – the preservation function. Too late, he realized he no longer had the power to switch any of them off.

The difference was that this time all the functions were on setting eight. The agony mounted and mounted, and mounted and mounted, fed by the super-senses silicon bones insisted, still, on giving him. He was back there. He was back with what he feared most, back in the pit, and Boaz howled his rage, howled his fear, screamed and screeched with his efforts to escape, to evade, to overcome, in any way at all to come to terms with torment as his bleak, twisted soul knew again its aloneness and its damnation. For the bones took the pain, took it, delighted in it, presented it to him enhanced to the ultimate. He journeyed a million years through winding labyrinths of exquisite, ecstatic agony. He dwelt in palaces of pain, he inhabited cities and civilizations based on the technology of torture.

And in that pain, as hellish super-fire whirled for the second time through his being, Boaz remembered. *He remembered.* With a depth of recall impossible to mistake he remembered this scene. He had lived it before. A thousand, a million times before. He remembered how he died, minutes from now, thrashing about the room and killing Mace in his uncontrolled spasms.

With that, he stopped screaming, though he felt system after system collapse within him as the somatic disaster deepened. He tried to speak, and words came out, the voice roaring, distorted, from a furnace of suffering.

'The – colonnaders – are – right . . . The – world – repeats . . .'

Hand to mouth, eyes wide, she stared at him in horror.

'But – death – is – not – an – end – to – be – sought, Mace . . . Go – escape – live!'

He turned from her. 'It need not be!'

He went crashing through the flimsy wall of the fun room. He staggered into the dusty arcade. It was deserted, fading into a dusk relieved only by a white glare beyond the low buildings.

This prospect was new. Never in all the infinity of ages had his eyes, at this instant, beheld it.

The ship, even while dying, still fought to preserve him. He knew the Rectification agents would not be content with killing him. They would search the town, find and kill Mace too, unless he gave her a breathing space. He moved down the arcade. He staggered up an alley, smashed through a wall, and was on the ship ground.

His ship was a streaming tree of withering white fire. The first flash he had felt, from bottom to top, had been the thermal grenades exploding and taking hold even on metal. A knot of men, three with guns covering two others, stood nearer to him, using their arms to shield their faces from the heat.

There was still strength in him. He leaped to them. His eerie, screeching voice seemed to fall from the sky.

'I – Joachim Boaz – have – altered – the – world . . . Never – again – will – you – destroy – me—'

His sense of liberty was absolute. He was transgressing physical law. He had stepped out from under Nature. Their terror did not register with him as he fell on them. Three he certainly killed, two more perhaps, but then his consciousness was cut off from the outside world. A series of images passed through his mind: Priestess, Vehicle, Justice, Strength, all the colonnader cards flashing by in sequence. Then he heard an immense trumpet blast that wiped out everything. Then nothing.

The Garments
of Caean

1

'I tell you I don't like it,' Peder Forbarth said nervously.

'Dammit, none of us can be expected to *like* it,' replied Mast. 'It's a matter of *guts*.'

Realto Mast lounged full-length on an elegant couch which was sumptuously cushioned and quilted and burnished in gold and lavender resins. It was without doubt the most prepossessing of several items of *arts nouveaux* furnishing the main cabin of the star yacht *Costa*. Mast had, indeed, taken particular care over the outfitting of the cabin, since he liked at all times to live in style.

Sighing, he poured himself another measure of purple liqueur from a swan-necked decanter. 'Now please stop moaning, Peder, and try to show a little spirit. You accepted this assignment, after all.'

'Accepted!' wailed Peder. 'I'm wishing I hadn't!'

'Considering the price I paid for your services,' murmured Mast, sipping his liqueur reflectively, 'it's disappointing to find you so eager to chicken out.'

Peder stopped his pacing of the cabin and sank down on a chair, the picture of a man defeated and frightened. The two other occupiers of the cabin, Mast's sidekicks Castor and Grawn, chuckled mockingly in the background.

Mast had him there, of course. He *had* fallen in with Mast's scheme lock, stock and barrel, hypnotized by the man's charisma and no less by his glowing descriptions – descriptions which a full-blooded, professional sartorial could hardly ignore. To begin with he had hesitated, it was true, because of the dangers and risks involved, but those misgivings had vanished when Mast had offered, as an advance on Peder's share, to pay off the debts that were about to ruin him.

Only now, thinking about it in retrospect, did Peder Forbarth reach the suspicion – rather, the certainty – that Mast had had a hand in calling in those debts. His creditors were not normally that pressing.

And only now, after locking up his shop *The Sartorial Elegantor* and journeying to within striking distance of the planet Kyre, did the full extent of his funk hit Peder. For one thing, Mast's image of faultless ability and impeccable planning was beginning to wear thin at the edges. He had noticed how the self-styled entrepreneur's (more accurately, racketeer's) carefully cultivated nonchalance hid an occasional ineptness, and a definite tendency for things to go slightly wrong on him. Peder was afraid that Mast would somehow mishandle the affair, that they would be caught trying to dispose of their illegal cargo or even worse.

The chief fear that loomed in Peder's mind, however, was of what lay in wait for him below. He no longer believed that Mast really appreciated what infra-sound could *do*. He was a calculating chancer, always ready to minimize the risks involved.

Suddenly Mast spilled a drop of liqueur on his green velvet waistcoat. 'Damn!' he mumbled, attempting to brush off the drop. He rose and swept out in search of stain remover.

A grin spread over Grawn's broad, ugly face. 'Don't bug Mast so much,' he told Peder good-humouredly. 'You're ruining the tone of the operation, for Chrissake.'

'Yeah, you've got too little faith in Mast,' Castor added. He was thin and below medium height, with square shoulders and a slight stoop. He had once suffered damage to his eyes, and the retinal function had been partially replaced by light-sensitive contact lenses which gave them an odd, metallic glitter. Castor exuded seediness: already the new suit Peder had given him – he had given them all new clothes as a gesture of good faith – looked grubby and crumpled.

'We've been with him a long time, and we've done all right,' Castor continued. 'He works everything out before he starts, and having sunk half a million in this caper he's not likely to go at it half-cocked.'

'Though he likes to take the odd gamble,' put in Grawn, his grin widening yet further.

'Like the gamble he took with your eyes,' snapped Peder to Castor, instantly regretting the words. Castor's accident, he had gathered, had been due to a mistake of Mast's.

Mast returned to the cabin, the stain only half eradicated and still spoiling the soft sheen of the velvet. 'I've just taken a look in the cockpit,' he said. 'We've arrived; the yacht's going into orbit now. Are you ready, Peder?'

'Y-yes. I suppose so.' Peder's stomach tightened up into a knot and he began to tremble slightly.

'Good.' Mast looked eager. 'No point in wasting time. Let's get down to work!'

He led the way to the hold below the cabin. The space here was quite large; everything extraneous had been cleared out of the yacht for the sake of speed and to gain maximum room for their expected cargo. At the loading end stood a small planetary lighter for descending to and returning from Kyre: Mast had no intention of risking the *Costa* herself.

Near the lighter, in pride of place, hung the baffle suit, a bulky object covered all over with clustered, variously sized tubes resembling organ pipes. Peder felt somewhat like a condemned criminal entering the death chamber as they approached it. There were three layers of baffle-tubes so that the suit, though vaguely manlike, was so gross and grotesque that it looked more like something designed to trap and encase a man than to protect him.

Castor operated a winch, lowering the suit jerkily to the floor. Then he unlocked its front, swinging it open like an iron maiden, and with a sardonic smile made a gesture of invitation for Peder to step into the cavity thus revealed.

Peder swallowed. By now the *Costa* would be in orbit, the auto pilot swinging her along those co-ordinates which Mast had obtained; mysteriously, but nevertheless somehow obtained (by means of a lucky break, as he would have put it) and which had made the whole mission possible. This was it. Peder felt that unfriendly forces, invisible hands, were impelling him forward against his will.

He hesitated, then stepped back. 'Why me?' he said. 'This is unfair. There are four of us.'

'Come, come,' said Mast, a look of complete reasonableness appearing on his lean, handsome face. '*You* are our expert. That's why you're here in the first place, to value the goods. How can you do that if you don't go down?'

'But that doesn't go for the first trip down,' Peder argued. 'We haven't found the wreck yet. Perhaps we won't find it for two or three trips, so you don't need my expert knowledge yet. You, Grawn, or Castor would probably be much better at looking for it than I would.'

Mast pursed his lips. 'I think you are pessimistic . . . but perhaps you have a point. We will cast lots.'

He took a small randomizer from his pocket. 'Choose your numbers. One to four.'

'One,' said Peder instantly.

Castor and Grawn seemed scarcely interested in the proceedings. Castor murmured a casual, indifferent 'Two', and Grawn followed with a grunted 'Three'.

'Then that leaves me with four,' Mast said animatedly, apparently entering into the spirit of things. He inserted the appropriately numbered domino-like chips. They rattled about the slotted framework of the randomizer for several seconds, shuffling and rebounding. Then one was suddenly ejected. Peder bent to inspect it.

One.

So it was Peder after all.

'Well, well,' exclaimed Mast. He gave Peder a look of comradely concern. 'I hope you feel happier about it now, Peder?'

Peder nodded dismally. He offered no resistance as they helped him into the suit and clamped it shut. He had worn it several times before, during their training sessions, and oddly, once he switched on the externals and began to communicate with his surroundings through them his panic abated and he began to consider the task before him more calmly. The motors came on; he turned and lumbered towards the lighter, negotiating the enlarged hatch awkwardly.

There was no question of sitting or lying down in the suit. Clamps reached out to hold him fast in the cockpit, so that the suit's maniples, several feet outside the reach of his real hands, could manage the controls. There was little for him to do, in any case; the lighter was mostly on automatic.

Mast's voice came to him through the suit intercom. 'Right,' he said, 'we've just heard that the survey sensors have located a large metal object. That might be it. The lighter knows where to go. Good luck.'

'Right,' answered Peder. And then, as his mind ranged over the situation, still trying to fight down his fears, a realization came to him.

'The lots!' he gasped. 'You rigged it!'

'Well naturally, old man. I have to protect my investment, after all. We can't have you chopping and changing plans at this stage. Good luck.'

'Let me out!' raged Peder impotently. 'I demand that we cast the lots again!'

But it was no use. He felt the lighter moving under him. On the screen, he saw that it was trundling through the air-lock. Seconds later he had been launched into space and the lighter darted down towards the glowing atmosphere of Kyre.

The rustling of the air over the outside surfaces, the buzzing of the lighter's mechanisms as it guided itself in, filled Peder's consciousness for some minutes. Seen from the outside, Kyre was an unremarkable, hospitable-looking planet. The atmosphere expanded and brightened as he plunged in. Nearer the surface it would contain a fair proportion of oxygen. The white clouds were water vapour. It would be a world fit for colonization, if it weren't for the habits of its denizens.

Once below the cloud layer, the features of the landscape began to take shape. There were mountains and plains, rivers and forests. All looked normal and innocuous. From a height, Kyre's special feature was not discernible.

The lighter slowed down and winged over a plain broken into a series of gullies, many of them fringed and hidden by tree-like vegetation. The lighter stopped and hovered about uncertainly in the air.

Mast came through again. 'You're on our sensor spot,' he said. 'Can you see anything?'

'No,' said Peder, 'but I get a reading too.'

He focused his attention on one of the tree-cloaked gullies. It could be down there, he thought.

Then he noticed that there was animal life on the plain. A big animal emerged from cover, looked around it, and trotted lumberingly towards a small body of water about a mile away. That reminded Peder of what a jam he would be in if the lighter was destroyed or damaged, and that he was asking for trouble by hovering about in the open. He would have to continue on foot – or on what, in the baffle suit, passed for feet.

He put the lighter down as close to the gorge as he could get. 'I'm down. I'm going out,' he said curtly. Mast's reply came faint and thoughtful. 'Right.'

Releasing the clamps, Peder backed himself to the hatch. Promptly it opened, and he backed straight out onto the ground. No sooner was he three or four feet away than the lighter took off again and went soaring skywards, back to the *Costa*. It was good strategy, but it still gave him the feeling of being alone and cut off.

For here he was at last, on the infra-sound planet.

Evolution on Kyre had reached a stage somewhat equivalent to the Jurassic. But the animal life here had developed a unique form of offensive and defensive armament: infra-sound, low-frequency vibrations that could, by hitting the right resonant note, shake to pieces any large object using very little power. Buildings, vehicles, machines, animals or men, all were equally vulnerable.

Several roving expeditions had landed on Kyre, and one of them had been lucky enough to get off sufficiently in one piece to report on the conditions there. The animals on Kyre attacked one another with infra-sound. Conversely, surviving species were those that had best learned to defend themselves against infra-sound. The use of infra-sound had developed biologically into a sophisticated spectrum of effects on Kyre. Even plants had been obliged to guard themselves against it and to generate it on their own account.

The baffle suit was Mast's answer to this deadly environment. Constructed at great expense, the suit's ranks of tubes were designed to deaden lethal frequencies before they reached the wearer. As a last-ditch defence the suit carried its own sound generator to try to cancel out or interfere with any attacking vibrations that got through.

'Are you getting anything?' Mast asked with interest.

Inside the suit, two screens confronted Peder. One gave a panoramic view of his surroundings: bright, clean air, a sky tinged with pale blue, a rocky foreground with boulders and trees in the farther distance. The second screen was an oscilloscope. Waggly traces ran across it. From a small speaker curious tones and squeals emerged; ranged-up analogues of infra-sounds the air outside was carrying.

'There seems to be some of the stuff about,' he replied. 'Must be some animals somewhere around. Nothing's coming through, though.'

'There you are, then,' Mast said reassuringly. 'I told you you had nothing to worry about.'

Peder silently cursed Mast. It was all very well for *him* to talk, safely up there in orbit. And Peder hadn't even encountered any of the infra-sound beasts yet.

Just the same he felt more confident. Curious stuff, this infra-sound, he thought. All it consisted of was sound waves of very low frequency, say five beats per second. Yet if it happened to hit any largish object's naturally resonating frequency, then that object simply crumbled. The principle had once been used to create weapons capable of levelling cities, so Peder had read somewhere.

'I'm moving towards a sort of gulch,' he announced. Be ready to send the lighter down if I tell you.'

The suit moved rapidly over the uneven ground, its tube-clad legs aping the movements he made with his real legs farther up in the metal body. As he came closer to the trees hiding the gully he could see the regular fluting on their trunks, and took it to be some sort of anti-vibration device.

The oscilloscope went frantic and the speaker began to squeal urgently as he approached and then passed between the trees. He paused, and placed a waldo hand on one of the trunks – and in the same instant snatched it away again. A numbing, shuddering sensation had passed right through him.

Peder wondered if there was any form of life on Kyre that was not in the infra-sound racket.

Below him the ground descended in a series of steps. Finding a shallow slope, Peder began to negotiate the first step. He had almost reached the cover of a small copse when his attention was caught by a drama being enacted to his right.

A huge brontosaurus-like beast had emerged from behind a slab of rock. At least, a brontosaurus was the first resemblance Peder could find for it, for it was of comparable size and was massively armoured. But it differed in an important respect: its gigantic head was almost entirely taken up by an enormous snout taking the form of a permanently open square chute. Peder recognized this as the sounding-trumpet of its infra-sound roar.

He panicked momentarily, thinking that the beast was after him. He scooted as fast as his suit would take him towards the copse. But then he saw that he had passed unnoticed; the object of the great saurian's attentions was a somewhat smaller creature that now turned to face its foe.

Peering from beneath tangled vegetation, Peder recalled some of the hasty pictures taken by the one surviving expedition to Kyre. The expedition had named the big bronto a 'shouter'. He was fascinated, as it lumbered closer, to see that its armour incorporated the same open-ended tube arrangements as his own armoured suit. The tubes were particularly close-packed around the shoulders, making it look as if it spouted rank upon rank of gun barrels.

The smaller beast, however, Peder did not recall seeing. Instead of a single square funnel, its head sported three barrel-like projections. Its body was even more covered with vibration-baffling devices than its enemy's; baffle-tubes, heavy movable flaps, thick masses of floss-like fur, as well as sharp spikes to ward off a more physical attack.

The two animals squared off, their baffle-tubes rising and arranging themselves. The shouter's sounding-horn gaped.

And Peder was flung back among the trees by the shock wave that resulted.

The monitoring speaker inside his suit let out a rasping noise. A strong, steady succession of peaks and troughs marched across the oscilloscope. He heard the sound generator coming into action, desperately trying to counteract the deadly, regular waves of compression and rarefaction.

Peder felt that some of it was getting through. Something seemed to be seizing his guts and turning them inside out. But it was not altogether a painful experience and he was able to watch what was happening with full clarity of mind. The smaller animal had extended long bony flaps like a ruff about its neck and these ablated or broke off before the assault of lethal sound, carrying away the effect of it. Both animals, it seemed, simply stood their ground and shouted infra-sound at one another. Judging from the oscilloscoped trace and the sonic analogue (the speaker had recovered, now, and was giving him a regular ululating yowl), they constantly varied their pitch, each seeking the frequency that would shatter the other.

Then the smaller, three-trumpeted animal began to sag. Cracks appeared in its armour; it trembled like jelly.

And suddenly it collapsed to the ground, its skin rupturing and spilling blood and intestines through jagged rents in a dermal wall that must have been all of a foot thick.

'What's going on down there?' came Mast's insistent voice.

'Quiet!' hissed Peder, as though the shouter could hear them. He was, in fact, frightened out of his wits.

Looking around itself once more, the shouter pointed its square horn to the sky and gave vent to a great infra-sound roar of victory. Then it stamped its feet up and down and turned about, as if affirming that the area was its own. Peder guessed that he had just witnessed a fight over territory.

Looking around itself once more, the shouter pointed its snout at a big boulder, perhaps ten feet high, some distance away. Its sound chute strained forward on its thick neck. Peder's scope and speaker came through strong.

And the boulder exploded into dust. With that demonstration of its might, the shouter lumbered back to its lair.

As concisely as he could, Peder related what he had seen. 'If I'm standing in the path of that sound beam,' he concluded, 'I've had it. You've chosen the wrong man for this caper, Mast. Send the lighter down. I want to come up!'

'No lighter until you've finished the job,' Mast answered firmly. 'Take hold of yourself, now.'

A cold wind swept through Peder's vitals. In the humming, clicking suit, he realized he was sweating – a cold, clammy sweat.

'But what if the shouter sees me?'

'You've got your gun, haven't you? Just make sure you get your shot in before it opens its mouth.'

Peder's hand moved unconsciously to the grip-hole that operated the heavy-duty energy rifle. He sighed.

A rustling sound made him turn. Shouldering its way through the ground-level shrubs came an animal about the size of a rabbit. He was fascinated to see that it reproduced on a small scale the same baffle-tube and head-trumpet arrangement of its more massive cousins. It made him realize that he had not yet made a real inspection of his surroundings at close quarters. He extended an arm and carefully pulled away some of the brush.

More small animals scurried away at his touch, some turning their heads momentarily to hurl at him beams of vibrations which were easily cancelled by his suit.

Looking overhead, he glimpsed a winged creature squatting on a branch, heavily rigged with scale-like feathers and bearing a conical trumpet in place of a beak. It peered down at Peder, then launched itself into the air and flapped clumsily away.

Peder's gaze fastened on the bark of the tree itself; insects could be seen crawling about on it. Turning up the magnification he made out several varieties, many of them top-heavy with various devices for casting vibrations. The frequencies with which creatures of this size battled could scarcely be called infra-sound at all, of course; they would intrude into the sonic range.

He reminded himself that he had not yet exploited all the suit's capabilities. He considered opening the direct audio link for a brief listen, but almost immediately cancelled the thought. The scene looked peaceful enough; but to let into the suit, even for a few seconds, any of the stray vibrations of infra-sound that he suspected pounded at all times through this woodland could prove fatal, or at least cause him serious internal injury.

Instead, he switched on the odour plate. Connected to a corresponding plate on the outside of the suit, it reproduced all the odours that struck that plate, automatically omitting any that could be poisonous. A resinous, fresh smell entered Peder's nostrils. He was reminded vaguely of a pine forest, except that this was more tangy and contained many altogether foreign undertones, some sweet, some repugnant. It seemed odd that a world so lethal and alien could, at the same time, smell so natural and familiar.

He switched off the plate. The smell, he decided, would become too cloying after a time, and besides he was here for something more serious. He began to consider how to cross the territory that apparently was guarded by the shouter.

After some hesitation he decided that his best bet was to advance through the trees away from the beast's lair, and make his way down the next step of the gorge behind the cover of some rocks. This he managed with only moderate difficulty, encountering some medium-sized animals which snarled low-frequency vibrations at him in a half-hearted manner, but desisted when he retreated. Only occasionally did he feel the protective capacity of his suit was being pressed to the limit, and he had no occasion to use the energy rifle.

It was impossible to move stealthily in the baffle suit. He crashed through brush and, once or twice as he careened down the slope, lurched into a tree. Then he broke through a screen of matted creeper-like vegetation and found himself on the lip of the gorge's deepest crevasse.

And there it was.

The crashed Caeanic spaceship had, he guessed, first hit the farther edge of the gorge a glancing blow, and then had bounced full-length into the crevasse where it now rested, filling it almost entirely. His eyes raked over the unfamiliar, alien lines – insofar as he could ascertain them amid the damage – and discerned a domed, semi-transparent guidance section, drive section, and a long, amply curved cargo section.

The ship must have come down at least partly under its own power, for the damage from impact was not all that great. The fauna of Kyre had done all the rest. The whole structure of the vessel had been broken open, shattered and cracked, by infra-sound. Through the vents Peder could see its structured interior, also crumbled and broken. Its cargo, though, should be intact.

'I've found it,' he clipped tersely to the *Costa*. 'It's in the gorge, as I said. Pretty badly broken up. I'm going inside.'

'*That's* my boy,' said Mast ingratiatingly. 'I told you you could do it.'

He picked his way down the overgrown slope and clambered through a rip in the hull large enough to take him. To his mind came the sketch that Mast had shown him (obtained, again, by some devious, unspoken means) of a typical Caeanic transport's layout. This section of corridor he was in must be one of those running the length of the ship just under its skin. He had entered close to the nose; opening a door to his left, he found himself looking into the main astrogation dome. The crystal canopy was in shreds, of course; reclining in semi-lounge control chairs were the decaying bodies of the ship's officers. Probably they had lost consciousness at the moment of impact and had been killed by infra-sound before recovering.

Peder cast an interested eye over their rakishly smart uniforms, so strange to him, and then withdrew. Decomposing human beings were not something his stomach could take too well.

He lumbered sternwards. Any minute now, he told himself. His heart began to thump with excitement as he thought of what lay so close.

He entered the first cargo section.

It was only a small hold, designed to store minor items. Its contents, now, had been thrown from their racks and were tumbled about in profusion. A little light entered through the broken roof. Peder switched on his suit lamp to provide more. His breath caught in his throat.

Hats!

Colours glowed; elegant shapes hypnotized his senses in the beam of the lamp. Hats of myriad descriptions: hats, caps, berets and bonnets; toques, trilbies and titfers; chaperons, chaplets, cornets and coifs.

Soft-crowned hats, stiff-crowned hats, low-crowned and high-crowned; feathered, plumed, winged and gauzed; bicorne and tricorne; boaters and bowlers, homburgs and turbans; gorgets, cowls and hoods; helmets, galeas and aegeas.

And these were just the hats!

Peder picked one up and held the sleek titfer at head level. He recognized the touch when he saw it. The cloth was like no other, the line, the design – the *creativity* – had the unmistakable flair found in only one part of the galaxy. This hat would do something for a man, would make him feel different, act different.

'Send the lighter down,' he said to the *Costa*. 'I'm ready to start loading.'

Mast had been right. The ship was loaded to the roof with freight of inestimable value: the clothes of Caean.

At one time they had been called tailors. Peder's father had been a tailor. And on Peder's home world – Harlos – as indeed on many worlds of the Ziode Cluster they were still referred to as tailors. But that was because in Ziode vestments did not have the esteem that, in Peder's view, they deserved. He, like others of his ilk, called himself a sartorial, and his was not a trade but a profession.

Twice before he had been privileged to handle garments from that strange, clothes-conscious civilization, Caean. They had been a brief, damasked gipon, and a simple flowered cravat, no more. But even then he had been captivated, entranced, and had realized that all the legends concerning Caean were true.

The Caeanic worlds occupied a section of a galactic spiral arm known as the Tzist Arm. It was a well-defined arm with a regular curve and nearly empty space on either side of it. The Ziode Cluster, looking like a sudden burst of sparks, was situated somewhere near the focus of this curve, but contact between the two political systems had been slight over the past few centuries and mostly confined to guarded hostility. The Cluster did not understand the ways of Caean; and Caean, for its part, was aloof and unyielding in its attitude towards raggedly dressed foreigners.

In Caean clothes were not merely an adornment but a philosophy, a way of life – *the* way of life. Even Peder Forbarth knew that he failed to grasp the fullness of this philosophy, try as he might; officially, in the Cluster, the covering of the body was of no importance and it was even sanctioned to go naked. But even there, despite any amount of official disapproval, the love of clothing – one of man's oldest arts – flourished and Caeanic articles were recognized for the consummate, sublime treasures that they were. In point of fact it was illegal to import, sell, or even possess a garment from Caean, and very few of them had ever crossed the black gulf of light years; but those few fetched fabulous prices.

In crossing from one extremity to the other of Caeanic territory, trading vessels entered the gulf defined by the Tzist Arm and traced a chord between the two points. In doing so they were, at mid-point, about half-way to Ziode. And somewhere in that region, where one of these trading vessels had suffered some accident and elected to try for a planet-fall, the planet Kyre orbited its lonely primary.

And Mast had heard about it.

Legally the cargo still belonged to the Caeanic trading company that owned the ship, but none of them felt much concern over that. Peder pressed forward through the Hat

Hold and nearly swooned at the delights that awaited him in the larger compartments: coats, trousers, breeches, shirts, shoes, and many garments that defied Peder's vocabulary. Then Mast warned him that the lighter was on its way and he hurried outside to guide it down to a spot where he could most easily carry the merchandise aboard.

In his enthusiasm, Peder once more began to feel admiration for Mast. He *had* managed everything superbly. For one thing, bringing Peder along was a master stroke; they couldn't possibly carry away the whole hoard and only someone of Peder Forbarth's knowledge and experience – he flattered himself that, though little-known, he was perhaps the best sartorial on Harlos – could choose the best prizes from this feast of splendour.

Having guided down the lighter he began selecting garments from the racks, scurrying with armloads to the dumpy little craft and piling them neatly in the small hold. His brain was forced to work as quickly as his hands, discarding the merely superb and taking only the super-excellent. Raiment that otherwise would have had him gasping with pleasure was now carelessly thrust aside, making him feel almost as though he was despoiling something sacred.

He sent up three lighter loads and then entered a compartment that, after a brief examination, had him wishing that he had examined the whole cargo before beginning the selection. At first he doubted his judgement; but then, feeling the material, its texture that seemed to bring the nerves and blood more alive than before, the dazzling twills, damasks, displays and culverts into which it could be woven, he decided that there could be no other explanation. This was the fabled fabric which no one in Ziode was absolutely sure existed. Even of those who had heard of it, not all knew its name. Peder had heard it called 'Prossim'.

If this was Prossim – Peder was sure now that it was – then he must take every scrap of it that the ship contained, even if it meant throwing out the loads he had already ferried up to the *Costa*. He didn't think that would be necessary, though. This compartment probably held all there was. Even in Caean Prossim was reputed to be rare, fine and costly, the stuff of kings, of arcane, mystic dressers. An aura of Caeanic occultism surrounded it, although Peder was not sure why. He only knew that a garment made of Prossim, whoever the maker, was ten times the garment that was made of anything else.

He said nothing to Mast immediately, but got busy emptying out the compartment. Its contents made up barely one lighter load, but when he was gathering up the last armful he noticed a small door in one corner which was unlabelled. Thinking that it might be a cupboard with a few more small items, he opened it, and despite his haste stood stock still for at least five minutes.

The chamber semed, at first, out of proportion to its content. It was a largish chamber, almost a room, and hanging in it was a single suit.

And yet, as one gazed at it, the arrangement was not so disproportionate after all. The suit seemed to command the space around it, to require it, much as a person requires space for comfort. Peder chuckled to himself softly. Some personally valued set of apparel, perhaps, or the private attire of an exalted personage. There was no knowing what customs the Caeanics observed in such matters.

For some reason he did not merely take the suit but continued to stand gazing at it. To begin with it looked like an unpresumptuous suit, the colours muted, the cut consummate but modest. And yet, while he stood there, the impression it made upon him grew. He realized that the subtle flares in trousers and jacket were executed with genius and displayed, to those who could see it, an electric, confident *élan*. The coloration seemed no longer matt, but to be radiant with eye-defying patterns. The more he looked, the harder he found it to brush aside a stupefying possibility. Finally he stepped forward, extended a waldo arm reverently, and lifted the skirt of the jacket.

On the rich inner lining was woven an intricate design of loops and whirls. Peder snatched away the arm with a gasp. He knew that design; his suspicion was confirmed.

It was a Frachonard suit!

Never in his wildest dreams had he imagined that he would ever behold, let alone possess such a suit. Frachonard, the crowning genius of Caean's sartorial art!

The great master, so he heard, had died but recently. He had never been profligate in his creations, and he believed that since his death all items that had come from his hand were known, numbered and named, and viewed in the same light that great paintings had once been. But Peder's good fortune was even more extraordinary; the use of the fabulous new cloth, Prossim, had but lately been perfected. Peder had been told, by a sartorial who claimed to have visited a planet within communicable distance of Caean, that Frachonard had completed five known suits in the new material.

'Peder!' Mast's voice said fretfully. 'What's keeping you?'

Steeling himself, Peder took the suit off its hook. 'Just finishing this batch,' he said.

He stepped carefully out to the lighter and stowed the suit aboard, closing the hatch to the hold. He was about to return to the cargo ship when his speaker gave him a warning squawk and the sound generator warmed up ominously.

Turning, he saw that the shouter was easing itself down the slopes of the gorge.

'Hold it,' he said, 'I think I've got trouble.'

The shouter seemed to have spotted him. Its long tail threshed the air for balance; its square sound-chute was aimed at the Caeanic ship, and suddenly Peder knew by the howl of his speaker that the chute was in operation. Frantically he reached for the hand-grip that operated the energy rifle. On the suit, baffle-tubes were fracturing and breaking off; something slow and rolling seemed to be grinding up his insides.

The energy rifle sent out a barely visible pale blue flame, like a wavering gas jet except that it went in a dead straight column to its target. It hit the shouter just below the snout. The beast squirmed to one side, injured but by no means dead, slithered farther down the slope and endeavoured once again to aim its beam of infra-sound towards Peder and the lighter. Peder fired again, taking more care over his aim this time. The energy column demolished the shouter's chute, bored through its dermis and apparently struck a vital organ, for it rolled on to its side and wallowed in agony.

Peder was praying that the lighter was still capable of taking off. He stepped towards it, and as he did so everything inside him seemed to vibrate. He recognized that he had taken a good dose of infra-sound.

But he ignored all discomfort and forced himself into the cockpit of the lighter. 'Take me up,' he gasped to Mast. 'I'm hurt.'

'Right,' said Mast, and the lighter rose. It creaked rather too much, but anyway it flew and did not appear to have any serious structural damage.

Fifteen minutes later he was back in the *Costa* and out of the crippled baffle suit. On the return journey, while standing still, he had felt all right, but as soon as he moved he got the same sensation of vibrations being let off inside him, and it was the same when he spoke. Castor, who had once flunked medical school, muttered something about 'Not much; maybe a little minor haemorrhaging', and, laying Peder down on Mast's couch, gave him some injections and massage. After half an hour or so he felt better.

'How much of the cargo did we get?' Mast asked him.

'About half, I'd say.'

Mast pursed his lips. 'There's still room in the hold . . .'

'I'm not going down there again,' Peder said quickly. 'Anyway the suit's damaged. If you want more get it yourself.'

Mast dropped the subject. They all went down to the hold to look over their merchandise, and for some time enjoyed themselves in picking items of finery for their personal use. Grawn and Castor bedecked themselves with gross indulgence. Mast, however, examined the clothes carefully but appeared to be uninterested in appropriating any for himself, choosing only a cravat of spider-silk, some handkerchiefs, and a small but jaunty titfer. Peder was surprised at this restraint, in view of Mast's usual attention to his personal appearance. He himself sorted desultorily through the garments, put aside a quilted Prossim tabard with vandyked sleeves and collar, a pair of soft slippers of lavender suede with silver inlay, and a set of thigh-hose in chiaroscuroed textural. Hesitantly, trying to appear casual, he looked out the Frachonard suit.

'One thing I must commandeer is this suit,' he said.

Mast looked at it askance. 'These people of Caean are pretty peculiar in their life-styles, so I've heard,' he said noncommittally. 'Don't let the clothes master the man, the way they do.'

Peder scarcely heard the remark in his joy at being the possessor – and soon, he promised himself, the wearer – of a genuine Caeanic Frachonard suit.

Wearing their new clothes, the four repaired to the cockpit where Mast proposed to initiate their return to Harlos. But before he could do so a warning gong sounded. Bending over the slanting control board, Mast studied a display screen with puzzlement.

'There's a ship heading our way,' he announced finally. 'A Caeanic ship.'

'Coincidence?' suggested Castor. 'We are close to one of their trade routes.'

'I don't think so. It appears to be heading directly for Kyre.' Mast frowned pettishly. 'I don't get it. They must know what sort of a planet Kyre is, even if the crew of the wreck didn't. You wouldn't think it would be worth the expense of making a baffle suit just to recover that cargo, not on the Caeanic market, anyway.'

Peder did not mention anything about Prossim, or the Frachonard suit. 'We'd better leave,' he urged.

'They would see us if we headed for home now,' Mast mused. 'Yet we can't stay in the open. We'll have to hide somewhere.'

'Down on the surface, boss?' Grawn gawped.

'Dolt, the *Costa* wouldn't last ten minutes down there. And besides, they could probably still trace us. Wait a minute . . . Kyre has a sister planet. There she is!'

A larger, closer trace appeared on the display plate. The second planet inscribed Kyre's orbit only a few million miles closer to the primary. Mast tapped out instructions on a set of keys, adding a verbal to the voice pick-up: 'Land on the planet if safe, orbit as closely as possible if not.'

The *Costa* swung out of its orbit, slipped into overdrive and arrowed for the inner planet. 'They're not expecting anybody to be here,' Mast remarked. 'I doubt if they'll spot us yet. After they get to Kyre we can slide away using the planet and then the primary for cover.'

'What sort of a planet is it?' Peder asked.

'Diameter, five thousand miles.' Mast shrugged. 'That's all I know. The expedition that came home from Kyre called it the Planet of the Flies. Don't ask me why.'

On overdrive, the *Costa* took little more than half an hour to cover the thirty million miles to the Planet of the Flies. As they dived into its atmosphere and descended almost to ground level the reason for the name became abundantly clear.

A type of fly lived on the planet. It was almost all that did live there – little else could have survived the environment the flies themselves had created. The atmosphere was jammed almost solid with them to a height of about a mile. Evidently they bred prodigiously; they had achieved a density of about three per cubic centimetre, and the *Costa* ploughed through this black buzzing mass as if through a wall of sludge. Briefly the yacht set down on solid ground, but those within, looking with horror at what surrounded them, ordered the auto pilot to take off again.

They crept into the upper reaches of the atmosphere and were able to observe the recently arrived Caeanic ship take up orbit about Kyre. Then they slid guiltily around to the other side of the second planet and departed, making straight for the Ziode Cluster, Harlos and (they hoped) riches.

2

Alexei Verednyev swept on through a familiar environment. Far down-range was the glowing light of the central sun. To all quarters, a pointillist background at the limit of vision, shone the unreachable stars, but he ignored those. Surrounding him, the medium in which he lived and moved, was the warm, cavernous dark of interplanetary space.

Playfully fleeing from him, Lana Armasova was some five hundred miles down-range. He could sense her metal body with his radars and his spirits mounted as he realized that soon she would let him catch her. Already they were a long way from the gas giant's girdle of rocks and masses that, to them, was Homebase. If they chased one another much farther sunwards they would stand in danger of coming within range of Shoji, the small arid world where the evil cyborgs lived.

Lana was breaking her speed, now. He saw her glinting in the starlight, and he called to her. She turned lazily, transmitting incidental signals of sexual excitement. He beamed his urgent demand; she responded quickly with rapid, vibrating love feelings.

Already their exchanges had passed beyond the range of ordinary speech; now those exchanges moved up to UHF, the only frequencies on which pure emotion could be directly conveyed. On rich high-frequency harmonies, tender, mutual sensitivities which words could never have handled passed freely to and fro. Alexei and Lana thrilled to one another's presence, and as the distance between them closed the delirious sensations increased. Alexei, for his part, felt faint with the impact of sheer *femaleness* which the UHF transmissions were bringing to him.

Then, when their bodies clinked together, a merging of magnetic fields heightened the delirium still further and a long, thin steel prong slid automatically out from Alexei. He grappled with Lana, jockeying her into position and finding the orifice into which that prong plunged. Instantly, ecstasy overcame them both and they clung together while the probe ejaculated his sperm into her.

With a gentle hiss of jets they drew apart. Neither said anything at first; but suddenly Lana broke the post-coital peacefulness with a cry of alarm. A shadow crossed them; something had come between them and the sun.

He turned to see a long, quite huge shape bearing down on them. He did not really have to pick out its features, for only the starlight illuminated this, its eclipsed side, and it did not seem to shine as metal did.

'What is it?' Lana screamed.

He did not know. He had never known cyborgs to build anything like this, in fact they did not come into space very often.

'Flee, Lana, flee!'

But she scarcely needed to be told. Her main propulsors burst into action, as did his, and they hurtled up-range.

The home rings were far away, and there was no cover here. Alexei veered away from Lana, ordering her to change course. His hope that he could draw the pursuer off Lana was fulfilled; it followed him, and he saw that its speed far outpaced his.

Something shot from the bow of the big object. Despite all his twistings and manoeuvrings Alexei could not escape it. Though little more than a flat platform with a dome set upon it, it was able to pace him easily, and soon was almost touching him. Alexei cursed desperately as strong, lash-like cilia extruded to entrap him, imprisoning his arms and dragging him inexorably towards the menacing black shape.

'Should we bring it aboard?' Estru asked. 'It might be dangerous. A robot bomb, perhaps?'

The middle-aged woman with purple tinted hair glanced up at him from the table, where she was watching the events on the vidscreen. 'You're too suspicious,' she reproved in a mature, controlled voice. 'We'll deep-sensor it in the lock before we bring it in any farther, but I don't think it's a bomb. What I'd like to know is, what were the two of them doing when we came upon them?'

Estru bent to look over her shoulder at the screen. The object being brought in was apparently metallic. It had arms, a bulky, interestingly accoutred main body incorporating a drive unit, and what looked like a helmet-like head section with tubes and antennae that presumably were sensors.

'What does it look like to you, then, Amara?'

She tilted her head. 'Well, it looks like some elaborate kind of spacesuit.'

'Who needs a spacesuit as big as that? Unless there's a giant inside. And anyway where's their vehicle? We're miles from anywhere out here.'

Amara shrugged. 'Well, we'll soon know.' She flicked a switch. 'Aspar, did you say those things were transmitting when we interrupted them?'

A man's voice came over the intercom. 'Yes. Some form of UHF, very richly modulated. Can't make anything of it; probably some kind of machine talk. Then there was a break, and then a fragment of spoken conversation.'

'What language? Caeanic?'

'Not Caeanic; I don't recognize it at all.'

'Let's hear it.'

Amara held down the record key while the brief exchange came through. 'Thanks, Aspar,' she said, then cut him off. A frown on her face, she played back the scrap of tape several times: first a woman's voice, then a man's.

'I don't recognize it either,' said Estru. 'What is it?'

Her face took on a wondering look. 'It sounds like – well, it *is*, as far as I can tell – some variant of Old Russian.'

'*Russian?*' Estru laughed disbelievingly, then recovered himself. 'But Caeanic isn't descended from Russian, is it?'

'No, not particularly. There are traces of Russian in it, but there are in nearly all languages. Russian itself hasn't been spoken as a living language for centuries.'

'Well, *they're* speaking it. What are they saying?'

'Not much. They're obviously referring to ourselves.' She played the frightened, urgent voices again. 'The girl says "What's that?" She's pretty startled. Then the man says something like "Run, run". I think he uses the girl's name; Lana.'

'Hmm. Lana.' Estru was thoughtful. 'Maybe they're spacesuits after all. I'd be more inclined to think they're on remote. Anyway, there's presumably some kind of civilization in this system, or at least nearby.'

'"Presumably" is the operative word. There's been precious little sign of it so far. You'd think we would have noticed.'

Estru nodded. As usual, Amara's observations were acute; she was, as a general rule, right.

But of course, Amara's knowledge was vast, as was evidenced by her unhesitatingly identifying a meagre four or five words as belonging to a long-dead language. She was, in fact, one of Ziode's greatest authorities on cultural anthropology, and that was why she was here.

In consideration of the possibility of war with Caean, the Directorate had ordered a closer study of that little-understood civilization, of its aims and origins. The *Callan* was part of that study.

It was necessary to proceed cautiously; they were, in the strictest sense of the term, trespassing. They had begun outside Caeanic civilization proper, on that part of the Tzist Arm along which it was presumed mankind had migrated. They hoped to find early settlements, by-passed outposts, which might give them some clues as to how the peculiarities of Caeanic culture had developed.

The Captain's voice interrupted them. 'Well, Amara, do we continue on course?'

They both turned to the Captain's face on a screen to their right. 'If it pleases you, Captain,' said Amara, 'we would like to break our journey here pending investigations. This thing might be significant.'

The Captain nodded. 'You're the boss,' he said sardonically. 'But please keep me informed of your findings, Amara. It's my job to assess possible dangers to the ship.'

'Of course, Captain.' The bearded face disappeared from the screen.

Another voice spoke from Amara's table. 'We've got him in the lab, Amara.'

'Him? There's a man inside it?'

'Yes.'

'We'll be right down.' She smiled at Estru, rising. 'Maybe you'll believe me next time.'

Sighing, Estru followed her down to the labs.

They had put the spacesuited man in a gravity-free vacuum chamber. Estru still couldn't understand the reason for such a suit. It was twelve feet tall, even though it had no legs. The drive unit also seemed disproportionate.

This, evidently, was a deep-space suit, capable of carrying its wearer over long distances.

Neither was there any face plate: the suit presented a totally mechanical, metallic exterior.

'What have you got him in there for?' Amara asked irritably. 'How do you expect him to disrobe? Give him some air; give him some gravity.'

Slightly embarrassed, the techs obeyed. Air whistled into the chamber. The suit settled gently to the floor as the gravity phased in, then as it came full on toppled over on to its side. The massive suit made an attempt to lift itself on its arms, but then collapsed and lay like a stranded whale.

'All right, skip the gravity,' Amara said in annoyance, waving her hand. 'Just fix it so he can come out of that suit and we can talk.'

The gravity was lifted. Amara got them to open the hatch to the chamber and addressed some words through it.

The spacesuit didn't answer.

'He probably can't hear you,' Estru suggested. 'It must be like being in a spaceship inside that thing. You'd have to talk to him through his communicator.'

'Just so.' Amara called for a radio transceiver and, using the same frequency on which Aspar had picked up the conversation earlier, faltered out some Russian which she hoped was heard by the stranger.

After a pause a strong, sonorous voice emerged from the transceiver. Amara raised her eyebrows.

'What does he say?' Estru asked.

'He says that we will answer for our crimes. He says that we may as well kill him quickly, because he will tell us nothing. He is, I might say, being brave and rather melodramatic about it. That was characteristic of the Russians, I believe.'

She spoke again, reassuring their prisoner and entreating him to divest himself of his suit. She was answered with florid curses. She turned to Estru.

'This is ridiculous. We can't talk to him under these conditions.'

'If he wants to remain suited up . . .' Estru shrugged. 'Maybe we should let him.'

'No, it won't do!' Amara was exasperated. 'It's . . . just so damned inconvenient! Besides, he might run amok or something.'

The last remark was perhaps, the most convincing. At Amara's insistence the prisoner was held under restraint again and, while he was clamped and lashed inside the chamber, the techs strove to unfasten the suit.

'This is very odd, Amara. There are no movable plates; no seams. The suit is completely sealed.'

'There *is* a way to open it, obviously,' retorted Estru. 'You just can't find it.'

Amara pushed the transceiver away from her. For the past few minutes she had been trying to reason with the prisoner on the point of his spacesuit, and it was as if he didn't understand her at all. Perhaps, she thought guiltily, her Russian was more fragmentary than she had believed, or else the dialect had drifted too far.

'I've lost patience with all this,' she announced. 'Get that suit open. If it won't open by itself, *cut* it open.'

She stormed out of the lab, heading for her library.

From the moment when they had dragged him inside the big space-cave, Alexei Verednyev had been certain that he was in the hands of the hated cyborgs. He had once seen some cyborg prisoners, so he knew how to recognize the soft, repellent little things. True, these cyborgs did not look *quite* like the ones he had seen in Homebase. Some of their organs seemed to be missing, such as the turrets in their heads and the metal boxes embedded in their chests.

But as these organs had actually been the most human-looking things about the cyborgs, the ones who had captured him were by comparison even more repulsive. He supposed that, being able to adapt themselves to different conditions to a limited extent, the cyborgs were able to change and modify their organs. Perhaps the fact that they had now taken to travelling in a space-cave had something to do with their altered appearance.

They had spoken to him in a garbled version of his own language, but little of what they said made sense to him. Vaguely he hoped they would kill him soon; their cruelty was renowned. And now the full extent of that cruelty was to be brought home to him. He was put in bonds again and taken to another part of the cave where he was laid down on a steel plate, still helpless. Several cyborgs were there, and there was a big mirror where he could see a reflection of himself. The cyborgs had instruments which they brought to bear on him.

They were cutting into his body! Alexei struggled and screamed, but these creatures were remorseless. Soon they had sliced through his outer skin and he saw his innards revealed. His consciousness reeled. And then they cut him open to reveal the *inmost* innards, and in the final moment of trauma in which he finally passed out, he saw in the mirror the pale worm-thing which he had never seen before, as unprotected as when he had first been born.

3

The most prestigious occupation in Caean is, of course, the sartorial's. As a profession it entirely supplants the functions of psychiatrist, priest and moulder of public opinion, none of which exist in their own right in Caean. If someone has a problem, he consults his sartorial, who runs up garments to help him find his own way out of his difficulties.

Despite this, Caeanic tailoring is not necessarily bespoke. No Caeanic would think of limiting himself to the output of a single sartorial, unless he is fortunate enough to have a special relationship with an all-round genius; he demands access to the whole range of the art. Consequently there is massive trade in ready-mades between Tzist planets.

All garments are, however, hand-made, whether bespoke or not. The mass manufacture of garments on a machine or factory basis could not possibly be envisaged. The very idea is regarded as a horrific barbarity, and Ziodeans, because of their willingness to wear garments so made, are looked on with pity and contempt. A Caeanic's raiment is his interface with the universe, the sole means by which his existence can be validated and his hidden abilities brought into play, and it is therefore imperative that it should be the work of a single artist who is both designer and executor. A Caeanic sartorial displays a marvellous unity between hand and brain. Using power tools and often working in the heat of inspiration, he is capable of producing a full suit of clothes in minutes, in an astonishing exhibition of skill and originality.

Caeanics would strenuously deny that their addiction to apparel has anything in common with the use of mood drugs. The Art of Attire is held to be a practical, extrovert method of fulfilling life, and not to rely on introspective mood changes. Arth Matt-Helver (see Travels in the Tzist Arm*) believes, however, that the more creative of the Caeanic sartorials are guided by subconscious forces. Hands that cut and stitch are responding to subconscious racial archetypes, which can then possess the wearers of the garments that express them.*

List's *Cultural Compendium*

The cab sped through the streets of Gridira, Harlos's capital city. Through the tinted windows the vague shapes of the metropolis fled by like angular phantoms, in alternations of light and shade.

Realto Mast was in an expansive mood. 'A most satisfactory conclusion to our enterprise, don't you think, Peder?' He raised his glass in a salute to his partner, downing the raw green spirit which was all the cab service dispensed.

Peder sipped his own glass. 'So far so good,' was all he would say.

But on the face of it all was well. The *Costa* had come down at the same provincial spaceport, used almost wholly by small-time commercial lines, from which they had departed, and was now back in the possession of its owner with an innocent trip to the antipodastral hunting reefs entered in the log. They had been cautious and circumspect about transferring the cargo to Gridira, but the transfer was now being completed by Castor and Grawn, who were storing the Caeanic garments in a suburban house previously rented for the purpose. All that now remained was the disposal of the goods, a leisurely business which would take years and which was to be entirely Peder's prerogative.

There was reason, therefore, to feel fairly gratified, and Peder had even begun to forgive Mast his various peccadilloes towards him. The cab stopped at a low entrance framed with jazzy pink and electric-blue mobile light-strips. Peder peered anxiously through the window. He saw a narrow, dusky street, tall buildings rearing up on either side, flickering with dimly glowing lights and signs. He recognized the *Mantis Diner*, a haunt in a part of Gridira all but inaccessible to the law, which he had visited in Mast's company once previously.

'Ah, here we are!' Mast enthused. 'Come in and let me buy you a drink and some dinner.'

Peder fumbled unhappily with a hold-all he was carrying. 'I'll take the cab home,' he said hesitantly. 'I was going straight to my shop in Tarn Street.'

Mast slapped him jovially on the shoulder. 'Nonsense! Reticence has always been your downfall, Peder. A success like ours needs celebrating! Besides – ' He tilted his head in a suggestive manner, raising his eyebrows

– 'I may be able to put a bit of business in our direction, and get some of this merchandise off our hands.'

The thought alarmed Peder. It would be like Mast, in his exhilaration, to do something rash and jeopardize all their carefully laid plans. He hurried with him from the cab, fearful now of leaving him unguarded, and went through the rectangular colour frame into the sleazy, smoky atmosphere of the all-nighter.

The *Mantis Diner* had, besides a walk-in restaurant open to the street, a private club whose rules of membership were all the more complicated for being arbitrary. In essence, it was necessary to be trusted by the owner. Mast was, and accordingly had become a member. He led the way through a screen of hanging gew-gaws at the back of the restaurant; after a nod to the doorkeeper they entered a six-foot-tall cylindrical capsule made of rainbow plastic.

The capsule descended fifty feet into the earth, then moved horizontally for about a quarter of a mile; they were heading into a semi-secret underworld, a world that had learned to protect itself simply by being, literally, underground.

The elevator in which they rode could not be commandeered by anyone seeking to enter the club uninvited. To raid the *Mantis*, or any of an unknown number of other clubs and hideouts clandestinely slotted among the legitimate installations beneath Gridira, the police would have had to bore their own tunnel. The cylinder slid to a stop. To the strains of soothing music they stepped into the underground club. It was a markedly different place from the all-night eatery, smelling of grease and sour wine, which they had left behind. The décor was plush, utilizing soft lighting effects, glowing carpets and embossed murals on the walls. Here food of good quality was served by pleasant young women, and the air was never foul or fuggish as it generally was above. Here those members of Gridira's fringe society who could afford it, and who met the owner's favour – rich fences, top racketeers, professional embezzlers, shady self-styled entrepreneurs (into which category Mast fell) and numbers of their associates and providers of technical services – could relax in their own special *milieu*.

Peder and Mast settled at a small table and ordered a dinner of spiced Protvian grasshoper legs, a delicacy Peder promised himself he would enjoy more often in future. Several people greeted Mast or came to exchange words with him. Peder did not really understand why Mast wanted to bring him here – a privilege never extended to Castor or Grawn. Perhaps it was because so much business was conducted here. It was here that Mast had conceived and planned the Kyre junket. The owner of the *Costa* was also a habitué of the *Mantis*. Here Mast had learned of the crashed Caeanic ship, buying the information together with the co-ordinates of the infra-sound planet.

He had also purchased certain technical assistance here. A short scrawny man with a wizened face, completely naked from head to toe, flung himself into a chair at their table. 'Hi, Realto, the suit work all right?'

Devilishly handsome in his Caeanic titfer, Mast tapped the end of his nose and gave a saturnine smile. 'Well enough, Moil. You should ask Peder here. He was our brave "infranaut".' He chuckled.

Since Moil had manufactured the infra-sound baffled suit, in a sense Peder's life had been in his hands. The sartorial felt uncomfortable as the technician's eyes flicked to him, not knowing how much Mast had told him of the purpose behind the project.

'It was a bit hairy, but I survived,' he said.

'Any of the stuff get through?' Moil asked him. 'Got the recorder box on you? I'd like to look it over.'

'No, sorry, I haven't,' Peder said, not realizing until now that there had been a recorder.

'We dumped the suit, I'm afraid, Moil,' Mast explained apologetically. 'We didn't keep anything.'

Moil nodded absently. 'Well, let me know if you need anything else,' he said, getting to his feet. 'Always glad to do business.'

'Likewise.' After he had gone Mast refilled Peder's glass. 'Fancy a game, Peder? Cards, or some shuffle? Luck's with you, I can see.'

'No,' said Peder, certain by now that Mast was a bare-faced, accomplished, habitual cheat.

One large table in the corner of the diner was sepa-rated from the rest of the room by cloth screens. Mast kept glancing at it from time to time, a speculative look crossing his features. Eventually he leaned across to Peder, speaking in a confidential tone. 'See that screen table, Peder? That's the permanent booking of the most powerful fence on Harlos. There's no saying whether he's here tonight, of course, until you get behind the curtain.'

'Who cares?' Peder responded desperately, gulping down his wine. But Mast was already on his feet, and oblivious of Peder's look of ineffectual anxiety, he made his way across the saloon to the tented table. A tall, cadaverous man appeared suddenly from behind the screen and held a brief conversation with him, punctu-ated by vigorous gestures.

Mast returned looking excited. 'Jadper *is* there, Peder. I haven't managed to obtain an interview with him yet — but there's a definite possibility that later in the evening . . . if so, I want you to come with me. You understand the merchandise; you'll be able to talk to him.'

He slurped his wine, unaware of Peder's nervous strain. 'You realize what this means? Jadper won't be interested in bits and pieces. He'll take the whole load in one go! By this time tomorrow you may be rich!'

'No, *no*,' Peder protested in anguish. 'That's not how to do it at all. I must sell them slowly, piece by piece over a period of years, through my contacts in the trade. That way they'll enhance their value. This is already *agreed*, Realto.'

Mast arched his eyebrows. 'How long must I wait to recoup my capital? You are too amateurish, Peder, one doesn't do things like that at all if one can help it. The thing is to make quicker gains to invest in new projects.' He lowered his tone. 'I haven't mentioned this before, but I know a way to tap the main root of the sap-oil forest on Tundora. The outlay is rather expensive, but we can draw off a substantial quantity of fluid before being detected, and it can be sold immediately at a large profit, no questions asked.' He tapped Peder on the knee. 'Come in with your share from selling the garments, and in a few months you'll get it back tenfold. What do you say to that?'

'No,' Peder said. 'I'm not in your line of business. I'm a sartorial, and that's all I ever want to be. I'm sticking to our agreement.' He folded his arms stubbornly.

'Are you aware of how risky it is to be in possession of Caeanic apparel?' Mast reminded him, wide-eyed. 'Leave it to the fences, the professionals. They take the risk, and they don't mind hanging on to the goods for a year or two.'

'Neither do I,' Peder said in a surly tone. Part of his resentment stemmed, in fact, from the prospect he had been savouring of doling out the merchandise to avid customers culled from all over Ziode; discriminating elegantors who would pay almost anything for such treasures as a pair of Caean-cut breeches or a Prossim cheviot.

Mast was undergoing one of his dangerous bouts of over-confidence. It had been a mistake to come to the *Mantis*, Peder thought. Without him Mast would make no move; he needed his expertise.

Peter had initially been seduced by Mast's glamorous aura of privateering, even imagining – falsely – that they were kindred souls; that the care Mast took to be a snappy dresser meant he was seriously interested in the sartorial art. But he was wrong in that, and he did not have the nerve to go along with the man's compulsive opportunism.

He jumped to his feet in a near-panic. 'I'm going home,' he said bluntly. 'I have as much at stake in this as you do. I'm using my right of veto.'

'You do *not* have as much at stake in it!' Mast exclaimed, leaning back and looking up at him. 'Who paid for the co-ordinates, hired the *Costa*, had the baffle suit made? Your own expenditure has been nil – and your share in the proceeds, correspondingly, is minor. Or had you forgotten that?'

'I risked my life,' Peder reminded him icily. 'You didn't – or ever intend to.'

Clutching his hold-all, he went stumbling for the rainbow plastic elevator. As it rushed him to the *Mantis Diner*'s greasy street-front, he hoped vacillatingly that he had not hurt Mast's feelings.

It was midnight when he arrived in Tarn Street, and the stars of the Ziode Cluster blazed overhead, a spangled ceiling to the city's night-glow. Peder unlocked his small shop, *The Sartorial Elegantor*, and stepped quietly within.

The closeted smell of cloth greeted him. In his imagination the populations of garments huddled on their racks, like a close-packed army on parade, seemed to welcome him. He brushed through them in the near darkness and descended a few steps to his cellar workshop, switching on the light.

Neatly arrayed before him in the cramped space were the tools of his trade: the pressing board, the dummies, the slender bodkins, the array of power needles for stitching and seaming in hundreds of different ways, the fibril-loom – a hand-held machine for joining cloth so that there was no seam. Another machine wove individual suits from the ground up, starting from reels of yarn, a procedure which ostensibly was personal tailoring, the sartorial sitting at the control board and feeding in instructions; but one which Peder rarely used – the work was too remote from the hands, it was something borrowed from a factory.

His eye fell on the half-completed garments bedecking the walls, and as he compared them mentally with the contents of the hold-all he carried Peder smiled the bitter-sweet smile of an artist who knows he is inferior, knows he is in the presence of a creativity transcending all he could aspire to.

And yet he would have to summon up what talents he did possess, for judging by his first hasty examination of it the Frachonard suit was a trifle too large for him, and would have to be adjusted. The thought of adjusting the work of a Frachonard sent prickles down his spine, but it would have to be done if the suit was to be his own.

He laid the hold-all on the table, and opened it.

He took out the lavender suède slippers.

He took out the Frachonard suit.

Handling it gently, he draped it on a hanger and then stepped back to view it.

Just as when he had first seen it on the crashed Caeanic spaceship, it took over the whole room. The Frachonard Prossim suit! How annoyed Mast would be to know he had appropriated such a rarity!

It could well be worth as much as the rest of the haul put together, he reflected. He directed all the consciousness he could muster on to the suit, dazzled by its simple elegance, an elegance which surpassed any he had known or imagined. He rubbed the cloth of a sleeve between his fingers; the texture was impossible to pin down and endlessly fascinating, neither sleek nor rough, somehow combining perfect drape with perfect structurality.

Caean had thousands of different fabrics, natural and synthetic, but the origin of Prossim was a mystery to Peder. He did not even know if it was grown or synthesized. He only knew that it was rare, and costly, and sublime.

Suddenly he frowned. Had he been mistaken? The suit now seemed a perfect fit for him. He lifted the panel of the jacket and glanced over the lining, but of course there was no size notation.

The excitement of the trip must have warped his judgement, he decided.

He was tired; it had been a long day. Tomorrow he would try on the suit.

He mounted a staircase to his living quarters above the shop. There he undressed, donned a long crocheted nightgown, and settled into a deep sleep on the divan bed.

He was woken by the chiming of the door bell. Blurrily he rose from his bed and peered out of the bay window. The false dawn limned the outlines of the giant emporia half a mile away. Down below in the street, two figures stood in the porch of his shop, but the light was too indistinct for him to see who they were.

He descended the narrow stairs to the shop. Thrown against the translucent front door by the street lamps were two silhouettes, one tall and slim, the other lumpy. With a grunt of annoyance Peder hurried through the racks of clothing and unlocked the door.

Mast and Grawn slid into the shop. 'Really, Peder, must you keep us in darkness?' Mast said petulantly. 'Let's have some light!'

Ignoring him, Peder led them through the darkened shop to his apartment upstairs. He turned to face them in his main room, which doubled as a sitting-room and bedroom, feeling slightly ridiculous in his nightgown. Mast found the most comfortable chair and draped himself negligently on it. Grawn simply stood there apishly, mouth ajar.

'What do you want?' Peder asked. 'I hadn't expected to see you so soon.'

'Good news, Peder,' Mast told him nonchalantly. 'My stake-out in the *Mantis* produced results. Well, I didn't actually get to see Jadper, but I'm visiting his villa next week. The deal is probably on. But to do business with him I'll need to know what the goods are worth, so could you start evaluating them today, finishing the job by, say, the weekend? I know it's a lot of work, but worth it . . .'

Peder had a presentiment of disaster and groaned inwardly. Mast was going to make a mess of things – he felt sure of it.

'I've already told you – I'm sticking to the agreed plan,' he said with stubborn exasperation. 'Disposal of the garments was to be in *my* hands – those were the terms of the project.'

Mast spoke with sudden sternness. 'I don't think you really understand our relationship, Peder. You were never really more than an employee. It's *my* operation, and I don't take orders from *you*.'

He jerked to his feet, angular, lithe and saturnine. 'Now don't be so unreasonable, Peder. Everything is going splendidly! Try to snap out of this silly mood. I'm going to get a few hours' sleep now. I'll call on you again this afternoon and we'll go to the storehouse together.'

Sick with frustration, Peder watched them leave.

Mast hummed softly to himself as his Cauredon saloon car, chauffeured by Castor, slid away from the kerb and whispered through the nearly empty streets.

Grawn, in the back of the car with him, spoke in a gruff voice. 'Why are you bothering with that creep, Realto? Heave him over the side, that's what I say. He's a comedown.'

'Hmm, maybe,' Mast replied patiently. 'But we need him for the evaluation. Never sell anything until you know what it's worth.'

'So? He's not the only goddam tailor in town, for Chrissake. Buy another.'

'There *is* the question of secrecy . . . but you have a point, Grawn. It might be as well to remove the merchandise from Forbarth's reach. That, at least, should secure his co-operation!'

He tapped on the window separating them from Castor. 'A change of plan, Castor! Drive to the warehouse!'

Castor pulled on the steering rod. The car swerved round a corner, then proceeded south.

Mast leaned back in satisfaction. 'He'll soon realize he's been bucking the wrong league,' he said confidently.

Unable to return to his bed, Peder paced the room in an agony of vacillation. He didn't know what to do!

Eventually he sat down despairingly, his head on his hand. In the end he would give in to Mast, he supposed. But where would that lead him?

To Ledlide, the prison planet, most likely.

For half an hour he must have sat there, until eventually the Frachonard suit began to come into his thoughts. It was getting light outside, and he might as well make a start to the day.

And today, of course, was the day of the Frachonard Prossim suit.

The great occasion of trying on the suit should be approached with care and respect. He washed slowly and powdered himself, and ate a leisurely breakfast before choosing his accessories: a lemon-coloured shirt with ruffled front and piped cuffs, silk underpants with a flowered pattern in gold thread, hand-knitted socks of real lambswool, and shoes of soft black leather with gold buckles.

His heart pounding with anticipation, he descended to his workshop and donned the accessories there. Momentarily, his hands trembled.

Then he reached for the hanger and dressed himself in the Frachonard suit, feeling instantly its electrifying effect.

Wonderful, wonderful! It fitted as well as if Frachonard had measured him up for it personally. The waistcoat was a superb personality support, making him feel erect, strong and alert. The trousers were lank and only slightly flared, like the fairings of a transsonic rocket, and gave him the extraordinary feeling of being long-legged and energetic. Under the prompting of this feeling he strode from one side of the cellar to the other and back again, the jacket's subtlety of line helping to control his movements, eliminating the slight awkwardness of gait that normally plagued him.

Stopping to view himself in the full-length mirror, he felt the suit appropriating his personality, taking it over and remedying its defects, forming his new interface with the exterior world. Here was a new Peder Forbarth, upright, rational and aware, the kind of Forbarth he liked to imagine, now in possession of his latent qualities. Even his face was artfully transformed. The same open, pleasant-enough expression was there, but the eyes held a new directness. The pliability and vacillation were gone, to be replaced by an unmistakable air of ability. Even the pudginess of jowl, which before had given an impression of weakness, now reappeared as the full-fleshed look of someone who had learned how to make his way in the world.

How could anyone attired in a Frachonard suit gainsay the tenets of Caeanic philosophy? Man's naturally evolved form was adventitious, lumpy and incomplete, and it did not fit his creative inner powers. If he was to exteriorize these dormant inner powers then he must acquire the appropriate interfaces with reality. Only then could he confront the universe in his true garb, become the creature of effective thought and action he should be, and experience all possible realms of existence.

But the evolution of his physical form beyond the status of the hairless ape could not be left to blind biological forces. It had to be done by conscious art. In a word, it was to be accomplished by means of raiment.

As he gazed upon his image these ideas, which previously he had never taken seriously, carrying as they did the taint of foreign subversion, struck him with full force. With every glance he discovered dazzling new effects. He thought he saw in the mirror's depths the foreshadowing of the future god-man, fearlessly apparelled, flashing through the galaxies, impinging by virtue of his glorious vesture on any circumstance. Who could compare such splendour with the sodden clay that was unclothed man?

An ecstatic thought came to him. He was now the best-dressed man in Ziode; and presumably, among the *five* best-dressed men in Ziode and Caean put together, Frachonard having made only five Prossim suits.

He was, therefore, *one of the five best-dressed men in the universe*.

He seemed to go dizzy, the room spinning and the harmonic colours of the suit becoming momentarily kaleidoscopic.

The delirium left him as he turned away from the mirror. All at once he realized that the problem that had plagued him minutes before was trivial. There was no need to make an issue of Mast's scheming obliqueness. It would be a simple matter for Peder to take his cut of the proceeds in kind, disposing of it as he saw fit, and severing all connection with his partners. Mast could then do as he liked.

He went back upstairs and dialled for an autocab, taking out three large suitcases from his storeroom while he waited for it to arrive.

All would be well. He stood in front of his shop, looking up through the plate window. The sun had already risen, but on Harlos the stars remained visible until several hours after dawn. The Ziode Cluster covered nearly half the purplish-green sky, a giant fluorescent puff-ball with a hazy atmosphere of less closely-packed suns. Among the thousands of stars in that puff-ball, nearly a hundred inhabited planets made up the Ziode nation. Beyond it could be discerned the rainbow-like wisp of the Tzist Arm; beyond that, the rest of the galaxy made an even dimmer background to it all.

He thought of the future man, transformed by raiment, who would one day rule that galaxy. The evolution of the transformed man would take a long time – thousands of years, even – but one thing was certain. He would spring from Caean, not Ziode.

The autocab drew up outside. Minutes later he was riding southwards through Gridira's still nearly-silent streets.

The sleek commercial buildings fled by. Soon the cab entered an outer ring of high-rise habitat tenements where the sky disappeared intermittently behind the criss-cross of overhead dwellings. After half an hour he was in the garden suburb of Cadra, whose streets were shaded by willow and bouquet trees.

He wound down the window, bringing the perfume of the trees clean and fresh on the morning air. But he frowned as the autocab came to a stop at the maisonette rented by Mast. A manual-control Cauredon – Mast's car – was parked outside. The door to the side garage was raised, and inside he could see someone loading bundles into the van kept there.

He left the autocab and padded down the driveway. 'So!' he exclaimed in a ringing voice. ' A fine trustworthy accomplice I teamed up with!'

Unabashed, with slow careful movements, Mast emptied the armful of garments he held into the back of the van. 'I too, it seems, have made a bad choice of partner,' he said pensively. 'What are you doing here, Peder?'

Peder spluttered. 'I guessed what you were up to and came to put a stop to it!'

'Remarkable foresight,' Mast commented. 'What are those suitcases I see on your luggage rack?'

Their arms filled with clothing, Castor and Grawn emerged through a side door leading from the house. 'Put those garments back at once!' Peder stormed. Poker-faced, they ignored him and dumped their burdens unceremoniously in the van.

Peder followed all three of them into the house. The Caeanic apparel lay neatly stacked against the walls of the storeroom, or hung in racks Peder had erected. While

Castor and Grawn continued their hurried transfer of the hoard, Mast looked Peder coolly up and down.

'I see you're wearing your new suit, Peder. It makes a new man of you. A new man altogether.' Mast seemed thoughtful.

Peder in turn regarded Mast, appraising the Ziodean suit he wore. At one time his stylish taste had impressed him. Now all his clothes – apart from the Caeanic titfer, of course – seemed unbelievably grubby. His dress was merely a shabby form of self-advertising; it had nothing in common with the true Art of Attire as it was understood in Caean.

He was sure Mast's tendency to meddle with plans already well-laid was a basic flaw in his character. Imagining he was looking through the eyes of a Caeanic sartorial, he began to speculate how he would repair the deficiency. He would prescribe garments making for care and caution, as a counterbalance to the initiative and enterprise Mast already possessed in abundance.

An idea came to him. What if he could select the appropriate items from among their haul? . . . but the idea was unfeasible. Mast would never co-operate. And Peder, for his part, was not a Caeanic sartorial and lacked the necessary insight.

He found his voice again. 'May I ask what is the meaning of all this?' he demanded. 'I'd like to know what excuse you can offer for trying to rob me of everything!'

'A precautionary measure only, Peder,' Mast replied easily. 'I wished to remove the merchandise to a safe place so as to forestall the possibility of theft. I can now, it seems, congratulate myself on my wisdom.'

'You are mistaken – I came to steal nothing,' Peder claimed. 'I'll tell you the truth. I don't like the way you are handling things. I want to take my share in kind, to sell on my own account. The rest can be yours.' He paused. 'I'll be satisfied with sufficient to bring me in, say, a hundred thousand units. A modest enough demand, all things considered.'

'Very well, Peder,' Mast said slowly, 'I agree. On one condition. Give me a valuation of the remainder, even if only a rough one. I have to have some idea of what I'm offering Jadper.'

Peder hesitated, stroking his chin and looking around him. 'They are worth whatever one can get for them,' he said dubiously. 'That's why I was anxious to dole them out one by one. Jadper himself probably won't get as good a total price as I would, in the long run . . .'

Mast snapped his fingers to Grawn who had just re-entered. 'Grawn, go and get Peder's cases from the autocab standing outside, will you?'

Peder began looking through the store, selecting a garment here and there.

'I'm putting a lot of trust in you,' Mast murmured. 'Only you know the worth of the items you're taking.'

'I am an honest man,' Peder declared. 'I keep my bargains.'

Carrying the bulky suitcases, Grawn ambled back into the room. Peder packed away his choices carefully, snapping each case shut as it was filled.

Finally he was satisfied and stood up. 'Don't accept less than five million,' he told Mast quietly. 'Better if you can get six.'

'All right.' Mast offered his hand. 'Then our association would appear to be at an end.'

Peder shook hands. 'To our mutual benefit, I hope.'

'Of course.'

But still Peder lingered. 'You know,' he said diffidently, 'there are garments here that could work wonders for you. Why don't you let me? . . . after all, you've never exactly been a *mezzak.*' *Mezzak* was a Caeanic word meaning 'one who dresses like a baboon'.

Smiling, Mast shook his head. 'I'll be frank, Peder. There's another reason why I'd just as soon off-load. I've begun to feel uneasy about holding on to them for too long, though not from any legalistic angle.'

'I don't understand.'

'Well, you know what they call the Caeanics, don't you – clothes robots. This sort of gear gives me an odd feeling. There's something un-Ziodean about them.'

'Prejudice, prejudice. Typical Ziodean xenophobia!'

Mast shrugged. 'Call it what you like. I simply have fixed ideas about what's healthy. I believe one should stand on one's own feet and walk without crutches.'

Inwardly Peder sighed. Poor Mast. Dressed in rags and tatters, imagining he was adequate. He had put his finger on the difference between Ziodean and Caeanic cultures, of course. The Ziodean *ethos* stressed individualism and self-dependence. It was diametrically opposed to the artificial augmentation of qualities and abilities such as occurred on Caean.

All of which, Peder now knew, implied a serious misunderstanding not only of the Caeanic sartorial art, but also of man's psychological nature.

He turned to Castor and Grawn, who were standing grinning at him crookedly. 'Well, goodbye then, chaps,' he said.

'Yeah, have fun,' responded Castor, his reconstituted eyes glittering.

As he departed, Peder heard their muffled sniggers behind him.

'Looks like Peder can pull himself together after all, when he has to,' Castor sneered when the sartorial had gone.

'You noticed it too, did you?' Mast remarked. 'His change of manner? There's a word for that. It's called *mien*. The Caeanic suit does that for him.'

He fell into thought. It had been on board the *Costa* that he had first begun to have second thoughts about the garments. Castor and Grawn, bedizened in their new finery, had suddenly started to adopt uncharacteristic mannerisms – nothing all that drastic, initially anyway, but enough to persuade him that Caeanic wear *was* as much a risk to one's mental health as it was said to be.

He had forbidden them to wear anything but Ziodean clothes ever since.

He looked up. 'Take the rest of the stuff out to the van, fellows. We'll move out anyway, just in case.'

He hoped the fence would soon take this junk off his hands.

The morning was now bright and full. Peder relaxed contentedly, gazing through the autocab window as Cadra went speeding past him.

How easy it was to solve problems!

But he would never have done it without the Frachonard suit – Mast, he believed, would not have allowed it. Peder would have dithered, would have felt impelled to go along with whatever Mast decided.

Even as he talked to Mast new horizons had opened up before him. Business possibilities which he had been too timid to spot until now became visible all around him. He would soon be moving out of Tarn Street. Zoide was his playground.

Which was as it should be, for a member of a galactic elite, one of the best-dressed men in the universe.

4

'Well, how the hell was I to know?' Amara Corl exclaimed in great irritation. 'It's not the sort of thing one can be expected to anticipate.' She drummed her fingers on the desk, her brow creased. 'What in Ziode shall we do now? What do you make of it, Estru?'

'Have you called the medics?' Estru asked.

'Yes, of course,' Amara snapped. Estru could see she was shaken by the incident, mostly because it reflected on her own judgement.

The business of opening the suit could, he felt, have been approached with more caution. 'Impetuosity,

Amara, is not a quality to be cultivated when in unknown regions,' he thought – but the words merely floated wistfully in his mind. To have uttered them would have been to throw the female sociologist, his team leader, into a rage.

They were in an office adjoining the engineering service room where the outsize spacesuit had been laid on a workbench and cut open. When summoned, Amara had taken but a brief look at its contents and then swept out again, obviously unpleasantly affected.

'Is he dead, do you think?' she said. 'He might have committed suicide.'

Estru, by means of a camera in the service room, still had a view of the suit on a vidplate, but Amara's eyes studiously avoided this. 'I reckon he's just fainted.'

'It's weird, I have to admit that,' Amara said distastefully, finally giving the screen the merest glance. 'Just look at him, all connected up with wires, tubes and catheters. The muscles are so atrophied, too. If you ask me he was put in that suit years ago! Who would do such an awful thing?'

'I'll go further than that,' Estru told her mildly. 'I'd say he's never been out of it. It's not just the muscles that are atrophied. His limbs haven't developed properly.'

'You mean he's been in it since *birth?*'

He nodded. Unlike Amara he had lingered with the technicians to inspect for a minute or so the workings of the suit. He had seen enough to indicate a permanent life support system supplying all aspects of biological existence. The man in the suit had been transformed into a new kind of creature: one able to inhabit space.

Suddenly Amara seemed to overcome her disgust. The scientist in her took over. She became thoughtful.

Two medical officers arrived. The sociologists accompanied them into the service room. They paused on seeing the suit and its contents.

One cast a reproving look around him. 'This should have been done in a properly equipped theatre, not in a mechanic's service shop.' Estru shrugged.

The techs had cut, not just through the suit's outer casing, but also through much of its interior equipment. Estru was worried that some of it might be vital to the health of the wearer. He watched anxiously while the medics made their examination, applying their probes and pick-ups. The figures and traces that appeared on the read-out plates of their instruments meant nothing to him, and their faces were professionally impassive.

Finally they closed up their cases and stepped out of earshot to confer, nodding in agreement.

'He's in shock, the catatonic kind,' the older medic said when they returned. 'Otherwise he's in good health, if one leaves his unusual condition out of consideration.'

Estru gazed down at the worm-like pallor of the shrivelled human being encased in the works of the suit. 'What would bring on that kind of shock?'

'Trauma of an unexpected, unacceptable kind. Something the mind just wouldn't be able to face up to.'

'Well, that's only a medical problem, isn't it?' Amara said hopefully. 'You can bring him round, can't you? We want to talk to him.'

The doctor hesitated. 'That depends on whether the cause of trauma is still present. If it is, bringing him forcibly to consciousness could be contra-indicated. In such cases, a safer procedure is to remove the patient from the source of trauma, and apply psychomedications in an environment familiar to him.'

'I get you,' Estru said. 'You mean put him back in the suit, right?'

'Right.'

'You're saying we were wrong to break the suit open,' Amara said heavily.

'That's not for us to comment on, madam.'

Estru screwed up his face in concentration. 'Let's get this straight. You're suggesting the suit is the natural environment for the man inside it – that cutting it open sent him catatonic? How long do you think he's been in it? Since birth?'

The medics glanced at one another, then at what lay on the bench. 'That would be our guess,' said the one who had remained silent up to now. 'Not in this suit, of course, but in some comparable kind of container. You realize, of course, what that means.'

'Yes,' Amara answered firmly. 'It means that his own body-image of himself doesn't include anything we would recognize as a human being. When he thinks of himself as a person, the picture in his mind is that of the suit's exterior. Probably he isn't even conscious of his biological body, except as a sort of internal organ or essential core.'

'And we forced him to look at himself,' Estru breathed. 'My God!'

'Psychologically it's a fascinating situation,' Amara said. 'An almost unique opportunity, in fact. It would be interesting to do some experiments – but that's not our mission.' She waved her hand dismissingly and her face became stern. 'We'd better stick to our brief. If this is a cultural norm then we're up against a pretty weird culture.'

A look of guarded relief had come over the older medic's face. 'I take it you have abandoned the idea of removing him completely from the suit?'

'That would be some job of unscrambling. God, where does the suit end and the man begin?' For the first time Amara stared without flinching at the bulky sawn-open cylinder and its unnerving contents. The inert flesh was, indeed, practically enmeshed in its surrounding web of transducers and catheters. 'Imagine what it must be like to be this man,' she said thoughtfully. 'He doesn't have the use of the limbs he was born with; only of the suit's devices and organs. I wonder if the suit is equipped with a kinesthetic sense? Probably so; in that case he's able to sense it and feel it the same way we do our own bodies. It *is* his body, as far as he's concerned.'

'It's so elaborate it's a misnomer to call it a suit,' Estru added. 'It's an integrated system in its own right: a space body-prosthetic.'

'And from his point of view you've inflicted savage injury on him,' the older doctor pointed out.

Amara turned to the techs. 'What about that? Can you repair the damage?'

The chief technician stirred. 'If I'd known you'd want us to make good we'd have been more careful. We invaded quite a few sub-systems by cutting into it in the way we did.'

'How would you assess the suit, technically?' Estru asked.

The other pursed his lips. 'A good solid job, very durable. But judging by what we've seen so far there's nothing too advanced for us to handle. Some of it's pretty quaint, in fact. We can patch it up if you want.'

'Good. Get on with it, then,' Amara said.

'It's really more of a job for a doctor than an engineer,' the medic said anxiously. 'I'd be happier having him in surgery.'

'Fair enough. You can all work on it together. Just before you seal him up give him whatever psycho-medications you think necessary.' Amara made for the door, giving Estru a glance to follow.

As they walked back to their own section she tapped him on the arm. 'There were *two* of them, remember? He called the other one *Lana* – in Old Russian that's a feminine name.' She screwed up her face in amusement. 'I *wonder* what they were doing!'

In terms of the interstellar velocity of which it was capable, the exploratory ship *Callan* had been almost stationary when it spotted the deep-space suits. In fact it had been engaged on a moderately-paced sweep of the planetary system occupying the near-space of the small nondescript yellow star. This was the forty-third such unremarkable star they had visited at random, following Amara Corl's theory that in this way they would uncover traces of the beginning of Caeanic civilization. Had their sensor scans not picked up the suits their stay would have been brief. The system contained no habitable planets. It was a bleak corner of the starry world, one among a million such bleak corners, and Estru, Amara's first assistant, had been about to suggest that they abandon the search for ancient beings and move closer to Caeanic space proper.

Now, however, Amara was excited. It would probably take the techs a couple of hours to close up the suit again. Meanwhile there was the question of where it had come from.

Two nearby worlds offered themselves as candidates. The first and most unlikely was a gas giant surrounded by a system of Saturn rings but lacking any satellites. The second, a tiny arid planet quite unfit for human life, lay at present scarcely fifteen million miles sunward of the gas giant. The *Callan* had picked up its prisoner about mid-way between the two.

'The small one, I think. Don't you, Estru?'

'Presumably. It's not much of a world. Less than two thousand miles in diameter, a thin carbon dioxide atmosphere and cold. But maybe there's a protected outpost there or something.' He reflected. 'Shouldn't we wait till we get a chance to talk to our specimen before going any farther? We might save some time that way in the end.'

She snorted. 'We didn't have much luck last time. He was raving.'

'Maybe we didn't try hard enough to meet him on his own terms? He seemed to be under a misapprehension regarding *our* nature, as well as we of his.'

'Yes.' She switched on the recording she had made, listening with a frown to the sonorous voice. '"You will pay for all your barbarities,'" she translated slowly and with difficulty. "'We have never submitted to you and we never shall. I shall tell you nothing . . ." As if we were an enemy he recognized, instead of complete strangers.' She switched off.

'I'd rather know more about his background before we go barging in.'

'You can carry caution too far,' she reproved. 'What if we hadn't opened the suit? We still wouldn't know the truth about him. But all right. A few hours of library research can't do any harm.' She turned away and held down her memo key, which carried her voice to every section of her fifty-member team.

Minutes later she had alerted them to what was happening and had put the department on a crash project: investigate late Russian history, with special reference to any incursion into the Tzist Arm. She herself settled down to brush up her knowledge of the language.

She had been at it for a couple of hours when the vid chimed and the bearded face of Captain Wilce appeared.

'I ought to tell you we've spotted another object heading our way, Amara. At a guess it's come from the small planet up-sun of us. Any suggestions or preferences?'

'Yes! Make contact!' Amara replied immediately. 'What is it, another deep-space suit?'

'Something larger this time,' Wilce relayed a blurred long-range sensor image to her. It was hard to make anything sensible out of the shape that emerged. The object could have been lozenge-shaped, or perhaps flat and rectangular. It was studded with smaller features which the scanner failed to define properly.

'It has a length of about a hundred feet,' the Captain explained. 'We might have been better advised to proceed under baffle. They doubtless know we're here by now.'

'There's no reason to think they're hostile,' Amara murmured as she studied the advancing space vehicle, 'and we can't stay under baffle all the time. How about meeting them half-way, Captain?'

'If you're in that much of a hurry.'

'Yes, yes,' said Amara eagerly. 'We have to get to the bottom of this thing just as soon as possible.'

'Right. Keep your eyes peeled – we'll be there in minutes.'

He went off-line. Amara turned to Estru as she tapped her vidboard. 'I've a feeling we're about to add a chapter to the annals of sociology.'

Carrifer, in charge of the information team, came on the screen. 'Anything on the region yet?' Amara asked him.

'Yes, Amara. The Russians *were* active here. But there's not much by way of details. Knowledge of that era is so scrappy.'

'Yes, I know,' she said impatiently. 'Well, I hope you can give us a précis pretty soon. Keep at it.'

She cleared the screen, then put it through to the *Callan*'s sensoring section, obtaining the same view that was being delivered to the bridge.

With perfect ease the *Callan* swept through millions of miles of void to a meeting with the space object. At a distance of a few hundred yards the bridge crew nullified the ship's motion. The object now showed itself to be a rectangular raft moving directly outward from the sun, propelling itself by means of two nozzles which emitted a bright blue discharge and looked like electrostatic impellers.

Clinging to the raft were about fifty passengers. Amara turned up the magnification and gasped. She had expected to see more examples like their captured specimen: men who had fitted themselves for life in space by burying their organic bodies in giant suits. But the people on the raft wore no spacesuits at all. Neither did they wear any kind of clothing, protective or decorative.

They were naked to the void.

But that was not all. So bizarre were the space travellers in appearance that it was some moments before Amara could confirm that they were in fact human. She focused the screen on one specimen to examine it closely. Like its brethren, it had been extensively modified by deep surgery and the incorporation of artificial organs. Embedded in its skull was a turret-like device which she guessed was connected directly to the brain. The eyes were hidden by the black goggles which seemed to be riveted into the eye-sockets. The nose had been removed.

She moved the screen's cursor down to the torso. The chest had been replaced entirely by a metal box-like structure. Likewise the abdominal wall was substituted for by a flexible corrugated shield, making it resemble the abdomen of some type of grub. Amara could imagine the problems of pressure and temperature involved in adapting people to an interplanetary environment. Below the abdomen, however, hung an incongruous indication that the creature was fundamentally human, and male. The genitals had been left intact and floated flaccid and loose.

The mixing of man and machine continued. From limbs, backs and sides projected an assortment of devices and turrets. Amara swung the cursor to other parts of the raft. The modified men were far from being identical to one another. The machine-organs they incorporated varied from individual to individual, as though a division of function existed among them. Some torsos were transfixed by lateral shafts in an eerie travesty of crucifixion. Other specimens were made to seem even less human than their fellows by the elaboration of their cuirasses and metal pipes. As the raft jetted through space the modified men clung to handholds so as to avoid being thrown off by the weak gravity the acceleration generated.

And all were naked – all but one. The exception, a burly figure wrapped in a voluminous brown habit or gown, his head hidden by a deep cowl, stood in the centre of the vehicle while those around him kept a respectful distance.

On the raft, too, was additional equipment that might have been primitive artillery, radar and the like.

Finally Estru took a deep breath and let it out in a loud sigh. 'Wow. How do you relate this?'

'It's fairly obvious, isn't it?' Amara responded excitedly. 'What we have here is a space culture in the real meaning of the term. People adapted to living in space, just as you and I live in an atmospheric medium. The giant suit was one answer. This is another. We'll call it Type Two,' she added, for the benefit of the recorder. 'Modified men, rather than ensheathed, protected men.'

'Evidently they've solved the breathing problem,' Estru said sardonically, focusing on one of the modified men again. 'They've fixed it so that they don't have to breathe.'

'To live in space biologically must require an entire systematic overhaul,' Amara supplied. 'Almost certainly the blood is replaced by a more suitable fluid that won't form bubbles under zero pressure. Just where their tissues get their oxygen from I can't fathom at the moment. As you can see the lungs have been excised in every case. Probably those chest boxes carry a store of oxygen, possibly in a solid state or locked in a compound, which they release into the bloodstream – or pseudo-bloodstream – at a regulated rate. I'll ask the medics to write up a report on it. The idea seems strange to us, of course, but technically there's nothing difficult in any of it. It's just that – well, who would want to do that to themselves?' She shuddered.

'I'll second that,' Estru said fervidly. 'I don't know which is worse, the man in the suit or these fellows.'

Amara had been searching for a word. Now she found it. 'Cyborgs,' she said.

'What?'

'Cyborgs. That's what these are. I knew I'd heard of the phenomenon somewhere before. The word occurs in several dead languages — it stands for "cybernated organism" — but more as a legend than a fact. This is the first time I knew for certain that any had actually been made.'

From Amara's board came the voice of Aspar, in sensor section. 'I'm picking up transmitted speech, Amara. Want to listen to it?'

She smiled. 'Yes. It will be interesting to hear what *they* have to say.'

But when the voices followed Aspar's, several voices speaking at a time, her smile changed to a frown which deepened by the second. The voices were high-pitched, with odd, alien-sounding inflections. The language, as far as she could tell through the gabble, bore no relation either to Russian or to any known to her.

Estru looked at her with concern. 'Well? What do they say?'

She shook her head. 'It isn't Russian. I don't know what it is.'

There was a sudden quickening of activity on the raft. Several cyborgs leaped to a large device mounted on the nearside periphery. In their hands the machine swivelled and emitted a bright flash.

A muted buzz from Amara's table informed her that the *Callan* was under attack. On the screen she was unable to see what kind of weapon the device on the raft was, but three more flashes followed in rapid succession.

Captain Wilce's voice came through to her. 'We have a decision to make, Amara,' he said firmly. 'They're firing rocket missiles at us. The electrostatic deflectors have prevented any hits so far, but we can't rely on that. I must insist that we either retaliate or withdraw.'

Amara bit her lip. She knew that Captain Wilce felt he had been given a slightly unfair brief for this mission. The *Callan* was only lightly armed, in recognition of the fact that they would be intruding into Caeanic space. Some attempt had been made to compensate for this with a purely defensive, non-aggressive measure in the form of electrostatic focusing, said to be able to lock on to and deflect any solid missile or non-radiant energy beam. The Captain did not believe in its efficacy, however, and exhibited some nervousness where the security of his ship was concerned.

'I want to take one of those specimens alive,' she said suddenly. 'Do whatever's necessary, Captain.'

'Fair enough.'

The cyborgs appeared to be infuriated by their gun's failure to damage the *Callan*. They began to quit the raft; about half their number surged towards the ship in an angry swarm, propelling themselves by means of cylinders with small, flaring nozzles. They carried a variety of hand weapons: ray-guns, recoilless rifles, big spiked hammers. One cyborg, a launching tube mounted on its back, lobbed a mortar bomb. Automatically the electrostatic deflector seized it and hurled it away into space.

At the same time the *Callan* was bearing down on the space raft. Narrow energy beams seethed harmlessly against the hull. Bullets, unnoticed by the electrostatic deflector, bounced off it.

The ship's bulk scattered the cyborgs like chaff. Their cacophonous yelling swelled, almost deafening Amara and Estru; high-pitched, ranting sounds full of hatred. A whiplash tentacle snaked out from the ship and wound itself round one of the modified men, dragging him inboard.

Amara gave a grunt of satisfaction. 'That's that, Captain. I think we can withdraw now.'

'Good.'

The scene on the vidplate dwindled. The raft and its crew vanished into the endless void.

Instantly Amara switched to the airlock. The handling crew were not having an easy time with the cyborg. Although still restrained by the steel tentacle, it had tried to shoot one of them with its ray gun and had left molten metal running down the side of the chamber. It struggled wildly, almost manically, as they strove to disarm it.

'Hmm, interesting,' Amara murmured. 'Both he and the suit-man exhibit responses on the barbaric level. They react to strangers with fear and hostility. Incongruous for a people whose entire existence depends on technology, don't you think?'

'They wouldn't be the first technologically-minded barbarians in history,' Estru said mildly.

'No, of course not. And yet their hostility *could* be due to their . . . peculiar condition. Perhaps they carry a repressed group memory that originally they were human beings – a memory containing trauma, guilt and self-mutilation. The appearance of a ship from outside their system might stimulate this memory – unconsciously, of course – and it would express itself in unreasoning hostility.'

'Maybe. It's highly speculative.'

The cyborg had finally been subdued and disarmed. It was strapped to a board, its limbs immobilized. Now that their spell of emergency was over, the inboard crew were able to stand back and take a good look at what they had caught, and they found time to be appalled.

Amara got through to the medical section. 'How is our Russian?'

'The operation has been completed,' the senior doctor told her. 'As you're always in a hurry, Amara, we gave him a combination of drugs designed to erase from his memory any recent event sufficiently charged to cause catatonia. In a sense we've replaced the catatonic effect with an amnesiac one. Not the most responsible way of dealing with psychic disorders, but . . .' He trailed off. 'We also gave him an arousal drug, and according to his brain reading he's coming round. He should be functioning normally.'

'Let me understand this. He won't remember what we did to him?'

'The memory isn't expunged completely, but it's not on complete recall. He might even be able to remember it vaguely, as if remembering a dream, but he won't be sure it really happened. It will be robbed of significance. I thought you would prefer it that way,' the doctor added drily, 'because later we could reintroduce the incident to him slowly under controlled conditions.'

'Ah! Excellent! Then we can discuss the business with him!' she chuckled. 'Congratulations, Doctor. Indirect methods of enquiry never were to my liking!'

She tapped her finger-tips on the table, thinking something over. 'Put him back in the vacuum chamber, will you?'

'He's there already, for the sake of continuity. It's the last thing he will remember clearly.'

'Good, good,' she murmured slowly. 'I'll get in touch later.'

As soon as the doctor went off-line the lock crew came in. 'What shall we do with it now?' the team leader asked, not hiding his distaste.

'Put him in the vacuum chamber with our first specimen, and then stand by. And take those restraints off. I want him to have freedom of movement.'

'Is that wise?' said Estru in a low, worried voice. 'It does seem precipitous, Amara. Our patient is only just recovering! Shouldn't we give him more time?'

'I reject the term "patient",' Amara replied icily. 'What's the matter with you, Estru? The Russian is going to be perfectly all right, you just heard medical section say so. Finding himself in the company of the cyborg will probably reassure him.'

'We have no idea what relations are between the suit-people and the cyborgs,' Estru pointed out guardedly.

'But they belong to the same culture!'

Estru coughed politely. 'That is an unwarranted assumption, if I may be permitted to say so. They speak different languages. And you were the one to observe that the Russian's outbursts against us suggest he already has enemies.'

Amara waved her hand imperiously, annoyed at her assistant's misgivings. 'Such possibilities are not lost on me, I assure you. This is a scientific test. I want to see what Types One and Two have to say to each other.'

Minutes later the cyborg prisoner had been taken to the vacuum chamber. In the vestibule the lock crew freed it from the restraining board, protecting themselves with difficulty from its flailing attacks, and pushed it through the chamber lock.

In free fall it floated into the metal vault. Up to now the giant spacesuit, its surface barely scarred by the welds that had fastened it up, had been motionless on the opposite side. On the entry of the cyborg, however, its huge arms stirred.

The two space-adapted men confronted one another.

The suit advanced.

The cyborg's gaze darted quickly here and there, as if seeking a way out. It drifted against a wall, and expertly jack-knifed its legs against it, leaping across the chamber and out of the path of the suit.

Unlike the cyborg, the suit had its own built-in propulsion. Its drive unit, which was capable of accelerating it to speeds in the order of hundreds of thousands of miles per hour given a sufficiently long period, needed only minimal activation for manoeuvres in this tiny enclosure. The suit flicked round in pursuit of the cyborg and zipped across the chamber, able to pre-empt any further evasive manoeuvre by its greater ease of motion.

Not a single word had passed between the two, although both species (as Estru thought it would be fair to call them) communicated by radio. Nevertheless the attitude of violence and implacable hatred which each displayed towards the other was unmistakable.

'Better put a stop to it,' Estru said tightly.

'Get the cyborg out,' Amara ordered.

Suit and cyborg had come together. The suit was incomparably the more powerful. The great metal arms flailed, smashing into the puny organic body. The cyborg's skull-turret broke and seemed to become dislodged. A thin, pale blood began to strew itself across the chamber in swaying rivulets which broke up instantly into a haze of droplets.

Those watching through the windows had tried to save the situation by switching on the gravity. The suit dropped clanging to the floor, accompanied by the limp body of its enemy.

They rushed into the chamber, fending off the arms of the suit with prods and chains, and dragged away the broken mixture of metal, plastic, flesh, pink blood.

'It's dead, Amara.'

'Oh well,' said Estru wearily. 'It all counts as data.'

Amara, too, after casting him a contemptuous glance for his sarcastic remark, took the news philosophically. 'Get medical section to carry out an examination,' she said with no trace of embarrassment. 'The details of the cyborgation process should prove interesting.'

She turned to Estru. 'Maybe we should go back and get another one?'

'We're being pretty free with other people's lives, not to say their liberty,' he objected.

'People? These aren't people, they're – well, at best, they're savages. If one wants to regard them as human at all.'

'I only hope we aren't going to behave in quite this fashion once we get to Caean.'

She snorted. 'Don't be silly.'

'Well, I don't think we should make any further contacts just yet,' Estru continued. 'We ought to try talking to the suit-man again. It's easy to see now why he was so hostile towards us.'

'Oh?'

'Well, think about it. He knows two kinds of beings, as far as we know. His own kind – outwardly a species of machine, or space-robot – and the cyborgs, whom he kills on sight. Look at it from his point of view. Which do we most resemble?'

5

Realto Mast's emotions were a blend of foreboding and resignation as he approached the home of Olveolo Jadper, a splendid villa set in ample grounds and partially hidden by a miniature wood. Among those who had dealings with Jadper, such feelings were apt to be the rule – not because Jadper was Harlos's wealthiest and most successful fence, but because along with it he belonged to a class of personality unfortunately fashionable in certain parts of Ziode. Jadper was a practical joker, infamous for regarding his clients as fair game.

Mast deplored the cult of the japer. He valued his dignity, and resented all arbitrary assaults on it, especially when in the form of crude and unsubtle buffoonery beloved of Olveolo – 'Jadper the Japer', to give him his cognomen. But, business was business.

Silver-plated gates swung lazily open in answer to Mast's arrival before them. Ahead, overhung by willow trees, a narrow crazy-paving path meandered into a profusion of blooms and bushes. In the distance, raising aloft their translucent green crowns, the villa's yellow travertine towers peeped through a tracery of silver birch branches.

Mast wore jodhpurs and a lounge jacket, the muted colours of which were made to glow quietly by juxtaposition with his lime green waistcoat. Notwithstanding his stern prohibitions to Castor and Grawn he still wore his Caeanic titfer, and in his hand he carried a small box which he waved in the air in the hope of sniffing out any suspicious electronic activity. Finally, taking his courage in both hands, he stepped through the gates and set forth along the crazy paving.

The path plunged immediately into a miniature jungle which practically cut off the daylight, twisting and turning in a confusing pattern. Mast was surprised, on emerging into the sunlight some minutes later, to find that the villa now lay behind him, but he continued nevertheless to follow the meaningless loops and curves. At the end of thirty minutes he was back at the main gates, having made a complete circuit of Jadper's home.

With chagrin he abandoned this fool's route and struck out directly for the villa across a bush-screened gravel bed. He was rewarded by the discovery of a proper path giving clear access to the villa's front entrance. Having progressed about half-way up this path, however, he was halted by the sudden eruption from the paving of a large box, or platform, which completely blocked his way. Before he could react in any way to this event the box sprang open with a rushing noise. Amid streamers of coloured paper there burst forth the corpulent figure of Olveolo Jadper, grinning and screeching, a large green bird rushing up from below him to flap around his head and go winging off. '*Hello!*' screeched Jadper, '*Hello!*' On his head was a white conical hat decorated with purple blobs which matched the red blobs of his ballooning white gown. His face was painted in the manner of a clown. Continuing to grin inanely, he bobbed up and down as if on a spring, only the top half of him visible over the rim of the box.

Mast suddenly realized that the figure was lifeless, and not Jadper at all. It was a jack-in-the-box. With a grunt of disgust he attempted to squeeze between the box and the close-packed cane shrubbery, but as he did so the dummy twisted round and seized him in two powerful rubbery arms, planting a slobbery kiss square on his lips. He fought violently to free himself from the embrace, the soft warm pseudo-flesh, the twinkling eyes. Jadper the jack-in-the-box giggled, caressing him intimately, then let him go.

At last, complaining bitterly to himself of Jadper's conduct, Mast reached the entrance to the villa, large double doors flanked by abbreviated barbican towers of the same yellow travertine, a sedimentary limestone quarried from deep hot springs which was used throughout the building. The doors opened at his approach, disclosing a cool and inviting circular vestibule. Restful light filtered through a green cupola supported by slim columns. The floor was a mosaic of tiles in various pastel colours.

Mast halted and peered hesitantly within.

'Olveolo Jadper?'

There was no reply. Cautiously he stepped through the doorway, noting the comic reliefs on the panels of tinted wainwood, and sauntered a few paces, and those warily, into the empty vestibule.

And then the floor seemed to open up all around him. All was confusion. He was being grabbed, tossed, interfered with. A flurry of movement and colour obscured everything. When the air cleared Mast found that he was stuffed feet first into a sort of cylindrical holder reaching to his waist. He was bouncing steadily up and down, supported above the floor by a giant spring. A clown's hat had been stuck on his head and, he suspected, a bulbous comic nose on his face. He wore a gaudy ruff. The entire arrangement was set in a large box, crudely painted in garish colours, with the lid gaping open to permit his regular oscillations. Facing him there bounced Olveolo Jadper, similarly situated, and looking very much like the articulated dummy Mast had encountered a minute or two earlier. As Mast rose Jadper descended, and vice versa. The inane motion, about which he could do nothing, infuriated Mast. He wondered how in Ziode it was possible to maintain any vestige of dignity in circumstances like these.

Jadper spoke to him in a voice of melodramatic hospitality, his eyes wide and staring. 'Ah, my guest has arrived! Greetings! The comforts of my house are yours!'

'For heaven's sake, Jadper!' cried Mast in strangled tones as he bounced up and down. 'Get me out of this!'

'Surely you don't wish to break off our business so soon?'

'Quit the joking!'

'First let us conclude our transaction.'

'Like this?'

'Why not? Whee! Up and down! Up and down!'

Mast struggled in sudden fury, and discovered that the cylinder holding him possessed no more binding power than stiff paper. He ripped it apart and clambered over the side of the box. Jadper followed suit, giggling to himself and throwing away his clown's hat, ruff and nose.

Once divested, Jadper was naked except for a phallocrypt held on by a silk string around his waist. He was a very fat man, with little twinkling eyes set in a bulging face. He approached Mast with a friendly smile, holding out his hand.

'Please excuse my little jest. Quite inexcusable, I know!'

Mast shook hands with him. His own hand came away covered in slime. He wiped it on his coat, then with a savage gesture tore off the clownish gear that bedizened him.

'As a joker you're a failure, Jadper,' he said peevishly. 'The essence of a joke is that it should come as a surprise. With you one is constantly expecting some sort of foolishness.'

The reproof seemed to have some effect on Jadper. His face became more sober. 'You're quite right, my dear fellow. It is very childish of me. Let's forget that nonsense, then, and get down to business. Please take a seat.'

He gestured. Mast glanced at the chair suspiciously, hesitating to accept it until Jadper had already seated himself opposite him. He sat down gingerly, expecting it to collapse. But it did no more than emit a rude farting noise, at which Jadper emitted a snort of repressed mirth.

'You have a load of garments to dispose of, I believe,' Jadper said.

'That's right. Caeanic garments.'

'Like this one, eh?' The Caeanic titfer appeared out of nowhere into Jadper's hand. He inspected it cursorily, then threw it across to Mast, who put it back on his head in place of his clown's hat.

'A neat little job, eh?' Jadper complimented. 'But of course, this is a bad time to be dealing in Caeanic stuff. You've heard the government's getting edgy, I suppose? I expect that's why you want to get rid of it.'

'No, I hadn't heard that,' Mast answered truthfully. 'I can't see that it makes any difference. The government's always worried about something or other.'

'Oh, I don't know . . . I had some inside griff the other day. Caean has made a formal protest. Something about a cargo of raiment stolen from a crashed ship. Coincidence, eh?' Jadper winked grotesquely. 'The Caeanics get paranoid about their togs, you know! The police might start looking for it. Things could be difficult.'

'Look,' said Mast, 'are you interested or not? I don't *have* to find a buyer. I'm told my goods are worth ultimately about twenty million, but I'm prepared to scale down that figure substantially to make a quick sale.'

'Hmm, I'd have to have someone look at them. Even if your valuation is right, what with all the risk and everything I doubt if I could even go as far as one million.' Jadper looked fretful, full of doubt. Mast was relieved; the fence had started trading.

'When do you want to inspect the goods?' he asked. 'Once they've been viewed even you will be ready to part with at least twelve million.' Then he became aware that something was happening to the chair he was sitting on. He tried to rise, but could not: he was fixed to it somehow.

The chair tilted back, rose from the floor and turned a half circle until he was facing Jadper upside down. It was as if his backside and spine were firmly glued to the chair. Presumably he was in the grip of an inertial field.

'I thought perhaps the day after tomorrow,' Jadper said seriously, displaying no sign that he noticed anything amiss. 'Where are you keeping them?'

'Let me down!' Mast cried in exasperation. 'This is intolerable!'

The chair released him and he fell sprawling to the floor, giving his skull a painful crack on the tiles. Jadper chuckled.

Mast scrambled to his feet, retrieving his hat and jamming it back on his smarting head. He brushed himself down and turned to Jadper gravely.

'I absolutely refuse to go through with this. How can I think straight when I'm being interfered with all the time?'

'I don't know,' Jadper said with a dismal shrug. 'It's not my fault.'

Mast deliberated. 'This house is as full of tricks as a rat-trap,' he said. 'If you want to carry on talking let's do it outside.'

'You want to go for a stroll? But of course!' Jadper jumped up with alacrity. 'It's a beautiful day! Let's go out on the lawn.'

Nervously Mast followed him through a door in the rear of the vestibule. They emerged on the other side of the house before an expansive, well-tended lawn of Harlos moss, a silky lavender-coloured growth which was generally preferred to earthgrass. Once in the open he felt safer.

Then, without warning, his hat deluged him with green ink. With a cry of frustration he snatched the titfer from his head, ripped it apart to see the cunning ink reservoir Jadper had planted there, and flung it away from him. He fumbled for a kerchief to wipe the dye from his face.

The prankster turned and grinned at Mast as they stepped across the moss. 'Lots of nice clothes, eh? Lovely!' He waved his left hand in a complicated motion and suddenly his flabby body was bedecked in dazzling finery. Glittering gold knee breeches, a tunic of silver and green stripes with puffed sleeves, and a gorgeous multi-hued sash. It was hardly Caeanic in quality, however – more like showy trash – and even as Jadper walked it was peeling from him, disintegrating and scattering until only ragged scraps remained.

How had Jadper performed the trick? Mast had seen nothing about his naked person from which to produce the coverings, flimsy though they were.

Jadper's tone dropped and became soberly confidential. 'I've been wondering if this lawn might be better with a pavilion on it,' he said. 'Something like this, perhaps.'

Again he waved his hand, making magic passes in the air. It was hard to see exactly what took place. The air shimmered and there were countless little rainbows, as if the sunlight was striking sprays of water. In seconds a small pavilion took shape, seeming to coalesce out of nothing. It had a façade of what looked like carved, painted wood, complete with arched windows and a brief veranda.

'Come inside,' Jadper invited.

'How do you do it?' Mast asked as they mounted the steps and passed to the shaded interior. He received no answer. The pavilion was unfurnished, and had a hurriedly erected, half-finished look. But it was solid. The floor sounded hollow beneath his tread. He tapped a wall with his knuckle. It was like matt plastic or fibrewood.

'A pleasant place to sit and drink with friends, perhaps,' Jadper suggested. 'What do you think? A better view of the garden might be in order.' He pointed with his finger and invisibly cut out large windows in the rear of the building, making available a view of the rest of the lawn and the flowers and trees beyond.

Jadper turned to him, his face bland. 'Well. How about the day after tomorrow, then? Where do you have your goods?'

'Tell your evaluator to meet me in the middle of town,' Mast said stubbornly. 'I'll take him to them.'

'Aha! Caution, caution!' Jadper tapped the side of his nose with his finger. 'All right, then. Afterwards you can come back here and we'll talk money.'

'I'd rather it was somewhere outside, preferably in public,' Mast said.

'Oh, come, come! Don't insult my hospitality!'

They sauntered back to the villa. From his manner one would think Jadper had ceased playing his jokes now. Mast pressed him once again to reveal how he was able to invoke clothing and buildings out of thin air.

'It's perfectly simple, really,' Jadper said. 'I'll show you.'

As they went into the vestibule Mast glanced back and saw that the pavilion had already begun to collapse and dissolve, the panels of the walls curling up like paper in a fire. Jadper disappeared through a side door and returned a few moments later carrying a cylinder with a handgrip and an array of nozzles.

'See.' He pointed the nozzles and pressed a grip. A set of furniture shimmered into being across the floor: a dining table, chairs, and a sideboard.

'There's an aerosol for everything these days,' Jadper chuckled. He opened the side of the cylinder and explained to Mast how the gadget worked. It was a programmed extrusion process controlled by insertable templates. Liquid plastic from a reservoir sprayed out in an atomized mist, hardening on contact with the air to form whatever structures the templates dictated.

The reservoir held an amazingly small volume of liquid. 'It mixes with the air to make practically any bulk you like,' Jadper told him. 'And those solid objects are ninety nine point nine per cent air.'

'Hence their lack of permanence,' Mast commented.

'Oh, they could be as durable as you like. But that would be in awful nuisance, don't you think? I use a mixture with an ingredient that makes them instantly degradable.'

'Ingenious,' admitted Mast, 'but I didn't see you use an aerosol in the garden.'

For an answer Jadper laid the gadget down on an occasional table and, using his right hand, disconnected his left hand at the wrist. 'I lost my real hand some years ago. Just making a virtue of necessity. Very *handy*, as you might say, for an amateur conjuror, eh?'

'Is that what you call yourself?' Mast responded drily. 'It's all very interesting.' He watched the dining table, the sideboard and the chairs suddenly lose strength and cave in on themselves, gradually dissolving to tatters and then to dust. It would make a good epitaph for the quality of Jadper's mind, he thought.

'There's an eating house called Mona's at the corner of Engraft Street,' he said. I'll be there at three after noon, the day after tomorrow. Can I look forward to seeing your man?'

Jadper fastened his left hand back on with a click. 'I'll let you know if he can't make it.'

'How many more gadgets have you got in that hand?' Mast asked, idly curious. 'No – don't show me. It doesn't matter. As our business seems to be concluded for the moment I'll be on my way.'

Hesitantly he stepped towards the door. Jadper raised the prosthetic hand in farewell.

'Good luck attend you!' he grinned.

As Mast passed through the doorway a bag of flour emptied over him from above. Jets of coloured fluid attacked him from several directions and he heard Jadper giggling and snorting behind him.

The step on the threshold gave way beneath his feet. He hurtled down a chute, where he felt metal fingers picking and tugging at him in the confused darkness. Seconds later he popped up again and found himself standing on the pathway some yards from the villa. He was wearing enormous pink pantaloons with purple spots, and an oversize baby's bib.

He tore the foolery from him, wiped his face free of flour and mush, and after a last acrimonious glance at the villa, dodged the flailing arms of the jack-in-the-box and fled towards the gate.

*

Peder braced his legs against the acceleration of the slim private elevator as it raced up the shaft to the summit of the 300-storey Ravier Building. The elevator was his very own now that he had rented the penthouse on the skyscraper's roof. It was one of several private shafts which served various levels of the tower.

The elevator slowed, giving him a momentary feeling of free fall, then slid smoothly to a stop. He stepped into the spacious main room of his apartment.

The view through the great curved window was still novel enough to cause him to pause to take it in. Gridira lay spread out below, sparkling in the sun. The River Laker curved round the south side of the city in the distance, glinting here and there where it became visible between buildings.

Definitely an improvement on Tarn Street!

He crossed the lounge to his desk. The vid had received a number of messages in his absence, mostly relating to his new business ventures. He replied to a few of these, giving instructions to his broker, to the manager of the new store he was opening in Gridira's main shopping avenue, and to his financier.

That done, he poured himself a glass of chilled mango liqueur and sauntered back and forth before the view window, his feet falling silently on the deep pile of the glowing carpet. It seemed to him as if he could fly through that window and wing over the cityscape, so perfect was his new-found sense of freedom and space.

A few months ago it would have seemed unbelievable that he could have made such swift progress. Yet facts were facts. Doors opened for him wherever he went. Possibilities became actualities. Bank managers offered credit. High-class social clubs did not refuse him membership out of hand.

He stopped to admire himself in the full-length mirror. 'No hesitation,' he murmured, repeating a private litany. 'No self-doubt, no solecisms.' It was true what he had read once in a book on practical psychology. If you maintained a positive attitude to the world it heaped benefits upon you.

The vid chimed. A red-lipped, violet-eyed face appeared on the plate, smiling at him. 'Hi.'

He drank in the curly black hair and curvy soft neck. In his imagination her perfume was practically wafting to him out of the picture plate. 'Hi.'

'I had no luck after you left the club last night,' she pouted. 'You took it all with you.'

'Well, it was my luck, wasn't it?' He recalled giving her his vid number when playing at the Coton, one of Gridira's most distinguished gambling clubs.

He had been learning to gamble with skill lately. It reminded him anew of how much things had changed for him, that he could now look forward to possessing so poised a creature and regard it as normal. Only weeks before he would have considered her quite unattainable.

Half an hour later she arrived in the penthouse. Peder offered her mango liqueur, and some smooth small-talk. It was not long before he fell on that delicious neck, nuzzling towards the source of her heady perfume.

In the bedroom he hesitated when it came to undressing. This is always the moment of uncertainty. Without the suit his old feeling of lumpish inadequacy came back, at the very time when he most needed confidence in himself.

But he flung his clothes from him and dived on to the big bed. 'No hesitation, no self-doubt, no solecisms,' he breathed in a private prayer, before his limbs entwined with hers.

Later, when the light had faded somewhat, they awoke from a drowsy sleep and she began to tease him. His body responded, but by this time he felt somehow unequal to her kittenish repartee.

On the ottoman, his Frachonard suit glowed softly in the dusk, as if calling to him.

6

Events perplexed Alexei Verednyev. They perplexed him not least of all because he was still alive. By now he should certainly be dead, killed by the cyborgs in some hideous and fiendish manner.

He must have slept, because there had been confused, horrible dreams. Then, when the cyborg had entered his prison, he had determined to sell his life dearly and had attacked and destroyed the monster. But the aftermath had not been what he had expected, because he was now being asked to believe that the *other* cyborgs, the new type with the missing organs, did not wish him any harm at all. Or at least, so the voice said. The female voice, which spoke his own language, but with odd pronunciation and strange words. The *new* cyborgs, she insisted, did not even come from Shoji; the cyborg he had killed had been their prisoner, just as he was. They had put it in his chamber just to see what the two of them would do. In fact, she said, the cyborgs of the space-cave were not the cyborgs at all. They were more akin to his own people, and had come from the distant stars.

'You are cyborgs,' Alexei had contradicted. 'I have eyes, I can see. You have altered yourselves a little, that is all. You have altered yourselves, as cyborgs are able to do, and have learned the Sovyan language, so as to trick me into giving you information about Homebase.' The more he thought about this the more obvious it seemed. The cyborgs were apt to roam uprange at this time, when Shoji and Sovya were in conjunction, and he should have been more careful.

Besides, it was common knowledge that cyborgs had no feelings and the female, like all other types of cyborg, was deaf and dumb on the emotional wavebands. His radio sense registered nothing at all from her in that respect, so her understanding of how Sovyans communicated was seriously deficient. She did not even respond to the insulting feelings of revulsion, disgust and defiance he was beaming at her.

Apart from that, these denizens of the space-cave were even more physically repulsive, if anything, than the usual vermin that came crawling up out of Shoji, were even more squishy, and resembled nothing so much as big mobile foetuses or internal core-organs. They were nauseating.

She showed him a picture of a new-born infant. 'You recognize this as a baby, don't you?' she challenged.

He turned away from the sight. He was squeamish about such things. They were only for doctors and nurses to see.

'This is how my own kind look at birth, too,' she said. 'It's certain the cyborgs look the same.'

'You are wrong. The young cyborg resembles the adult. The cyborgs cut their females open and operate on the foetuses.'

'Really? That's fascinating. But doesn't it all go to prove what I've been trying to tell you – that you, we and the cyborgs all belong to the same biological species?'

'No. It is impossible.'

She seemed exasperated by his obstinacy. 'Don't you realize that we saved your life?' She said angrily. 'If we hadn't picked you up when we did the cyborgs would have got you – there was a raft loaded with warriors on its way to you. And haven't we given you all your biological requirements, both oxygen and liquid nutrient? Would the cyborgs have bothered to do that?'

'Not until now.'

But eventually he had begun to believe her. Her patience wore down his brave tirades and he found himself following her arguments.

She did not try to wheedle any military information out of him, but in the end she did ask him to describe his life in Homebase. And so he began to talk of home, that happy Eden of rocky islets girdling gassy Sovya . . .

For many years Amara Corl had cherished a scientific ambition: to transform sociology, her chosen subject, into a branch of knowledge as exact as the sciences of chemistry and physics, able to calculate the social forces acting on an individual as precisely as the forces of gravity or nuclear energy could be calculated.

All that was needed, she believed, was to find the underlying principles by which these forces operated. But her search for such principles had so far been frustrating. Ziodean civilization was too capricious for one to be able to pin individual characteristics to a graph-board as neatly as she would have liked. For that reason she had turned to the study of aberrant cultures, such as the Caeanic – though even that did not go far enough for her purposes, her reasoning being that the major signposts of social consciousness would best show themselves at the limits of extremity and bizarreness. She had even toyed with the idea of creating a suitable culture artificially, perhaps taking over an orphanage for the purpose, but unfortunately the government had declined to co-operate in such a scheme. Sociology was not officially regarded as a practical science, and the Directorate always wanted change out of any projects it financed.

Nevertheless Amara's approach to the subject had given her a useful reputation for toughness. She flourished in the study theme set up to make an appraisal of the Caeanic menace. When the *Callan* expedition had been mooted, she had grabbed at the opportunity with both hands.

'We are going to have to fight a war with Caean,' she began when, shortly after her sessions with Alexei Verednyev, she addressed the ship's company of officers and social scientists for an important orientation meeting. 'That is Fact Number One. All reputable psychologists are agreed that the Caeanics will not, in the long run, be able to control their quasi-religious conviction that their way of life is the only one for mankind. When their desire to convert their neighbours becomes irresistible, as we believe is now happening, they will launch their crusade.

'That is why we are here – to try to find weaknesses in the Caeanic aberration that can be used to our advantage. Ladies and gentlemen, we can now claim *to have solved the essential mystery of Caean*. We have discovered the historical origin of the Cult of Attire!'

Her eyes gleamed with triumph as she delivered this news, which though already known to most of her staff was a bomb-shell to many of the ship's officers. After a pause to let it sink in, she resumed.

'As you all know, three weeks ago we hauled aboard a metal object which turned out to contain a man in a much atrophied state. The metal "suit" in which he was encased proved to be his habitat. He thinks of it, in fact, as his "body".' She operated the playback, taping pictures of their 'suit-man' – the metalloid, as Estru had dubbed him – to the demonstration screen. The edited sequence showed him jetting through space, then being pulled through the lock. Briefly she let them see him in the engineering service room, the suit cut open to show its organic cargo.

'The subject's name is Alexei Verednyev, and he speaks a variant of Russian, an ancient Earth language which was thought to be extinct. I have now talked to him extensively and have learned a great deal about his life and the society he comes from. It is a life spent completely in space – indeed his countrymen imagine no other kind of life – during which he never consciously leaves his suit. After birth a child lives in a nursery canister until he can be fitted with his first space-suit, which occurs at the age of three months. At intervals the suit is changed until the child grows to full size, at which time he is fitted with his final suit. During each change-over he is anaesthetized. He never in his whole life sees his organic body.

'The suits are elaborate machines supplying every need. The man – or woman – as we know him has vanished into the suit. He has no consciousness or memory of his organic body; the suit has become his body. Its systems are *his* systems in just the same way that his native biological systems are. The data-processing unit that regulates these systems could logically be regarded as an adjunct to the motor and autonomic functions of his organic brain.

'So complete is the identification that the recipient has even been persuaded to accept the exterior of a spacesuit as an erotic stimulus. Watch this.'

With a wry smile Amara rolled the playback to show their first sighting of Alexei with Lana. The two suits were grappling, jockeying for position, thrusting together.

'Copulation between male and female suits.'

The gathering watched the brief exhibition in fascination. One of Wilce's officers uttered a sigh. 'Imagine living your life cased up like that. It must be awful.'

'You're looking at it the wrong way. This is *not* a man in a suit. It's a new kind of creature: a metal space-creature with an organic core. In fact the suit-people are no longer capable of descending to a planetary surface: they are space-dwellers in the fullest sense of the word. Their home is in a Saturn ring system belonging to a nearby gas giant they call Sovya. The rocks comprising the rings provide all the materials they need. They also hollow out some of them for various purposes, such as to make protected nurseries.

'The Sovyan suit-people also have enemies, and here they are.'

She showed them the pictures of the cyborgs. First the prisoner strapped to the board like a specimen awaiting dissection. Then the scene aboard the raft. She panned in on the cowled figure in the middle.

Then she showed them the giant suit butchering the captured cyborg. 'We'll come on to those in a moment.'

She licked her lips. 'You'll want to know how this extraordinary situation arose. That's something Alexei

Verednyev wasn't able to tell me. As far as he knows things have always been that way. I had to resort to the ship's library to put the picture together. So prepare for a little history lesson.

'A thousand years ago Earth was still the focus of political power for the whole of mankind. By that time there had already been a great spread of activity throughout the galaxy, and there was a great rivalry between various nations, but all those nations were Earth nations. This seems odd to us, of course. We are used to thinking of a nation as something consisting of many planets, hundreds of planets as likely as not, and for a number of autonomous cultures to coexist on the same globe strikes us as contradictory. Yet this was the case on Earth, not only prior to the galactic expansion but for some decades afterwards. And despite their small base many of these Earth-rooted nations managed to retain their power during the initial years of galactic exploitation, and not only that but actually to increase it.

'Two such national powers were the USSR – also called Russia – and Japan. There had always been a traditional feud between these two countries. At the time we are speaking of they had managed to be at war with one another in various parts of the galaxy for nearly a hundred years – including, for a brief time, in the Tzist Arm. Perhaps they felt themselves to be over-extended here, for apparently they withdrew. But it seems certain that in the process both sides left behind them sizeable pockets of personnel and equipment, cut off and marooned, with no way of getting home, right here where we are now. How did this happen? We'll never know. Perhaps this tiny system was simply overlooked in the drama and confusion of the withdrawal. Perhaps the task forces fighting here were thought to have been destroyed.

'Most human beings would have seen no alternative but to die in such a hopeless situation. This system is not a fit abode for human life. There are no habitable worlds. There is only one planet where man can set foot at all – Shoji, a tiny world a short distance sunward of here. These old enemies, however, were both of them peoples possessed of an unusual tenacity. They both developed remarkable, though different, adaptations to their circumstances. And they both, after a fashion, survived.

'The Russian survival tactic we have already seen in the society of the suit-people. The Japanese solution was something else again. They were already in possession of Shoji, fifteen hundred miles in diameter, arid, cold, with a thin unbreathable atmosphere, and totally inhospitable. To survive these horrid conditions the Japanese "cyborgated" themselves, that is to say, they redesigned the human body, blending it with artificial machine-organs.'

She played the cyborg pictures again. 'Respiratory, vascular and homeostatic systems have all been entirely replaced, and there have been serious inroads also into the nervous and hormonal systems. Remarkable as it seems, these modifications can adapt the human organism to the most unlikely of environments, including the void, without any need of protective covering. The surface of Shoji is their natural habitat, but they make frequent forays into space, usually in order to attack the descendants of the Russians – that is to say, the suit-people.

'Alexei Verednyev has not been too forthcoming about cyborg life, but what details I have gleaned from him are fascinating. The cyborg *ethos* would seem to be a fairly direct derivative of certain strains of Earth Japanese culture, going on what little we know of the latter. Here we have a *yakusa bonze*.'

She stopped the tape at the picture of the cowled figure on the space raft. 'A *bonze* is a religious priest; *yakusa* originally meant gangster. Religion and gangsterism seem to have gone hand in hand in Japan; a *yakusa* organization led by a Buddhist abbot once forcibly took over the Japanese government. Though it's rather hard to say whether the cyborgs still have religion, the individual in the cowl is doubtless by way of being a "warrior monk" wielding considerable power.

'The cyborg culture is fanatical and aggressive. To a cyborg, death means nothing. Suicide missions against enemies – which necessarily means the suit-people, of course – are traditional. It's a pity we can't take time off to investigate them fully, but that would be too lengthy a digression from our main task. We lack so much of the starting data, anyway. We don't even have a record of the Japanese language, for instance.'

Captain Wilce interrupted in surprise. 'Why is that, Amara? After all, you can speak Russian well enough.'

Amara smiled indulgently. 'Most aboriginal Earth cultures are a closed book to us, as it happens. Remember that cultures tend to be mutually exclusive; they don't like being crowded together on one planet. When the expansion into the galaxy took place they demonstrated their natural magnetic repulsion for one another. They separated out on a large scale. Our knowledge of ancient Earth is confined mostly to the culture called the Euro-American, from which both Tzist and Ziode are descended. There must also be regions of the galaxy dominated by the Japanese, the Arabs, the Afros and so on – all peoples with whom we have no contact. The cyborgs are an oddity, a remnant of a war the Japanese lost.'

The screen died as she switched off the playback.

'Now let's see what we can deduce from these facts. Although we have no proof of it as yet, I think we can take it for granted that at some date in the past some of the suit-people escaped from this system and migrated farther along the Tzist Arm. Possibly they managed to build a relativistic drive, or perhaps Sovya was discovered by later explorers who took them along as passengers or captives. In time the suit-people abandoned their suits and colonized habitable planets, becoming human again. They became, in fact Caeanic civilization; there is little doubt that the Sovyan phenomenon is the source of the entire Caeanic aberration!'

Her words provoked a stir among the ship's officers. 'You mean the Caeanics are all descendants of these Sovyans?' Navigator Hewerl asked.

'No, not all by any means. The Sovyans were the *first* settlers, the cultural matrix to which later migrants had to conform. This is usually the case when new territories are opened up. The first culture to arrive pre-empts all options and absorbs later arrivals. In the process some watering-down of the original aberration occurs of course, but – God, you can imagine what it must have been like when the Sovyans first came out of their suits.

'Well, there it is. Everything we find bizarre and exaggerated in Caeanic mentality can be traced back to the time when their Sovyan forebears, the prototype Caeanics, buried themselves in their space canisters. The correspondence really is quite remarkable in all details. The Sovyans replaced the natural body form with an artificial exterior – *ergo* the Caeanics are obsessed with bodily covering. To the Sovyans the natural body is physically repulsive – as repulsive, in fact, as we find our own intestines – *ergo* the Caeanics have a horror of nudity.'

She paused. 'Another aspect of this business is also quite interesting. Although the Sovyans have conditioned themselves to see their machine-nature as beautiful, and have arrogated to the human body the distaste we would feel for our internal organs, it's doubtful if the brain's instinctive levels can ever really forget what a human being *should* look like. It's worth nothing that, for the sake of his sanity, a suit-man must avoid looking at his organic body. The danger is probably that he will subconsciously recognize the body as his *real* body, repulsive as it is. Along with this would come the repressed knowledge of what was done to that body in the collective past. So we have self-disgust, and for another reason, racial guilt all in the same emotional charge. I needn't enlarge on the implications of that.'

'A version of original sin, as it were?' Captain Wilce said.

She nodded to him, politely amused.

'Is that why the suit-people hate the cyborgs so much?' someone else asked. 'Because the cyborg body stimulates this subconscious memory?'

'They have good practical reasons for hating them, also. But it explains the totally irrational element in that hatred, yes.'

'Do you think the Caeanics themselves know how they originated?'

'I'm quite confident that they don't know, which already gives us an advantage over them – an advantage we must learn to exploit. So unless there are further questions we can now discuss our future programme. First we must investigate Sovyan society as thoroughly as we can, then we must travel farther along the Tzist Arm and try to trace out the pattern of the early settlements. I have no doubt that as we research the worlds stretched out between here and central Caean we shall unearth the cultural bones and fossils – the customs, mores and mythologies – that will show us how the mentality of the suit-people evolved into the Art of Attire.'

She frowned. 'But first we have a little problem. We have to gain the co-operation of the suit-people in *Domashnabaza* – that's what they call the ring system encircling Sovya. It's proving a difficult enough job to win the trust of Verednyev, though I'm slowly bringing him round. In view of our closer resemblance to the cyborgs, our reception there is likely to be anything but friendly.'

There was silence for a while. Suddenly Estru's lined face puckered with amusement. 'There isn't any problem, Armara. We'll go out to meet them in spacesuits

– those big jobs, self-propelled with plenty of armour and opaque face-plates. Provided we don't let them see the interior of the *Callan*, the Sovyans will take us for a species cognate to themselves, not to the cyborgs.'

'Yes, of course,' Amara replied slowly. 'All we have to do is keep them out of the *Callan* and represent ourselves as "metalloids" like them. But it means we won't be able to use Verednyev as a liaison, as I had intended. We'll have to keep him under wraps or he'll blow the gaff on us.'

'So we are to keep him prisoner,' Captain Wilce said gravely.

'It's better we retain control of him for a while. I've put in a lot of work on him.'

'Presumably we are going to let him go eventually,' Navigator Hewerl added uneasily.

'Any more questions?' Amara snapped.

But Hewerl would not let go. 'What do we say to his people about him? They must know we have him – there was a witness to his capture. They'll want to know where he is.'

'The cyborgs . . .' Amara began, then checked herself. She disliked this kind of interrogation. 'I'll handle that point when we come to it. Doubtless Verednyev will still be able to play some sort of role in our dealings. Right, then, everything's settled. If Captain Wilce is agreeable we can make the move at the beginning of the next shift.' She raised her eyebrows to Wilce, obtaining his nod. 'So get a good night's sleep, everyone. We have a busy day tomorrow.'

Abruptly she turned and departed through a door to her left. The briefing was over.

You had to hand it to Amara, Estru thought. She was overbearing, but she brought results.

There had been a time when he had privately scorned the whole idea of searching for pre-Caeanic origins. Yet here they were, right on target, suited up and smack in the middle of the Caeanic prototype – a prototype that was as unsuspected as it was incredible.

He and Amara emerged from the mouth of a caverned-out asteroid where they had been inspecting a food factory. Accompanying them was Sarkisov, their Sovyan guide. His bulking metal form waited patiently on the threshold while they paused to take in the view once more.

It was quite a sight. All around them were the spreading fields of rock and ice chunks, a seemingly limitless labyrinth that shifted and slid together as the rings orbited, creating the illusion of grottoes and deep canyons constantly merging and melting into one another. It was the constant motion that made the perfect silence so eerie, Estru thought. And then there was the light – a limpid, soft, lucid radiance which made the fragmented rock and ice glow, which was sent endlessly spearing and reflecting through the apparent infinity of slowly dissolving grottoes.

Sovya, the gas giant, filled more than a third of the sky, her vast globe glimmering, glinting and flashing with the storms exploding deep within her atmosphere. Compared with that angry, raging world the airless realm of the rocks was calm and idyllic, a paradise that was to the suit-people what meadows, forests and lush watered valleys were to planet dwellers.

What Estru thought of as the eternal silence of the rings was in one sense spurious, however. It did not extend to the world of human intercourse: on the radio wavebands *Domashnabaza* was alive with talk. Yet a casually traversing eye might have failed to notice the Sovyan civilization at all, given the rings' span of two hundred thousand miles. Only if one knew exactly what to look for did the miracle make itself evident. Estru, turning up his helmet's vid magnification, could pick out the larger, asteroid-seized rocks that had been converted into permanent caves, platforms and casemates, many of them sculpted into elegant shapes. Some maintained group formations by automatic course adjustment. Others were linked together by chains. Many carried powerful steel buffers to absorb the shock of the collisions that frequently occurred, albeit gently, as the rocks drifted along. Also visible were metallic glints that were crowds of suit-men on the move. A large glint, intermittently visible as the rocks shifted, was the *Callan*.

Amara, encased like himself in a brass-coloured, heavily armoured spacesuit, spoke to their metalloid guide.

'*Ochen interesno. Nu, mozhete nam pokazat dyetkiye sady?*'

With difficulty Estru followed her Sovyan Russian: 'Very interesting, but how about letting us see the nurseries?'

Sarkisov's reply was deep-bellied and indignant. '*Takiye lichnye veshchi nye ochen piyatno smotret!*' 'Such matters are not pleasant to see, or for our eyes!'

Estru sighed. Determined to keep treading on taboos, Amara had persisted in her impudent demands throughout their stay in *Domashnabaza* (literally, Homebase). She had even pressed to be shown the hospitals – a suggestion which to the Sovyans was nauseating.

She just didn't seem to appreciate, either, that her metalloid disguise was far from perfect and that to the Sovyans she was a far from reassuring sight. The Ziodean suits measured only seven feet in height as compared with the Sovyans' twelve, so that they must have resembled fantastic little goblins in Sovyan eyes. There were other physical differences, too. The Ziodean helmet was quite different from the Sovyan head, which was a robotic type of structure lacking any organic content. Even more discerning, from the Sovyans' point of view, must have been the fact that the Ziodean spacesuits possessed legs, which were quite redundant in a purely spatial environment.

Estru did not blame them for becoming both exasperated and suspicious. Several times they had asked to see Alexei Verednyev, and were far from satisfied with Amara's evasive explanations as to why he did not appear.

Peremptorily the huge suit-man motioned them along the lip of the food asteroid's slot-like opening. While Amara continued to argue, Estru taped in his recorder and added notes to his running commentary.

'Life in the rings is highly mobile. Although there is no weather, leaving aside bursts of solar radioactivity, and therefore no proper need of shelter, the Sovyans maintain private dwellings which have propulsors and can move about the rings at will, each emitting a coded radio address by which it can be located at any time, thanks to a public triangulation service.

'The economy of the rings is centrally directed and rests on communal decisions alone. Food, fuel, artifacts and services are distributed free, every individual sharing in their production as a matter of obligation. This unusual arrangement possibly springs from the early Russian economy, which also prized group activity above individual enterprise. On the other hand it could have arisen as the best answer to the difficulties of wresting survival from extra-planetary surroundings.

'We have found out why it is that the metalloids frequently emit UHF. It seems that these emissions are emotional, non-verbal communications. The Sovyans, of course, are unable to communicate by facial expression, possessing nothing you would care to own as a face. We surmise that these UHF transmissions compensate for this deficiency.'

He broke off as Amara suddenly spoke to him. 'Sarkisov is getting hostile,' she said. 'Do you think I've pushed him too far?'

'Yes, I do.'

'He's been going on about Verednyev again. Claims we've got him in a Faraday cage!' She sounded annoyed.

'We *have* got him in a Faraday cage,' Estru said resignedly. 'If you think we're in danger I'll call Captain Wilce.'

She seemed not to have heard him. 'There's something going on,' she said excitedly. 'I think he's talking to someone a long way off. See if you can pick it up, Estru.'

Obediently he tuned his receiver, more elaborate than hers, up and down the scale, trying to find the wavelength Sarkisov was using. Whistlings and hummings, together with momentary babbles of Sovyan Russian, the living background of the rings, assailed his ears. Finally he pin-pointed a transmission which appeared to be beamed directly this way. Several voices were speaking on it, but from the rapid talk he picked out one repeated word.

Kiborg – Kiborg – Kiborg.

Cyborg!

Abruptly the voices stopped. Sarkisov's head section rotated slightly, as though searching the sky.

Amara spoke up brightly in Sovyan. 'Well then, we'd be interested in seeing some more public utility installations. What about—' But Sarkisov cut her off.

'Instead *I* would like to see the inside of *your* installations, the *Callan*,' he said brusquely.

'Well, it's difficult . . .' she said slowly.

'Where is the difficulty? Our comrade Alexei Verednyev is already there – as a prisoner!'

'No, no, not a prisoner,' objected Amara. 'He is with us by choice. You have spoken to him!'

'He speaks only when you take him out of the Faraday cage. The rest of the time you keep him in the cage so we cannot hear him. What would you tell us if he could speak freely?'

'He is *not* in a Faraday cage,' Amara lied.

'I will tell you what I think,' the Sovyan said calmly. 'You have told us you are our cousins, creatures like us from a far star. We have accepted your word and answered your questions, expecting to learn of your people in return. But perhaps you have deceived us. It is possible you are cyborgs wearing body-masks, seeking to trick information on *Domashnabaza* out of us.'

'Your surmise is *completely* unjustified,' she told him. Then she made an aside to Estru. 'Better call Captain Wilce.'

But before he could do anything Wilce's own voice came through his earphones. 'Is anything happening out there? We are being surrounded by Sovyan militia. They have some heavy equipment.'

Sarkisov spoke again. 'Well, in any case we must take you to a place of safety. There has been a large cyborg attack and there is fighting nearby.'

'We are sorry to hear it. But we would prefer to withdraw to our ship,' Amara said coldly.

'Out of the question. Follow me, please.'

Estru replied to Wilce, 'We have trouble too, Captain. I think we are being arrested on suspicion of being cyborg spies. We need a rescue party.'

'Very well.' Wilce's tone was clipped and efficient. 'We'll pull you out.'

With astonishing speed, four more Sovyans now jetted in to assist Sarkisov. It was useless to try to escape the towering metalloids; compliantly Amara and Estru obeyed Sarkisov's order and rose from the surface of the asteroid, to be escorted at high velocity on a winding path through the shining rubble.

The journey lasted several minutes, until finally there loomed ahead of them one of the few wholly artificial structures Estru had seen in the rings. It was a huge metal dodecahedron, drifting among the rocks like a giant shimmering diatom, all of two hundred yards in diameter. Suit-men flitted through a single huge portal, reminding Estru of the entrance to a beehive.

He heard Captain Wilce again. 'I'm sorry, but we're having trouble getting a party to you. We are under attack ourselves. What's your situation?'

'We are approaching a big artificial asteroid,' Estru told him. 'Can you see it?'

'Yes we have been tracking you. Are you in any immediate danger?'

'It's hard to say how decided the Sovyans' conclusions about us are. It seems the rings have just come under cyborg attack, which has made them edgy.'

'Understandable. Keep me informed.'

They passed into the dodecahedron. Estru examined the interior with some interest. It was constructed on some complicated open-plan system. From the peripheral walls jutted a maze of metal screens, but the central space, across which Sovyans soared to and fro, was left undivided apart from being criss-crossed by slender retaining girders. Estru found the place impressive.

Now their guards were herding them through the peripheral maze until they arrived at a meshed and gridded cage. For a moment Estru heard Captain Wilce beginning to speak to him again, then he and Amara were both pushed roughly into the cage and the gate closed behind.

He became aware of a sudden deadness in his transceiver.

They were in a Faraday cage, blocking them off from all radio communication.

Up until now Estru had not really been able to think of the Sovyans as anything more than truncated, rather pathetic human beings huddling inside their protective metal encasements. When he had coined the word 'metalloid' it had been as a disparaging joke. But the suit-men's swift and unhesitating actions had changed all that. Suddenly they seemed more capable and intelligent than his prejudices had formerly allowed him to admit. They had become what Amara had always said they were: a new species, wholly at harmony with their own nature.

One small detail during the journey to the dodecahedron had struck him with particular force – the way the antennae arrays surrounding the suit-men's heads and shoulders automatically shifted and turned as they darted unerringly through the rock fields. It was such a natural movement, yet completely non-human. The Sovyans really had adopted a new form of physical existence.

Yet in a purely technical sense the suits were not even particularly sophisticated. Ziodean technicians could have produced a version half the size and twice as efficient. Still, for their purpose they were fully effective. The biological and the technical parts of the new entity functioned as a unit. Oxygen was required to be imbibed only once every thirty hours, and then only to top up the reserve tank since the suit was able to split exhaled carbon dioxide. 'Biofood', a thick fluid whose waste content was minimal, was taken once in ten hours. 'Technofood' consisted of a small amount of lubricating oil and energy for the electrical systems, which came from an isotope battery replaced every fifty days and a solar cell back-up.

For the next half-hour Estru and Amara kept themselves busy, adding notes to their running commentaries on everything they saw. The scene put Estru more and more in mind of a beehive – and the Sovyans reminded him particularly of the bullet-bees found on his home planet of Migrat.

He could not deduce the purpose of the dodecahedral building. It contained a great deal of machinery which was being evacuated through the exit as time went on, and the numbers of suit-men in it also decreased. It could, he thought, be a military centre. He reflected that the Sovyans had suffered these attacks for centuries, and presumably knew how to deal with them. The assault would no doubt be followed by a retaliatory raid on Shoji – though the suit-men, being unable to land on the enemy planet, could do little more than bombard its surface.

At length Estru and Amara ran out of remarks to put on record, and still no rescue party arrived from the *Callan*. They looked at one another. Estru knew that, though she tried not to show it, Amara was even more scared than he was.

'What do you think's happened?' she said hesitantly.

'I dread to think.'

'Could the *Callan* . . .'

'Have been captured? It's possible. But don't write us off too soon. We haven't been waiting all that long. Maybe it's taking Wilce a bit of time to extricate himself.'

'It will be really awful if—' she began, and then a gasp of shock caused Estru to look the way her helmet was facing.

One of the dodecahedron's pentagonal walls was bursting inwards. Through the imploding rent, accompanied by the icy light of the rings, floated a dozen space-rafts crammed with cyborg warriors.

What followed was horrifying. Only a few Sovyans remained in the dodecahedron. The cyborgs swarmed throughout the structure, hunting them down and slaughtering them in a frenetic orgy. The suit-men were shot, burned, battered to junk with huge hammers. They fought back as best they could, occasionally blowing pale bodies to shreds with rocket-driven shells, but they were outnumbered and their situation was hopeless.

The ferocity of it all terrified the two Ziodeans, floating in their cage in frozen fascination. Then a moan of fright escaped Amara as one of the rafts drifted slowly by them only a few yards away.

The gowned figure they had encountered a week earlier stood on the raft. Leisurely the cyborg gangster abbot turned his body to look them over, his cowl thrown back, his face, with its bizarre mouth and black eyes, appearing cruel, supercilious, amused. Estru felt like a hypnotized rabbit.

The *yakusa bonze* was gross. The loose gown was open and drawn aside so that he could rest his puffy hands on the pommels of two huge curved swords which were thrust into a sash-like belt, to which also were clipped dozens of appurtenances. Swelling over the belt was a vast belly, corrugated and metal-studded.

A semi-circular plate of gold apparently bisected his brain and jutted out from the skull, each half of which sported its own control turret. The psychological implications of that division intrigued Estru, but he had no time to think about it. He felt only relief when the warrior abbot turned away from them, his attention taken by something else.

A captured Sovyan was being goaded across the dodecahedron by jerking cyborgs. The *bonze* floated up from his raft and went out to his meet his enemy, drawing the two great swords with a swift, vigorous motion.

His divided brain clearly did not detract from his physical prowess. A normal man, in normal gravity, would have needed two hands to control just one of those unwieldy blades, but the *bonze*, a sword in each hand, executed a dazzling series of movements, using each weapon to counterbalance the torque of the other. Then the shimmering blades whirled like propellers as he fell to destroying the suit-man, slicing through the metal body with astonishing ease. In less than a minute the Sovyan had been hacked to pieces and his gruesome wreckage drifted through the void.

It was impossible not to feel the tribal energy of the exulting cyborgs as the abbot turned his back on the scene, his twin swords smeared with blood and oil, and again approached the Faraday cage.

In panic Amara and Estru retreated to the far side of their prison. The incredible swordblades flashed, hacking their way through the meshed gridwork. A tumult of Japanese babble burst through the Ziodeans' earphones the instant the wires were scythed away. Then more of the creatures joined in, tearing the cage apart and reaching for its contents. The hysterical babble became deafening.

Then, at that moment, the whole dodecahedron seemed to implode. A great gap was riven in the side of the building. Shrieking hoarsely, the cyborgs turned to face the new threat.

The bulky shape of the *Callan* was visible hovering beyond the shattered wall. Driveboats were steering themselves into the dodecahedron, firing on the cyborgs and picking them off in dozens. Captain Wilce's promised rescue party had arrived at last.

Amara patted her frizzled, purple-dyed hair into place. Though badly shaken, she was rapidly recovering her composure.

'You certainly took your time,' she chided in a carefully controlled voice.

Knowing how close a thing it had been, Captain Wilce was not inclined to take the reproof as a joke. 'It was the best we could do,' he said gravely. 'We had some nasty moments. The Sovyans managed to do us a bit of damage, I'm afraid. As a matter of fact the arrival of the cyborgs took them off our backs and enabled us to get to you.'

The explorer ship had withdrawn from *Domashnabaza*. Through the bridge's observation dome they could see the ring system a couple of million miles away, arcing through space like a rainbow. Wilce, his back to the view, was stuffing herbs into a smoking tube. 'We've spoiled our welcome all round one way and another, I reckon,' he said equably. 'It might even be our brush with the cyborg raft that brought on this onslaught. What are your ideas now, Amara?'

'We'll move on,' she said shortly. 'We've collected enough data here to be going on with. It wouldn't be very easy getting more, anyway. The defence problem, as you point out, Captain.'

She laughed nervously. As they had left she had seen the cyborgs sacking what might have been a nursery or a hospital.

Estru had been gazing at the rings. He turned to her. 'Before we move shall I release Verednyev?'

Amara frowned. 'Eh? What for?'

He shrugged. 'I presume it was our intention eventually.'

'Well you presume wrong,' she snapped. 'These people are nothing but savages, cyborg and Sovyans alike. We've right to collect specimens where it bears on the security of Ziode. I want him for study, do you hear?

He stays with us!' She barely refrained from stamping her foot.

Resigned, Estru shrugged again.

Captain Wilce issued orders. The *Callan* moved into the interstellar velocity bracket. In minutes they had left behind the tiny, dark, forsaken planetary system where, against all the odds, man had survived, and set themselves to go probing yet farther along the Tzist Arm.

7

It must be admitted that the psychology of Caeanic Man differs substantially from that of Ziodean Man. Caeanic culture has performed the extraordinary feat of projecting its consciousness entirely into exterior forms. The upbringing of a Caeanic, indeed the whole of his social training, conditions his mind to respond in a chameleon-like manner to the adornments he dons. A naked Caeanic is a mental blank, like a man without limbs or a man paralysed, and he almost never allows himself to be so discommoded. For all occasions there are suitable garments; sleeping, taking a bath, fornicating, even childbirth. In normal circumstances it is never necessary for him to see his naked form, and if he does it is a private glimpse devoid of self-image.

A Caeanic, even an educated Caeanic, will be amused if a foreigner should suggest to him that his dependence on raiment is a cultural weakness. To him the benefits of the Art of Attire are self-evident. He will point out that these personality assists with which he invests himself are donned entirely by choice, and give him a greater command over his own mind than is possessed by the average Ziodean, who is subject to all kinds of uncontrollable moods and deficiencies.

Arth Matt-Helver, *Travels in the Tzist Arm*

'Just look at that guy! He's riding on a cloud!'

Castor's eyes glittered enviously as he read the newscast. The cast sheet showed a picture of a social function at the manse of an important Directorate minister. Among those raising their glasses to toast the minister, plain as day, was Peder Forbarth, outshining everyone, even the minister, as a paragon of elegance, of charm and grooming. By some photographic accident he, not the government supremo, seemed somehow to be the object of the occasion.

Mast sat wearing a pale heliotrope frock-coat and a cyan chemise. He glanced at the picture, eyebrows raised in affected unconcern, as Castor brought it over to him.

'I wouldn't have believed it,' Castor said in a gruff voice. 'A creep like that, making out like he was some sort of genius. How does he do it, boss?'

Mast sniffed delicately. Castor's revelation was not news to him. Anyone who paid even cursory attention to Gridira's social columns – as Mast did – might have noticed that a new star had appeared in the firmament: Peder Forbarth, successful entrepreneur (and so far as could be judged, legitimate to boot) and fast-rising social-ite, a man who had found the path to fortune and fame and was travelling it at speed. Lesser socialites, to whose gossip Mast was also occasionally privy, even rumoured that Forbarth could be in line for one of the much coveted posts in the Directorate's Economic Co-ordination Net-work, a loosely-knit organization of great power, where the opportunities for self-aggrandisement were not far short of enormous.

And all in the space of less than a year! Mast did not successfully hide from himself the thought that he would have done better to continue cultivating his relationship with the one-time sartorial.

'It's never a good idea to get too close to the govern-ment,' he said nonchalantly. 'Did Grawn go for my food?'

'Yeah,' answered Castor vaguely, still studying the picture. They were in Mast's own apartment in Rata, a reasonably opulent district of Gridira. The apartment was tastefully appointed, though a little flamboyant, perhaps, and of sufficient size for his needs – not too spacious but large enough so that he did not feel cramped.

Mast also rented a room in the cellar of the same building for the use of Castor and Grawn. Every day he allowed them up to spend a short time with him, so that he could keep an eye on them.

Grawn entered bearing a covered tray.

'Ah!' said Mast with gusto, uncovering the tray. He began to eat fried pork balls with centres of chilled pineapple, garnished with sautéed purple legumes. He washed the meal down with swigs of plum wine. Meanwhile Castor, to his faint annoyance, was loudly advertising Peder Forbarth's new career to Grawn.

When he had finished eating Mast pushed aside the tray, swallowed the last of the wine in the carafe and wiped his mouth with neat dabs of a napkin. He turned to face his sidekicks.

'I'll tell you how he does it,' he said firmly. 'It's that suit.'

Grawn's face became a ludicrously ugly picture of puzzlement as he squinted again at the newscast sheet. 'The suit he's wearing?'

'That's the suit he got off the Caeanic ship,' Castor said.

'That's right,' Mast concurred. 'The suit I let him have when we were on our way home from Kyre. He owes everything to that suit.' He snorted contemptuously, gesturing to the sheet with a limp hand. 'Remember the creep? He could never have made the grade in a high-class setting like that. He'd have been falling all over the tables. It's the suit that does it.' He became thoughtful.

'That can't be it,' Castor said finally. 'A suit of clothes can't make all that difference.'

'*This* suit can,' Mast explained. 'The Caeanics have some secret skill when it comes to making clothes. They can make you a changed man, make you become something you're not, give you new abilities. All Caeanic clothes have that quality to some degree. This suit,' he added, 'is obviously something special. Whoever owns it becomes rich and famous, that's clear.'

'Caeanic clothes can be *that* good?' Grawn exclaimed. 'But that's magic, boss!' He laughed in glee. 'A magic suit!'

'Science,' Mast corrected with condescending patience. 'It's a particular science that Caeanics have. Like hypnotism.'

'You should never have given it to him, boss,' Castor said reprovingly.

'Hm. Perhaps not.' Forbarth, Mast reflected – not for the first time – had evidently tricked him. He must have known there was something special about the suit, but he had said nothing so as to keep it for himself. No wonder he had been so willing to pull out.

'Well?' Castor looked at Mast challengingly, his re-paired eyes glittering more brightly, as they always did when he was excited. He also had jumped to the obvious conclusion. 'That punk robbed us! That suit should be ours!'

'I can see it on you now, boss!' Grawn crowed, as if in congratulation. 'You'd look great in it!'

'Then maybe we could start moving again,' Castor con-tinued earnestly, hunching his shoulders forward. There was something snake-like, almost predatory, in the way he was importuning Mast.

'Are you calling me ineffectual?' Mast retorted.

'You said yourself, that suit gives Forbarth the edge over everybody. Okay, so maybe it hypnotizes everybody around him or something. I've heard of stranger things. We could use some of that. If we sit around like this much longer we'll be broke.'

Mast hummed to himself. Castor was exaggerating, of course. The Caeanic merchandise had been sold to Olveolo Jadper for an acceptable profit – but only just in time. Things were so much more difficult now. The

Directorate had tightened up in all directions and he did not envy the japing fence his possession of a store of enemy goods. 'The joke's on you, Jadper,' he had thought when reading of the government's intensified propaganda campaign against Caean.

But much of the money was now gone, and the word was out to lie low to escape the attentions of the newly-vigilant Directorate Investigators. Castor had even suggested another sortie to Kyre but Mast, naturally, had vetoed that. He almost wished the war would start and open up the black markets every war entailed.

'It wouldn't be difficult to get it,' he decided. 'A quick burglary, perhaps. People don't usually bother to lock up their daily wear.'

'He might do with this one, though,' Castor said quickly. 'If what you say is right, it's a horn of plenty.'

'A cornucopia,' Mast smiled dreamily, pleased by Castor's unexpected literacy. 'Or a Pandora's box?'

'What's that?' Castor demanded.

Mast did not bother to explain. 'Find out where Forbarth lives,' he instructed. 'What his habits are. Then we'll decide on the best way of getting the suit.'

He paused, thinking the matter through afresh. 'You understand these moves are exploratory only. We'll experiment with the suit merely, to find out what its capabilities are.' He lowered his eyes. 'I don't think I'll wear it myself,' he murmured. 'You can wear it, Castor.'

Castor fingered his grubby jacket.

At that moment the signal chime sounded. 'Who can that be?' Mast wondered, looking up. 'Find out, Grawn.'

Grawn moved to the annunciator and held down the switch. 'Yeah?'

But instead of a proper answer they heard only bangings and stamping of feet as the outer door was forced open. The whine of the elevator sounded distantly over the annunciator.

Grawn gaped at Mast. Moments later the door to the apartment crashed open. Four big men, wearing formal business clothes, came through the short vestibule and entered the lounge.

Their leader flashed a card. 'Police. Realto Mast?'

Mast nodded.

'You're under arrest.' He gestured at Castor and Grawn. 'These yours?'

'We was just leaving,' Grawn offered, sidling towards the door.

Two of the men moved to block the exit.

Mast laughed uneasily. 'Really! How melodramatic! Just what is the charge? What could it possibly be?'

A square-jawed plain clothes man moved round his boss to look Mask up and down. 'A dandy,' he announced. 'Wouldn't you know it.'

'It figures,' said a third. 'You expect them to be pervy in a set-up like this.'

The leader turned to Mast. 'You're charged with importing subversive enemy contraband. That's just two degrees below treason on the criminal scale, Mast. Come on, let's all go.'

'*Treason?*' cried Mast in alarm. 'Since when?'

'Don't you read the Directorate Codesheets?' the captain asked sadistically. 'Since last month, that's since when. Tzist is an official enemy now.'

'It is absolutely ridiculous,' Mast said with finality. 'I have no connections with any importation of contraband or anything else. I am a loyal Ziodean. Obviously you have no evidence. You are arresting me by reason of rumour, or malicious gossip – or something.'

'Don't argue with me. We've got evidence.' The police captain gestured to him to stand.

Mast came to his feet. 'You'll never prove anything,' he said peevishly.

Castor lowered his head and spoke in a rasping whine. 'We don't know this man. We came up here in answer to an advertisement – '

'Sure you don't know him. That's why you've been everywhere he goes for the past seven years, that's how well you don't know him. Move, all three of you, and stop wasting time.'

Castor and Grawn continued to protest weakly as all three were herded out of the apartment and taken down in the elevator. In the ground-floor hallway Mast was most unpleasantly surprised to meet Olveolo Jadper, flanked by yet two more non-uniformed policemen. The japer, looking mildly unhappy, wore a silver-grey quilted boiler suit which made him seem even fatter than he was.

'You!' Mast accused.

Jadper grimaced, shrugging his shoulders in a show of embarrassment. 'Sorry, old fellow. Had to buy some leniency.' He made a wan attempt to giggle. 'The joke's on you, eh?'

'Is that him?' demanded the captain.

Jadper nodded.

Three big cars were waiting in the street. At the front door Castor gave a low strangled growl, ducked, twisted, and ran towards the back of the house. He disappeared down the steps to the cellar, his footsteps clattering in frantic haste.

One of the policemen drew an energy pistol and gave chase. He emerged from the cellar a minute or so later, looking frustrated.

'The little rat had a bolthole down there. He's probably two streets away by now.'

'Don't worry about it. We'll pick him up eventually.'

The police captain nudged Mast in the ribs. 'Come on.'

Resignedly Mast allowed himself to be led out to the waiting car.

8

Always on awakening lately, Peder was filled with fearful apprehensions, invaded by confused and perturbed thoughts, made to feel abandoned, alone and miserable. But he could never summon the will to make any sense out of his feelings. He could only, as today, stare blankly at the ceiling and move feebly under the covers, terrified of leaving his bed.

Eventually he forced himself to rise and flex his muscles with zombie-like movements, trying to clear his brain of its undeclared war. He had a headache. He took a pill, and padded to the bathroom.

On returning he stood and stared at the Frachonard suit, which hung on a rack near the wardrobe. His face was slack, his body like lead.

'I own you,' he said dully, trying to spark life into himself. The thought alone had once been enough to leave him brimming with joy. Now his words seemed cheerless and disappointing.

But the urge to wear the suit was still there. Of late he wore it every day – there was an enormous let-down in wearing anything else. Moving as if drawn by magnetism, he put on undergarments and a suitable shirt, then dressed himself in the superb Prossim cloth, adding slim shoes of soft lavender leather and a cravat to match. He adjusted the garments before the full-length mirror, his eyes flicking here and there.

Suddenly everything zipped into place in his mind. It was like switching on a power supply. The future tumbled through his head, showing him where he was going. He felt invigorated and in command of himself, strong and in his prime.

He gazed for some moments longer at the suit. There were new aspects to it every time he looked at it. Its ingenious lines were always revealing dazzling new effects. He had still not fathomed how the scyes and shoulders had been cut and fitted, for instance.

Frachonard had buried secret upon secret in his masterpiece.

It was a pity he was so vulnerable during that short period between waking and dressing, he reflected ruefully. That was the old Peder Forbarth returning and blinking in the light of the renewed Peder Forbarth.

He dialled the service hatch for breakfast.

He was still eating when the door opened. Two men in dark conservative clothes entered uninvited, looking around them warily. It was obvious they were security police. That they had gained access to his private elevator and neutralized the door lock without arousing the building's watchdog circuit told him that.

'You Peder Forbarth?' demanded the taller of the two. He nodded.

'Come with us. You've got some questions to answer.' The plain clothes man flashed a card.

'Quite impossible!' declared Peder loudly with a flourish of his arm. 'Whatever your business is, it must be settled right here. Tonight I am to attend the birthday ball of the Third Minister, so there is a great deal to attend to. Will you have some coffee?' he finished politely.

They glanced at one another, utterly disconcerted. Peder was inwardly complacent. The suit had stalled them. They did not even know why they felt so paralysed, why they had undergone a loss of confidence immediately on entering his presence. It was a phenomenon he had learned to use. People would even disbelieve the evidence of their senses if he wanted them to – provided he was wearing his Frachonard suit.

'Then may I know your names?' he asked with an ironic smile.

'I'm Lieutenant Burdo,' the tall security man said. He took a folder from his pocket and began shuffling documents. Finally he decided to get on with it. 'Where were you between the eighty-fifth and hundred-twentieth of last year?'

Peder paused as if searching his memory. 'I was vacationing on Hixtos part of that time. For the rest of it I was here in Gridira.'

'Can you prove that?'

'Certainly.'

'Where did you stay on Hixtos?'

'At the Pearl Diver Hotel in Permerand. It's on the Holiday Reefs. A big vacation area.'

'Yes, I know.' The lieutenant scribbled on a pad. Then he took out a picture of Realto Mast and laid it on the breakfast table. 'This man disputes your story. He says you were with him, on a star yacht called the *Costa*.'

'What would I be doing with him?'

'You tell us.'

'All right,' Peder said, smiling. 'Probably smuggling Caeanic contraband, the way you read it.'

'So you admit it.' It was the other plain clothes man who spoke, his voice determinedly tough.

'No, of course not. But I did meet this man once, when I used to keep a shop on Tarn Street. He came in there and tried to sell me Caeanic garments.'

'Did you buy them?'

'No. I don't deal in them.'

'You didn't inform the authorities.'

'I should have, I know, but I didn't want my customers driven away by any publicity. The line of work I was in . . .'

'That's right,' Lieutenant Burdo said brusquely, 'you're a specialist in bizarre and outlandish garments. A freak tailor, the kind who's always been regarded as a security risk. Usually with good reason.'

The other man waved a hand at the walls. 'What's all this, for instance?'

Peder had adorned his lounge with paintings of Caeanic scenes, some fanciful and imaginary, but others depicting identifiable Caeanic landmarks. One such was the famous tower of Quest, built in the shape of a man with outstretched arms, face raised to the sky, wearing a stiff garment trailing finlike structures down from his shoulders to the ground. In the original the tower was five thousand feet high.

It was admittedly embarrassing to have these pictures on show when the security police called. 'An interest in the bizarre doesn't necessarily mean approval of it,' he said.

'Why would Realto Mast try to implicate you in the smuggling of Caeanic contraband?' Lieutenant Burdo asked him.

'Who knows? I dare say the more people he drags down with him the lighter his sentence will be. That's how justice works these days, isn't it?'

The lieutenant gave a wry smile. 'Well, we'll have to check this out,' he finished in a more friendly tone. 'But don't leave Gridira without permission.'

Peder dialled the service unit to clear the table and rose to his feet, turning to the two men. All his movements had absolute elegance and precision. The suit was still working for him, subjecting the intruders to a subliminal bombardment of line and gesture, fractional poses whose effect on the unwitting perceptions could be remarkable.

'I am a loyal Ziodean,' he drawled, 'and these aspersions affect me unpleasantly . . .' He held out an arm and tweaked the cloth of his sleeve. 'Feel this: good old crabsheep twill, Ziode's native fabric. If you want someone to vouch for my loyalty, get in touch with the Eleventh Minister.'

'The Eleventh Minister?' Burdo repeated.

'A personal friend. I am also acquainted with the Third Minister, as I have intimated.'

'Yes, sir, I see,' Burdo said respectfully. 'Forgive us for taking up your time . . .'

After they had gone Peder wondered if his fake alibi would stand up. To cover some of the time he was away with Mast he actually had booked a vacation on Hixtos, but he had given the booking to a customer of his to use in his name.

What did it matter? A man garbed in the art of Frachonard had no cause to fear anything! Even when given incontrovertible evidence of his guilt, even when his increasing obsession with all things Caeanic, his mounting desire to see the Tzist Arm for himself (impossible though that was) was obvious beyond all reasonable doubt, men would still prefer to believe the front he showed them. Even though face to face with a man in a Frachonard Prossim suit, Caean's highest artform, they would still imagine he was wearing some factory-produced piece of Ziodean wretchedness. That was part of the suit's genius – its seeming conventionality. It was the perfect disguise. And, at the same time, it became a powerful social weapon.

Peder laughed, and went striding from the penthouse to go confidently about his day's business.

He arrived fairly late at the birthday ball of Baryonid Varl Vascha, Third Minister to the Directorate. The main mass of the Minister's palace was hidden from view of the ground by an ascending series of hanging gardens, up which Peder, after tendering his coded invitation, was escorted to the main entrance on the roof. The palace was already thronged with guests and the affair promised to be a splendid one.

But before he could join the revelry he had to wait nearly half an hour in an ante-room to be presented to the Minister. Baryonid Varl Vascha was a thickset man, his grip muscular and firm as he shook hands with Peder, growling a perfunctory greeting. His jet-black hair was greased sideways across his nearly flat pate, and his face wore a habitually ironic, knowing smile. His glance flicked to the present Peder had placed on the gift table: an engraved drinking goblet in gold and tantalum-silver alloy which Peder had commissioned specially.

Peder felt the Minister's unsettling eyes on his back as he left the audience room. He passed through a wide, brightly-lit connecting passage whose walls were decorated with meandering veins of gold, and set off to explore as much of the palace as had been made available for the occasion.

There was a main ballroom and three subsidiary ballrooms, and in each room music of a different type was being played. In interconnecting salons luxurious food and drink were laid out in such profusion, and footmen were so numerous, that no guest felt any whim unsupplied. Third Minister Vascha had spent a fortune on the arrangements. It could hardly have been otherwise; unstinting extravagance was expected of all high-ranking members of the Directorate, and Vascha was certain to have his eye on the Second and even First Ministerships.

Peder took himself to the radiant main ballroom, where the Master of Ceremonies took his name and bellowed his arrival to the company.

'*Citizen Peder Forbarth!*'

Leisurely Peder sauntered beneath the blazing overhead curve of the ceiling, whose golden lights and delicately tinted frescos made a hazy impression of some distant heaven. A number of heads turned at hearing his name, and he began quickly to pick out those he knew and those whom he would take the opportunity to get to know.

Soon he found himself dancing with Aselle Klister, daughter of the Thirtieth Minister, a comely girl with sparkling brown eyes and flushed, peach-like cheeks. Her hair was daringly *bouffant* and sparkled with diamante. They made a handsome couple as they capered about the floor together, and he knew they were attracting attention.

The orchestra struck up an angular, lively tune. Peder stepped out, long-legged and energetic, and the girl allowed herself to be swept breathlessly after his lead. Peder had never been much of a dancer before he came into possession of the Frachonard suit; now it was as natural to him as flight to a bird.

'Oh! Such thrilling music!' she gasped.

'Yes!' He whirled her round even faster, and she clung to him, laughing.

When the orchestra stopped playing they stood clapping with the other dancers. Peder gazed around him, taking stock once more of the celebrities present. There was no sign, he noted, of either the Second or First Ministers; none of their aides, servants or representatives seemed to be present. The disdain befitting their station would require that they make only a perfunctory and barely polite appearance at a festival in honour of one who was both their underling and a close rival, and no doubt they had performed this ritual very early in the evening.

Back at the tables Peder gravitated to a group discoursing with Eleventh Minister Severon, a prominent politician already known to him. A few weeks earlier Severon had hinted to Peder that he might find a place for him in the Economic Co-ordination Network, or as he liked to call it, 'the E-Co-Net'.

Now he was expatiating on the advantages of supervised – in other words bureaucratic – resource allocation as apposed to the free decisions of market-oriented entrepreneurs. 'It works like this,' he said in a dry voice. 'Whenever the government wants something done it can go about it in one of two ways. It can invite tenders, that is to say, it can buy whatever it is it wants on the open market. Or it can interfere with the course of business, dictating which firms will do what. That is the method I favour and which we are putting into effect with the E-Co-Net, and it is the best method, and I will tell you why. Take the first method. Governments invariably have more money than prudence. When a firm finds it has the government for a customer then that government gets swindled for all it's worth. Now take the second case. Government officials who have the power to dictate to firms will be bribed. Those firms who do not want the work will bribe the officials not to allocate it their way.

Firms who can complete the government's requirements with ease will, for the sake of profit, again bribe the officials. A bribed official takes care to acquaint himself with the business of both ends. He is much more knowledgeable than the honest civil servant living off his salary. He makes a fortune, but the government gets the job done for less money. In a phrase, graft serves the Directorate better than incompetence. What do you say, Forbarth?'

Peder, already aware that corruption and self-seeking were so cynically accepted that they had become an established instrument of administration, was not surprised to hear this rationalization. He had already heard it from Severon's lips, in a indirect way, when the Minister had insinuated how much good they could do one another once Peder was installed in the E-Co-Net. He laughed suavely. 'A realistic appraisal, Minister.' He launched into his own animated version of Severon's words, arguing that only a man who knew how to do himself some good could do his nation good, and illustrating the argument with countless anecdotes. Severon nodded sagely, his lips curling in amusement. 'True, Peder, true.'

'Enjoying the ball, Forbarth, huh?'

Peder was startled to hear the rasping, commanding voice behind him. He turned. Baryonid Varl Vascha stood eyeing him with narrowed brows, as if weighing him up.

He smiled and put on all his charm. 'An unqualified success, Minister!'

Vascha grunted and lumbered away.

Peder did not allow the Third Minister's apparent grumpiness to spoil his own enjoyment of the evening. There was plenty here for him to take advantage of. He talked, he drank, he danced, he won the infatuation of Aselle Klister. He did not utter a word or make a move that was not, from the point of view of the social graces, flawless. He moved through the gathering with all the elegance and panache of a gorgeously plumed cock through a barnyard full of hens.

A press photographer moved in and took a shot of him with Aselle clinging to his arm. Directorate officials, including the Thirteenth Minister, and their wives framed the couple.

'Oh, we'll be on the newscast tomorrow!' Aselle giggled.

'If we're lucky.' The newscasts would publish few pictures that did not feature the Third Minister himself.

It was still several hours before dawn when a footman approached Peder and coughed deferentially.

'The Minister would appreciate a word with you, sir.'

'With me?' Peder gazed at him imperiously. 'Which Minister?'

'Why, Third Minister Vascha, sir. Would you care to follow me?'

The footman's face was professionally blank, but Peder was puzzled by his slight stiffness of demeanour, which seemed to betoken something wrong.

He frowned and glanced to where Aselle was talking with her father. Leaving the footman to wait, he stepped over to her.

'I have been called away for a short while, my dear,' he said solicitously when he had caught her attention. 'The Third Minister requests my presence. I hope he will not keep me too long.'

He followed the footman down a broad, winding staircase. While they were leaving the ballroom one of the displays arranged for the evening burst into life. Canisters were opened to release clouds of coloured smoke which wafted through the hall, eventually taking on a semi-solid consistency and assuming the forms of fantastic dragons and imaginary beasts. The multi-hued phantoms went slithering and twisting through the ballroom, knocking over tables and chairs, grappling with the guests, and creating general pandemonium.

Then the sounds of the ball were left behind. Peder descended into the deeper reaches of the palace where a calm, almost stifling silence prevailed. They entered a wing displaying a more modest style of architecture, the colour scheme consisting of harmonious blues and pale greens. Peder guessed that this was Vascha's own private wing.

The footman paused at a circular nexus of five radiating corridors. The flat ceiling bore a golden starburst. From one of the corridors emerged two dark-garbed men, and Peder was disconcerted to find that one of them was Lieutenant Burdo, his visitor of the previous morning.

Burdo's present companion waved a detector box down the length of Peder's body, then frisked him expertly. 'What is this?' Peder protested.

'You're under arrest.' Burdo's face was closed, almost hurt.

'But why?'

'You might be able to fool us,' Burdo told him, 'but you can't fool Vascha.' He nudged Peder forward. The two policemen fell in behind him.

Peder was mystified. He followed the footman, who led them down a long corridor whose colours, seen in perspective, gave the impression of a box-shaped rainbow. As they walked by them the walls phased through purple, russet and gold, like a technicolor autumn, until finally the footman stopped at a door of carved wood.

Peder was pushed into a room breathing luxury. The walls, painted delicate peach, were lent an odd impression of texture by embossed murals of the same colour. All the furniture was antique. If Peder was any judge one or two pieces dated from before the settlement of Ziode itself.

Baryonid Varl Vascha stood before a huge open hearth in which timber logs blazed and threw out an enjoyable warmth. Peder was amazed. Never in his life had he seen an open fire inside a closed room before. Vascha wore a purple smoking jacket and was puffing at a curious smoking instrument of some ancient design. He nodded to the footman to leave; the security men arranged themselves by the door.

Vascha looked at Peder hard with eyes nearly as black as his greased-down hair, pulling thoughtfully on the smoking-pipe. His face was square and pock-marked, making him look like a hoodlum. Peder shivered inwardly. For a Ziodean, he had to admit that the Third Minister had remarkable presence.

'Sir, why have I been arrested?' he asked.

Vascha took the smoking instrument from his mouth and laid it on the mantelpiece over the fireplace. But he ignored Peder's question. He looked past him to Lieutenant Burdo.

'Do you know much about the Caeanics, Lieutenant? At first hand, I mean?'

'No, sir,' Burdo told him.

'They are strange people,' Vascha said slowly in a gruff, musing voice. 'Not like us at all. It's as if they don't have souls. Take you or me, for instance. Our personality, our mien or whatever you like to call it, comes from our own inner qualities. Theirs comes from the clothes they wear, pure and simple. It's a weird phenomenon. You don't get to recognize it right away. Not for a long time, in fact. But when you do, you realize these people are no more human than a robot. It's the same as if they were some alien kind of life-form.'

'I guess there's no accounting for foreigners, sir.'

The Minister gave a short barking laugh. 'You're right there, Lieutenant! No accounting for foreigners! But unfortunately that's not all there is to it. The Caeanics plan to conquer on a wide scale, spreading their perverse way of life everywhere. They'll come here and turn you into a clothes-robot.' He nodded with self-assurance. 'Caean poses a terrible threat to Ziode, in fact to the whole inhabited galaxy. "Caeanic Tzist lies curved above Ziode like a threatening maw" – that's from an official government pamphlet, and I wrote it.'

He walked across to Peder and fingered the cloth of his suit. 'Prossim, isn't it? You must be highly placed.'

'No, sir!' Peder cried, shocked. 'Crabsheep twill!'

The Minister went back to the fireplace, leaned against the mantelpiece and warmed his hands in the heat of the flames. He laughed softly. 'You made a real mistake in coming to this ball tonight. It so happens I once spent two years as ambassador to Caean! We had diplomatic contact in those days. By the time the two years were up, I had learned to recognize what it was made Caeanics different from real people. Almost as soon as I saw you tonight I knew you were Caeanic.'

'No sir, I am Ziodean! I was born here in Gridira!'

Vascha waved his hand.

And Peder's further denials faded away. He was almost totally bemused by everything the Minister had said. He had never really looked on Caean as an aggressive force, and not having taken the feud between the two nations seriously, had never expected to find himself in this invidious situation.

'Well, you've brought me a real birthday present after all,' Vascha said with evident gratification. 'Yourself: our first captured Caeanic agent, and a person of some importance if I'm any judge.' He glanced up at the security men. 'Bring him this way. ZZ want to take a look at him.'

The rear of the room contained a second door giving access to an elevator. All four men entered it, and the elevator first descended, then travelled horizontally for a distance. They emerged into a garage containing a handsome Maxim car. Peder was bundled into the back, while Vascha climbed into the front compartment. The garage doors opened. They were driven down a ramp, along a shuttered drive, through an automatic gate and on to the streets of Gridira.

The sky was beginning to lighten slightly. The car turned on to the North Axis and crossed the city. The Minister pulled a bandanna from his pocket, handing it to Burdo through a connecting window. Burdo blindfolded Peder.

After a while Peder spoke out loud into the silence.

'What's ZZ?'

Lieutenant Burdo's voice came in reply. 'You know all about them.'

'No, I don't. What are they?'

There was a pause. 'Zealots of Ziode. A secret patriotic society.'

Peder asked no more questions. Twenty minutes later the blindfold was removed. The car was standing on gravel at the rear of a tall, old-fashioned house, close to a well-tended garden bounded by twelve-foot walls. The baroque outlines of other buildings thrust up beyond. This was an antique, well-heeled part of the city.

After being taken from the car Peder was herded into the house and down some stone steps. They were in a small cellar, facing a steel door.

The Minister turned to Burdo. 'After we go inside, wait upstairs.'

The door opened. Vascha entered, and Peder was nudged in behind him. At his back the door closed with a thump.

In keeping with their rejection of artificial constraint on human individuality, the council of the Zealots of Ziode met stark naked. There were six of them sitting at the crescent-shaped table. Above and behind them, the starburst of the Ziode Cluster blazed on a dark backcloth. Above that, the initials ZZ were emblazoned. The walls of the room were draped with banners and flags.

Looking into their set, determined faces, Peder recognized at once that he was facing rampant nationalism.

Baryonid Varl Vascha divested himself of his clothing, piling his garments neatly on a nearby chair. Naked, looking flabbier and pudgier than he had appeared when dressed, he went and stood to one side of the crescent table.

For the first time since he had begun wearing his suit, Peder felt a loss of confidence. He even wondered if he should confess the whole story of its acquisition. That might be better than to be arraigned as an enemy agent, he thought.

No. These toughened fanatics would show him no mercy. He made an effort to call on the suit's supernal elegance, performing slight, casual motions – extending one foot an inch or two, lifting his shoulders and turning them in a gesture that was almost effete in its ambiguity.

His *élan* began to return. These near-subliminal manoeuvres were usually guaranteed to bring opponents to a state of fawning ingratiation. For a moment Peder saw the familiar semi-hypnotic look flicker over the faces of the Zealots, but they were plainly less susceptible than the average citizen to foreign wiles and their self-willed sternness soon returned.

They began to fire questions at him.

'How long have you been in Ziode?'

'What kind of information have you passed back to Tzist?'

'Who do you report to?'

'How many agents does Caean have in Ziode?'

Peder remained dumb before the barrage. 'You're on your own now,' one of them reminded him. 'No one can help you, you know that.'

Another Zealot made a remark to Vascha. 'I wonder if he knows the invasion date?'

'Invasion?' Peder echoed. 'Who says Caean is going to invade?'

'We say it,' Vascha said gruffly.

'You should look on Caean as a friend, not as an enemy,' Peder replied in a clear voice. 'Caean will do you nothing but good. We—' The response had come out of Peder's lips without any volition on his part. He stopped, realizing he was condemning himself out of his own mouth.

But still the words came, prompted by some secret impulse in his brain. 'We bring you a new life. Cast off your sleep, enter the new morning of revivifying apparel.'

He raised his arm in a strangely awkward, dramatic gesture, tilting his face towards the ceiling. Dimly he was aware that the suit had taken over his *persona* and was making him behave like this.

'Watch out, he's up to some kind of trick!' Vascha said sharply. He stepped forward and shoved at Peder, delivering a mild rabbit punch to the side of his neck as he went down.

'Don't underestimate Caeanic garments,' he told his fellow Zealots. 'Some of them can exercise a kind of mesmeric influence.'

Sullenly Peder climbed to his feet, rubbing his neck awkwardly. 'I have no information for you,' he muttered.

The Zealot chairman grunted and opened a drawer under the table. 'We've prevaricated enough. Let's begin the interrogation. Succinyl will soon get him talking.'

Peder shrank at mention of the interrogation torture drug. The chairman took a hypodermic from the drawer. But Vascha laughed without humour.

'You don't need that. There's a quicker method. Just take his clothes off him. Caeanics can't stand to be naked. It reduces them to some kind of animal state and you can do anything you like with them – I've seen it before. I told you, they're not like us.'

The chairman hesitated, then replaced the hypodermic in the drawer. He nodded to two of those who sat with him. They rose to their feet and approached Peder, their naked bodies, so pale and flabby, filling him with a purely physical revulsion.

The cellar oppressed him. He should have felt relief at his reprieve, but instead another, deeper terror had taken hold of him. The terror of being disrobed, of being made to go naked in front of these men. *To stand naked, stripped of his Frachonard suit!* No, no, he could not permit it, it was impossible, he could not!

'The succinyl!' he shouted desperately. 'I'll take the succinyl!'

They all laughed. Then, as they laid hands on him, something snapped. A feeling of gigantic orgasmic release ripped through every fibre of his body. It was like a sudden discharge between the electrodes of an arc light, an eruption of unsuspected power, and everything seemed to go dim, his perception to withdraw itself, to enter a far darkness. He was only aware, in a vague and incomplete manner, that blinding shocks of energy were vibrating through the room and creating turmoil.

He must briefly have lost consciousness. When he came to he was still standing, and was still unmolested. The cellar looked as if a small explosion had gone off in it. The backcloth bearing the Ziodean starburst was burning. The table and chairs had been overturned, the Zealots having been flung about the room like rag dolls. The air carried a strong acid smell of electrostatic discharge.

At first Peder was too nonplussed to know what to do. Then, quietly and carefully, he moved about the cellar, examining the forms of the unconscious Zealots.

The first two he looked at – the same two who had attempted to undress him – were apparently dead. He moved to a third, but at the same time heard a groan behind him.

He turned. Two other Zealots had been stunned, not killed. Now they lurched to their feet and staggered at Peder, their eyes feral with hatred.

Peder knew how to react without knowing why. He clamped a hand to each man's forehead. He felt a vibration issuing from his palms, passing through skin, skull and brain.

They both fell back dead.

He took one last look round the cellar to make sure there were no more survivors. Then he left, closing the steel door behind him, and mounted the steps to the hallway on the ground floor.

Lieutenant Burdo and his colleague were surprised to see Peder. Wordlessly he beckoned them, his Prossim-sleeved arm moving in a smooth, repetitive arc. They obeyed him involuntarily, though their hands hovered nervously near their guns.

Again using the palms of his hands, Peder killed them.

He decided to leave the house by the front to avoid the chauffeur waiting at the back. There was no sound in the building as he walked softly through it; it appeared deserted. The front door opened on to a short flight of steps giving direct access to the street.

Calmly Peder closed the door behind him and walked towards the centre of Gridira.

It was now early morning and the street was light. Suddenly Peder felt utterly drained. He had never felt so feeble and exhausted. It took a superhuman effort just to put one foot in front of another.

Sugar! He had to have sugar!

He put a hand to his face. The skin hung loose, all the flesh gone from his cheeks. He knew he was the same all over. He was a gaunt travesty of himself, his chubbiness lost in the explosion of energy in the cellar.

For that energy had not come from the suit, as he had at first presumed, but from himself. Like some sea monster he had discharged a lethal wattage of electricity, and to gain that unnatural level of power his body had drawn on all its reserves of fat, instantly converting it – and a good deal of protein – into a controlled, momentary blast.

That the suit could manage his body in such a fashion was a startling development. Had it a mind of its own? Was it alive, inhabiting him like a parasitical creature – or rather, symbiote? Peder still did not think so. He did not believe that the suit was sentient or that it had any powers of its own. For all its incredible qualities it was only a work of art which aroused the dormant powers of its wearer. It was, he concluded, a psychological template: his abilities flowed into it and were shaped and adapted by it. In time, flowing more freely, they could bring about even such remarkable physical effects as he had just witnessed.

Such was his explanation. The suit sometimes seemed to rule him, he decided, because it aroused the powers of his unconscious, and as every psychiatrist knows, a man's subconscious is a stranger to him.

He staggered on, letting himself be guided by the suit. It was a strange experience, having surrendered his will while his mind was yet active. He was himself, yet he was not himself. He could think, feel, and make decisions. But the thoughts, the feelings and the decisions were not those of which he would normally have been capable.

He went into an automatic food store and bought four cartons of granulated white sugar. Then he took himself to the cafeteria on the upper floor and bought a quart of coffee.

He was alone in the cafeteria. He sat in the corner, half-slumped over the table. He emptied the sugar into a bowl and spooned it into himself as fast as he could go, helping it down with the coffee.

When the sugar was gone the craving was less, but he was still dizzy. He rested for an hour, panting softly and watching the handful of people who entered the cafeteria for breakfast.

Then he bought four more cartons of sugar and devoured those too.

Eventually he began to feel a little better. But he stayed where he was. He wondered how the Third Minister's ball was progressing. Probably it was over by now.

He could not remember if he had killed the Minister or not. Everything had been so confused.

He fell into a half-doze. He could not say how much later it was that he awoke with a start. Four men stood by his table, gazing down at him. As he looked from face to face they bowed slightly, as if in acknowledgement.

'May we sit with you, sir?' asked one respectfully.

His mind blank, he nodded.

They sat down. 'We have been aware of your presence for some time, sir,' the same speaker told him quietly. Then he lapsed into a language Peder did not know.

'Why are you talking to me like that?' he asked.

The other made a self-deprecating gesture. 'My apologies, sir. I should have been more careful.'

Another of the four took up the conversation. 'It puzzles us that we were never informed of your arrival, sir, and we debated on whether we should contact you. Not knowing the nature of your mission, we decided merely to keep you under observation, and to be on hand should we be needed. We observed your attendance at the ball of the Ziodean Third Minister and by means of a spy-ray ascertained that you were being conducted from the palace. We followed you to the house used by ZZ, and hence here. Now, with great reverence, we make ourselves known to you.'

With great reverence . . .

Peder scrutinized the conservative, dark-coloured suits the four men wore. In an unobtrusive way they were exceedingly well made – better than anything ordinarily obtainable in Ziode – and cunningly designed to seem modest and inconspicuous. The strangers sat in these humble suits with a peculiar kind of confidence, exhibiting a *rapport* between the person and the cloth that did not exist in the society Peder was used to.

'So!' he exclaimed softly. 'There *are* Caeanic agents in Ziode!'

They looked at him in puzzlement. 'Naturally, sir.'

Another spoke, in a confidential tone. 'We will not enquire the purpose of your coming to Ziode. We merely make our presence known to you, to assist you in any way you deem fit.'

They all fell silent. They had probably spotted him by accident, Peder thought. A suit of Frachonard quality would be instantly noticeable to Caeanics, just as it had been to Baryonid Varl Vascha. But their subservience surprised him. It did not accord with what he knew of Caeanic attitudes. Then again, there was something odd in it, something *indirect*.

Suddenly it came to him just what bothered him about their manner. Their respect was not to him; it was, rather, to his *suit*.

They knew he was wearing a Frachonard suit! But they could scarcely have learned that such a suit had been lost, still less that it had fallen into Ziodean hands. He looked past them and around the cafeteria. He felt lost and deserted, drifting alone in a void. Unaccountably, with no wish on his own part, the lines and forms of the cafeteria scene began to transform themselves in his sight, and to depict designs and hieroglyphics he knew only he could see.

For months now the urge to go to Caean had been building up in him. The pictorial code was exteriorizing that desire; it was as though his brain were interpreting random data to form but one message, a painted perspective pointing in a single direction.

'I want to go to Caean,' he said suddenly, urgently. Then he stopped short. *He* didn't want to go.

The suit wanted to go.

He recollected the self-serving rationalizations by which he had still tried to picture himself as his own master. Such pretences were a delusion. The truth could no longer be evaded – the truth that he could not, now, claim to be the owner of the Frachonard suit. The Frachonard suit was a suit that *owned its wearer*. Without sentience it might be; passive and without powers of action, a mere object, but by degrees it could so change a situation that he, the wearer, became the recipient partner. The sleeping partner.

Dimly he realized that the Caeanic agent was speaking to him again. 'Unfortunately it is currently impossible to make physical contact with Caean. Ziodean forces have sealed off the Gulf.'

Peder jumped up. 'Forget what I said,' he told them thickly. 'Do not approach me again.' Staggering from the table, he negotiated his way across the floor of the cafeteria, feeling like a drunkard on stilts.

Once in the open air he seemed to recover his strength. The streets were filling now with Gridirans going about their daily business, and as far as he could tell the Caeanic agents did not follow him.

What if he got rid of the suit? he thought. What if he tore it off him right now and threw it in the gutter? Could he do it?

No, he couldn't do it. He did not have the will to break its bond with him. He paced the sidewalk, the tussle continuing in his mind, and paused at the corner to look about him. The perspective of streets and buildings was forming into a corridor leading off the curve of the planet and into the sky, across the void to an immensely distant destination. A one-way corridor to Caean!

How did his brain perform this trick? Was it the first stage of a total separation from reality?

And yet, the delusion offered the only certain solution to his predicament. Anywhere in Ziode, he was a hunted man. Only Caean was a safe haven.

Besides, was he not by now more of a Caeanic than he was a Ziodean? Even Caeanics themselves mistook him for one of their own. Yes, he would go to Caean. Perhaps if he journeyed to where the outer Ziodean stars straggled off into the Gulf it would be possible to find a way across it. The suit would help and protect him, as it always had. Help him also because thereby it fostered its own plans, whatever they were, plans which had been sewn and cut, by some arcane sartorial science, some coded language of psychic intentions, into its fabric.

With this decision his brain cleared and he applied himself to immediate details. Once the events at the ZZ house became known it would be difficult indeed to evade the ensuing police net, especially if the dead included the Third Minister. There might still, however, be an hour or so remaining in which to leave Harlos unimpeded. Hailing a cab, he went to his penthouse atop the Ravier Building and quickly collected together money, credit cards and a few documents, leaving everything else behind.

He took the elevator to the street again. As he emerged from the foyer a small, square-shouldered, slightly stooped figure sidled up to him.

'Hello, Peder. Havin' fun?'

Castor's eyes glittered at him. He was even grubbier than usual and his hands moved uneasily over his crumpled clothes. His face was deadpan, his jaw slightly fallen and his unhealthy skin drawn grey and slack over his bones. Peder, having presumed him to have been arrested along with Mast, was astonished to see him.

Before he could prevent it Castor waved away Peder's cab. 'You going somewhere, I take it? Think smart, Peder. Go everywhere in the same cab and the police know your movements just by asking one guy. Where were you goin'? Spaceport?'

Peder nodded. 'How do you know?'

'It stands to reason Mast will have ratted on you. Me, I got away. Mast wasn't so smart in the end.'

He touched Peder's arm and coaxed him along the sidewalk. 'The spaceport's not a good idea. They'll pick you up there. Come along with me. I've got a safe gaff where you can put up for a while.'

'Why should you help me?' Peder self-consciously moved his elbow from Castor's grasp.

'We can do each other some good.'

'What is it you want?'

'All in good time.'

Castor walked him a short distance to where a battered runabout was parked. Peder squeezed himself into the unaccustomedly cramped space while Castor took the driving lever and they shot off, heading east.

Peder did not to any degree trust Castor, but the man was an accomplished criminal and in his present circumstances that was a valuable asset. He probably wanted money. Peder reflected. There was always the possibility, of course, that Castor was trapping him on behalf of the authorities in return for leniency, but overall Peder did not think that likely.

Castor drove the runabout on a wandering, zig-zag route. They entered Deberon, Gridira's example of a type of district possessed by every city of any size and age: an old run-down warren of an area sprawling between the city's commercial and entertainment sectors, the home of crime, vice, jaded artists and adventurous young.

Mast's ex-sidekick eventually parked the runabout in a mews that could not be seen from the street, and took Peder to a windowless room buried deep within the shapeless mass of an adjoining centuries-old building. The room, lit by a yellow glow-bulb, smelling foully of Castor's habitation, contained a dirty palliasse without covers, a drab armchair and begrimed table. The walls were poorly painted with a cheap distemper which was peeled and soiled. A curtain hanging over part of one wall hid a cooking closet and larder.

'You just take it easy here for a while,' Castor said softly. 'I'm going out now. Is there anything I can get you?' He stared at Peder, his lips stretched in a parody of a smile.

'I just want to get some sleep,' Peder replied.

'Sleep? Sure. You sleep!' With alacrity bordering on eagerness Castor leaped to a sliding panel and opened it to reveal a wall cupboard. Inside was a set of brand new clothes hangers. 'You can hang your gear up here, see? Huh – ' He floundered for a moment, looking about the room wildly, then came up with a dusty mat-like counterpane from the floor of the cupboard. 'Here's something to cover yourself with.'

'This is all right, thanks.' Peder lay down fully clothed on the palliasse, leaving Castor fingering the counterpane, his expression unreadable.

Eventually Castor dropped the counterpane on the floor and shut the cupboard. As he slouched from the room, Peder's eyes closed.

*

His host's return awakened Peder some hours later. Castor smelled of drink and swayed slightly on his feet. He carried in both arms a bulky package which he unrolled and erected into a low travelling bed, placing it against the wall opposite Peder. He had also brought two clean coverlets which, though thin, were scarcely needed in the heated room.

'Just like old times, huh?' he reminded Peder in an attempt at camaraderie. 'Remember the Kyre junket? Aboard the *Costa*?' He chuckled, then rounded solicitously on Peder.

'Hungry?' he said vaguely. 'Want something to eat?'

'Just some sugar,' Peder answered weakly.

'Sugar? Just sugar? How much sugar you want?'

'All you've got.' Peder felt ill. The unnatural drain on his body's energy had been severe.

Castor shuffled to the larder and returned with a carton of sugar and a spoon. He sat watching Peder eat it.

'Has there been any news today?' Peder asked between mouthfuls.

'News?'

'I thought you might have seen a newscast.'

'No. What would be in the news? There won't be anything about you, if that's what you mean. The security police don't work in a blaze of publicity.'

'I suppose you're right.' Still wondering if he had killed the Third Minister, Peder licked up the last of the sugar.

'Thanks.'

He lay back on the palliasse, trembling slightly with his exhaustion. Castor flung him a coverlet. 'You always sleep in your clothes?' he said, speaking hesitantly. 'You'll rumple that fancy suit you've got.'

'I'm all right,' Peder murmured.

'Oh.'

Busying himself for sleep, Castor stripped to grey underwear, carefully laying his own dishevelled suit suggestively on the back of a chair. Settling down on the travelling bed, he turned his face to the wall. Soon Peder heard deep breathing.

The weight of his own form on the palliasse was burdensome to Peder. There was little life in him. The suit seemed to be quiescent. Perhaps it was letting him recuperate.

He shouldn't be sleeping in it, at that, he thought. He was misusing it. When a man slept, his suit should hang.

He rose shakily and undressed. To prevent Castor from stealing his wallet he tucked it in the waistband of his underpants. He draped the suit in the wall cupboard, leaving the panel open so that it continued to look down on him, a reassuring psychological glyph.

He turned out the light and quickly dropped back asleep.

The stealthy sounds that, some time later, impinged blurrily on his consciousness might not have woken him at all had not a dreadful feeling of loss been simultaneously tugging at his mind, expressing itself in doleful, disturbing dreams. The main light was still dead, but a dim hand-torch flickered by the wall cupboard, where a manlike shadow moved and shuffled.

Peder sat up and rubbed his eyes. He saw that his suit no longer hung in the recess. Instantly he leaped from the palliasse and switched on the ceiling light.

Wearing an acid, frowning expression, the stealthy figure by the cupboard turned to face him.

Castor was wearing the Frachonard suit. Since he was considerably smaller than Peder it looked ludicrously ill-fitting on him. The jacket and waistcoat hung loose, the sleeves flopping over his hands. The trouser legs were rucked up over the tops of his shoes.

Castor's face twitched. His eyes glittered. As Peder stepped forward a twinkling sliver-knife appeared in his sleeve-enfolded hand.

'Watch it, Forbarth.'

'My *suit*,' Peder snarled.

'Done you real good, hasn't it? Now let somebody else have a go.'

Castor backed to the door. Unwisely, Peder lunged forward, grappling with him in an attempt to get the suit off him. To his surprise Castor turned the knife aside to avoid doing him any harm. The thief began to utter outraged grunts.

The jacket was half off when Peder suddenly broke away from the tussle and flung himself sobbing to the other side of the room.

'*Take* it,' he groaned. '*Take* it from me! Let me be free of it! It won't own me any more. Ohhh . . .'

Agonized, he fought the urge to retrieve the suit, but he knew he couldn't hold out for long. Seeing it there before him was like being a junkie on withdrawal.

'*Take* it! Go!'

'Sure,' mumbled Castor, and he edged to the door, opened it and slipped through. The door closed again. He was gone. The suit was gone.

Peder collapsed on to the palliasse. An arid desolation overtook him. He was free, and empty, and dead.

He couldn't really understand why the suit had let it happen. Why hadn't it immediately induced Castor to discard it? He would have expected the suit to have rejected Castor straight away.

Then he understood. In the first place the suit did not make decisions on its own account. It merely mobilized the faculties of the wearer. Secondly its influence over Castor would be weak until he had worn it for a while. How it would ultimately affect Castor, a person for whom it was totally unfitted, he did not like to think.

After a while Peder tried to leave the room. The door was locked. Castor had trapped him.

He went back to the palliasse, sat down and waited.

9

Castor, immediately on waking, jumped out of bed and pulled on the suit with savage speed. It was always that way now. The suit didn't like him to be awake and not wearing it; sometimes he was even obliged to sleep in it.

But Castor didn't mind. He didn't care what the suit did, as long as it helped him to get the one thing he really wanted above all.

As long as it got him to Caean.

He sat on the edge of his bed, stretching his greasy face into a yawn. Then he jumped up and began to jerk his body in an awkward parody of physical exercise. That done, he wiped his face with a wet cloth, got rid of his stubble with some shaving cream, and devoured a scanty breakfast of blue milk and germ bread.

Feeling better, he stepped from the shack where he had been living for the past week. The shack stood on waste ground at the edge of Kass, a ragged town on Vence, a tattered planet on the fringe of Ziode where the star cluster straggled off into the Tzist Gulf. To one side of him were the domes and humps of Kass. To the other the flat terrain was punctuated by spear trees: tall, straight masts, lacking branch or leaf, that stood out against the whorl-like, bluish-tinted sunrise.

Castor had done a considerable amount of wandering since stealing the suit. But Vence was to be his last stop in Ziode. If all went well, today he would plunge into the Gulf towards Caean.

What he would do when he got to Caean was something his mind had not dwelled on with any clarity. The suit did not encourage that degree of deliberation. It amused him, though, to think that in traversing the Gulf he would be passing – at a distance of some light years, of course – the prison planet of Ledlide where both Peder Forbarth and Realto Mast were incarcerated. Castor smiled every time he recalled how neatly he had tricked Forbarth, locking him in the hideout and alerting the authorities as to his whereabouts. The one-time sartorial was on Ledlide for life, which in a way was surprising because Mast himself had only drawn twenty years.

Castor had to admit that his act was an unprincipled one, but tying up loose ends was a matter of simple prudence, after all.

He stumbled once or twice as he crossed the waste ground, as though his nervous system was not firing in proper sequence. The Frachonard suit fitted him badly. At first he had simply pinned it up to take out some of the slack and shorten the limbs, intending to have it tailored later. After a while he had been puzzled to find that the suit seemed to have shrunk; if he wasn't fussy about his appearance (and Castor wasn't fussy) he could wear it without pins, even though the suit still flopped and hung askew on him, making him look as if he was being moved like a puppet, on strings. Castor wasn't fussy.

It had other strange effects on him, too. Made for a man of Peder Forbarth's type, it was badly attuned to him – or he to it. It caused him to break into fits of nervous tics and twitches, and to undergo deranged mental episodes. Castor, accustomed to following his impulses without enquiring where they came from, scarcely noticed.

The bizarre and infelicitous relationship between himself and his apparel might in other circumstances have led to the suit's abandoning him for a more compatible wearer, but for the moment he answered its limited programme. And so Castor had wandered through Ziode, delighted with the bursts of jangling erratic talent the suit gave him, and making full use of his new-found power to influence others.

Like Mast had said, it was like being a hypnotist. And that had meant money. But he could never keep the money he made. The suit gave excessive self-confidence, but events did not always deliver on that confidence. Castor was always sure to pour everything he gained on to the gaming tables and lose it.

On Zenda and Arraseos he had operated a quack practice

making use of his one-time medical training. That always meant one had to move on quickly, of course, especially if any of his patients died as a result of treatment. On Julio he had simply pimped. On the Harriet circuit of worlds he had worked a type of con he found delightfully easy, known as switchback steering. It was on Kaylo, one of the Harriet planets, that he had finally become entirely ruled by a passionate urge to get to Caean by any means, and he had selected his present partners.

Kass's space field lay some distance from Castor's shack. To get there he had to walk through the empty dawn streets, passing between wax-coloured buildings. 'Beehive Town', some people called the place. All the buildings were rounded in shape, to ward off the two-hundred-miles-per-hour winds that came racing across Vence's plains during spring and autumn. At least half the town, in fact, was underground.

The *Little Planet* was one of half a dozen spacecraft parked on the space field. Vence, on the periphery of Ziode, was not a route to anywhere and received very little traffic, being very much the terminus of a minor branch as far as interstellar commerce went. The *Little Planet* had been parked for twenty days, watching other ships arrive and return whence they had come, while Castor tried to wheedle what he wanted out of the local governor.

He undogged the hatch and pulled himself through into a smelly corridor whose grey-painted walls were dimpled with rivets. The *Little Planet*, he had to admit, was a step down from the *Costa*. She was an out-of-service short-haul freighter that had spent forty years plying between two adjacent stars. But, with extra fuel, Castor was confident she could make it to Caean.

He squeezed through the inner door and climbed a ladder to the crew compartment. His partners were still sleeping on beds against the walls. Leecher and Rabbish both were snoring. Gadzha slept soundly, pressing the body of his girl possessively up against the bulkhead. Raincoat, who never slept without a weapon, had come adrift from his bedding and was sprawled on the bare floor, the stock of his gun protruding from under the vacated pillow.

The stale odours and clogging air went unnoticed by Castor. He began kicking his partners awake. Raincoat (Castor had never found out whether it was a nickname or a real one; they had once tried to dub Castor 'Eyes', but he had soon squashed that) came awake with a start, groping for his missing gun before he oriented himself. The others stirred resentfully.

They all hated him, and all with reason. Gadzha chiefly because Castor had raped three of his girl-friends in the months they had known one another. It was surprising he had risked bringing his current girl along on this jaunt, but the truth was he simply didn't like to be without a woman. The others hated Castor because he had cheated them, robbed them, insulted them. But that hadn't stopped them from putting up the money for the *Little Planet*. Violent and dangerous men, they were nevertheless under Castor's spell; he had baited them with his tale of the riches to be picked up from the crashed Caeanic spaceship on Kyre. They could take everything he owed them out of his share, he had promised, and there would still be plenty.

But they were growing impatient with the delay, not to say with Castor's company. For that reason Castor had moved out of the *Little Planet* to the shack on the edge of town.

'C'mon,' Castor urged. 'This is it. Today.'

Gadzha squinted at him blearily. 'Sod off. You've been telling us that all along.' He turned back, clamping himself to the girl.

Castor kicked him again. 'Get up. Ready the ship for take-off. I'll be back today with the pass.'

Grudgingly they stirred while Castor made them a rough breakfast. Afterwards he spent two hours helping them check the ship. It was all routine, but Castor was being careful.

Eventually he left and trudged across Kass to the Governor's office. The sun had risen in the sky and the streets had come to life, or what passed for life on Vence. Men in drab coveralls, mostly gem miners, blended like phantoms against the uninspiring background. There were few women: Vence was more a workplace than a colony.

The official residence of the Governor was underground, but he maintained an administrative office in the centre of Kass: a modestly sized building shaped like a long lozenge. At the moment all its slats were open, letting air and nearly horizontal sunlight into the interior compartments.

The Governor sighed as Castor was shown into his office, and gave a smile that was half embarrassed, half resigned. 'Hello, old chap. You're early today.'

'Thought I'd drop in ahead of the queue, and collect what you promised.'

The Governor frowned. 'Now I didn't exactly *promise*. . .'

Castor threw himself into a chair and stared fixedly. 'C'mon, we resolved all our difficulties, didn't we?'

'Well, I still feel I need more *assurance* . . .' The Governor lowered his head and tucked his short goatee beard into his throat, tailing off.

'Where's the risk?' Castor said reasonably. 'You are the Governor of a gem-bearing world. We are gem prospectors who know of another world out in the Gulf, and you are giving us permission to check it out. You're entitled to do that, almost. Even if we're lying about this world you're not to know: okay, we deceived you. What'll they do, demote you? There's nowhere to demote you to after this dump! Anywhere else has to be better! So that's the worst that can happen, but it won't because when we come back we'll simply report there are no gems there and you close the file.' He pulled out a plastic bank account card, idly fingering it and whistling suggestively. 'This is untraceable, after all.'

The Governor took the card from his fingers and looked

at the figures on it, smiling. 'You don't suppose there *are* any gems on this planet of yours, do you?' he asked. 'Maybe you could bring back a few samples or something.'

Castor laughed explosively. 'Of *course* we'll be bringing back some rocks and soil samples for your records, Governor. We are not amateurs.'

Castor had been working for the past twenty days on the Governor, who had been aghast at the first suggestion that he connive in Castor's putative scheme. Yet without the pass he could provide it would be impossible to get past the government patrols. Castor was certain that this would be the day; by now the Governor knew in his heart that he would yield eventually.

Before long he was handing Castor the travel pass in the form of a coded tape. 'Transmit this continually on the specified waveband,' he instructed. 'The patrols will let you through.'

In return Castor erased his own odour signature from the bank card and replaced it with the Governor's, putting his thumb print on the transfer square and thus activating it into the identity of its new owner. The bank deposit represented by the card, had there been anything genuine about it, was now legally the Governor's.

'It will run like a dream,' Castor lied.

Just after midday the *Little Planet* took off for the Gulf.

The chips rattled through the randomizer and Castor ejected them around the table. Leecher, Rabbish and Raincoat looked at the numbers. 'Mine takes it,' said Raincoat. Pieces of paper, written IOUs, passed to him.

'I'll stake a thousand,' Raincoat said excitedly. 'Who'll put up a thousand?'

'Me,' Castor replied in a flat, uninterested voice. He pushed papers into the centre of the table. Leecher followed suit. Only the gaunt Rabbish dithered, then hung on to his notes.

Raincoat won again.

It was the worst possible habit: gambling with joint proceeds that were yet to be gained. Castor didn't care. It was no part of his policy to foment harmony among his following.

They were three days out from Vence, and Castor's relations with his partners had deteriorated still further. He had grown more openly contemptuous, had quarrelled and jeered at every opportunity, giving orders in a coarse, insulting manner. Not even his inadvertent largesse – for he had gambled wantonly, making no effort to win – had softened his companions' view; for Castor was growing day by day almost inhumanly repugnant. He seemed to be turning into a bizarre travesty of a human being, his movements becoming increasingly unco-ordinated so that he flapped and jerked about the ship like a demented bat. Only the peculiar fascination he exerted prevented his companions from turning on him and, probably, killing him.

'Hey, Castor,' Raincoat taunted, 'how much you got left?'

'Plenty,' Castor scowled. 'I told you, there's plenty.'

'Plenty for me, all right,' Raincoat crowed. He had benefited most from Castor's recklessness.

Suddenly Gadzha's voice broke through the communicator from the bridge. 'Hey, we're being challenged.'

'Who by?' Castor snapped.

'Defence patrol.'

At a run, Castor went charging up to the bridge, hotly followed by the others. The face of a patrol ship captain stared at them on the comvidplate.

'Who's in command there?' he demanded.

Castor leaned over the vidplate. 'Me!'

The patrol captain flinched slightly. He seemed puzzled and displeased to see the disarray aboard the *Little Planet*. 'You are in a closed area. Return to Ziode.'

'Your coder bust or something?' Castor burst out. 'We're showing a pass signal issued by the Governor of Vence!'

'My orders don't come from Vence.' The captain's expression changed to one of cold distaste as he inspected the faces of each of them in turn. 'Return to Ziode.'

Castor persisted. 'You're out of order. The Governor is empowered to issue passes for travel to specified destinations. Examine the co-ordinates on our signal if you want to know more about it.'

The captain paused. 'Okay,' he said at length, 'I'll refer back to Vence. Check your velocity and proceed no farther.'

'How long will that take?'

'Oh, three, four days.'

Behind Castor, Gadzha was muttering. 'No good,' Castor said. 'That throws our schedule off. Our pass has a time limit. It would run out before we've finished our business here.'

'That's your problem,' the captain answered. 'Take it up with the Governor.' His face relaxed and he became a fraction more affable. 'Tell you what, I'll channel through a request for an extension for you. Meantime heave to so I can keep you in range – that's an order.'

'*Stuff it!*' Castor half-shrieked, his face swelling. He killed the screen, then moved to the guidance board and before anyone could stop him he had turned the engines on to emergency boost. The *Little Planet* shot ahead, temporarily doubling its trans-C velocity.

'You goddamned crazy loon!' Rabbish raved. 'What in hell do you think you're doing? He'll fire on us!'

'Nah. He's just a pipsqueak defence officer. He won't risk an inquiry by firing on a ship that has a legit pass. We're in the right.'

'Like hell we are,' Gadzha said tersely. 'Things have tightened up. There's going to be a war with Caean. We're right out on a limb.'

'He suspects us,' Leecher said dully.

Castor spoke placatingly. 'Fringe planets are full of rough types, always nosing out into the Gulf. The patrols are used to it.'

'Maybe, but now they're certain to board us on our way back in,' Gadzha reasoned slowly. 'Why did you do it? You've finished us.'

Castor ignored him, watching the drive indicators. The ship would soon be coming out of boost and back to cruising speed. The engines couldn't keep up the extra strain for long.

Gadzha took a step forward. 'Something funny is going on,' he announced. 'Why should Castor get us in trouble with the patrol for no reason, when everything was running smooth? There's something about this jaunt he hasn't told us. I've suspected it before.'

Castor turned and found himself staring into Gadzha's broad, unfriendly face. He huffed his shoulders aggressively. 'Maybe I didn't feel like hanging around,' he jeered, his mouth turned down in an ugly sneer. Then he sidled away from Gadzha, pulling himself into the oversize jacket of his suit like a crab.

Now they were all interested. Surrounding Castor, they all eyed him speculatively, but as yet still keeping a respectful distance.

'You know something? Castor owes us all,' Rabbish pointed out. 'That's how he got me interested in this project in the first place. How about you, Gadzha? Didn't he say he knew a way to clear his account with you?'

'What he owed me would be a drop in the ocean, the way he put it,' Gadzha agreed.

'Me too. It certainly saved his skin for a while, leading us out here.'

Leecher spoke up. 'Well how about it, Castor? What have you got to say for yourself?'

'So worried about your money,' Castor muttered contemptuously. 'You're all dirt.'

'There'd better be a Caeanic freighter out there, that's all. With everything on board like you said.'

'That's what I'd like to know,' Gadzha interjected. 'What about this ship?'

Castor didn't answer for a moment. 'The Governor will

keep the patrols off our backs,' he said. 'It's just as bad for him as it is for us if they come on board. Worse. You should have worked that out for yourselves, you poor schmooks.'

He turned to confront them, glaring into one face after another. 'The ship's there all right, I guarantee it. What do you think? I came all the way out here just for the view?'

He shoved his way through them and went to the door.

Leisurely he went below and sauntered along the corridor that ran the length of the *Little Planet*. Rabbish had nearly guessed the method he had used to set up the operation. He had intentionally got into debt with them all, then when they came to collect had dangled the carrot of the crashed Caeanic ship in front of them.

But Rabbish's observation would do them no good, not unless they could imagine some more substantive reason why Castor should want to visit the Gulf.

The door to the sleeping compartment was ajar. Castor peered in and saw that Gadzha's girl was there, alone, lying on a palliasse, either asleep or drowsing.

He gazed at her long black hair and pale skin. He had heard her name several times, but he didn't remember it. She was no beauty, but appealing in a sluttish kind of way – like all Gadzha's girls.

Softly he stepped inside, a leering grin on his lips. His eyes almost sparkled in the dim light.

Formerly Castor had always been obliged to pay for sex, which had lessened the pleasure he took in the act. Since acquiring the suit he had learned a new facility in obtaining it: he simply raped women. They found the experience revolting, but in some perverse way oddly fascinating; they never talked about it afterwards. Even if, by chance or sheer lack of precaution, Castor was discovered by a husband or boyfriend, the spell seemed to extend to them also, inflicting on them a kind of paralysis of the will. Gadzha had already suffered this effect a number of times.

When Castor was nearly upon the girl she came suddenly awake and started up. With a grunt he fell on the palliasse, bearing her down under him, his hands clutching and snatching inside her clothing.

She twisted her head to escape his fetid breath. Squirming and kicking, she tried to claw his face. He sniggered. She gave a loud, squealing cry, and then merely panted.

After a minute or two her struggles subsided to slow spasmodic movements of protest. He had her legs apart and was humping away with regularity when Gadzha came into the room.

With a low-throated growl Gadzha pounced. He seized Castor by the collar, lifting him bodily off the girl and throwing him across the chamber. Somehow or other Castor landed in a crouch, more or less on his feet. He slouched against the bulkhead, his face slack, his flies open and his still-erect penis exposed. The front of his trousers was stained.

Raincoat and Leecher appeared at the door, staring at him. The girl gave a moan and turned her face to the wall.

For the remainder of the journey to Kyre, Castor kept to himself. Their course was pre-programmed and on the coded pass-tape, so to change course before they were out of the area covered by Ziodean patrols might have been to invite trouble.

Two days after his fourth rape of Gadzha's successive girlfriends he heard Raincoat tap on the door of the store cupboard he now used to sleep in. Lying sprawled among the junk of the cupboard like a rag doll, he pushed the door outward with his foot. He had abandoned all thought for his appearance, yet it was amazing how much charisma he still carried.

'We're in orbit,' Raincoat announced. 'Kyre's below.'

'Big deal,' Castor grunted. He hunched himself to his feet, pushed Raincoat aside and made for the bridge.

His arrival there was greeted with excitement, if also with ill-concealed revulsion. Kyre was spread out on the main vidplate, a fair-looking world of blue oceans and fluffy white clouds. He took one glance at it and walked to the guidance board.

'Do you know exactly where to find the freighter?' Leecher asked anxiously, following him. 'Which continent is it on?'

'I know where it is,' Castor said. 'I've been here before, remember?'

'Where is it?'

'It's on the pear-shaped continent.'

Castor's hands moved over the board. But instead of descending towards the planet's atmosphere the *Little Planet* gathered velocity and left orbit, heading even deeper into the Gulf.

Castor turned and looked at his companions with a sneer of triumph.

'What are you doing?' screeched Leecher in alarm. 'We're leaving Kyre!'

Gadzha sprang forward and examined the controls. 'Where are you taking us?' he demanded angrily.

Hatred shone from Castor's face. '*I'm taking you to Caean, you fools!*' he screeched, mimicking Leecher. Then he spat. 'Caean!'

This turn of events perplexed them. They looked at one another.

'But why?' Gadzha asked. 'What about the freighter?'

Castor smiled malevolently. 'Bait, you poor pigeons! I needed a ship to take me to Caean. I could have off-loaded you all on Vence, but I thought I'd enjoy seeing your faces when the crunch comes.' Contemptuously he turned to the board again, leaving his back undefended.

But this time they were not overawed. Gadzha shouldered him away from the guidance board. The ship lurched as he cancelled some of its acceleration. Guided by the instructions he fed into its computer, it entered a flat, fast ellipse that once again orbited the planet below them.

Castor, however, ignored this and turned to face the others, who were edging menacingly towards him. He had been looking forward to this moment. His gimmicked eyes blazed and glittered. His lips jutted out with maniacal ferocity. He flung out his arms in a gesture of repulse, and at the same time imagined himself to be swelling up to an enormous size. It was a technique he had used before, and one which apparently involved some deformation of the senses, for he seemed in reality to expand, the bridge and its occupants dwindling to toy-like insignificance. The phenomenon, whatever it was, affected the others, too; after only a couple of steps they halted and stared at him as if at a vision.

'Quieten down, scum, I'm taking over this ship,' he said in a rasping voice. 'Just accept the fact that you're dirt. If you want to live –'

Castor had always been confident of his power at this point. He had believed that no matter how much his victims detested him he could always turn them into frightened rabbits as long as he wore his suit. But now the unexpected happened. The bubble of his mental expansion suddenly seemed to burst. He staggered. His arms flapped wildly. A convulsive tic seized one side of his face and he grimaced and jerked.

His partnership with the Frachonard suit, fragile at the best of times, was breaking down. His nervous system had been interfered with too much, and for too long.

'*Ugh*,' he grunted. '*Ugh – ugh – ugh –*'

A pathetic, helpless object, he cringed and twitched in front of the men he had tricked.

'He's flipped!' Rabbish said, amazed.

'He's a Caeanic agent,' Leecher grated. 'That has to be it.'

'That would explain it all right,' Raincoat muttered. 'Him being so weird, I mean.'

This interpretation of events was cause for added disgust. They forced the helpless Castor into a chair. Gadzha stood over him, legs apart. Castor breathed deeply, in gasps.

'So there never was a Caeanic ship on Kyre.'

'There's a ship there all right. We already took one load from it.'

Gadzha spoke to Raincoat. 'We'll give it a try. Take us down.'

'Hold it!' Castor giggled weakly. 'You can't go down there. Kyre's an infra-sound planet. The atmosphere's full of subsonic.'

'Subsonic?'

'Low-frequency vibrations. You've heard of infra-sound, haven't you? Put a ship down there and she breaks up in minutes.'

Gadzha paused uncertainly. 'What are you trying to sell us? I never heard of any infra-sound *planet*.'

Briefly Castor tried to explain about Kyre's unique fauna and flora. 'What do you think happened to the Caeanic ship in the first place? Try going down there if you like. See what the hell I care.'

'You've already been there, you told us. How did you do it, if we can't?'

'We had a special suit. A baffle suit, to cancel out the infra-sound. Mast had it made. It cost a fortune.' Castor sighed deeply. He felt abandoned, shrivelled.

'Mast?'

'My boss.'

Gadzha glanced at his companions. 'Looks like we teamed up with the wrong partner. Where's this Mast now?'

'On Ledlide.' Castor attempted to grin, but failed.

There was a long silence. Leecher snorted. 'This is ridiculous. We've been gulled by this Caeanic spy, might as well face up to it. Nothing for it now but to go home.'

Raincoat gestured to Castor. 'What about him?'

'Leave him on Kyre.'

'You *can't*,' Castor insisted. 'The ship will break up if you go down there.'

'Do what you like with him,' Leecher said. 'But let's not hang around here any longer. I'll set course for Ziode.'

He moved to the guidance board. The *Little Planet* swung away from Kyre and began to traverse the tiny solar system.

The others sat down and glared at Castor with hatred.

'Let's just shove him through the lock into space,' Rabbish said.

'I forgot to tell you,' Castor said with a smile. 'There was nothing for you down on Kyre anyway. The ship's probably still there, but with the cargo gone. Last time we were here we saw a Caeanic salvage ship making for it.'

They ignored him, making further suggestions for the disposal of his person.

After a while Leecher joined them. 'Why don't we give him a shot of something?' he suggested. 'Something that would leave him conscious and suffering for a long time. Like succinyl.'

'What's that?'

'You're fully conscious but you can feel yourself dying of pain and suffocation. They reckon there's nothing like it. It's an interrogation drug. I don't like people who mess me around the way this creep has.'

Castor had been spending the last quarter of an hour trying to get his charismatic powers back, knowing that if he did he would be able to command the situation again. But the suit seemed quiescent, and he began to grow worried that his verve would not return.

When Leecher made his malignant suggestion he acted on his own initiative. Surreptitiously he eased a sliver-knife from inside his jacket and jumped up, the knife waving in the air, to make a dash for the door.

It was Leecher who stepped into his path, unaware of the extremely thin, near-invisible blade. Castor's lips jutted out again in determined savagery. The sliver-knife sliced through cloth, bone and lung tissue. Leecher coughed, a choked, barely audible sound, blood foaming from his chest, and slid to the floor.

Castor gestured triumphantly with the knife, easily visible now as a shining line of blood. His eyes blazed and sparkled. 'Get out of it! Get out of it! Get out of it! –'

Gadzha was on him. He clamped an immensely strong hand on Castor's wrist, forcing the fist down until the fingers opened. The sliver-knife hit the floor and broke into a dozen fragments.

He flung Castor back in the chair. 'That does it,' he rumbled. 'That just does it. Have we got any of that succinyl, Raincoat?'

Rabbish was bending over the blood-soaked Leecher, who was barely conscious but was giving out tortured moaning sounds. 'What'll we do?' he appealed helplessly. 'He's in a bad way.'

Gadzha looked down at the injured man. 'Give him a shot from the medikit,' he said briefly, then turned back to Raincoat.

Raincoat seemed uninterested in the fate of his comrade. He had stepped to the guidance board and was studying it.

'No, we wouldn't have any succinyl,' he said after a moment. 'Anyway, a dose of poetic justice is what's in order. He's brought us all this way for nothing – let's just leave him here.'

'We've already left Kyre. You mean push him into space?'

'No. There's a second planet; we're close to it now.' He peered at the chart. '"The Planet of the Flies". Peculiar name. Let's see if it makes a suitable place to dump our friend.'

He killed the overdrive, turned the ship and instructed the auto pilot to land on the inner planet. Castor was appalled. He shivered.

Then, at long last, he felt the suit's guiding influence beginning to return slightly. He let the support flow into him, soothing his disharmonized nerves.

When he spoke it was the voice of a smoother, suaver *persona* that came through his mouth. He laughed in almost friendly fashion.

'You won't maroon me here, you know – that would be simply too inhuman. You don't know why they call it "the Planet of the Flies", do you?'

They all ignored him. Gadzha watched while Rabbish inexpertly gave Leecher a spray injection.

Soon Leecher stopped breathing. 'What was it, a metabolic stop shot?' Gadzha asked.

Rabbish checked the words on the capsule. 'No, it was a death shot,' he explained.

'You damned fool, why did you do that?' Gadzha shouted hoarsely. 'We might have got him to a doctor!'

Rabbish looked hurt. 'Well, he shouldn't have got stabbed,' he complained peevishly. 'It was you who told me to give him a shot.'

'*Flies*,' Castor interrupted desperately. '*Flies.*'

The ship descended through the planet's atmosphere. At a height of a mile it began to settle into the black sludge of flies, sinking as if into a swamp. From the hull came a faint thrumming noise.

They all stared in fascination at the main vidplate as the ship found a solid surface.

Gadzha spoke in a choked voice. '*God!*'

'Awful, isn't it?' Castor commented lightly. He looked about him hopefully, with raised eyebrows. 'Oh well, let's be up and on our way.'

Raincoat was staring glassily at the plate. 'It's perfect,' he intoned in a shaky voice. 'Just what we need. He's nothing but an insect himself.'

Castor stood up as Raincoat turned to him. The suit at this point made a brief attempt to invest him with grace and beauty, but his fractured nervous system interpreted the impulses so badly that he merely leaped up and down like a mad puppet, baring his teeth in a weird grimace and uttering animal-like sounds. The horrid spectacle goaded Raincoat, Gadzha and Rabbish into action. They dragged him kicking and screaming from the bridge and down to the package ejector port at ground level. Castor's screams became increasingly terrified as the import of events came home to him, but only in the last minute or so did he plead, and then it was to no avail. They locked him in the ejector chamber and worked the ramrod that pushed its contents into the open air.

Afterwards they looked at one another, gasping.

Castor ceased to scream once the outer hatch was opened. Foolishly he had tried to breathe; the flies, which had already flooded in to clog his nasal cavities, had evaded all his apertures and formed a layer between his skin and his garments, in seconds filled his lungs and stomach.

In spite of that he was still alive when the ramrod ejected him from the chamber. He staggered and floundered in the dense atmosphere of living, buzzing flies, which clustered around him like iron filings on a magnet, creating a manshaped blotch of near-solid consistency.

The flies were voracious: they lived by eating a semiorganic rock-like substance that rumbled up constantly from beneath the surface of the planet. In an astonishingly short time they had devoured Castor. Tissue, blood, bone, and all trace of undergarments entirely disappeared.

They did not, however, eat the Frachonard suit.

Over the past year it had gained much experience in the monitoring of sentient activity. It had reached the point where it could, if need be, control living systems directly, wherever they stood on the evolutionary scale. What was more, the primitive nervous systems of the flies offered no problems of incompatibility, as had the advanced human one possessed by Castor. The suit, despite its setback, had not abandoned its mission and was in no way faltering or reticent.

It did not collapse or even become slack when Castor disappeared. Instead, it filled itself up with flies, organizing them into a collective pseudo-body which powered it in a stiff mimicry of human action. Falteringly it turned to the closed hatch of the ejector port, and directed the combined efforts of thousands of flies to push loose the dogs. That done, it floated from the ground, entering the chamber and allowing in only as many flies as suited its purpose, leaving the rest to cover the open hatch like a black wall.

Behind it the hatch closed automatically prior to take-off. The *Little Planet* swayed into the air to rise rapidly above the fly layer. Minutes later, after opening the inner door of the package ejector port with difficulty, the suit was free and walking the passages of the ship by means of its humming pseudo-body.

In the long corridor beneath the level of the bridge it encountered Gadzha's girl. She stopped and stood stock-still with a petrified snarl of fear on her face, staring at the apparition: at the suit recently worn by her rapist Castor, but worn now by a body of flies. The head, hands and feet were each composed of a black fuzzy mass. The legs, even though they floated a foot above the floor, persisted in striding slowly in walking fashion as the monster came slowly towards her.

A breathy sound from the girl's throat signalled her vain attempt to scream. Then, recovering her power of movement, she turned and fled in the direction of the bridge.

The Frachonard suit arrived there scarcely half a minute behind her. Gadzha, Raincoat and Rabbish all froze to see this phantom return, as, for the second time, did the girl.

In the seconds remaining to them only Raincoat had the presence of mind to reach for his gun, a futile gesture he did not even complete.

He did not complete it because the suit released its hold on the flies, sending them exploding in all directions to fill the interior of the bridge. While it collapsed neatly on the floor, the flies began to feast on their victims; but shortly, with the bodies only partly devoured, the suit recalled them again. They streamed back, causing the suit to rise up from the floor as if lifted by a string.

It floated over to the guidance board. The pseudo-hands hovered over the controls; clumsily, exerting all their puny force, the flies began to manipulate them.

The *Little Planet* changed course and went hurtling obliquely through the Gulf.

The Frachonard suit was in search of its property.

And that property was Peder Forbarth.

10

Ledlide, in terms of geological time, was but recently accreted, a slagheap of a planet still drifting through a miasma of gas, dust and rubble that was the detritus of sister planets yet to form. It orbited a primary which was itself no more than a dimly glowing cloud of gas, more a proto-star than a star in the true sense, yet providing a modicum of heat and gloomy light.

To the Ziodean mind such a remote and dismal spot made an ideal prison site. Ziodeans did not view the social offender as a candidate for reform or rehabilitation. Responsibility for misdeeds was seen as personal and absolute: the criminal got his deserts, and the logical punishment, short of death, was for him to be removed from society, the farther the better.

Accordingly the convict, on his journey to Ledlide, looked back through the prison ship's viewports and saw the Ziode Cluster receding into the distance. Thus he was made to feel how decidedly he had been rejected.

The Frachonard suit experienced considerable difficulty in locating this six-thousand-mile heap of cosmic garbage. Finding the partially condensed cloud that was Ledlide's solar system was not so hard, but once within the cloud it was unable to use the ship's instruments and so had to rely on its own growing powers of apprehension. Guiding the ship at this stage was even more difficult, for the flies having fed on the remains of the bridge's previous occupants until nothing was left of them, were unused to a human-type atmosphere and were dying off despite the suit's strict control over their vitality.

Out of Ledlide's smog-like sky, the *Little Planet* descended towards the vicinity of the leaden prison roof, which jutted a few feet above the gravelly surface. Drifting northwards, the ship landed just beyond the horizon, behind a low ridge.

Once the ship was down, the depleted swarm of flies finally died, and the now-flaccid suit collapsed to the floor in a neat pile. The stench of decomposing flies filled the bridge.

After a while a door opened in the prison roof, and a man wearing a breathing mask appeared. Pausing once to orient himself, he trudged the mile or so to the ship. After a brief inspection he opened one of the hatches and went inside, exploring all sections of the ship and calling out to announce his presence.

When he reached the bridge the brittle bodies of the flies crunched under his feet. He still wore his breathing mask and did not notice the stench, or he would instantly have vomited. Otherwise the only sign of occupancy was the suit heaped on the floor near the guidance board. For some moments the man gazed at the suit. Then he bent down and carefully picked it up, straightening the folds and draping it over his arm.

After one last look round he retraced his steps and left the ship to trudge back to the prison. He reported that the ship was empty and appeared to have landed on automatic, but to make sure the governor ordered an air search of the surrounding terrain. The possibility of that unheard-of-thing – an escape attempt – was raised, but the governor quickly dropped it, secure in the knowledge that Ledlide was deemed escape-proof. The crew of the *Little Planet* must have suffered some accident, he decided. The craft must have flown itself here. He would ask for it to be taken to Ziode with the next supply ship.

For no apparent reason the suit was placed in a cupboard in the staff common quarters. Patiently, it waited.

*

Peder never discovered quite how large the prison was or how many inmates it contained. The population might, he conjectured, be as much as a million. It certainly could not be less than a hundred thousand, for Ledlide was a successful prison and had become a general dumping ground for Ziode's undesirables.

In view of such large numbers, tightly confined and marshalled by a relatively nugatory warder force, the chance of a revolt was surprisingly small, almost non-existent. The reason was simple. Should a revolt occur, no more food would be sent from Ziode and the prisoners would starve. The fact that they earned their food anyway, by working in the prison factories, was usually enough to keep them quiet.

The entire establishment was underground. Day by day Peder's consciousness became submerged into the environment of grey galleries, grey cells, the smell of men (he had heard there was also a women's segment somewhere), grey factories and workshops, and black-uniformed warders. He particularly hated the prison uniform, which was grey and baggy and humiliating. He had become shrunken and shrivelled since losing the Frachonard suit, and his flesh cringed away from the coarse hard fabric of his new clothes. He lived, moved and worked in a perpetual daze.

Once or twice, in the endless routine processions along interminable galleries and ubiquitous ramps, he had glimpsed Realto Mast, who had arrived in the same intake as himself, but he felt no desire to seek him out. He wished only to huddle in himself and die a little more each day.

So it caused him no pleasure when one evening during the association period, when Peder was sitting in his cell ignoring the murmur of talk on the landing, that the figure of Mast appeared in his open doorway. Framed in the yellow-grey light from the gallery, Realto looked much reduced in stature in his shapeless uniform and cropped hair. Peder turned away and hunched his shoulders sullenly, trying to rebuff him, but unabashed, Mast stepped into the cell, invading the tiny cubicle that was Peder's only privacy.

'Hello, Peder, how are you?' he said, the gaiety of his tone quite out of keeping with their circumstances. 'How long a sentence did you get?'

'What are you doing on this landing?' Peder grumbled.

'I've been moved to the end of your gallery – for the time being, at any rate. People get shifted around pretty often in this place, you know – that's to stop them forming permanent attachments, you see. So let's not quarrel. We might not be together for long.'

'Good,' Peder said in a stubborn, accusing mutter. 'You informed on me.'

'How can you be sure?' Mast asked him with a small, apologetic sound. 'It could have been Grawn.'

'Was it?'

'As a matter of fact it *was* me – but I had every excuse, Peder. You see, it was poor old Grawn I was thinking of. *I* would have kept you out of it, but they would have dragged everything out of poor Grawn, the defenceless old thing, and he would have suffered in the process. So I blabbed to spare him that. After all it makes no difference from your point of view – does it?' Mast adopted the frank, open-eyed camaraderie Peder had learned to mistrust.

'Very altruistic!' Peder sneered. 'But no doubt you collected your due reward!'

'Oh, I don't know. Grawn came off much better, in the event. He only got five years. I managed to convince the court that his part in the affair was minimal – they realized he was too dim to be an instigator, I think. But it worries me to think I won't be around to look after him when he's released. I don't know what will become of him, he's quite hopeless.'

'Oh, yes, you're good at looking after people, all right.'

Mast seemed genuinely disappointed by Peder's bitterness. He smiled painfully. 'Come come, now. Circumstances do occasionally get out of hand. Risk is proportionate to the potential reward, and so forth.' But Peder remembered Mast's smoothness on previous occasions, and remained unrelenting.

Mast hummed meditatively to himself, looking out on to the landing where the other prisoners were playing with improvised cards. He essayed one or two further remarks, to which Peder made no reply, and after a while wandered off.

Several nights later the humming of the lock on his cell door woke him from his sleep. He raised his head from his pillow. The cell was in darkness, the infra-red bulb, which allowed any passing warder to survey the cell through the sensitized peephole, being invisible to him. But normal yellow-grey light from the landing was filtering through the outlines of the door as it swung open. Peder became aware of a presence moving into the narrow cell.

The interior light came on. A warder stood there, though Peder knew him as a warder only because he recognized his face. He was not wearing his usual black serge uniform. He was wearing the Frachonard Prossim suit.

A chilling thrill of fright and shock ran through Peder. He shrank to the farther end of the bunk, his eyes wide with terror, trembling with anticipation. The warder's expression was glassy and unseeing. Without a word he undressed, neatly laying out the Frachonard suit on the bunk.

Then both face and body crumpled. The warder collapsed on to the floor.

How the suit had found its way here was too large a concept for Peder even to think about. But he knew now, accepting the fact with a dumb, animal-like resignation, that he could never be free of it. Slipping from the bunk, he stood up. With deft movements he removed his sacklike sleeping garb, took undergarments from his locker – hesitating at the thought of bringing Prossim in contact with their rough, churlishly cut cloth – and drew them on.

As he donned the suit its field of influence settled on him once more. There was the usual instant change of outlook, but this time in a way that was different from before. Impressions of a hitherto unknown order crowded into his brain, as though the whole prison around him was open to his inner gaze.

Nor was that all. Never before had the suit buried his ego almost completely beneath the thoughts and actions it suggested. It had always allowed him some independent consciousness. Now this changed. It was still his own brain that formed his thoughts, but that brain took its cue from something that was outside of him, something that surrounded him and supported him.

In the face of this invasion his ego at first struggled feebly but it had time for only one complete thought of its own.

Clothes robot.

Then it gave up as an entity on its own account, collapsing into a pale reflection of what went on around it.

And Peder the New Man, creature of Prossim, emerged. He went through the pockets of his suit and found several electronic pass keys. Kneeling, he inspected the unconscious warder. The man's breathing was light. He was in a deep coma.

He straightened. The beat of Ledlide prison was all around him. He became aware of facts, details, names that the unaided senses could never have told him, all interlocking throughout the huge ramification. The sleeping shifts, the working shifts, the rest-and-association shifts.

And he realized that escape from Ledlide *was* possible.

Leaving his cell, he padded the length of the silent landing. Men snored and muttered in their sleep behind the locked doors. On his left-hand side was a railing. The gallery well, screened at regular intervals by safety nets, dropped down for a thousand feet. On the opposite side of the well Peder could see the standard historical pattern of large-scale prisons: tier upon tier of landings and cells, a giant honeycomb of prisoners.

At the end of the gallery he halted. Using one of his electronic keys, he opened the door to Mast's cell. Quietly he went inside.

Mast was a light sleeper. He awoke immediately the light came on. He greeted Peder with a befuddled frown, then climbed from his bunk and stood staring at him.

'Peder . . . how did you do it? They are letting you wear your suit!'

'I'm leaving here,' Peder announced. 'You may come with me. It will be convenient.'

'Leaving where? Ledlide?' Mast chuckled softly, still puzzled, and shook his head. 'That isn't possible, Peder. You have to stay here. Better just to accept it.'

'I can get us out. To Caean. That is better than Ledlide, even for you.'

'Caean? . . .' Mast frowned. 'But there just *isn't* any way out.'

'I know a way. A ship is waiting for me on the surface. But it is difficult for someone like myself to man it alone. Better if you come with me. Caean is a long way.'

Mast took a step back. 'No,' he said in alarm. 'It's an automatic extension of sentence if you do anything . . .'

He trailed off. Peder leaned against the door jamb, the lines of his jacket falling away in a codicil of grace and perfection.

'Twenty years,' he reminded Mast. 'Twenty years of this grey routine, of never seeing outside. Come with me and you'll be *freeeee* . . .' His voice soared and caressed. 'Free on new worlds.'

Mast gave a cynical quirk of his lips. 'Free?'

He sighed.

'All right, Peder,' he said, 'I'll try you out.'

He reached for his prison clothes. Together they left the cell. At the end of the gallery one of Peder's pass keys gained them entry to a door which opened on a tiny station where waited a bullet-shaped vehicle containing two seats, side by side. The shuttle service was normally never used by prisoners unless accompanied by a warder, but at

a gesture from Peder they took their places in the seats
and the shuttle moved forward on its guide rails, coursing
along the efficient transport system. They traversed the
sleeping silence of their own segment and entered others
which, though identical, were like foreign territory to
them. Here men were awake and working, for the rota-
tion of shifts was designed never to leave a machine idle.

Other shuttles swept past them in a blur of motion.
Peder steered the vehicle unhesitatingly. When they
eventually came to a stop it was in a factory area where
the hum of machinery mingled with the bustling of prisoners shuffling to the canteens, to the sleeping galleries, or
to the baths and the recreation halls.

Peder's stride was unhesitating as he led Mast along the
outside wall of one of the factory workshops. Mast was
becoming increasingly nervous to see so many warders
about, and he stiffened as one approached them. But the
officer strolled on with only a passing nod to Peder.

'Relax,' Peder murmured. 'I am a warder; you are a
prisoner I am taking to the medical room.'

'But you're wearing civilian clothes!'

Peder smiled. 'I'm in disguise,' he said.

'It's some kind of hypnotism?' Mast asked after a
pause. 'People see what you want them to see?'

Peder did not answer. The truth was not quite as
Mast had stated, but in a sense it was close to it. The
suit could make itself inconspicuous; it could cause its
wearer to adopt a role so convincingly that a detail like
the absence of the correct uniform went unnoticed. The
warder's mind had been subliminally tricked, distracted.

He had considered tricking his way in this manner
through the official portals in the prison roof, but had
decided it was impossible. Even if he could get through
the cage that separated the prisoner compound from the
outer administrative shell, he still would not be able to
leave the prison without setting off the automatic alarms.

Besides, the suit had a better way. Peder turned into
a narrow down-sloping passage ending in a metal door

which needed no pass key. They stepped into an engine room filled with row upon row of power units.

The high-pitched whine the machines gave off made a din in which hearing was difficult. As they passed by, the prisoners tending the power units looked up once, then took no further notice. Peder made his way to the far corner of the room and moved aside one of a series of what looked like filing cabinets or store cupboards. He beckoned to Mast, then began testing the wall behind the cabinet.

The cabinets were cleverly arranged so that the two men were screened from view, enclosed in a triangular space in the corner. At first nothing happened. Then, with a click, a section of wall slid aside.

Feet first, Peder dropped through the hatch-like opening to a floor about four feet below. As Mast followed, the concealed entrance sprang automatically back into place behind them, and the noise of the machinery faded somewhat.

They stood in a dimly lit chamber, or cellar, that appeared to have been hammered together from sheets of scrap metal. Its only occupant was a grey-clad prisoner who was hunched over a glowing screen. The figure whirled round to glare at them in fear.

This, as Peder knew, was Grashnik, a lifer like himself. Grashnik was almost unique among the inmates of Ledlide, however, in that he refused to accept that escape was impossible. He had always clung steadfastly to the belief that he could – and would – break out.

The first reward of his optimism had come twenty years ago, when, on a working party that had been extending the prison a few hundred yards farther into the rock, he had discovered a fissure leading to the surface.

He had kept this knowledge to himself, watching dumbly as access to the fissure was sealed off with the building of the prison's new outer wall. He had spent the next twelve years regaining that access. The route he had finally established was tortuous. First he had located

a small hole in the sensor field that surrounded the prison.
Over a period of seven years he had manufactured pass
keys for twenty-three different doors and hatches so as
to take him up to, through and beyond this gap in the
electrostatic web, always by little-frequented passages.
Then had come the laborious business of boring a hole
through the wall itself, bringing him to the fissure.

The enterprise had taken genius, care and much
patience. Grashnik had worked always in secret, always
alone, making use of his training as an engineer and his
position of trust in the factory where he had been made
a permanent overseer.

He calculated that, given another twenty years, he
could have got this far without ever having discovered
the fissure; that was how long it would have taken him
to burrow up to the surface. It was plain why no one had
ever embarked upon such a scheme, for Grashnik's own
motivation rested on stubborn faith. The chief problem
was not to gain the surface, but to leave Ledlide once that
was done. Grashnik had racked his brain to try to think of
a way of getting aboard the regular supply ship, but since
it did not even touch down but offloaded its cargo from
a mile in the air, the idea seemed impossible. And so he
relied on hope. Grashnik's whole scheme was redundant
unless some day, for some reason, a ship – any ship –
landed in the dirt near to Ledlide prison. Then the route
to the surface would make sense, even if he had to wait
another thirty years for that ship.

At the entrance to the route Grashnik had built this
hide-hole, and equipped it with a low-output scanning
set that could surreptitiously survey the terrain around
the prison, without interfering with any of the official
equipment. Once a week he slipped in here and used
the set for half an hour or so, a practice he had kept up
now for eight years.

All this Peder knew through the Frachonard suit, just
as he seemed, looking at Grashnik now, to be able to read
his mind. The criminal rose slowly and backed away from

the two intruders. Peder glanced at the screen of the scanning set. It bore the blurred image of a spaceship parked on uneven, gravel-like ground.

'*Whassamarrerdoinhere* . . .' Grashnik whispered hoarsely, unable to formulate coherent speech in his confusion.

Peder waved a hand at the screen. 'All things come to those who wait, it seems.'

Grashnik found his voice. 'How long have you known? Who are you guys, anyway?'

'Unfortunates like yourself, Grashnik.'

'Well get out of here and keep your mouths shut, or I'll kill you.' In his excitement Grashnik began to stutter. 'There's a ship out there! There's a ship out there! It worked! I'm free!' His eyes narrowed. 'Get out of here or I'll kill you.'

'The ship landed in order to take *me* off,' Peder informed him. 'I'm afraid you will have to wait your turn until another ship chances to call. Meantime I shall need to use your route to the surface.' He spoke equably but with chilling self-confidence.

Grashnik glared, spittle forming at his lips. 'This is *my* route and nobody's taking it from me. I've spent twenty years setting it up!' He whipped a hand-ground knife from inside his baggy tunic and crouched low, shifting his weight uncertainly from foot to foot.

Mast interrupted, pointing to the screen. 'One moment. Is that the ship you're talking about? It looks big enough to take us all. What is there to quarrel over?'

Peder shrugged. 'Grashnik has only one set of breathing apparatus to take us to the surface. Even with the two of us, that presents difficulties. Still, if you insist . . .'

But Grashnik was in no mood to be reasonable. 'Nobody uses the route but me. Nobody! I spent twenty years setting it up!' His eyes went glassy and he edged towards Peder.

From the way he held his blade it was plain he was not one of Ledlide's most skilful knife fighters. Peder did not even try to meet him on his own terms. He held up a hand commandingly, bringing Grashnik to a halt.

'You can escape from Ledlide,' he said softly. 'I know a way out. A much better way than this.' He stepped forward. Grashnik's lined, tired face stared up wonderingly at the sartorialist, the knife limp in his fingers, and Peder had time for fugitive feelings of pity and admiration as he put his hands on the prisoner's brow, the tips of his fingers touching the greyed hair.

Grashnik gave a barely audible gasp. Peder stepped back. The lifer's face had gone slack and dreamy, his eyes vague. He was reliving the happier times of his life; all awareness of his presence in Ledlide prison was gone. With a faint moan he slumped to the floor.

Peder located a hidden square in the floor and lifted it. In a space beneath were the pass keys Grashnik had manufactured so painstakingly over the years. Peder took them out, briefly inspecting each one and placing them in various pockets. Then he pulled away a section of wall on the opposite side of the chamber. The roughly cut sheeting came loose easily, revealing a gap between the floor of this level and the ceiling of the level below them.

Grashnik had stopped breathing by the time Peder beckoned to Mast to follow him, and they set forth on the lifer's slow, persistent project: a route to the surface.

It took them nearly three hours of crawling, dodging and ducking, of fiddling with Grashnik's sometimes faulty pass keys, before they came to the hatchway he had built into the outer perimeter wall. Nearby, in an improvised locker, they found the breathing set.

'One of us will have to go first, and return for the other,' Mast said.

Peder paused. He filled his lungs, breathing deeply as if experimenting with his respiratory system. 'It may not be necessary,' he murmured. 'Ledlide's atmosphere contains *some* oxygen. Not enough to sustain one normally . . . but I may be able to manage. You don't mind if

I lean on you to save my energy? Occasionally I may ask for a lungful of air from your mouthpiece. If I should collapse, carry me the rest of the way to the ship . . .'

'But you can't live out there,' Mast objected.

'Do as I say.'

'How long will it take us to get to this ship?'

'I don't know.'

Thinking him mad, Mast donned the breathing set. The Frachonard suit slowed down Peder's metabolism to a minimum as they went through the tiny airlock Grashnick had built. Ledlide's young atmosphere was thick and cloying, filled with unpleasant gases. By the light of a torch, also supplied by courtesy of Grashnik, they found a low-roofed tunnel, and then the fissure, made scalable by metal ladders hammered into the rock.

Steadily, foot by foot, they began to climb.

11

Casting off one's body and assuming larval form was, after all, something the human mind could not be expected to take without strain. Amara admitted this as she peered anxiously through the window of Alexei Verednyev's chamber. Alexei, *sans* suit, filled to the eyeballs with de-sensitizing drugs, was tottering about his prison in a daze.

The surgical revamping given him by the *Callan*'s medical section had left him seriously ill. His limbs were new, grown in a gene tank since his original ones had been too atrophied to be of use. Some of the torso and neck muscles had also been replaced, while others had been coaxed to work against the pull of normal gravity by an extensive course of massage and protein injection. His present digestive system would probably never be able to absorb normal food, and therefore there was talk of replacing that also with a new alimentary canal.

But the physical problems were nothing to the psychological ones. Alexei's rebirth would not have been endurable at all had he not been subjected to a process known as 'neutralized effect'. This technique, accomplished by a combination of hypnosis and a whole battery of psyche-controlling drugs, robbed all experience of emotive content, so that anything, however bizarre or traumatic, was viewed with the same complacent equanimity. The drug dosages were supposed to be decreased by stages as Alexei grew accustomed to his condition, but in practice the withdrawal simply could not be carried out at the planned rate without his quickly regressing into what Estru flippantly termed 'the horror syndrome'.

In deciding to undertake the experiment Amara had acted from mixed motives, not all of which could be subsumed under the heading of scientific curiosity. When speaking to her team she had reasoned that it would be a useful exercise in researching 'the mentality of encasement'. Possibly it would give them a line on how to decondition the Caeanic aberration. But she was also prompted by a genuine compassion for the hulking metalloid, who was cut off for ever from his own kind and could not even negotiate the ship without help, – or so she had told herself; she had also conceived an aggravation with him, an exasperated feeling that he would not really co-operate until he had been cut down to size.

In one corner of the chamber stood a mock-up of the suit Verednyev had once possessed, into which he was permitted to retreat in moments of stress. With old-man weariness he leaned briefly against a wall, then made for this refuge. Amara spoke to him quickly, using the outside microphone.

'You're looking well today, Alexei. How are you feeling?'

As she had intended, he halted his retreat to the mock-up. 'As well as could be expected, Amara,' he said dully, keeping his face averted. Even his own voice, vibrating directly on the air without the mediation of radio transducers, sounded alien to him.

'Good,' she responded briskly. 'I'd like to come in so we can talk face to face. How about it?'

'Not yet, Amara. I don't think I'm ready for it. I still wouldn't be able to bear it.'

'All right,' she said, making no attempt to hide her displeasure. 'But just try to understand that you've got to make an *effort*. Before long we'll be cutting down your medications to absolutely *nothing*. Then you'll *have* to learn to face us. You're got to live as we do.'

Maybe I'll take his mock-up away altogether, she thought as she left. It's time he did without a funk-hole.

Back in her section, she faced up brazenly to Estru's scepticism. 'He'll adjust in the end,' she assured him. 'Learning to walk in only three months is pretty good going, if you think about it.'

'But you said he'd be strolling through the ship by now and chatting to the crew,' Estru reminded her.

'He will. The important thing is that he's realized there's no other way out for him. He's co-operating.'

'Oh, I've no doubt he'll make some sort of adjustment in the end. Then when we stop filling him with drugs he'll be able to perceive his situation clearly for a change. A week later he'll commit suicide. I doubt if lifelong conditioning can ever be permanently set aside.'

'Then we won't stop giving him drugs,' Amara countered. 'We'll find a balance, whatever keeps him sane.'

She cut off any further talk on the subject. There were more important things to do than to argue over the Verednyev experiment. The latest field research report to be delivered by the 'planetary probes' (as she called her spies) lay on her desk. She leafed through it attentively before speaking on the vidcom to the head of her staff in the adjoining room.

'Has this report been taped yet?'

'All ready to roll, Amara.'

'Right, run it through to me.'

She and Estru turned to their official terminal and watched a flow of symbols and diagrams (the specialized jargon of their trade) dance across the screen. 'Leave it keyed in,' Amara told her staffman. 'I'll integrate the results myself.'

Her hands moved over the keys, instructing the sociological computer (the department's main piece of hardware) to integrate the report's findings into all the rest of the data they had gathered so far. Then they both sat back and studied the emerging updated pattern.

'Well, it's shaping up as I had expected,' Amara congratulated herself. She stopped at the summation diagram, a graph displaying various curves and coded figures. 'See, the habit-cohesiveness index is down – less rigidity. The Ries-Hammond factor is down, too. The implication is quite clear – the "Sovyan effect" is beginning to abate.'

'But the sartorial index is increasing,' Estru commented. 'Apparel is richer in variety and content.'

Amara nodded. 'Of course it is. As the more restrictive consequences of the Sovyan experience fall away, the basic Sovyan mode manifests itself in a compensatory blossoming of sartorial techniques. Somewhere farther along the Tzist Arm – mid-way along it, perhaps – I think we shall see a culmination of Caeanic culture; clothes-consciousness will reach its peak. Then that, too, will decline as we proceed towards the farther end of the Arm. We can predict that the people at the extremity – those farthest from the seminal Sovyan event – will be almost normal. That's what we can extrapolate from these figures, anyway.'

Estru grunted. 'The Directorate will be interested to hear that.'

'They will indeed,' Amara nodded emphatically. 'If the planets at the farther end of the Arm turn out to be closer to us in outlook than to more typical Caeanics – as I think they will – they will provide us with a lever for subversion.'

She sighed with satisfaction, feeling the excitement of expanding knowledge. Sovya had given her an anchor-point from which to forecast a whole range of Caeanic characteristics right along the Tzist Arm. It thrilled her to see her predictions being borne out by observation.

Privately Estru was more cautious. For the past few months, under heavy baffle to avoid detection, they had been scouting along the inner curve of the Tzist Arm, taking 'cultural sounding samples' from the more accessible inhabited planets. This they did by stealthily dropping trained observers, Caeanic-speaking and wearing Caean-made garments, who were supposed to index certain 'cultural variables' identified according to parameters chosen by Amara herself. Surprisingly, all the agents had so far returned safely. Amara swore that the method was reliable and objective, and Estru did not dare to contradict her, but sometimes he amused himself by imagining what sort of picture a similar operation carried out on Ziode would produce.

'What's the itinerary now?' he said as Amara cancelled the summation diagram from the terminal. For an answer she keyed a map of the Tzist Arm on to the screen. Wandering along part of the inner curve ran a jagged line, each kink and angle marked by a symbol and denoting a planet they had surveyed.

'Logically we should head for Verrage, the nearest regional capital, but that will bring us into the commercial space routes where we might be detected.' She bit her lip, then zoomed in on the approaching stretch of the Arm.

'We ought to try to get as close to Verrage as possible,' he commented.

'True enough.' Stars and star groupings were sliding past in glowing colours on the screen as she tried to pick a tortuous path that would avoid the main space-faring lanes. 'There's a lot of information to be gained from this region.'

'Perhaps we should ask Captain Wilce to pick a route,' Estru suggested. 'Safety is his responsibility, after all.'

'I don't want to give Verrage too wide a berth. But I dare say you're right.'

She turned to the vidcom asked for Captain Wilce.

12

The Diask: *a garment unique to Caean, composed of independent panels of stiffish, chunky cloth cut into various shapes. Lacking stitching, seams or fastening, the panels maintain position solely by reason of the cloth's natural tendency to adhere to itself, a quality which is heightened by friction. The garment thus clings during motion and relaxes somewhat when still. Wearing the* diask *brings a sensation of security and containment.*

The Bliaut: *a garment of ancient origin but much developed and variegated in Caean. Consisting basically of a corset-like bodice with wide, sweeping sleeves, elaborately decorated, low, curved waistline and heavily folioled skirt or breeches.*

The Cyclas: *a loose garment cut from a single piece of cloth with a single hole for the head. In the same class as the* chiton (*a long loose tunic with overfold fastening on the shoulder*) *and the* kalasiris (*a long-sleeved or sleeveless robe*) *but unlike them an essentially simple garment. To cut a new* cyclas *is regarded as one of the tests of a true sartorialist, since originality can only be achieved by means of tensions and warps in the weave. The* cyclas, *like its cousins the* chiton *and the* kalasiris, *imparts a sense of airy freedom.*

The Houppelande: *a gown made in a bell shape and of rich cloth, sometimes reaching only to the thighs, but more often falling in increasing fullness to the ankles. Gracefulness of the heavy folds, both in skirt and sleeves, is an important feature. The* houppelande *gives a feeling of graciousnesss, richness and slow dignity.*

The Arras: *a broad hanging garment consisting of flat,* *tasselled front and back curtain-panels depending from wide shoulder-rails, usually worn with a matching rail-like head-dress and veil. The arras gives an impression of screened secrecy and withdrawal. Faintly reminiscent of a mandilion or some kinds of herald's tabard.*

The Leviathan: *a set of clothes covered in moving human images, so that the wearer seems to be clad in a living multitude. Variations on the leviathan use fewer, perhaps only one, image – a face set in the chest, perhaps, furnished with a voice and a certain degree of computer-backed personality able to respond to the wearer's social environment. The leviathan can express sociability and extreme extroversion, but also multiple personality, instability of mind, and extreme distraction from one's surroundings.*

The Remontant: *a garment in which the human frame is utilized as the supporting stem for a flower theme. There is an infinite variety of remontants, most of which express a springlike quality denoting delight in new life, blossoming energy and artistic talent.*

These are but a few examples of the garments commonly worn in Tzist. It would be impossible to give any really adequate idea of the vast diversity of Caeanic apparel, which perhaps is best indicated by the fact that nearly one third of the Caeanic vocabulary is concerned with clothing. Oddly, the concept of fashion does not exist in Caean; the country is subject to no sweeping changes of mood or mass imitation. An important feature of the national structure is supplied, however, by sub-cults which could be described as 'fashion societies', but which are known in Caean as 'sodalities'. There are innumerable of these, some small and local, some nationwide, each with its own historical, philosophical or cultural theme or goal which is pursued by means of suitable costume.

All the above, and most other distinct categories of garment, could be regarded as having specialized applications. If a dress of universal potential exists then it is the form of attire most commonly worn in Caean and Ziode alike, and known simply as:

The Suit: *consisting essentially of trousers, a jacket, and more often than not a waistcoat. In this form the suit can be traced as far back as pre-expansionist Earth, reaching a peak of inventiveness in the twenty-first century of that era. In all known succeeding cultures it has survived as the predominant mode of dress among males and sometimes even among females, by reason of its convenience and flexibility of expression. In the hands of the Caeanic sartorialists it has radiated into a whole universe of styles, often losing its original character and merging into other, more specialist, classifications. Many established modes are known by apt names: the* Scythe *(making a man incisive, speedy), the* Skyscraper *(bringing a feeling of tallness, uprightness and commanding power), the* Zipflash, *the* Suit of Light, *the* Airplane, *and so on.*

The Caeanic ideal is a suit of clothes that encompasses the whole man and not merely some aspect or potentiality of him. Only the near-legendary Frachonard is believed to have accomplished such perfection, and then only in a limited number of his creations.

Arth Matt-Helver, *Travels in the Tzist Arm*

Sinuating through the velvety curves of superphotic space, the Caeanic battle cruiser had been shadowing the *Callan* for days. Captain Wilce, preparing to make a fly-by of the star group containing Verrage, had continued to entertain the faint hope that it was merely flying on a course coincidentally parallel to their own. But he had not been so impetuous as to veer away in order to put that hope to the test. Sudden changes of course attenuated the effectiveness of their baffles.

On the fifth day, however, he was forced to acknowledge the failure of their mission. His face grave, he made a call to Amara.

'We have just received a transmission from the commander of the Caeanic ship,' he told her. 'He tells me we are to be escorted to Verrage. He also instructs us to pipe aboard a party of his officers.'

Amara went white. 'Is there no chance of getting away?'

'None at all, from a fully armed cruiser. They've clearly broken our bafflement.'

'But we *must* get our research findings back to Ziode,' she insisted.

'We could try launching a message boat. It probably won't get far.'

'Do it anyway. We'll have the tapes ready in five minutes. After that I want time enough to destroy our records.'

'I should be able to delay things that long. I'm sorry about all this, Amara, but we really don't have any choice but to comply.'

'I know.' Amara shut off the vidcom and turned to Estru. Even in defeat her look of stubbornness remained.

'Damn,' she said. '*Damn.*'

Then she issued the orders which kept the department frantically busy for the next quarter of an hour. Two complete copies of all their findings were made. One went to the launching bay. The other they hid where the Caeanics would be unlikely to find it unless they took the *Callan* apart rivet by rivet – in which case the record would burn up before it came to light.

Then all records, reports and dissertations contained in the sociological computer were erased.

At last Amara sat back with a sigh, satisfied that the Caeanics would not discover the highly strategic secret of the existence of Sovya. Then she sat suddenly upright, her mouth set.

'We shall have to destroy Verednyev too.'

'No! I mean, not yet anyway.' Estru was disturbed. 'His background isn't immediately evident. They won't learn it unless they interrogate him – in Russian.'

She clenched and unclenched her fist indecisively. 'They'll interrogate everybody. It's too much of a risk.'

'It wouldn't be a very nice thing to do,' he protested, 'unless we absolutely have to.'

Grudgingly she conceded. 'We'll leave it for the

moment. I don't like having to kill him any more than you do. But I want his guards armed and informed of their duty, should it become necessary.'

As the Caeanic officers came aboard the message boat was launched. It was equipped with self-destruct, but this precaution proved superfluous. Before it could even slip into overdrive a pin-point ray shot out from the Caeanic cruiser and vaporized it.

Minutes later the *Callan*, accompanied by its escort, moved off and headed deeper into the Arm of Tzist.

The Ziodean ship was approaching Inxa, Verrage's sparkling main city, when Captain Wilce again called Amara's department. He sounded slightly embarrassed.

'Captain Grieuard – ' he gestured to a bearded Caeanic standing behind him, just visible on the vidplate – 'requests that the head of the sociology department joins us on the bridge.'

'We have no sociology department,' Amara answered adamantly.

'It's no good, Amara. He *knows*. He seems to know everything except your name.'

'All right,' she said, becoming sullen and downcast. 'I'll be along presently.'

She cut the connection and spoke furiously to Estru. 'This is *intolerable*. We should ram the cruiser and self-destruct.'

'Don't start thinking of suicide yet, Amara. Maybe we can still get back to Ziode.'

'Hmph. I can just see these people ever letting us into the light of the day again.' She folded her arms across her chest.

'Well, let's hang on to our scientific objectivity for a while,' he said drily. 'Would you like me to come with you?'

Dumbly she nodded.

Estru had been watching on the vidplate as the *Callan* glided over Inxa and put down near the centre of the

city, which in contrast to the uniformly rectilinear style
of Ziodean towns was built on the principle of curving
terraces. Clearly the Caeanics displayed in their architecture some of the flair they put into costume. He was put
in mind of an aerial whirlpool of frosted colour, a titanic
amphitheatre, or a vast swirling orchid.

It was tempting to compare it with some Ziodean city,
such as Gridira, also a state capital. Although neither
side would ever admit to any similarity in their political
institutions, they both followed the system of maintaining several equivalent capital worlds, none having pre-
eminence and each capable of exercising government.
The difference was that Caean seemed to have no regular machinery for policy-making. Ziode saw this as a
dangerous source of instability and indicative of a lack
of self-control. Ziodean propaganda was always warning
of 'the mindless hordes of Caean'.

Estru was surprised to see no sign of activity on the
landing ground. He took his eyes from the screen as
Amara coughed. She was ready to leave.

On the bridge the four Caeanic officers who were keeping awkward company with Captain Wilce and the bridge
crew turned and smiled charmingly at the entry of Amara
and Estru. While they were being introduced Amara
stared fascinated at their jet-black uniforms, which even
to her untrained eye made those worn by Wilce and his
men seem shabby and desultory. The Caeanics wore a
type of galea, or helmet, which curved closely round the
skull and flared outward at the front in a paradigm of
the Mintov formula for space strains. The supple lines
of tunic and leggings further suggested the relativistic
curves and tensors of the void. The whole uniform was
a paradigm of deep space. If she let herself gaze at it too
long she seemed to be hurling through long black light
years, deep into infinity.

Captain Wilce's voice brought her out of her trance.
'Captain Grieuard wishes to assure us that his government has no hostile intentions towards us,' he said stiffly,

'and hopes we will consider them as hosts, rather than captors.'

'We have no wish to molest you,' Captain Grieuard added in heavily accented Ziodean, flashing Amara a dark grin.

'But you *have* molested us,' Amara replied indignantly. 'You have waylaid us, destroyed one of our boats – '

'With respect, madam, you *were* trespassing, ignoring all diplomatic procedures – and have been doing so for some time. Our actions are not unreasonable. But let us not begin on a basis of hostile feeling. If Captain Wilce and yourselves will be so good as to accompany us into Inxa, there are certain personages there who are earnestly desirous of meeting you.'

'And while we are gone the *Callan* will be turned inside out,' she retorted.

Captain Grieuard waved away the idea with an elegantly dismissive hand, pursing his lips in amusement and shaking his head. Amara had to admit that he *was* disarming – *and* handsome, *and* vigorous, *and* winning. A dashing young officer . . .

She arrested her train of thought. The space-clad Caeanic spoke again. 'Take the view that you are making a diplomatic call, even a social call. Those are my instructions.'

'And afterwards will we be permitted to return to Ziode?' Amara asked coldly.

Captain Grieuard shrugged.

She took Captain Wilce to one side. 'A tactfully put piece of coercion, Captain. Still, not quite what we had expected. Are you coming with us?'

'In the present circumstances my duty is to stay with my ship. If they'll agree to it I'll send Second Officer Borg instead.'

'All right. But what happens if they don't let us back on board?'

'Let's be realistic, Amara. We always knew this might happen. We are entirely in their hands. Just see what pressure you can exert on whoever it is you'll be seeing.'

'Perhaps they won't be eager to make too much of the incident, after all.'

'Let's hope so.'

Grieuard affected uninterest when Wilce offered Borg in place of himself. 'It is a matter of choice on your part, Captain, though my principals would certainly be displeased not to receive Madam Corl. Frankly I am more concerned that we should not keep our dignitaries waiting any longer than we must. Perhaps we could now debouch? . . .' He made an elaborate gesture that was almost gallant in its insistence.

A few minutes later Amara, for the first time in her life, breathed the air of a Caeanic planet.

While they had been negotiating, a traction platform had quietly moved the *Callan* away from its point of touch-down. By the time the seven-strong party emerged from the main port it had been deposited amid a complex of graceful buildings, and nestled among them so neatly as to seem to be one of them.

Amara took a deep breath, inhaling the warm scents of a summery afternoon.

Before them, somewhat below the level of the platform extruded by the port, stretched a pleasant esplanade on which had gathered a small crowd. Her first impression was of a fancy dress ball, all dazzling colour and finery.

Then she seemed to suffer a momentary paramnesia. The esplanade became a stage. On it, standing motionless and frozen, the figures in the crowd were no longer recognizably human, but were transformed into archetypal caricatures, primeval and menacing.

The dream-like experience passed. To clear her brain she shook her head, telling herself that the paramnesia must have been brought on by stress.

The crowd was waving and gesticulating. A cry went up. There was jeering, or cheering, she could not tell which. But Second Officer Borg had few doubts, and looked grim.

'It looks as if we're in for a rough time, madam,' he murmured.

Amara frowned with discomfiture, trying to assess the crowd's costume for herself from her somewhat inadequate knowledge. The gathering's adornment could fairly be called sumptuous even by Caeanic standards, she hazarded. Nearly all present were of high rank, or at any rate prestige.

Captain Grieuard urged them down the ramp to meet two men of mature years who stepped from the crowd to meet them. The apparel of one of them was enormously self-assertive: a blazing-hued panoply, flounced, scalloped and bombasted, with flying lappets of lucent fabric so that to the observer's fancy the wearer seemed to be throwing off fiery splashes of verve and energy; spurting feathery jets of *panache*. There was enough ostentation, enough magnificence, clearly to denote a man of leadership. And there was more than enough wildness to suggest that he was not bound by rules of convention.

Keeping a step to the rear, the second of the two was of a different style. He wore a variant of the diask known as the grid, exemplifying rectitude and dependable rigidity. Amara peered closely at both faces, hoping to see the look of passive, stylized consciousness a Ziodean automatically expected of a Caeanic. For a fleeting instant she thought she discerned it; but confessed that the impression was probably due to imagination. Far from appearing robotic, the faces confronting her were disconcertingly natural and individualistic.

Captain Grieuard made introductions: Abrazhne Caldersk, Director of Harmonic Relations; and – wearing the grid – Svete Trupp, his Foil (the title baffled Amara; she could not tell if Trupp were merely some kind of servant or private secretary, or himself an official of high rank).

Warmly Caldersk shook hands all round. 'This is a splendid occasion!' he exclaimed in a vigorous voice, speaking his native Caeanic. 'It is not every day that we receive distinguished visitors from Ziode!'

Estru and Borg looked at him sourly. But Amara's reaction was much more positive. She giggled, glancing again at Caldersk's extraordinary features, and even the handsome space officer Captain Grieuard faded into nonexistence in her mind.

Her male companions aboard the *Callan* had been a dour lot. Caldersk was going to be entertaining, she promised herself.

Then she checked her thoughts, aware that she might be succumbing to some particularly seductive brand of Caeanic blandishment, and wondering if it might not even be naïve to read anything but sarcasm into Caldersk's welcome.

'I trust you treat your visitors with humanity, Director,' she said stiffly.

The other threw up his hands in shock. Then he laughed, loud uninhibited laughter. 'Surely you do not fear for your safety? You know nothing of Caeanic hospitality if that is the case. Why, you are celebrities, dear lady. Celebrities!'

'If I may say so, you credit us with little percipience,' Abrazhne Caldersk said affably, about half an hour later. 'It is practically impossible for a complete foreigner to live in Caean without being noticed, however well he knows the language.'

'Even if he wears Caeanic clothes?' Amara asked.

'Especially if he wears Caeanic clothes!' The Director seemed amused. 'There is more to wearing apparel than merely pouring oneself into it!' He paused, and raised a hand reflectively. 'Suppose a foreigner in Ziode were to – well, to wear all his clothes back to front, to wear garments totally unsuited to his nature and the circumstances. That is some indication of the impact your agents made among us! We were aware of them from the beginning. From there it was easy to guess the location of your ship, to penetrate its bafflement and to track it from planet to planet.'

Amara responded huffily: 'Then why did you not arrest us all immediately? Why wait until now?'

'For what reason? What harm were you doing? We are an open society, dear lady. Anyone may come and go as he pleases. No visas are required!'

'But you *have* taken us into custody now,' Second Officer Borg pointed out.

The grid-wearing Trupp spoke. 'We are concerned that you should not return to Ziode with misinformation about Caean,' he said in a gentle but firm voice. 'We are perturbed by the reports of increasing fear and hostility towards us in your country. We wish to correct any wrong impression you have gained; and since you are on a sociological mission this is an excellent opportunity to remedy misunderstandings that apparently are rampant in Ziode.'

'Does that mean you will allow us to return home?' Amara said in surprise.

Caldersk clapped his hands, causing the flying lappets on his upper garment to make volatile, feathery leaps. 'We have arrived!' he announced with enthusiasm.

Riding through Inxa's concourses in an open carriage, the Ziodeans had been given the opportunity to see the sights of the city, the serried terraces, the hanging gardens and the throngs of people, many of them in fantastic garb, and to enjoy the invigorating, exotic atmosphere. Now they halted alongside an oval-shaped bowl or depression about the size of a stadium, set apart from the main avenues. Here a banquet had been prepared. A huge table was burdened with food. Footmen, stepping neatly in black, carapace-like suits, were busy completing the arrangements.

And there were guests: perhaps a hundred in all. The brilliance of their costume was bewildering. It was like entering some novel zoological garden where evolution had run riot. The Ziodeans descended from the carriage and moved hesitantly into the stadium, feeling the strangeness of it all. Amara wondered how *her* dress seemed to their hosts – and then firmly shut her mind to the thought. She was a Ziodean, she told herself sternly. She did not have to worry about what foreigners thought.

Shortly they found themselves seated at the long table, after being introduced to a score of guests, all flowered, flamed, bedizened and bedecked so as to resemble a tropical menagerie. Abrazhne Caldersk sat on the left of Amara, plying her with food and drink, while Estru and Second Officer Borg were ranged stiffly to her right, being entertained somewhat more formally by Svete Trupp. Amara, herself refusing to unbend, consumed as little as was politely possible. Like her companions, she felt herself to be Caean's enemy and had expected to be dealt with as an enemy. It was unnerving to be fêted instead.

'Will you have some syllabub?' offered Caldersk, providing her with a dollop of aromatic jelly. She tasted it, and unfamiliar flavours melted in her mouth. Then she turned to him challengingly.

'I wish you always maintained such a friendly attitude towards Ziodeans,' she said in a suspicious tone.

Caldersk chuckled. 'That is exactly what I want to set straight between us – these ridiculous notions you have about us. You think we are "clothes robots", having no individuality. You think we want to invade Ziode and enslave you all.' He laughed. 'It has its comic aspect, I must admit.'

'Do you actually claim that you *have no* aggressive claim on Ziode?' Amara snapped sharply.

'Absolutely none!' Caldersk's laughter nearly punctured her eardrums. 'Caean has neither the intention nor the desire to embark upon a career of conquest. It would be contrary to our way of life.'

She reflected for a moment, taken aback. 'Well, do you claim that you have *never* had such ambitions?'

'Again, absolutely.'

'Oh, I know better than that!' Amara flared.

Noting that she had rejected the syllabub, Caldersk reached across the table and drew close a succulent meat dish. 'Try this.'

Amara waved it away.

He shrugged, raising his eyebrows with an air of deliberation. 'Remember that we see the Art of Attire as being the essence of civilized life,' he said. 'It is true that, in the past, idealists among us have wished to spread Caean's unquestionable superiority in this field to the rest of mankind. But their plans were of a missionary, rather than a military, nature, and took the form of loading up fleets of giant spaceships with sumptuous apparel with which to bombard the barbarian planets. Even this scheme was abandoned, owing to the hostility of other nations, chiefly Ziode – though for a fact many of the ships still lie in their hangars, fully laden. I expect it is stories of these efforts that have produced the fears prevalent among your people.'

Amara became aware that by her side her assistant was listening intently. 'So you do admit that you have expansionist leanings,' Estru remarked drily.

Trupp answered him from farther up the table. 'That is so, but only in a cultural sense. The urge to propagate one's cultural values is nowhere regarded as reprehensible.'

'It is where those values are inimical to one's own – which is our case.'

Caldersk made a jovial, explosive gesture. 'Come, come. We no longer think of swamping Ziodean culture beneath our own – until, that is, the superiority of Caeanic attire becomes evident to the Ziodeans themselves. I have just explained that the missionary zeal of an earlier generation has abated. You have nothing to fear from us – nothing but your own ignorance of our nature.'

'So you say,' Second Officer Borg put in. 'But if I may put matters bluntly – how can we confirm this? The Ziodean Directorate will take a lot of convincing.'

'Exactly!' Caldersk agreed with satisfaction. 'I am glad you asked that. We would ask you to confirm for yourselves that our society is peaceful, our natures unaggressive. To demonstrate our good faith we give you liberty to travel about Caean at will, without let or hindrance, to carry out your sociological investigations.'

Amara glanced wildly at Estru, unable to conceal her amazement. 'You will let us take the *Callan* anywhere? Survey any planet? Talk to anyone – obtain information from universities, cultural scientists, military establishments? *Without supervision?*'

'You may regard yourselves as free agents,' Caldersk said, 'though I must draw the line at giving you *carte blanche* with the military – that will have to depend on the local commanders.'

'But that's wonderful – that's just what we need.'

'There was never any need to go sneaking about the fringes,' Caldersk told her. 'All you needed to do was come and ask. We are a much more easy-going society than you are in Ziode.'

'One thing needs to be said,' Estru put in. 'You are trying hard to represent yourselves as reasonable and harmless. If that's the case how could our people be so wrong about you, even to the extent of preparing for war? Our people at home think of you as being far from harmless.'

He was answered by Svete Trupp. 'As sociologists, you must be aware of the theory of cultural repulsion. Disparate cultures repel one another, is that not how the theorem goes? In fact the bad relations between us are solely the result of mistrust and misconception. We are probably not as unalike as you have always imagined. You believe, for instance, that we have some kind of obsession with clothing. This is not true.'

Amara raised her eyebrows and seemed about to laugh.

'I am sure your coming researches will show you that you have exaggerated our preoccupation with costume,' Caldersk took up, seeing her expression. 'Very few Ziodeans have studied Caean, after all. What reference sources do you use?'

'Matt-Helver's *Travels in the Tzist Arm is* the standard text,' Amara told him defensively.

'Ah yes, Matt-Helver. Full of inaccuracies – a very amusing book! Yet in the end Matt-Helver settled here himself and came to know us better, I believe.'

'You mean he was wrong about the place of sartorialism in Caeanic society?'

'Every civilization has typical artforms, does it not? Ours is dress. It has nothing to do with religion, as some foreigners have supposed. It is a matter of practical psychology, that is all. We have found that our science of adornment has the power to lend life a positive, forward-looking aspect. To us it is *you* who are obsessed – obsessed with man's evolutionary past, unable to escape from the single shape arbitrarily imposed on man by nature.'

It did not escape the Ziodeans that despite his disclaimers Caldersk was already interpreting the significance of dress in terms that to them were bizarre. 'Let's examine this business of *obsession*,' Amara suggested. 'To be obsessed is to be unnaturally preoccupied with one thing to the exclusion of others. Now, we in Ziode have no objection to imaginative dress. But likewise we have no objection to nakedness either. Both are a matter of indifference to us. So who is obsessed?' She was tickled to see both Caldersk and Trupp blush deeply at her mention of nudity.

'But you disparage raiment and let your minds dwell on . . . vulgar biology. That way lies decadence.'

'We are *not* decadent,' Amara said indignantly.

Caldersk drank a deep draught from a tankard of fizzy yellow liquid. Trupp once again took up the thread.

'What is man when he is born? He is nothing; his mind is in neutral; not switched on. Only when he begins to interact with his environment does his life burgeon. Such interaction means that he must have an effective inter-face; he must clothe himself with suitable psychological instruments. Thus it is the lot of the shabbily clothed to sink into morbid introspection, to take on a depressing uniformity. The skill of our sartorialists, by contrast, ensures that we maintain a healthy contact with external reality.'

'Yes, we of Caean enjoy life, thanks to the Art of Attire,' Caldersk agreed. He turned to Amara with a smile. 'And you say we have no individuality! Do I look like a "clothes robot" to you?'

'No, you do not,' she admitted.

He leaned closer, his eyes roving over her. 'Let me send a sartorial to you. Experience for yourself the benefits of our art. A rich houppelande, perhaps? A graceful pelisse? You will soon notice the difference.'

'No, thank you,' she said primly.

Estru looked about him at the picturesquely garbed people feasting at the table, and wondered if there could be any truth in what Trupp and Caldersk had just said. Was Caean indeed a case of exotic social insanity, as he had always believed, or was it merely that Ziode had lost some quality Caean had retained? His gaze came to rest on two women sitting on the other side of the table a little farther down. One wore a dress which consisted of interlocking diamond-shaped panels, making her torso look like a crystalline explosion, while on her head she wore a fontange, a tall, fan-like headdress. The other wore a polonaise, a simpler willowy dress made of a cream-coloured material decorated with wandering lines of pearls. Her headdress, however, was an extravagant vision from the past: a full-blown model of a three-masted sailing ship, complete in every detail, proud and tall with sails and rigging, and apparently being buffeted by the complicated waves and curls into which her hair was set.

Noticing his attention, the girl in the sailing-ship hair-do smiled at him. Estru received an inward jolt. Her smile

was at once winsome, proud and tempestuous, exciting
him quite against his will.

Amara, too, was realizing that they were being subjected to a clever propaganda exercise. It was becoming
easy to let small, treacherous doubts contend with their
Ziodean upbringing. Were the results the Caeanics gained
from their practices – or imagined they gained – really
harmful? More and more people were coming into the
stadium now, giving the place the air of a festival. Amara
watched one young woman saunter shyly across the soft
moss which covered the floor of the bowl. She wore a
gauzy outfit which was known generically as a flimsy,
though this version was doubtless named after some species of bird. She even walked somewhat after the manner
of a bird, stepping delicately and nervously, as though at
any moment she might take to the air in fright, and go
winging away over the surrounding towers and terraces.

Caldersk beckoned to a footman, who handed him a
moulded purple control box.

'After all, the Art of Attire merely gives life a civilized
texture,' he remarked. 'But enough of this talk about *your*
obsession that *we* have an obsession. Your tour of Caean
should show you that we *do* have interests other than
pride in our appearance. For the present, how about
some entertainment?'

His fingers went to touch the controls on the box. The
centre of the stadium glowed slightly, then came to life.

For the next hour the Ziodeans were obliged to view
a spectacular extravaganza, a kaleidoscopic documentary
on various Caeanic pursuits. Caldersk was clearly at pains
to illustrate that, as he had stated, there was more than
one aspect to his countrymen's existence. They saw
drama, ballet, stratospheric racing, and sporting and
scientific activities that were not always easy to follow.
Caldersk explained that some of the scenes were record-
ings, while others were being transmitted directly from
various parts of Verrage and from other nearby planets.
He was able to modify the programme at will by means

of the control box, bringing in relays from a thousand different locations.

His efforts to give Caean a more balanced image were largely unsuccessful, due to the fact that to Ziodean eyes costume played an almost manic part in everything that was portrayed. For every single activity there was a form of dress. The stratospheric racers wore outfits made up of brilliantly flaring yellow panes that gave them the look of hurtling gods out of some fiery pantheon. Scientists working to perfect a new industrial process were god-like in a more abstract manner, robed in gowns of dispassionate simplicity on which the signs for the scientific constants shone in luminous gold. Strangest of all was a short, incomprehensible drama in which the players were accoutred in machine-like rig-outs of silver and black, robbing them of any resemblance to human life.

All of this was apparently so normal to the Caeanics that they scarcely noticed it. Probably for this reason. Caldersk did not neglect to represent the Art of Attire specifically. He showed a short sequence in which a master sartorial produced garments in a dazzling display of virtuosity. He gave them a tantalizing glimpse into the semi-secret, labyrinthine world of the sodalities, or sartorial sub-cults, concentrating on the historical sodalities. Those societies, each steeped in one or another phase of history, had succeeded in resurrecting entirely the spirit, the life-style and even the personages of their chosen time. The Ziodeans were fascinated by the segue-created procession of period costumes, going back thousands of years as far as the Egyptian era.

In what might have been a veiled warning, Caldersk ended by asserting the usefulness of Caeanic attire in the military field.

'Although we are not by inclination a military race, every nation must be prepared to defend itself,' he said. 'In the wardrobe of every Caeanic is a military uniform, specially styled to inculcate the qualities of a soldier. Furthermore it facilitates his receptiveness to military training, so that we would be able to field an enormous army in a remarkably short space of time.'

The figure that was projected to illustrate Caldersk's words amused Amara at first. It was like nothing so much as a toy soldier, of an antiquated variety at that, wearing a bright red tunic with gold braid across the chest, stiff buff trousers with a broad stripe down the side of each leg, and shining black boots. The headgear was a shako with an unusually large peak. The soldier marched stiffly, jerkily, as if worked by a spring mechanism, and carried a dull green pack on his back, also bearing a doubtlessly efficient force rifle at the slope.

But as he marched closer her comic impression of him began to change. There was a certain wooden ferocity in the face. A look of unrelenting will to win that she found quite frightening. She imagined a million such men, marching in rank after rank. It was terrifying.

The soldier halted and performed a number of machine-like drill movements. A transparent face-plate snapped down from the broad peak of the shako, converting it into a complete space helmet. The whole uniform, indeed, served as a spacesuit equipped for all conditions.

The image faded. The show was over.

'Impressive,' Amara commented.

Caldersk rose from his place and stretched his arms luxuriously. 'The night is but begun,' he said. 'Plenty of time to enjoy ourselves!'

Dusk was falling on Inxa. Amara felt overloaded with the new and strange sights that had been forced upon her. The richness and variety of vesture was almost too much for her senses. She rose also, feeling a need to exercise her limbs.

And then the paramnesia came over her again, much stronger this time. Instead of smiling, lively faces around her she saw – masks, glaring from within their multicoloured casks of cloth. Humanity was gone; instead there was something alien and incomprehensible, something implacable and malevolent.

I've been overworking, she thought. Momentarily she swayed, and as Caldersk chanced to move nearer her hand touched the scalloped front of his tunic. The feel of the cloth was something odd and thrilling.

'What's that made of?' she asked wonderingly.

'Prossim. The finest cloth in the universe!'

She took a deep breath, at which her head seemed to clear. There was a hubbub of talk and laughter all around her. She lifted her eyes to the bowl of the stadium and the greater bowl of Inxa beyond that, with the dusk settling all over it.

Suddenly there was a flurry far up on one of the topmost terraces, and what she took to be a flock of birds exploded across the sky, soaring and swooping towards the stadium. Only when they made ready to land on the moss did they become distinguishable as human beings wearing various types of bird costume – including the girl in the flimsy Amara had noted earlier.

I should have anticipated it, she told herself wryly. Personal antigrav units.

The bird-people alighted all over the stadium. A flamboyantly plumed flier, wearing on his head a gilded balzo which completed his likeness to a scintillating, strutting cock, came striding towards the banqueting table. Caldersk, evidently recognizing him as a messenger, stepped forward and they spoke briefly.

'Apparently you are not the only Ziodeans in Inxa,' he said when he returned to his guests. 'Two others currently living here have arrived to join the party. Perhaps you would like to meet them.'

'Do you get many of our expatriates in Caean?' Second Officer Borg asked in some surprise.

'Very few, but that is probably because there is so little traffic between the Arm and the Cluster.'

'And not because of the difficulties they would find in making out in Caean?' Estru put in.

'Oh no. It is an easy matter to live here. No one is ever made to feel out of place, however eccentric.'

'Unless – ' Amara tittered, then caught herself before mentioning the forbidden subject again.

The newcomers came stepping diffidently through the throng. One was of medium height and slightly pudgy. He wore what seemed to her a perfectly ordinary conventional suit which would have passed without notice even back in Ziode. His companion was taller and slimmer, rather handsome in a lean, sardonic sort of way, his apparel more fetching: a brocaded lavender frock-coat, matched by a blue satin Bourbon hat trimmed with pearl fleur-de-lis. The outfit suited him perfectly.

They introduced themselves as Peder Forbarth and Realto Mast, both of Harlos. Forbarth, the pudgy one, puzzled Amara straight away. He was greeted with an inexplicable deference by both Caldersk and Trupp. Bearing an unmistakable look of authority, he yet behaved in a distant and offhand manner, keeping his gaze averted elsewhere.

The stylish Mast, however, expressed effusive pleasure at meeting his fellow-countrymen.

'How long have you been living here?' Amara asked him.

'A few months.'

'Oh? And what brings you here?'

Mast dodged the question. 'May I ask what brings *you* here? Is this an official visit?'

She nodded dubiously, after a sidelong glance at Caldersk. 'A fact-finding tour.'

'Relations must have improved, in that case.'

'Possibly.'

He sidled closer. 'Perhaps I could be of some help. Not many people have lived right in the middle of Caeanic society.'

Amara could not disguise her suspicion of anyone who chose to live among foreigners. 'What are you looking for, passage home?' she said in loud, challenging voice. 'Or are you wanted by the law?'

Mast looked uncomfortable, then uttered a feigning laugh. Caldersk, still giving no indication as to whether he understood their conversation, which had been in Ziodean, moved in. 'You are still governed by a mistrustful, angry mood, dear lady. I wish you would take some pleasure in the evening. Come, this will soon help you relax.'

He poured her a large goblet of the fizzy yellow liquid and handed it to her. Amara sniffed it suspiciously, and made to put it down.

'It won't do you any harm,' Peder Forbarth said in a disinterested voice, still not looking her way. 'It is a mild stimulant, that is all, similar to alcohol. Drink it.'

She quaffed the goblet. The liquid tasted sweet and delicious.

An effervescent, warm sensation started up in her stomach. What the hell, she thought.

Already she felt better.

She turned to Peder. 'And what about you? Are you looking for a job too?'

'Oh, take no notice of him,' Mast said lightly. 'He's not really Ziodean at all any more. He's gone native.'

She tossed her head in disapproval. 'Is that so?' she asked Peder.

Peder smiled superciliously. 'Yes, madam,' he answered politely. 'In Ziode I was a sartorialist. Here I find I am a natural Caeanic.'

'And if there is a war, whose side will you fight on?'

Peder made no reply. He drifted away and procured for himself a drink which he sipped slowly and reflectively.

'Frankly I would have thought it more of *you*,' Amara said to Mast, eyeing his elegant frock-coat.

'Appearances can be deceptive,' Mast said smoothly. 'I am Ziodean to the core. But I have never been anything of a *mezzak* – excuse me, that's a Caeanic word.'

'You speak the language well?'

'I'm not an expert, but I don't find it difficult. One can master the basic vocabulary quite easily in a few days, with the help of light hypnosis. But after a while one longs for the sound of one's native tongue. Are you sure there's no place for me in your work?'

'Well, we shall have to see about that.' She accepted a refill of her goblet. 'I'm not quite sure exactly what's going on around here yet.'

A good deal of the yellow beverage was imbibed in the ensuing hours. The Ziodeans began genuinely to enjoy themselves. The Caeanic were uninhibited hosts, and it was impossible not to be caught up in the festive mood. When full darkness came a magnificent fireworks display was set off to go blooming over the whole of Inxa. Then there was more drinking, dancing and general conviviality – a garden party to which it seemed the whole city had access.

Estru succeeded in keeping company with the girl in the sailing-ship hair-do. Towards midnight they slipped away.

She took him to an apartment some distance off, then left him alone while she went into an adjoining room. He hummed to himself, gazing absently through a window.

Softly she called to him from the other room.

He stepped tentatively into a spacious boudoir. The girl, having changed her dress, stood at the other end.

She still sported the sailing-ship, but the polonaise had been discarded in favour of a quite different affair. He did not really notice her corsage; his attention went to the skirt. Cinched tightly at the waist, it flared out into a full dome-like shape. Smiling, she came towards him, and as she moved he saw that the skirt really consisted of numbers of leaves which seemed capable of free movement.

On coming to the apartment Estru had not felt particularly aroused. But when she walked towards him those leaves lilted and swung in curvy motions which, inexplicably, evoked an irresistible sexual desire in him.

He realized suddenly that there was even more to the garments of Caean than he and Amara had known about. The Caeanic tailors had analysed the basic vocabulary of form, line and movement that spelled out sexual allure. The skirt was fashioned according to this vocabulary. It was a sartorial aphrodisiac. His instincts reacted of their own accord, and there was absolutely nothing he could do about it.

Not that there was anything he wanted to do about it, except to go along with what was happening. But what was he supposed to do? he wondered. How did they go about it? The worst thing he could do would be to undress himself – or try to undress the girl.

She came up to him and tugged him towards the bed. As she sank down on the coverlet she lifted her legs on to it and her skirt belled, apparently supported by hoops. Beneath it he caught a glimpse that sent his blood pounding. Under the skirt were – petticoats, endless intricated, waved, ruched, rose-pink petticoats. Like the skirt itself, they utilized the full fury of erotic sartorial knowledge, and Estru's senses went exploding in heady images of flowers opening in an infinite series one into the other, leading to a hot, intense, delirious centre.

She was looking deliciously wanton. The petticoats rustled and curled like the combers of an aroused ocean as he joined her on the bed, and she began to teach him the Caeanic ways of love.

Realto Mast's evening ended on a slightly less felicitous note. He was caught off guard, having drunk more than was his habit of late. His intemperance sprang from the fact that he knew Peder was shortly going to desert him – would probably abandon him that very night, in fact – and that since his survival rating without him was slim, he was zealously eager to find a place aboard the *Callan*. After much importuning, and much imbibing, he had eventually extracted from Amara Corl a grudging promise that she would interview him on board ship the following day.

Caean was definitely not the place for Mast. He could never be happy here. It depressed him unspeakably that he seemed unable to exert any influence over anyone. When he had heard that a Ziodean ship had landed on Verrage he had decided to risk the consequences and attempt to get back among this own kind. Now the thought that he might soon be free of this crazy society intoxicated him and he even began to enjoy himself.

During the course of the evening he fell in with a rather strange young creature calling himself Reggae Elphis, and at length acceded to his suggestion that they adjourn to a nearby wine-tavern. Mast found it refreshing to be accepted as a companion. They sat sipping persimmon wine, which had a fine, bitter flavour. He looked across the table at the young man. Reggae wore an open-jacketed zoot-suit whose incredibly padded shoulders thrusted sharply up and out so that the pointed ends were more or less on a level with his pixie-like ears. The garment set off perfectly his almost phthisic thinness, his jerky, rapid movements. Yet Reggae, for all his youth, had a strikingly self-assured manner. His face was unusually mobile and expressive, though wasted, the skin being drawn close to the bone, the eyes at once restless yet showing a considerable power of concentration. His unhatted hair was high and oiled and combed back in a prow-like manner.

He caught Mast's eye and smiled enigmatically. Mast looked away.

'How do you like the place?' Reggae asked, raising his glass in a salute, the timbre of his voice colourful but slightly off-balance. 'Do you have taverns like this in Ziode? What's it like there? Can you have a good time? Or is everything dull and lifeless, like they say?'

'Oh, you can have a good time, all right,' Mast drawled. 'There are some differences, though.'

He started to tell his new friend about Ziode. But his story soon turned into self-pitying complaints about the life he was leading in Caean. 'Nobody takes any notice of me,' he said peevishly. 'I'm just a rotten foreigner here. Everybody makes me feel it.'

Reggae jerked his pointed shoulders sinuously to the rhythm of some music coming from the other end of the tavern, moving his arms back and forth slightly at the same time. 'You're unhappy,' he murmured, his eyes half-closed. 'We've got ways of dealing with that.' He leaned forward. 'Nobody need to be a foreigner in Caean. Caean is for all mankind.'

'Not for Ziodeans.'

'It's easy to find yourself with the right gear. You can really get in phase, get coherent. You just need the right *sort* of . . .' Reggae's voice was caressing and oddly thrilling.

Mast guessed what he was talking about. Reggae probably realized that his clothes hadn't been made by a native sartorial. But Mast kept quiet. To tell Reggae what he thought of Caean clothing would probably insult him.

He sat back with a sigh, wondering how in the galaxy he came to be sitting in this Caeanic tavern, which even at this hour was half-filled with its weirdly caparisoned patrons and presented as alien a sight as was possible. It seemed like a dream. Sometimes he wondered if he *was* dreaming. It still seemed unbelievable to him, for instance, that the *Little Planet* could lumber openly into the Tzist Arm and actually put down in the Verrage countryside without being challenged! After landing, he and Peder had simply walked into Inxa. No one had ever questioned their presence, from that day to this.

Peder had found them a room and they had learned the language from hypno-tapes. Mast, however, had obstinately refused to wear the Caeanic clothes Peder had obtained for him to replace his quite unsuitable prison wear. 'I'm Ziodean,' he had said stubbornly. He had been afraid of draping himself in those seductive shapes, and spent the days skulking indoors, refusing to go out.

Peder had been patient with him in those early days, taking pity, perhaps, on his helplessness. Finally Mast had compromised. He wouldn't wear Caeanic clothes proper, but he would wear garments made by Peder.

At first Peder had demurred at the thought of having to produce something to be worn in Caean; but then he had risen to the challenge. He had purchased tools and fabrics. He had gone to a professional sartorial for tutelage. And, by dint of effort, he had surpassed himself. The results were in fact barely up to Caeanic standards, but Mast thought them magnificent.

Reggae performed a frenetic hand-jive, his lips puckered and his face intent. He seemed miles away, yet Mast became aware that the youth's attention was still full on him.

'I'll do you a favour,' Reggae said. 'I'll take you to my sodality tonight. I belong to a *special* one . . . I can take you in as a guest.' He reached across and patted Mast's knee comfortingly.

Two more bottles of persimmon wine later Mast's speech was more slurred and, not really resisting, he went with Reggae to a large house with shuttered windows tucked away in a back street. Within, however, the house had the inward-looking, sated atmosphere of a temple. They passed through a number of rooms, each more cushioned and quilted than the last and clad in perfumes hinting at depravity. Mast was aware of the induction process only vaguely – the murmured explanations, the searching glances in his direction, the discreet air of special privilege.

'I say,' he drawled at one point, ' I won't have to go through any ceremonies, will I?' Not until he was ushered into the adytum, with Reggae by his side, did he begin to sober up.

The walls of the interior were broken at intervals by arches which led to screened passages or else to cosy alcoves. The atmosphere was one of luxury and indulgence; the adytum had lavender walls brocaded

with extraordinary erotic murals, *chaises longues* of soft
magenta fabrics, and deep armchairs. Several members
were present – all males, this being a male-only sodality
– and they turned to greet the newcomers with friendly
smiles. Some were of a commanding appearance, looking very smart and handsome in military-style uniforms.
Others seemed to exude an almost repugnantly intense
masculinity. And there were others, mostly younger,
who exhibited the same svelte quality of deliberate sexual ambivalence he had up until now chosen to ignore in
Reggae. One or two of these wore slashed doublets that
allowed glimpses of frilly chemises and undergarments –
Mast knew that slashed over-garments were considered
daring and even indecent in Caean.

But it was the phallocrypts that informed his befuddled
mind most plainly of the nature of the sodality into which
he had wandered. Projecting from trousers, breeches
and hose, curving sharply upward before the belly, the
horn-shaped penis sheaths exaggerated the member they
enclosed in such a magnificent way that they altered the
entire stance and character of the wearer.

'Oh no,' Mast groaned. 'Sorry, Reggae, I'm not . . .'

'No one's a hundred per cent,' Reggae murmured in
a voice that was like rough diamonds. 'It just has to be
brought out, that's all. Come on! It won't hurt you to let
yourself go for once.'

Mast learned with a shock that the Caeanic sartorials
did indeed know how to 'bring it out'. There was something about the slim, erect lines of the young man by
his side that sent a shivering, trembling sensation right
through him, and in his own breeches he felt his own
horn rising, responding to the horn sheaths worn by the
others.

'I have to change now, Realto. Come along and I'll give
you something suitable to wear.' Reggae gave his hand
a squeeze and made for one of the arches, taking Mast
willy-nilly in tow.

*

At some stage during the evening Amara lost track of Abrazhne Caldersk, her hoped-for consort, but she did not let that disappoint her for long. As the party wound down she went on a night tour of Inxa with an acceptably presentable, if slightly intense, man, much younger than herself, who had been pursuing her for hours.

He went by the name of Holosk. His pudgy face showed, perhaps, a rather unconfident attitude for a Caeanic, being once both eager and hesitating. The outlines of his body were practically obliterated by a dark-coloured suit, and he seemed to hang on Amara's every word, to be fascinated by any details she could tell him of Ziode. Amara could not help but sense something behind his pressing enquiries, though she was at a loss to understand what.

'What do *you* do, Holosk?' she asked him. 'Are you in the government?'

'No, I'm in business,' Holosk explained. 'Export-import. My firm trades with fifteen planets in this sector.' His voice was quiet, almost inaudible. 'Tell me, in Ziode . . . do the women . . . er . . .' He trailed off.

They were leaning against the balustrade of a terrace overlooking a great plaza where coloured fountains played. Amara looked at her watch, which she had already adjusted to Verrage time. 'Oh well,' she said, 'I'd better be getting back to the ship.'

'I live very near here,' he told her quickly. 'Why don't you come up for a nightcap?'

'Well . . .' With a doubting expression she went with him across the terrace to the street.

Holosk lived in an apartment block only a few hundred yards away. He fumbled with the key as he opened the door, clearly in a state of excitement. Flattered but also filled with curiosity, Amara entered. The apartment was small and unpretentious, but moderately comfortable. Holosk gave her a drink then paced nervously back and forth.

'Sit down,' she said. 'You'll wear a hole in the carpet.' She held out a hand invitingly.

For answer he suddenly went down on his knees before her. To her astonishment his lumpy face was filmed with sweat and he was tense and trembling. He was in a sexual frenzy!

'Come on!' he cried with bulging eyes. 'I've heard all about you Ziodean women! It's true, isn't it? That you – that lovers – ' He swallowed and choked, unable for a moment to bring out the words. '*Undress one another!*' he gasped hoarsely.

'But of course,' Amara replied lightly. 'What else?'

'Oh God, oh God,' moaned Holosk, writhing on the floor.

All at once Amara understood, and struggled not to burst out laughing. She was in the hands of a Caeanic pervert – one so depraved that he actually gained erotic excitement from the thought of uncovering the body!

Was his type common? Probably not – Amara's guess was that it was very rare, and that such as there were kept the vice secret. News of a Ziodean woman would bring them running, of course.

Taking his courage in both hands, Holosk clutched at her skirt and began to mouth the Caeanic equivalent of obscene sex talk.

'*Unclothe me,*' he begged in a hot breathless voice. 'Undrape me, disrobe me, leave me naked! Strip me, peel me, expose me! Unlace, untie, unbutton and undo me! *Oh, take my clothes off!*'

Giggling, she obliged him while he lay back shivering in a near-swoon. Then he whimpered in ecstasy while she helped him to do the same to her.

13

*Every creature having a complex nervous system makes use
of body image. Body image is self image: the creature's
knowledge of its own physical existence, a knowledge which
hovers between conscious and pre-conscious perceptions. It has
been a matter of argument as to whether body image has a
genetic basis, or whether it results from conditioning. Experiments designed to resolve the question have subjected human
volunteers to total amnesia and then attempted to induce them
to accept alternative images, of animals or robot waldos, as
their own. Results were never conclusive, due to the difficulty
of occluding the volunteer's own body with another body,
and also to the mentally deranging effects of the drugs used.
Some subjects reported that they had 'dreamed' they were
the replacement body – a dog, a bear, in one case, even, a
butterfly.*

*Pliability of body image is clearly of interest in the study of
bodily adornment, a feature of all human cultures. In the case
of Caean it would seem to be specially important. Is Caean
a proliferation of divergent body images? Are the Caeanics
dreamers, lost in a state of hypnotic sleep, imagining that they
are exotic and arcane as suggested by their apparel? These
questions remain to be answered by social science.*

List's *Cultural Compendium*

The Tzit Arm contained in excess of ten million suns.
The section covered by Caean alone embraced one million. Among that million were about a hundred inhabited
worlds, connected by threads of commerce and national-
ity: phantasmagoric sodalities, fantastic fetishes, cultural
displays which bedecked planets like floral growths.

Peder made his way in Caeanic society with automatic
ease. The suit he wore meant that he was treated with
utmost respect everywhere he went. Whether people realized it was a Frachonard suit he was wearing, let alone the
one that had gone missing, he did not know. Here, where
style was understood, such questions were not asked. The

suit had found its wearer; he was the acme, social man made perfect. That was all there was to it.

That was, indeed, all there was to it. As Peder sank deeper into Caeanic ways an inhuman detachment came over him. The suit, having indulged him for a while, sent him on his travels again, wandering from star to star, tending always, as if by chance, towards the other end of Caean.

In the city of Quetzkol he one day happend to stroll beneath a continuous stone awning that sheltered a long esplanade paved with hexagonal grey flagstones. The farther end of the esplanade broke into a cascade of descending ledges that resembled the slope of a ziggurat. It was here, standing staring at him, that he saw the first of his brothers: a wearer of one of the other four existing Frachonard suits.

Peder examined the other suit. In superficial style it might have been thought much like his own, but he knew that philosophically the two were radically apart. 'A different paradigm,' he thought to himself. The suit denoted a man of unbending will, a man who set his face in one direction and never retraced his steps. In keeping with this paradigm it had one accessory Peder's lacked: a sinister hat with a wide brim, low and flat, in whose shadow the man's eyes were cold, grey and hard.

Peder paced the length of the esplanade to meet him. 'I am Peder Forbarth,' he said.

'I am Otis Weld,' the other replied. His voice was deep and brusque, with a metallic timbre. 'We have been waiting for you. But time is not important. A forest takes time to grow.'

Peder's conversation was without any un-necessary verbiage. 'You know where to find the others?'

'One more resides already here in Quetzkol. We shall take ship to meet the others. A symposium will be arranged. When the petals of the flower are joined, the whole plant flourishes.'

They made their way through the city. The architecture

of Quetzkol was quite unlike that of any other Caeanic city, being redolent of the style referred to as the Incan or Aztec. Flat, grey horizontal slabs slotted and criss-crossed to create a three-dimensional maze. Rakish tiers piled into one another, forming countless interstices that served as streets and passages. The unremittingly clean outlines, the lustrous grey of the building material, all gave an impression of decisiveness and willpower. Above, the sky reflected back a clear, watery blue.

Quetzkol's idiosyncratic character was typical of this end of Caean. It was as if evolution had started anew in numerous local enclaves, using not biological forms but creatures of cloth and dye. There was Palco, whose people were robed in cool saffron and spent their lives placidly and calmly, reflecting on thoughts that could not have been conceived outside Palco. There was Farad, whose inhabitants wore only blue in all its shades and cognates and fought a ritualized war whose motives would have been incomprehensible to the Ziodean mind. There were the Cabsoloms, absorbed in a new type of sculpture equally enigmatic. And here in Quetzkol there was this stoic severity, exemplified *par excellence* by Weld himself. Nowhere was the carefree hedonism of Verrage to be found. There was passivity; there was also febrile activity which extended in unthought-of directions. But even there, a kind of inactivity reigned within the activity, a submission to action rather than an initiating of action.

Peder was close now to the very verge of Tzist.

'I see that much Prossim is worn here in Quetzkol,' he remarked as they walked. 'Almost to the exclusion of anything else.'

'True. Who would wish to wear other fabrics when perfection is available?'

'How soon can I meet our other companion?'

'I shall arrange for him to visit the sodality I own.'

Peder was puzzled. 'One does not *own* sodalities,' he said.

'I do,' Weld told him.

'Are you then, by any chance, yourself an exponent of the sartorial art?'

'Not professionally. Occasionally I make experiments for my own amusement.'

'Your sodality is one of these?'

'Yes.'

Weld took him to a cool, unpretentious building, a flat grey slab buried in a mass of flat grey slabs. The interior consisted of a single room having the same shape as the slab itself. Peder quickly learned not to touch any extrusion such as the doorframe with his bare hands. The edges were as sharp as a knife.

A few members of Weld's sodality arrived and sat silently, making no greeting to Weld. To Peder's eye their suits were cruder versions of Weld's own, except that the fabric had a leaden sheen to it and seemed very substantial. Their faces, too, were stern and uncompromising, though unlike Weld they went bare-headed.

'There is a unique character to my sodality,' Weld said. 'Let me show you.' He beckoned one of his members forward, and bent back the cloth of the man's sleeve.

'Cutaneous raiment,' he explained. 'I have integrated garments into the cuticle, taking the place of the epidermis. They are part of the person – or more strictly, the person is the biological content of the raiment. They can not be removed.'

Peder felt the metallic texture of the Prossim, noting where it was joined to the skin of the member's wrist, then let his hand fall. 'It is an aberration,' he said in a supercilious tone while the member stood there stony-faced. 'The essence of the Art of Attire is that one is not bound to a single shape. Thousands of paradigms are offered to the individual by his sartorial. Your invention reverts to pre-Caeanic biological forms of evolution, where every creature had but a single nature.'

'Quite right, it is an aberration,' Weld agreed.' 'Yet it is an interesting diversion. It would have displeased me not to see this possibility explored.' He waved the member away, then picked up an object lying on a nearby table. 'You're from the Verrage sector, aren't you? Have you ever seen anything like this before?'

He handed Peder a circular mirror, which at first appeared perfectly ordinary except perhaps that its surface seemed to shimmer rather oddly, which could have been a trick of the light.

But as Peder looked into it, it seemed to flame with a pale effulgence. He gazed entranced at his face in the glass. His features were undergoing a subtle transformation. They were still his own, but evincing some indefinable alien cast.

And while he remained staring wide-eyed, the eyes of his reflection closed. The face settled into a sleeping repose.

He was inexplicably alarmed. 'How is this done?' he exclaimed.

Weld showed a rare hint of amusement. 'Although it looks like an ordinary mirror it is not, quite, a mirror. The image is formed not by reflected light but is a reconstituted image produced by a micro-computer backing. The device is fully perceptive.'

Peder turned the mirror over. Beyond a few barely visible etched lines there was nothing to see, and it had only the thickness of a normal looking-glass. That meant little, of course. Micro-electronics could put the contents of an entire brain into an even smaller space.

'A sentient mirror,' he murmured.

'Yes. Computer sentience, of course. Not quite as real as the human variety. But even so, perhaps it has a quality we lack. It is able to experience, nothing more. It doesn't have to perform actions, as we do.'

'It's purely passive. A passive sentience. A strange thought.'

'Yes. Yet sometimes the face that looks back as one gazes into it is not quite the face that an ordinary mirror would show. It's really quite percipient.'

Peder laid down the mirror. Similar devices were

becoming common in this part of space: electronic machines which did nothing but soak up influences from their surroundings devoid of any power of action. The phenomenon was symptomatic. The colonization of the latter half of Caean had apparently produced a sort of photographic negative to the earlier culture, the ebullience of Verrage and similar places being replaced by passive receptivity, as though – to continue the analogy – the human mind had decided to turn itself into a universal camera plate.

His gaze fell on Weld's jacket. Although Prossim was of vegetable origin, the fibres were much too minute to be visible to the naked eye – yet suddenly, in his imagination, he seemed to be seeing them, and he entered into a green, microscopic forest of living fronds, fibrillous networks and clumps of tiny bracken-like folioles, a forest which spread and rustled all around him, filling his horizon. As if from a great distance, he heard Weld speaking.

'Ah, here comes Famaxer now.'

In answer to Weld's summons the third Frachonard suit to be seen by Peder entered the cutaneous sodality. Peder moved forward. He seemed to walk though the matted forest, brushing aside the fern fronds. Or was the forest instead moving through him, reaching with its fibrils into his nervous system, replacing his thoughts and perceptions?

The vertiginous hallucination vanished. 'Good day, brother,' Famaxer greeted in a dry, cynical voice. 'I hope Otis has not been mistreating you.'

'No, he has been most hospitable,' Peder answered.

Famaxer's suit had the apparent texture of forrel, a vellum-like parchment at one time used for covering books. It imparted to Famaxer a quality of dryness, of a dusty, wind-blown environment, of a man much weathered by sun and air. His stance signified leathery cynicism, sprightly confidence – and other qualities Peder could not readily define.

It gave Peder no cause for wonderment that the Frachonard Prossim suits could guide their wearers across hundreds of light years. Apart from a flickering curiosity as to what might be Frachonard's master plan, he never asked himself why he did what he did, any more than a man waking in the morning asks why he wakes.

As if saluting the sun, his mind was filled with the glory of Frachonard's genius.

The three came close together. Peder was dimly aware that subtle radiations were passing between the three suits, too rarefied to be detectable on any scientific apparatus, perhaps, but nonetheless real.

'We must call together the others, and travel,' Famaxer said.

'Yes, we must travel,' Peder agreed. 'The time has come.'

'Something is *wrong*,' Amara announced. 'This just doesn't make *sense*.'

'It has to make *some* kind of sense,' Estru argued. 'We just haven't found out what it is yet.'

'This type of calculation can't be simply set aside, not if we are to be in any way scientific,' she insisted. 'Sociological decay-time is a fact, not a theory.'

They were in the late stages of an extended session in the department's operations room. Amara was revelling in all the data she could handle. But that data simply did not tell her what she wanted to hear.

According to Amara, those regions of Caean farthest from Sovya should be relatively free from garment fetishism, and even those parts settled earliest should by now be discovering more normal ideas. Yet field reports, as well as the personal observations of anyone who cared to venture outside the ship during its frequent landfalls, made it perfectly clear that quite the opposite was the case. Caeanic culture was not phasing into normalcy. The farther one got from Sovya, the weirder and more aberrant it became.

The calculations on which Amara placed such stock made used of the sociological notion of 'decay time' – the time taken for cultural forces to lose their impetus and die. A passing fad or fashion might have a decay time of weeks or months. An obsession like the one ruling Caean could, at the other end of the scale, persist for centuries. Amara's parameters, she believed, were solid. The 'half-life' of Caean was even shorter than she had at first supposed. By this time Caean should have grown out of its specific syndrome, should be a nation more nearly resembling Ziode.

'This is a sick nation,' she said. 'But something is keeping it sick – making it sicker. We have to find out what.'

'Maybe the computation is wrong?' someone suggested bravely.

Amara scowled.

Estru took up the thread. 'It could be we have underestimated the staying power of the Sovyan experience. Our equations don't allow, for instance, for total erasure of body image.'

'*Total* erasure?' Amara came back at him indignantly.

'The Sovyans clearly demonstrate that the normal body image – the image that exists in the mind for purposes of personal and species identify – can be overlaid with an alternative image,' Estru said. 'The Sovyans see themselves as big spacesuits. But suppose the original *human* body image has *no* instinctive or genetic component? What if it can be erased *permanently*? Then the Caeanic syndrome could be stable – not subject to decay.'

'Plausible,' Amara admitted. 'The Caeanic phenomenon would then emerge as a form of accelerative evolution, analogous to biological evolution. Psychologically, in terms of outward image, the Caeanics could be diverging into countless new species.'

Estru felt encouraged. 'That's right. Especially if some of these images are archetypal, dragged from the subconscious as Matt-Helver believed. A Caeanic puts on a fox-type suit and it makes him into a foxy individual, because he feels like a fox. I recall that List had something to say along those lines in his *Cultural Compendium*.'

'It's plausible, but it's *wrong*,' Amara stated. 'The natural body image *is* genetic. It *can't* be permanently obliterated.'

'Arms and legs are genetic, but Alexei Verednyev didn't have any to speak of when we first found him,' her staff chief said.

She waved a hand in exasperation. '*Proliferation. Proliferation* is the very thing that knocks Estru's argument down. Caeanic sartorials are enterprising enough not to leave stones unturned. Even if the basic image *had* been erased, what's to prevent it appearing again? How long before some sartorial whizz-kid discovered that the naked body is an exciting object in it own right? What's to prevent garments becoming increasingly scanty until nakedness becomes acceptable, as it is with us? Yet in fact the naked body, where it *is* an erotic object, is such only as an unspeakable perversion.'

As she said this she blushed deeply, then to hide her embarrassment turned to study the display screens again. 'There is something blocking the natural process of normalization,' she said.

There was a silence in which they all stared at the screens. Suddenly Estru spoke up again.

'Isn't there something else we should be talking about, more important than this? What we have also failed to find is any aggressive intention towards Ziode.'

Everyone murmured. 'Yes, that's so,' Amara said with a frown, almost reluctantly. 'It seems Abrazhne Caldersk was telling the truth in that respect.'

'Well, shouldn't our first priority be to explain this to the Directorate? We ought to be giving some thought to it. After all it might not be as easy as it sounds.'

'Oh? Why not?'

'After gearing up for war, to some people it can seem a pity not to go to war,' Estru said.

'Yes, it is unnerving,' Alexei said mildly, in reasonably intelligible Ziodean. 'All the time.'

Mast responded feelingly. 'You poor bastard. God, I thought *I* was a villain until I met some of these scientific types we've got here.'

'I'm managing to cope,' Alexei said. 'They give me drugs to keep me moderately schizophrenic. That's the only way to get through this type of experience, I'm told.'

As he spoke Alexei's face was deadpan. He probably never would learn to use facial expression, even though all the requisite muscles had been revitalized.

Mast was aware that Alexei could tolerate human company only with difficulty. But, he told himself, the Sovyan must also be lonely.

They were walking along one of the belly passages that ran the curve of the *Callan*'s hull, Alexei stepping awkwardly and falteringly so that every now and then Mast automatically put out a hand to save him from falling, though in fact the Sovyan lost his balance only rarely. As they reached an observation window Alexei stopped, as if to regain breath. Mast stood by, embarrassed, while he gazed with homesick longing into the vacuum of space.

Then he hurried on. They turned aside from the belly corridor and came to Amara Corl's sociology department, which Mast took care to visit at least once a day. A murmur of agitated talk was coming from behind the door of the conference room. No one took any notice as Mast rudely pushed the door open and went in, followed by his limping companion.

The team had drifted apart into two groups. One, bunched around Amara, was busy with some kind of calculation using a computer terminal at the other end of the room. The rest didn't seem to be doing anything very much, except to talk aimlessly in the sort of crass jargon which Mast found irritating.

He listened patiently to their drivel for a minute or two until Estru, who had been gazing into a mirror, suddenly interrupted the discussion.

'It's wouldn't surprise me to learn that *this* is the sort of clue we're looking for,' he announced.

Mast came closer. The mirror was oval, set in a frame of wrought gold. It seemed unremarkable, unless it was that its surface was a little too bright.

'What, that mirror?' someone asked.

Estru chuckled. 'Yes, just a mirror, an ordinary silvered glass reflector. Only it isn't. While you're looking into the mirror, the mirror is looking back at you.'

He turned it over in his hands, explaining. 'The glass isn't ordinary silica glass; it's hologram glass. Instead of bring coated with mercury in the usual manner, it's painted with a micro-computer backing of about the same thickness. The hologram glass digitizes the image that falls on it, absorbing all the incident light, and passes it into the computer, which then puts it through the perception process. Eventually – a few nanoseconds later – the reconstituted image bounces back into the hologram glass and is re-emitted by fluorescence.'

'What in the galaxy is the point of all that?'

'Yes,' someone else joined in, 'that's a very complicated method for a simple convenience.'

'The difference is that the mirror has machine sentience. Only in an extremely receptive, passive way, of course. It has no output leads whatsover; no outcome. It's a mirror with a mind that reflects what it experiences. So you're looking at yourself being looked at – the more you think about that, the less simple it seems.' He chuckled again. 'You could say it's a mirror with an open mind.'

Mast peered at the artifact over Estru's shoulder. 'But what practical use is it?'

'None at all. It's an ornament, a typical Caeanic conceit. Though there's a little more to it. Sometimes it modifies the "reflected" image, and occasionally quite drastically. The effect can be pretty scary if you don't know how it's done. But it still doesn't invent or add anything. It brings out latent qualities, points out what the human eye might miss.'

The other speakers edged forward, staring at the mirror. 'So what's this got to do with Caean?'

Estru gripped the mirror, his eyes going dreamy. 'What if Caean is trying to turn itself into such a mirror . . . trying to lose its specific human consciousness . . .' He shook his head, aware that he was floundering.

Mast laughed mockingly.

At that moment Estru spotted Alexei Verednyev hovering nearby. A sudden ruthlessness flitted across his features.

'Here, Alexei, take a look at yourself.'

'No, I don't like mirrors – ' Alexei, however, could not avoid the shimmering oval surface as it was thrust before his face. For a moment he stared, his expression still wooden, before he turned aside with an agonized cry.

'What's wrong, Alexei?' Mast said with concern. But the Sovyan turned his back on them all and went stumbling through the door. Mast moved to follow him, then changed his mind.

'Now that wasn't very nice,' he said accusingly to Estru.

'Forget it, he needs these shocks as part of his treatment. Besides, it was an interesting result. I saw what showed in the mirror.'

'Oh?' And what did show in the mirror?'

'A metal space helmet. Verednyev's face wasn't there at all.'

Estru's co-workers, embarrassed by the incident, looked away and began to inspect some Caeanic garments that hung in a mobile rack. The clothes had been obtained during their last stop. By now the *Callan* had a big enough store of them to go into business, Mast thought.

'Everything we pick up lately is made of Prossim,' one of the sociologists said, fingering the cloth of a tabard. 'The locals seem to scorn anything else.'

Unaware that it was his own conduct that had prompted the change of topic, Estru joined in. 'Caeanics have always prized Prossim,' he said. 'It *is* a remarkable material.'

'But further back in Tzist history fabrics are as varied as styles.'

'A question of cost. Prossim is actually versatile enough to take on any texture, to serve as any other kind of material according to how it's processed. But it costs a lot. Reputedly it's grown on some secret planet whose location is known only to the merchants who supply it. Probably the reason why it's prevalent hereabouts it simply that we are close to the source.'

He pulled out a suit of the type known as a suit of light. It was a close-fitting set of garments consisting of trousers, a zouave jacket and a pouch-like hat sporting two short horns, one on either side, like stumpy antennae. The suit was resplendent with synthetic gems and gold piping which seemed actually to shine and to cast out dazzling rays.

'Why don't you try this on, Blanco?' Estru mused, offering it to the other. 'Let's see how it looks.'

Surprisingly the Ziodeans rarely tried on any of the garments they acquired. Blanco shrugged. 'All right.' He slipped out of his clothes and donned the suit with deft movements.

They all agreed he looked really smart. Immediately he was apparelled his back straightened and his shoulders squared as though of their own accord. His eyes cleared and seemed to sparkle.

'It really does something for you,' Estru told him thoughtfully. 'I had no idea it would – you've got the right physique, somehow. How does it make you feel?'

'All right,' said Blanco in a new confident voice. 'Fine. Like – ' His eyes took on a far-seeing, penetrating look 'Like nothing can be hidden from me– '

He took a few steps back, dancing away from them, his movements light and nimble. It was as if they saw him on a faulty vidplate which was giving after-image on the highlights. The glittering gems, the glowing goldwork seemed to leave traceries of light in the air, and as he moved he filled the space around him with radiance.

Amara came striding up from the back of the conference room, her helpers in tow. 'I see you've dealt your own death-blow to your body-image theory, Estru,' she boomed. 'Notice how that suit clings to the shape of his body? Proving that the basic image is very much alive in Caean.' She gave Blanco a sharp glance. 'Get that rubbish off, Blanco. I'm not having you turn into a subversive.'

Obediently Blanco disrobed.

'I guess you're right,' Estru conceded.

'Of course I am. Behind all these garments is the tacit assumption of the naked human form. Any kind of adornment would be redundant without it. Here, I'll prove it to you – I'll bet those clothes exert no psychological effect on Verednyev. The basic image *is* dormant in him. Where is he? I thought I saw him with you just now,'

'He left,' Estru said. 'But I've already explored that avenue, and you're quite right about him. He doesn't respond to Caeanic apparel, or to any kind of apparel – unless you give him a spacesuit.' He sighed. 'Well, how have you been getting on?'

'Excellently!'

She beckoned to all present. 'I'd like your attention, please. I want everyone to hear this.'

They crowded round as Amara took up a lecturing stance under the big terminal vidplate at the rear of conference room. Currently the plate showed the elongated curve of Tzist, dramatized so that the inhabited planets stood out as bright blue blobs while the rest was faded to a ghost-like glow.

'On the evidence of the utterly reliable parameters we have adopted, we have already ascertained that the situation as we find it in Caean is theoretically impossible,' she asserted. '*Ergo*, some other factor must be present of which we were unaware. So first, let's set the problem up in structural terms.'

She inclined her head to the screen, her hand straying to the terminal console. Under her prompting the image began to transform. Arrowed pathways connected up the blue blobs, then these themselves began to shift position, many of them coalescing into one another, so that the whole display bunched itself up and the picture became simplified and formalized.

'Right. This is Caean reduced to a network of cultural influences,' Amara explained. 'Now to identify those influences. The aberration coming from the direction of Sovya should have worked out in this fashion.'

The network had a lozenge shape. From its left-hand vertex a red stain appeared and spread through the connecting pathways. On reaching the middle of the network it began to fade, so that the lozenge's right-hand quarter was left in its original white – the colour of sociological normalcy in the accepted code. Amara tapped this part of the graph with her baton to emphasize her point.

Then she turned to face them triumphantly. 'Yet instead of cultural conditions returning to norm we find that the Art of Attire is even more thriving, with new unpredicted features developing. Only one circumstance can explain this. Our original appraisal of Caean can be only half right. The impetus coming from the direction of Sovya is being reinforced by a *second* impetus coming from the opposite direction. By using the same kind of cultural mapping we have just established roughly whereabouts the source of this impetus lies.'

Amara's hand went again to the terminal. A green stain began at the lozenge's right-hand vertex in complement to the red stain, spreading until it met and blended with it, producing a spectrum gradated from buff orange to a murky mauve. 'There is even a likely candidate planet. Selene, the last Caeanic planet in Tzist and – as it happens – the farthermost from Ziode. So there it is. We repair full-speed to Selene.'

Those who had not helped Amara to arrive at this conclusion stared in fascination at the diagram. There could be little doubt of the cogency of her logic. Remarkable as it was, the thesis answered the facts.

'What do you think we're going to find on this planet?' Estru asked. 'Not another Sovya, surely? That would be stretching things a bit too far, wouldn't it?'

'No,' Amara said seriously. 'I think both source-points must have originated in Sovya. I imagine what probably happened is this. I think Sovya must have been responsible for two different planetary settlements, one close to Sovya and the other much farther away: Selene, or possibly a now-abandoned planet near Selene. Having no contact with one another they will each have developed in their own way. We all know that there can be a thousand reasons why societies diverge – perhaps they sprang from different strains within the Sovyan culture, or possibly climatic conditions were unusual on Selene at that time. At any rate, when they eventually met it was to produce a society with mutually reinforcing impulses.'

Blanco rose to speak. 'This is all very interesting, but on the subject of going to Selene, haven't we hung around for rather too long already? It's some time since we established the most important fact – that Caean is not a military threat to Ziode. Shouldn't we be heading home with that news?'

A murmur rose from the group. 'Captain Wilce is of the same opinion,' Estru said, raising his eyebrows enquiringly.

Amara could see before her the inception of one of those divisive quarrels which end by making team-work impossible. She licked her lips.

'I am well aware that there are differences of opinion on board this ship,' she said in a hard voice. 'By virtue of the special authority invested in me by the Directorate, I have already overruled the view that says we should go directly home. We are *not* going home until we have completed our researches in an exhaustive manner. There will be no further discussion of the subject.'

That should shut them up, she thought to herself.

Estru tried to remember if Amara had ever looked into the computerized mirror. He wondered what it would show in her case.

Mirror, mirror on the wall, he thought, who is the fairest of us all?

14

One person who was equivocal on the desirability of returning to Ziode was Realto Mast. During a harrowing interview Amara had dragged his story out of him and he had told her all about his sentence to Ledlide, his subsequent escape and the amazing qualities he had witnessed in the Caeanic suit worn by Peder Forbarth. She had listened superciliously, obviously believing only about half of it, and disdaining to make any comment.

Ever since he had been coquettishly trying to court Amara with a view to getting her to intercede on his behalf with the authorities in Ziode, convinced that she could arrange a pardon for him, or at least obtain a drastic reduction of sentence on the grounds of 'patriotic services rendered'. She had off handedly encouraged him in this belief, but was far from magnanimous when it came to keeping the score.

'But you haven't actually *done* very much, have you?' she said severely when he taxed her on the subject, as they were about to land on Selene.

'Well, there was that time I cleared up the data for you on Kurdoc,' Mast suggested tentatively. 'When your interpreters couldn't understand idiom.'

'Hm. That hardly adds up to getting out of twenty years on Ledlide.'

He became peevish. 'Stop reminding me of that savagery. Instead of looking at the sentence all the time, you should measure my services against the offence, which was comparatively trivial.'

'The degree of guilt has already been settled by a court of law,' she told him primly. 'I'm not prepared to discuss it. You're in the market for remission, not a retrial.'

The bitch, Mast thought to himself as he went away. I'd like to . . . His thoughts tailed off, unable to imagine anything horrific enough to befall the research ship's *de facto* matriarch.

Displaying by vidcast the 'unfettered freedom' status conferred on her by the Minister of Harmonic Relations on Verrage, the *Callan* settled on to a landing compound within the city of Yomondo. Within an hour Amara's people were preparing for a sojourn into the city, and Mast disconsolately wandered down to the disembarkation bay, hoping to make himself useful.

No one took any notice of him. It was the same old story; he was not a trained sociologist. 'Leave this sort of thing to the professionals, old man,' a staffman had told him once, with infuriating condescension, when he had tried to attach himself to one of the team projects.

As soon as the bay doors were opened Mast went off to explore Yomondo by himself. As usual in Caean, there were no formalities at the spaceport, and no officials. The egress roads led directly into the city proper.

If Selene had initially presented any climatic or geological problems, then the planet must long since have been tamed. The air was warm and balmy. Yet there was an ambience to the place, a kind of lulled calm, that was off-beat and disturbing. The atmosphere was invested with a clear, purple twilight. The breeze wafted the scent of lavender. Odd twittering sounds came from all around, echoing from twisted towers and crazy air-ramps which made up the city's skyline.

Mast searched for Selene's sun. He found it – or rather, them – low over the southern horizon. A double star, the large one mauve, the smaller blue-white, both of them soft and fuzzy in outline. Which meant that Selene, in all probability, had seasons lasting centuries. The habitable planets of double stars nearly always had large orbits.

What was the season now? Spring? Summer? Autumn? Probably not winter, Mast decided.

Beyond the fringe of the city a forest grew. Mast could see the olive-green fronds waving like dark seaspray behind the twisted towers. Birds with glorious plumage of silver and lilac, gold and mulberry, shot out of that forest to go soaring, sweeping and hovering all over Yomondo, giving the city the impression of being a vast open-air aviary. The birds were of all sizes. Some were very big – Mast peered closely to see if any of them were human – and the smallest were tiny purple and pink humming birds, darting hesitantly hither and thither, their long curved beaks, made to dip into the nectar of orchids, craning forward as if pointing out mysterious messages.

Yomondo had a single flat floor of a pale lilac colour. Above it the twisted towers, the air-ramps, the tortuous corridors hanging in the air seemingly without proper support, made an open-plan framework. The nearest comparison Mast could find was that the city resembled a huge fairground, with helter-skelters, roller coasters, barkers and innumerable stage-shows taking place in the open air. The impact on the eye was indeed unexpected and bewildering. He could make no sense of the multifarious and apparently disjointed activities taking place. Was a festival in progress? Or was this, fantastic as it seemed, normal business?

An individual whose broad, snub-nosed face bore an idiot grin stepped from behind a blockhouse and approached Mast. Of the young man's rig-out, Mast noticed clumpy steel-shod boots and flared pink trousers, held up by broad blue braces worn over the top of a chemise, or tunic, which fluffed and frothed all around his torso and arms. The impression of bucolic brutality was made complete by a crude, broken hat made of straw.

He walked with an ungainly stomp, body bent forward, thumbs thrust into his braces. Moving to block Mast's path, he stood flexing his knees.

'Har! A dude, eh? Come on then! Put up yer dukes!' Even to Mast's ears, his dialect was uncouth. He began to buffet the Ziodean with ham-like fists, in a manner both playful and aggressive, and Mast, surprised and alarmed, put his arms before his face to ward off the blows.

But suddenly the ruffian ceased his assault and looked sidelong at something to Mast's left. Mast followed his gaze. A woman was walking the floor of the city, making for a twisted tower some distance off. Her movements were swaying and willowy, and her long graceful robe, with its streaming pagoda sleeves, made her seem as if she were being bent by the wind. Gauzy veils were blowing away from her face, which was dreamy and distant.

The ruffian reached up and removed his straw hat, stuffing it into a pocket in the seat of his trousers, from which he drew another piece of headgear. This was an abbreviated cloth casque, or galea, boasting a modest panache and decorated with ornate ribwork of gold. As he placed the casque on his head, adjusting it carefully, an amazing transformation came over him. No longer was he gormless and belligerent. The light of intelligence came to his eye. His back straightened, and his features moulded themselves into a different countenance. He was a new man.

At the same time he was tugging at the frills of his chemise, altering it into a different type of garment entirely. Gone from sight were the braggart braces, the insolent cut of the trousers waistband. The chemise became a sleek doublet, striped heliotrope and cyan, ruched at the hem, the body purled with twisted cord of silver and cobalt. In proximity to these new colours the pink of the trousers took on a mauve tint; their cut seemed no longer boorish but elegant.

Now the essence of courtliness, and with perfect comportment, the erstwhile tough stepped to accost the fresh object of his interest, introducing himself with a bow and a flourish. He seemed to have forgotten Mast entirely.

Mast moved on, mingling with the sparse throng that was abroad in Yomondo, and pausing to watch what was happening on a raised platform. To pounding music young men performed a jerky, ritualistic dance. Their tight-fitting cladding blazed with baroque curlicues, arabesques of gold and silver glitter-work and glowing art-gems. Suddenly they stopped of one accord, clapping their hands over their heads. The platform – really the floor of a box skeleton – rose from the ground and swept vertically upwards, gathering speed. Mast now noticed many such aerial boxes gliding through Yomondo's sky, guided by force-beams between the towers and air-ramps in seemingly meaningless, maze-like patterns. In each box a different but equally mysterious scene was taking place.

Not far from him a woman in the red and gold plumage of a tropical bird uttered a joyous shriek and took to the air, trailing fire behind her. He watched her trajectory as she went hurtling like a rocket right over the city, coming down on the far side. He found himself hoping she had made it safely.

At the centre of Yomondo was a great open square. Mast arrived there in time to witness the sudden evanescent crystallization of a crowd phenomenon. All present began to surge together, all turning to face the same direction. All faces, men's and women's, momentarily presented one identical face. A tribe-like dance step took hold of the mass of people. Forward . . . back . . . forward . . . back . . .

Then, as inexplicably as it had come, the spell dissipated. Everyone went his separate way, or undertook unfathomable activities with smaller groups.

Mast became aware that here, more than on any other Caeanic world he had visited, human nature had gone over the top; had taken a turn in a new, irrevocable direction. People no longer seemed to be human beings in the Ziodean sense of the word. They were loose collections of roles, play-actors switching parts at random, no longer having any visible conscious direction in their lives.

Clothes robots, he thought.

He wondered what Amara would make of this.

Peder could not quite plumb the psychological system by which Frachonard had designed his five Prossim suits. It was not a system a conventional psychologist would have devised had he wished to delineate the qualities of the human race – for such a delineation, complete within its own terms, was what the set of five undoubtedly comprised.

There was Peder himself, with his urbanity; there was the unbreakable will of Otis Weld, the caustic dryness and irony of Famaxer; there was Cy Amoroza Carendor and his athletic sprightliness, and the retiring imperturbability of Poloche Tam Trice. Yet these were only the most obtrusive characteristics. There were others. Each suit was itself a symphony of indefinable qualities, chosen according to concepts of humanity foreign to conventional thought, and all of which when taken together added up to an equally off-beat definition of human ability.

In a room where lilac light shone through turquoise windows, the five stood facing one another formally, as if arranged on the limbs of a pentagram. Peder could sense a communion between them; it was as if they were the various organs of one single man.

'Only one more journey now,' said Trice.

'Then the bright new universe will begin.'

'How shall we travel?'

'I have met a harvester,' Otis Weld said. 'He will take us. He knows the location.'

'Such people practise their trade in greatest secrecy. They can never be persuaded to accept passengers,' Peder pointed out.

'Us he cannot refuse. I know where his ship is. He will take us.'

'Why delay?' Carendor said lightly. 'Let us embark on this ship now.'

They all concurred. 'Yes. Let us go now.'

They left the building, Otis Weld leading the way.

Realto Mast had stopped for refreshment when he spotted Peder walking with four others dressed, as far as he could see, in identical suits.

At a gilt-bedecked booth he had bought a chunk of sweetened goldbread, washing it down with purple blackcurrant juice. The vendor, rigged out in a piratical costume and an eye-patch, had doubled the price on handing over the viands, speaking an archaic dialect and making good his demand by flourishing a fancy force-pistol, but Mast had paid up without argument.

Peder was just disappearing through a magenta arcade. Mast, gulping down the last of the goldbread, ran after him, calling his name in astonishment.

'What are you doing here, Peder?'

Peder stopped, glancing after the retreating backs of his companions. He did not seem at all surprised to see Mast. 'I am glad that you are broadening your mind by travel, Realto,' he said, 'but you really must get yourself some decent clothes.'

'What? But this is the frock-coat *you* made for me, Peder. Don't you remember? The trews are your work, too.' He held his arms akimbo, displaying the garments.

'Tawdry rags. You deserve better. You should dress like a Frachonard. And so you shall. I must go now, Realto. We have business to attend to. When I return I shall have something better for you to wear.'

'You have business here, Peder? Where are you going?' He paused, trying to think of some topic to detain the other. 'Amara Corl thinks this planet is Caean's wellspring.'

Peder smiled. 'Not so, Realto. The wellspring is farther off. A secret, holy place.'

'Oh?' Mast opened his eyes wide in excitement. 'Tell me more!'

But Peder padded away, ignoring Mast's further questions.

Mast stood dazed and perplexed. The strangeness of this twittering city, with its crystalline purple atmosphere, its mass psychosis, struck him anew. Something was going on here. But what?

Cautiously, keeping his distance, he began to follow the five sartorial brothers.

'You're sure about this?' frowned Amara, looking suspiciously at Mast.

By now she had been able to confirm for herself, from her probes' first tentative talk-back, that Yomondo was an insane city.

'I've told you what Forbarth said,' Mast replied. 'It agrees so perfectly with your theory. Besides, what's Forbarth doing here? What's he up to? I've already said there's something special about that suit he wears. Why did the Caeanics try to recover it from Kyre? I'm pretty confident that's what they were after. And here are five of them, all together in a bunch.'

He was still out of breath from running nearly all the way back to the *Callan*. He had followed Peder and his group out of the city to a rendezvous in the forest, where they had entered a battered space freighter hidden beneath the cover of the huge ferns. Nearby Mast had found a camouflaged warehouse filled with stringy plant fibre. To his mind it all fitted together. He felt positive that Peder had been doomed to pursue his enigmatic quest from the very moment he had first put on the suit.

'It could be possible,' Amara mused. 'Other cultures have had holy places – holy groves, holy cities, holy continents even, whose locations were secret and which ordinary people were never allowed to visit, and certainly not foreigners. So why not a secret holy planet?'

'Peder said something else odd, too.'

'What was that?'

'He said when he came back he would dress me like a Frachonard. That's a historic figure. Their greatest-ever sartorial.'

'This suit must be some sort of totem-figure,' Estru said. 'Perhaps if you wear it you can visit the secret grove.'

Amara nodded. 'Possibly the suit is part of some quasi-religious rite that takes place on the secret planet. We were so close, and we missed it!' She brought to mind her brief meeting with Forbarth on Verrage, and tried to recollect if she had noticed anything unusual about his suit. It had looked comparatively ordinary, she recalled.

'If nothing else you might discover the source of Prossim,' Mast said. 'But if you're going to discover anything at all you'll have to move now. I nearly broke my guts getting back here in a hurry. Leave it any longer and you won't be able to pick up Forbarth's ship.'

Amara snapped her fingers at Estru. 'He's right. Get on to Captain Wilce. And call in the probes immediately.'

Within minutes the *Callan* took off again, its sensors searching surrounding space until they found the ancient freighter that had recently departed. The ship's baffles came full on. Locked on the Caeanic merchantman, keeping it just within sensor range, the Ziodeans followed their prey.

15

The owner-captain of the harvester ship was a brooding man who spoke but seldom. His Prossim garments covered him like a protective shell, whorl patterns in their purple-and-heliotrope stripe generating intense moiré effects. The eye was befuddled whenever he moved; he seemed at times to disappear, to leave the ship with an impression of emptiness, of lack of pilotage.

The journey occupied two days and took them well beyond the bounds of inhabited space. During that time the five men in Frachonard suits either wandered separately through the rusty, echoing freighter, or else sat silently together around a table. It was a period of introspection, confused daydreams vying with vacancy of mind, each keeping his mental state locked away from the others. The captain kept to the bridge, only occasionally venturing into the saloon to sit in the presence of his passengers, looking like a glowing purple lobster, awed and unspeaking.

No one apart from the six of them was on board. The harvesting machinery lay in the cavernous hold below, but the crew that usually operated it had been left behind. The captain did not even know why these men wanted to visit the source of the Guild's wealth. Somehow he did not think it was in order to poach on that wealth – why should men clothed in perfection desire anything else? When word of his treachery got out, as was bound to happen, he was a dead man, but he had found that he simply did not have the will to resist their wishes, even though it meant betraying the supreme secret of the Harvester's Guild.

The freighter slipped through a cloudbank of glowing suns, finding hidden behind it a region of waste raddled with trails of concentrated dust, sporting a scattering of flickering stars but few planets that consisted of much more than amorphous masses of rubble. The area was too out-of-the-way, too poverty-stricken, normally to attract interest. But even here, as in many unlikely places, the universe did not fail to surprise. The harvester ship homed on a small lone planet circling a dim sun. Better-favoured systems might have incorporated it as a moon; it had little water, a calm atmosphere and a bland geology. Yet in its billions of years of solitary existence the forces of evolution had not left it entirely untouched.

Peder Forbarth had received in a flash from the brain of Realto Mast, at their passing meeting in Yomondo, knowledge of the theories and discoveries of Amara Corl. The encounter had given him his first intimation that Caean's uniqueness sprang originally from a planet called Sovya and the peculiar culture existing there. He had learned, too, of her belief that at Caean's opposite extremity there existed an additional cultural source complementing the first. He smiled now to think of the woman's cleverness. She had come so close to the truth. Caean was, indeed, stretched as if between the poles of a magnetic field between two nearly equal forces: Sovya the ancient prototype and ancestor, the home of the space-dwelling people in their huge suits, and the gloomy, poorly endowed world towards whose surface they were now decelerating. But on one important point Amara was wrong. Never at any time had this planet had any contact with Sovya. It was, purely and simply, the source of the wonder cloth, Prossim.

The freighter descended gently into the calm, quiet light that bathed the surface of the plain, its drivers on retroactive phase. Standing in the observation blister, Peder could see the mats and fronds of the Prossim plant stretching for mile after mile over the plain like a tatty fibrous carpet, dull green in colour, worn through here and there where the bare rock showed.

Looking at the unprepossessing green mats, it was hard to realize that the growth was sentient.

A strange form of sentience, perhaps. Not sentience at all in the accepted sense. Yet – sentient.

Nature habitually cast her creations in two opposite forms. Positive and negative electricity, north and south magnetic poles, matter and anti-matter, forces of attraction and repulsion, male and female sexes.

And of sentience, after the same pattern, she had made two basic types: active and passive.

Human consciousness was active. Man was a thinking, doing, imagining being. Perception itself, as it took place in the human brain, was an act: to perceive meant to put some sort of mental construction on what was seen. Man could be forgiven for presuming his own consciousness to be the only kind the forces of nature would permit, for the animal nervous system had a compelling logic to it; an intelligence that lacked this type of nervous system, that lacked any power of thought or action, would have seemed a contradiction in terms. What properties could it possess that would compensate for its incomprehensible deficiencies? Man would almost certainly fail to recognize a passive sentience should he encounter one, just as he had in fact failed to perceive that the vegetable growth from which Prossim was woven comprised such a sentience.

Prossim had no power of action. It had no faculty of conceptualization, even. Its fibrous floral mentality perceived not by performing acts of recognition but by a totally different type of chemical and mental reaction whose nature allowed only the passive acceptance of incoming data, unselectively and unmodified. It did not think further on anything it perceived; it simply experienced the universe, a dreaming mirror, without alteration, without further constructive process.

A private ear on the radiations that came to it from all quarters, during untold aeons the Prossim growth had basked in the impressions it received. It recorded the movements of heavenly bodies, the tumultuous energies of suns, the faint traffic of radio-using civilizations, the dancing sleet of particles which, though invisible to the human senses, on another level brings space to life. It was receptive to the whole of the electromagnetic spectrum, to cosmic rays, to relativistic electrons, in lesser measure to the neutrino flux, the tachyon flux, and to even subtler radiations little-known to man and which carried charges of a near-mental nature.

It knew almost nothing of other biological lifeforms except for the related flora and bacteria on its own planet. It had never formed a thought. It had a memory, in which some form of selective ordering did occur, but here it was the impressions themselves that provided the ordering principle, and the experiencing sentience, as always, retained its negative polarity. It could not make the crucial breakthrough to imagined concepts. Still less could it arrive at the idea of intentional actions.

And yet this idea, by a rare coincidence, had come.

It was a billion-to-one chance that might never again in the history of creation be offered to a passive sentience, and it had begun with the landing of Caeanic explorers on the Prossim growth's planet. The clothes-conscious Caeanics quickly recognized the sartorial potentialities of the new material. Within years Prossim cloth had been fashioned into millions of garments and was being worn all over the inhabited Tzist Arm.

Nothing else than to be worn by this clothes-fetishist people could, perhaps, have forced the Prossim plant to comprehend the presence of active intelligences in the universe. Although it had no individuality – personal consciousness being unique to the active mode of sentience – the microscopic fibres composing its structure were good mental conductors. Even when harvested and transported hundreds of light years away, they could still experience; processed and woven into garments, they behaved as silent mirrors to the nervous systems of their wearers, remaining *en rapport* with the parent mass behind the screening star bank.

As it increasingly clothed the doings of human beings, the Prossim forest became more and more drawn into those doings. Willy-nilly it experienced the nature of *doing, thinking, striving,* even if at a distance. Dimly, it began to understand that evolution had sold it short.

A revolution, a quantum jump, occurred in the Prossim growth's perceptions.

It formed a project.

The new world of sentient activity attracted it magnetically. Automatically it accepted the main aim of Caeanic philosophy: to open up every possible area of conscious life. There was nothing, to the Prossim plant's mode of being, that was not material for experience. Life *was* experience, undifferentiated experience of everything that chanced to arrive within its field. It undertook to enter into every nook and cranny of this amazing novel universe that had been opened up to it.

But it could only ever achieve the new sentience vicariously, by sharing it with human beings, by clothing them and eventually controlling them – just as, in the first place, it had come to this realization by vicarious use of human reasoning powers. It decided it must create a dual sentience; one that was active and passive together, humanity and the Prossim plant forming opposite poles of a complementary system.

Of which, in short order, Prossim would become the dominant partner.

To do this it had to become the garment of all humanity. But simple garments were not enough. What was needed was a *whole suit*, made with such artistry that it encompassed the whole of man. *Five* such suits, the Prossim plant judged, would give the gamut of human potential for the entire species.

Only one more preliminary was required: the suits would need to mature by 'growing on to' suitable wearers, so as to fix the qualities that were to be brought to the Prossim plant. They would need to move through society, to interact in innumerable situations, before, fully charged, they returned to source.

This, then, was the strategy that was enacted through the agency of the greatest genius in tailoring ever to live, the inestimable Frachonard.

The weirdest fate ever to befall an intelligent species was nearing culmination. As the ship sank to its destination the picture became clearer and clearer to Peder, emanating from the electromagnetic mental field surrounding the Prossim jungle, relayed into his mind by the Frachonard suit. The freighter settled into the green Prossim, creaking slightly and transferring its weight to the tough mats. There was a long pause before he heard a whining and a clanking from below, signifying that the hold doors were being opened.

The blister's inner port irised apart. The others were standing on the gallery, waiting for him to join them: Weld, Famaxer, Cy Amoroza Carendor, Poloche Tam

Trice, their faces appearing one behind the other. He even glimpsed the captain, staring with a stricken, intensely dour look from beneath his purple morion, eager to see what was to befall, though he had little intimation of what was afoot.

'We must go outside now,' Otis Weld told Peder.

'Of course.'

Peder walked with them along the encircling gallery, down the iron steps to the hold.

The ramp-like doors had been let down directly on to the green verbiage. They moved past the harvesting machines that were ranked on either side in the hold's spacious cavity and stood for some moments on the lip of the port. The landscape was bathed in a gloomy, though oddly translucent light. The fronds, ferns and tangles that comprised the Prossim mats could be seen extending to the horizon. There was scarcely any undulation in the ground. The plain was level and flat, and vegetable green – cabbage green. Peder raised his eyes to the sky, which was dark purple in colour and glistened with stars. The star bank that cut off this sparse region from Caean would also be seen, glowing like a silvery cloud far off in the mid-heaven.

The harvester captain stayed behind, peering out over the landscape from the port's rim, as the five elegantors set forth from the ship. The Prossim mats, growing to a depth of several yards, their roots deep in a rocky soil, made a springy carpet underfoot. Peder looked down to where his slim shoes of lavender Prossim leather trod the bracken-like surface. He had the impression he was looking from an immense height on to a gigantic forest. The rustling fronds were titanic trees, the ferns and stems, with their myriad tiny flowers, hid a million minute countries bedecked with greenery, containing endless forested depths.

For several minutes they walked in silence, until they were some distance from the ship. Then they stopped of one accord. With dream-like motions they laid themselves down on the mat-like masses. For a fleeting instant Peder had the feeling that he was stretching himself out on a grassy meadow on a sunny afternoon.

Then the Prossim growth seemed almost to open up to receive him. He was sinking into it, though probably by his own weight since he knew it was incapable of voluntary physical movement.

He turned his head, finding himself shaded by over-hanging ferns. Viewed from close up, the green of the Prossim plant took on an oily sheen, breaking up prismatically into mother-of-pearl colours, while the tiny flowers that covered the stems glowed like point-sized jewels. He saw now that the plant, of unremarkable appearance when observed from a distance of a few feet, actually contained an amazing variety of structures. There were countless bolls from which the Prossim fibre itself was spun. There were little mushroom-like spore propagators. And each fern and frond was made up of thousands of leaves and spikes of an astonishing diversity of delicate antennae-like shapes: spirals, whirls, ingeniously reticulated arrays.

Antennae. That, thought Peder dimly, was what they were. But very few thoughts were occurring to him by now. He was removing his garments, his hands moving by no will of his own. Jerkily, hastily, he was divesting himself of his suit and, as though by nervous momentum, of his underclothing as well.

Naked, he pulled himself free from the miniature Prossim forest. He climbed to his feet. Dotted around him on the verdant plain, standing some tens of yards apart, the other four elegantors were likewise coming to their feet. They gazed around them like bewildered children, staring at their naked forms, their faces expressing total horror.

One by one they keeled over again in a dead faint, flop-ping back on to the vegetable mats. A Caeanic could not remain functioning if denuded – it was too unacceptable, too unthinkable a rape. Peder also tottered, his senses swaying. But he was not, after all, a native Caeanic, and he stayed conscious. He stumbled over to the nearest of his companions, Poloche Tam Trice, and knelt by the naked body to examine his pulse. The man was dead. Traumatic cardiac arrest, Peder guessed.

He went in turn to each of the others. Otis Weld and Cy Amoroza Carendor were likewise dead. Famaxer was breathing faintly when he first went to him, but shortly he, too, expired.

A breeze swept over the Prossim plain, causing the fronds to shiver, sending waves rippling across the surface of the jade-coloured crop. In a daze Peder began to walk disconsolately hither and thither, scarcely knowing where he was. It did not even occur to him to return to the harvester ship, or to try to recover his suit, which in any case had entirely disappeared beneath the interlocking ocean of Prossim. He had no idea how long he wandered about in this manner, except that the dull sun seemed scarcely to move in the sky: but it was long enough for him to discover that in one respect the Prossim growth had learned to be adaptable.

In genetic terms, at least, it was no longer completely helpless.

It could control its growth, and the manner of it.

Using the five Frachonard suits as a pattern, the new harvest was appearing with astonishing rapidity. The bolls had already broken open to add their fibres to the plant in the accustomed way. But they were being incorporated into the Prossim growth in accordance with new templates. Suits. Hundreds, thousands of suits, accompanied by matching undergarments and accessories, were growing all over the plain by an accelerated building up of the basic Prossim fibre. Already Peder's practised eyes could discern, even though the suits were as yet but partially formed, the five basic types that in the planet's view made up the complete glyph of humanity.

It was all over.

Everything – the whole world Peder had known before meeting the suit – was over. The new world had begun.

A shadow fell on him, blotting out the coolly shining sun. He looked up, to see a ship falling out of the sky towards the plain.

A ship of Ziodean design.

16

'Now let's go through this once more,' ordered a pinch-lipped Amara. 'You're saying that the source of Prossim fabric – this flora growing outside – is a vegetable inteligence. That it can control people through the clothes they wear. Right?'

'Right,' muttered Peder.

He sat shivering in a chair, draped in nothing but a blanket. Half an hour earlier they had found him half out of his mind, stumbling ankle-deep in the Prossim.

Peder's present experience of events was that he was slowly waking from a long, inescapable dream. His feverish explanations had confused and dumbfounded his rescuers, but it was not possible for them to dismiss his claims.

They were forced to take notice, because all around them was the spreading sea of Frachonard suits, a fact that was as undeniable as it was astonishing.

'It has sentience,' he repeated, 'but a sentience that's purely passive. One could never communicate with it, for instance. It's like some of those gadgets you can find in Caean, mirrors and so forth, that have only passive functions. They exist because of its influence, in fact.'

Amara's staff chief took up her recap. 'And the suit you were wearing is a basic pattern, from which the plant can grow millions of copies organically. Right?'

'Millions, trillions,' Peder told him fatalistically. 'The whole planet will become a never-ending crop of suits. Every human being in the galaxy will wear one eventually. It's the end of the world.'

'And the suit was using you as a wearer, so as to bring it to maturity?'

Peder nodded.

The staff chief glanced at Amara before continuing. 'Why did you co-operate?' he demanded. 'Especially when you got down here on the surface – why didn't you fight it, destroy the suit? You're still a Ziodean, aren't you? Do you like what you see happening?'

'But you have to understand! I was the plant's proxy! I didn't have any ego, any will of my own!'

'That's just what I *don't* understand,' Amara said. 'If this intelligence is purely passive, without the mental quality of action, how could it control minds like ours?'

Estru understood Peder's meaning more clearly. 'Like the mirror, Amara, remember? It only reflects – but sometimes it modifies the reflection.'

'Well how can it do that if it doesn't *do* anything?' she retorted.

'The Prossim mind works by comparing and collating, nothing more,' Peder said. 'It compares one impression with another. Think about it. You'll see you can get a lot of interesting effects that way.'

Momentarily they fell silent. On the conference room's biggest vidscreen the Caeanic freighter was visible, standing silent and unmoving while all around it stretched the green plain, speckled with the suits that were relentlessly growing. Estru gestured to the ship. 'What will happen now?' he asked Peder. 'Is that ship going to harvest the suits, and take them back to Caean?'

'The Captain doesn't have the crew to do it. Not yet. He'll have all he needs, though, in an hour or two.'

'Where are they coming from?'

'From the *Callan*,' Peder said. 'You will be the gatherers of the first crop.' Suddenly he surged to his feet, the blanket falling from his naked body, his eyes blazing wildly. 'You will be the first members of the new order. Man made perfect! Cosmic elegance! The galaxy ablaze with sartorial glory!'

Then he crumpled. The sociologists stepped forward, helping him back to his chair and draping the blanket around him.

Amara took Estru on one side. 'Well, what do you think?' she asked him. 'Could this lunatic's story have anything to it?'

Estru nodded slowly. 'I think we should treat it with the utmost seriousness.'

'But this – *monster*. Could there be such a thing?'

Estru screwed up his face in thought. 'Remember Bourdon's *Imaginary Numbers of the Mind*? He pointed out that every act of perception, every mental intention, resembles a positive vector in physical space. By applying the square root of minus one as an operator he produced theoretical descriptions of *negative* mental vectors. He claimed that the negative dimension was implicit in mentality as a whole, that the positive component couldn't exist unless it had its own mirror image. It's an idea that's close to the notion of passive sentience.'

'Could Forbarth have read Bourdon?'

'No. He'd have to be both a mathematician and a trained psychologist. But I don't think he could have invented what he's told us either.'

'His mind might be warped enough to accept some kind of mythical interpretation, or analogy, as the literal truth,' she suggested dubiously.

'And the suits?'

'A new Caeanic enterprise – tailoring by genetic manipulation, perhaps?'

'But there are four dead bodies out there.'

Amara's staff chief, having sidled close, joined in the discussion. 'I agree we should act on the assumption that Forbarth is telling the truth,' he said. 'There's something very logical about his story. It explains a great deal about what we've seen in this neck of Caean.'

He broke off as Peder started rambling, speaking to nobody in particular. 'It will be irresistible. An alien culture on the move, clothes-robots in Frachonard suits, sweeping across the Gulf in their millions . . .'

'What's he talking about?' Amara demanded.

'He's talking about the invasion of Ziode,' Estru answered in a flat, dry voice. 'We've all been fooled – the Caeanics themselves have been fooled. An invasion *is* afoot, or shortly will be – an invasion which will appear to be the work of the Caeanics, whereas in fact they'll only be proxies. You heard what Forbarth said. The Prossim intelligence plans to clothe the whole of mankind.'

'I knew we should never have trusted foreigners,' Amara grunted in disgust.

'There's an awful kind of grandeur about it in a way,' Estru said meditatively. 'We are familiar with the idea of physical invasion, or of invasion by disease in the form of epidemics. But this is a psychological invasion. The total remaking of mankind.'

'I like my mind as it is, thank you.'

He smiled with ironic humour. 'Be objective about it, Amara. Cross-fertilizing is usually a good thing. This is mental crosss-breeding between lifeforms literally poles apart. Something quite unbelievable ought to come out of that. Perhaps the Caeanics know what they're about.'

Amara cast him a look of withering scorn before turning her gaze to the vidscreen. 'You're being flippant. Luckily we are in a position to nip this horror in the bud. We can hardly destroy the entire Prossim species, of course, since it grows all over the planet, but if I understand Forbarth aright the scheme depends on those suits it's growing. This is the only patch of them so far. Destroy it and Ziode is safe – for the time being, anyway.'

'We don't have any external armament to speak of.'

'It can be done manually. We have portable atomic flamethrowers.'

Overhearing them from where he sat, Peder Forbarth began to laugh weakly. 'But you won't be able to! You won't be able to!'

★

They found out what Forbarth meant almost as soon as Captain Wilce sent out a pair of his crewmen to burn up the Prossim growth.

The two went out on a disc-shaped grav platform that skimmed over the surface of the plain. One steered the platform, while the other handled the flamethrower, a telescope-like affair he held under one arm, supporting its weight with a harness that went over his shoulders. Both wore protective suits of a silvery heat-resistant light metal, complete with visors.

The sociological team, watching while they glided some distance away from the *Callan*, waited to see the flamethrower come into action. Nothing of the kind occurred, however. After a puzzling delay the grav disc settled on the plain. The two men divested themselves of their protective clothing until they stood naked on the green Prossim.

'What in space are they *doing?*' Amara squeaked in alarm. 'Have they gone mad?'

Peder was giggling like an idiot. Now they saw the two crewmen, ignoring all orders that came through their headsets from Captain Wilce, bend down and detach something from the growing greenery. For a minute or two they were busy, probing and poking in the leafy tangle. Soon they had picked an assortment of newly-ripened garments: underpants, shirts, jackets, waistcoats, trousers, ties and cravats. Then, apparently absorbed in what they were doing, they carefully dressed themselves.

Finally, fully attired, they stood upright on the verdant plain. At a nod to one another they remounted the grav platform, leaving the flamethrower where it had been thrown, and headed back towards the ship, landing in full view of the external scanner.

They were transformed men. They stood before the *Callan*, flexing their limbs, exhibiting themselves to those within, stepping back and forth and pirouetting as if in a fashion show.

'I told you you couldn't do it,' Peder gasped, gurgling with laughter. 'Go on, give in – you've got to eventually. Don't you feel it getting to you?'

Estru felt like hitting the renegade Ziodean in the face. 'What do you mean by that?'

'Those suits create a field of mental force. It'll get to you soon, even through the walls of the ship.'

'I don't feel anything.'

'Not even when you look at your men in those suits?'

Estru stared at the disporting pair on the vidscreen. 'I'm not sure . . .'

'All right, focus the screen out on the plain. Let's see a close-up of all those suits growing out there. Then you'll know . . .' He stood up, staggering to the screen controls. The image zoomed, blurred and sped until, with dazzling clarity, it showed an enlarged spread of garments.

Suddenly Realto Mast sprang forward. He pushed Peder away from the controls and hastily refocused the screen. 'Don't let him do that,' he warned.

Peder sniggered. 'See, he knows, don't you, Realto? There's no defence against those garments. They just call out to be worn – and they are so perfect that the human mind can't resist that call. The Prossim plant can conquer humanity by sheer mental force, simply by displaying the garments it has created.'

'I *definitely* felt something then,' Estru declared, looking around at the others for confirmation.

'And Ziodeans say the sartorial art is a delusion!' Peder derided.

Blanco came forward and leaned over him belligerently. 'Whose side are you on?' he shouted. Then he turned to Amara. 'What about you, madam? Perhaps the garments are ineffective against a woman.'

'I felt something too,' Amara admitted quietly.

'The Prossim plant is something of a male chauvinist,' Peder told them in a sarcastic voice. 'Male qualities are more active than female ones, so it elected to delineate mankind by using masculine garments only. It views female garments as accessories. But it isn't oblivious to sex – far from it. Stand up in one of those suits and no woman can resist you.'

Silence reigned in the conference room.

'Well?' Amara said grimly. 'Has anybody got any ideas?'

'You can do it, Alexei,' Mast said earnestly. 'You're the only one who *can*.'

'I simply don't understand what you are asking of me,' the Sovyan replied. 'I don't understand why simply anyone cannot do it.'

Mast sighed. 'No, I don't suppose you could understand. But you can understand that the growths are menacing us.'

'If you say so.'

'We can't leave until the growths are destroyed.'

Mast was in Alexei Verednyev's cramped private cabin. Alexei had painted the walls a metallic grey. There were only three items of furniture: a table, a hard chair on which the Sovyan was now seated, and a pallet on which he slept. His face, as always, was dour and immobile.

Mast had slipped away unnoticed from Amara Corl's section. He was sure she was too insensitive to be able to persuade her victim to help her.

'On this whole ship, you are the only one who has been a friend to me,' Alexei said at last, emotion entering his accented voice. 'I will do what you ask, since it is you who is asking.'

He rose, his arms moving in a waving motion reminiscent of the typical arm movements of a Sovyan metalloid. Mast led him out of the room. They went down to the exit bay where he explained to him what had to be done.

The doors opened. Alexei, armed with a handgun Mast had given him, ventured out.

The breeze that swept over Alexei's skin as he emerged from the *Callan* was an entirely new phenomenon to him.

It frightened him at first. Realto Mast had not warned him of this.

He stood on the Prossim mats, which were depressed into a shallow bowl by the ship's weight, and gazed about him. He had seen planetary landscapes before, but only on the *Callan*'s external screens when she landed on some world or other. With the flowing of air on his skin, assaulting his intimate feelings, it took on a completely different aspect. The spaciousness of the land, the colour of space seen through an atmosphere – not black, but with a purple tint in this case – made him appreciate all the more the *alienness* of such an environment.

The cyborg world must be much like this, he thought.

The exit bay port closed with a thump behind him. The two crewmen who had preceded him were standing out of the shadow of the ship, where they had been looking up at its bulk and shouting to be let in.

On seeing Alexei they stopped shouting. His feet unsteady on the yielding surface, he made his way towards them, and they responded by moving to meet him. Their mouths were stretched in what he had been told was a facial signal called a *smile*. But the grace of their movements, the display of manly beauty by which Mast had explained they would try to hypnotize him, all that was lost on him. The human body was a hated object to him. It was easy to imagine that he was killing repulsive cyborgs as he let them get near enough for him to take steady aim, then kill them both with his hand beamer.

He walked on to the grav platform. Although the dead men had been crewmen on the ship which was now his own home, he felt no compunction over killing them, knowing that they had been enslaved by the malevolent force within the green vegetation. Such sacrifices came naturally to him. Sovyan society made every individual understand that he was expendable in terms of group survival.

Flying the grav platform was easy. He sent it skimming over the ground at a height of about twenty feet, until he came to where the crewmen had discarded the flamethrower. Stepping down from the flying disc, he collected together the components of one of the protective suits. Immediately upon donning it, with clumsy, unaccustomed movements, he felt a little better. To be clad in metal always brought him a slight relief from his personal agony of mind.

He picked up the flamethrower, pulling the harness over his shoulders. Feeling it in his possession also brought a marginal improvement in his spirits. He was in his element when handling pure instrumentalities, machines and the like – a fact of which the hideous female and supposed mind technician, Amara Corl, had never made any use, if it had occurred to her at all.

After outfitting himself Alexei paused, staring down at the vegetable fabric structures which comprised the blossoms of this surplanetary growth. What did his captors find to fear in these rags? He bent down, stretching out a hand to feel the front of a jacket.

His hand twitched, entirely of its own volition. Peculiar thoughts passed through his brain, a series of extraordinary images.

Quickly he pulled the hand away. It was not his own hand, he reminded himself. It was a grafted hand. A space-cave hand.

Standing erect, he triggered the flamethrower.

Atomic fire gouted from the nozzle. The roaring lateral column reached almost to the horizon, incinerating everything in its path. Alexei swivelled the long tube, cutting a blackened quadrant out of the landscape and extending it into a near-circle.

Smoke rose in masses and obscured the sky. Alexei mounted the grav platform again and flew a short distance away, surveying the ground below him. The crop of garments had by now spread to cover a patch about five miles across.

Handling the flamethrower was too awkward when controlling the grav disc as well. Alexei worked by choosing a new area for destruction and landing in the centre of it. The air shimmered and heat smote at him through the protective suit.

Barely fifteen minutes later the task was almost done. Alexei paused, standing by the platform after having employed the flamethrower yet again. He was in a fog of smoke and crackling heat, through which the shapes of the two spaceships, standing a mile apart and so far ignoring one another, bulked shiftingly like slumbering beasts.

Suddenly Alexei saw that one of those beasts had stirred to life. It had lifted itself off the ground and was surging towards him. He immediately guessed its intent. It meant to crush him, in defence of the vegetable mats.

He adjusted the nozzle of the flamethrower to its narrowest aperture. The space-cave – it was the other one, not the *Callan* – was approaching fast. Instinctively he backed away, stumbling in the black dust that had been Prossim, and sent a narrow jet of atomic fire hissing at the ship. The flame splashed against the hull, melting the metal and causing it to run in glowing streams down the curved side.

In a second or two the flame jet had lunged through the hull and was busy devouring the interior of the ship. But by then the hull was blotting out everything, expanding and descending on him with terrifying swiftness. For a moment the metal monster seemed almost friendly. He imagined it as a righteous Sovyan weapon that was crushing an evil cyborg – the cyborg being himself – then it was all over.

The harvester ship had come down like an avenging fist on Alexei Verednyev, with such determined force that it broke its own back in the process and lay crippled on the plain. Amara, watching from within the *Callan*, viewed the whole affair with satisfaction.

'We should have thought of this ourselves,' Estru said. 'It's this business of body image again. Alexei's mind lacks a human body image. So the Prossim suits couldn't get to him.'

'They would have eventually,' Peder told them. 'If put to it those suits can control the nervous system of animals and even insects.'

'And to think you wanted to leave Verednyev behind in the Sovyan Rings, Estru!' Amara crowed. 'Sometimes I think I'm the only one around here who makes the right decisions. By the way, remind me to put in a good word for Mast when we get back to Ziode. Where's he got to?'

Mast had returned to the section to explain his ploy, but had left again following the death of the Sovyan. 'Probably gone to sulk,' Estru said. 'He was quite friendly with Verednyev.'

'Really? Well, you can't expect a layman to have any objectivity.' Amara was manipulating the screen controls, searching the great carpet of soot that had once been the Prossim plant's garment beds. There were still a few garments left here and there, mostly charred or partly burned, passed over by the main force of the flamethrower's flood. Those remnants would have to be cleared up.

Suddenly she switched off the screen and turned to face Estru and those of her team who were still in the room. Her face recovered its former grimness.

'The most immediate peril has been averted, but the Prossim intelligence remains as a continuing threat,' she declared. 'It will not relinquish its ambitions. Sooner or later it will find another Frachonard, or it will continue to extend its control by means of lesser garments. Now, we have two options. We can make our way back to one of the Caeanic capitals, preferably Verrage, apprise the government there of what Prossim really is. Personally, I rule that out immediately. They would never trust us. They would be insulted by what would seem to be foreign criticism of their life-style.

'Or we can return to Ziode and inform the Directorate of the facts, leaving the decision to them. I have little doubt as to what that decision will be. They will order an expeditionary force to this part of Tzist to annihilate this planet utterly.'

'The Caeanics simply aren't going to accept such an action on our part. There will be war,' the staff chief said.

She nodded solemnly. 'That's so. But we have to face up to it. The Prossim flora must be wiped out. There isn't any alternative – and we can't trust the Caeanics to do it for us.'

She leaned back against a table, gripping its edges with her hands. 'As a matter of fact I doubt very much if Captain Wilce would permit us to go for the first option. The Caeanics would be too likely to impound the *Callan* and kill us all just to suppress our story. But on an issue as important as this I'm prepared to record the feeling of the department. Who's for going straight to Ziode?'

Slowly, aware that they were voting for war with Caean, they all raised their hands in the air.

The last people were coming back into the ship, trudging over the soot beds. It was time to be lifting off; Caeanic harvesters no doubt arrived here with regularity.

Amara's team had taken cuttings of the Prossim plant to be conveyed, under sterilized biokiller seal, for study in Ziode, and they had gathered up the remaining pathetic scraps of the garment crop, also for study. Peder stood on the lip of the exit bay port, looking out over the scene for the last time. He wore plain garments given him by Estru. Though pale and shattered in spirit he had recovered his composure and was no longer mentally unbalanced. He even managed to nod in friendly fashion to Estru when he joined him at the port.

Together they shared the view. In one direction a rim of green could be discerned where the unburnt Prossim began again. The wrecked freighter was slumped in the middle of the dead area like a slaughtered mammoth, black dust piling up against it in the breeze.

Estru sighed, shaking his head, then chuckled cynically. 'You know, I'm wondering if they're going to believe any of this back in Ziode. How many other intelligences of this type do you think there are? It's odd we haven't come across any before.'

'I don't think it's very common,' Peder said slowly. 'It's too anomalous. The universe is a place of motion and conflict where passive sentience can't easily get a hold. Perhaps it's an evolutionary counterpart of anti-matter – equivalent to normal matter and just as probable in theory, but scarcely ever encountered in fact.'

They moved aside as the last man came aboard and the port was closed. Together they made their way up the ramp and into the belly corridor. As they were about to part, Estru paused reflectively.

'By the way, we shall want to carry out some investigative psychoanalysis on you,' he said. 'You've been through a unique experience, you know. Don't worry, though, it isn't painful – well, a little stressful occasionally, perhaps. We should have finished by the time we get home.'

Peder felt the ship lifting off as he made his way alone to his cabin; which not altogether by chance happened to be the one so recently vacated by Alexei Verednyev. In a way it was decent of Estru to be so friendly. Very few on the *Callan* felt any sympathy for him at all, and it was by no means clear what his eventual fate would be. Still, he believed he had a fair chance of being given parole and of being allowed to live as a private citizen. Even in a Ziodean court of law one could justifiably plead alien mental interference as a mitigating circumstance, he would have thought. And if Mast was to get off, why shouldn't he?

Perhaps he could even become a sartorial again.

He entered his tiny cabin, locked the door and sat down with a thankful sigh.

It was good to have all the pressure off.

He opened the buttoned pocket of his crumpled work jacket and took out its precious cargo.

His little memento: a tie, of a captivating magenta colour. He ran it through his fingers, feeling its gorgeous silky texture, caressing his cheek with it. Marvellous! It was like something alive!

Carefully he draped it under his collar and tied a loose knot in it, peering into the cabin mirror and admiring its effect even on the grubby shirt he was wearing. He was grateful now that they had let him out to poke among the ashes with the others, before the place had been given one final burning to eradicate all trace of the Frachonard crop. They had seemed glad to have someone to help them gather up all the bits and pieces – the fragments of cloth, even one or two whole garments. It had been easy to filch this one little item.

There was something else. He opened a handkerchief in which something soft and fleecy was carefully wrapped: a spore pod. Like the tie he had found near it, it had escaped the searing heat of the flamethrower – or almost. It was a little singed round the edges, as indeed was the tie. It was hard to say whether it would still be viable.

Peder would never really be able to forget his Frachonard suit, despite all the hard times it had put him through. His reasoning was that the spores in the burned patch of Prossim might already have been imprinted with the genetic information to grow Frachonard suits. If he let a spore germinate, it might grow him one. Just one – that was all he would allow. With the main mass destroyed by the Ziodean Navy, it wouldn't be able to control him as the first one had.

He couldn't see any risk. He would be the plant's gardener. It would be cultured. He would be able to restrict its growth.

He would only allow it to grow one suit. To begin with, anyway. It would be wonderful to have such a suit that was his helpmate, not his master.

Only one suit.